Go for Shakedown

Go for Shakedown

Stephen Robertson, CD, BA, ATPL

To order additional copies of this book, contact:
Xlibris
1-888-795-4274
www.Xlibris.com
Orders@Xlibris.com
728032

Contents

Author's Note

This is a fictional story based on true events.

Some names, timelines and details have been changed;
characters blended in order to make it easier to tell the story.

To my loving children, Josh, Tim and Abby
who loved and supported me through my dark days.
I can't begin to think how this affects you.

And thank you to the GSH gang
who watched me toil, type and shed tears over my
computer in the northern forests of Alberta putting
this manuscript together for two years.

Special thanks to C.Wiggins (Wiggy) for his amazing photography.

Cover photograph: C. Wiggins, of G. Juurlink,
KAF Ramp Christmas 2009.

And my dearest, Florence.
You inspired and encouraged me to resurrect this work
from its long hiatus. I can't thank you enough.

In Memory of:

Master Corporal Patrice Audet

Corporal Martin Joannette

Corporal Zachery McCormack

Sergeant James Patrick MacNeil

Private Andrew Miller

Master Corporal Kristal Giesebrecht

Foreword

From 2009 to 2010, I was a Canadian forces helicopter pilot, serving at the pinnacle of my career in Afghanistan as a Griffon Weapons Section leader. Although probably the most stressful time I have endured in aviation, it was also the most fulfilling. The mission, the people, and the place made it something that I hope to remember forever.

During the commander's end-tour speech, he said to the new vets, "Go tell your stories." This is my story. It is based on real events and inspired by real people. The timelines and characters were blended for ease of telling the story. I hope to build empathy toward the intensity of continuous, dynamically changing operations, often culminating in life-and-death decisions. And how this chronic pressure affects our character and transforms our souls.

Our veterans are special people. They are driven, focused, and hard working. More than anything, they are willing to sacrifice. But I don't mean that to come across arrogantly noble because let's face it, we do this shit because we like it. It's exciting, crazy, and sometimes a little stupid—well, more than sometimes. More than anything, we find courage through camaraderie, compassion in fellowship, humility through peer roasting, and humanity through empathy towards those friendly, enemy and innocent people we fly over every day. Yes, we love to tell stories and this is just another story.

One forefather of tactical aviation in Canada stated, "There is no hell like Tac Hel." We are Tac Hel (tactical helicopters). We're proud, and we're cool! Tactical aviators have unique perspectives. Sometimes from only a few meters away, we look eye to eye at our combatants, see the terror in the child-victims of the enemy, and put suppressive fire only feet away from friendly troops to watch our own ricochets reflect over us if not bounce off our aircraft, thus justifying the expression.

Unfortunately, history often goes scripted into the technical archives, and the human side disappears; the passion is forgotten. I hope this will spark some empathy for the exciting times as well as sympathy and compassion for those who wish to flush the horrors. So on that note, my first story is about pride—how we arrived in Afghanistan is a proud achievement in itself.

Flying over Panjwaii District in Southern Afghanistan near Kandahar, the pilots of the griffons would routinely hear a voice over the radio blurt out for help. Our radio call sign was "Shakedown."

"Shakedown Flight, TIC in progress—can you respond?" an excited voice would call over the radio. This meant friendly troops were in contact with the enemy, often under fire and often following an explosive attack from an IED. There was usually someone hurt if not dead.

Often in those moments, there were many cases to justify not immediately responding and flying toward the threat: low on fuel escorting Chinooks, or overwatching ground patrols. However, despite the risks of sitting in thin-skinned metal aircraft and despite not being to see the enemy that would often shoot at us, our teams were always sprung loaded for that call. And the reliable reply was always:

"Roger that. Go for Shakedown!"

Chapter 1

The Canadian Aviation Battalion Is Born

From 2002 to 2011, Canadian troops were deployed to Kandahar Province. 2002 was shortly after the final battle called the Taliban Last Stand (TLS), which is the KAF airport terminal building, where the American Forces finally forced out the Taliban government. That building today is still known as the TLS; it remains riddled with bullet impact marks.

The Canadians task was to provide the interim government of Afghanistan (GOA) with security forces until the new government could establish, train, and equip an Afghan National Army (ANA) to provide their own security. Canada was given the Kandahar area, Panjwaii District, and north up the Arghandhab River to the Dalah Dam. This area had millennia-old irrigation systems nurturing a lush beautiful area of fruit orchards, grape fields and contrasted with orangey brown desert and brittle rugged mountains. Most of these areas were a mix of opium poppies and marijuana fields—the cash crop forcefully encouraged by the insurgent forces to finance their war effort. The legitimate fruit orchards were neglected to wither because efforts to take legal produce to local markets were often ambushed; farmers sometimes even murdered by Taliban.

The area was large. The troops were few, and often our soldiers became easy targets for IED (improvised explosive devices) attacks as they patrolled communities trying to provide security. It was common to have weekly combat situations—often with injuries and death. It wasn't long until our first soldier was returned under a Canadian flag instead of holding it. When I was serving, it was a daily occurrence to have TICs occurring in the region. (TIC means troops in contact fighting with the enemy.)

1

Frustrated—yes, but perseverance and commitment continued, and the Canadian troops continued in this "whack-a-mole" game of clearing out Taliban from small towns just to have them pour back in after they egressed to a new location.

Being moved by helicopter was the safer method. However, the Allied Forces were limited in their ability to lend support to the Canadians. The government of Canada was reluctant to provide the air and land equipment required by the Canadian troops at that time, sending only Special Forces units. In 2006, a battle group combat component was sent by the newly elected government in Canada.

Finally in 2008, the Canadian government released the Manley Report. This was the long-awaited political justification to increase the air force by acquiring Chinook helicopters to conduct troop and logistical lift to the forward operating bases (FOBs). The aim was to keep soldiers off the vulnerable rural roads. However, there would be the risk of air ambushes. Initially, it was hoped that the American forces would provide gunship escort to the Chinooks. However, the Americans had their own forces to protect, so the resources to provide escort to Canadians was limited.

During 2007 through 2008, the Canadian government briefed by military seniors that Canada was the only country in NATO to not have gunship capability to escort our own Chinooks. Nor could Canada provide armed overwatch (protection) to troops on the ground that come into enemy contact.

Further to the Manley Report, decisions were made as the Canadian forces were quickly converting the CH146 into a platform that could provide such combat support. In 2008, Shakedown was born. The Bell 412 helicopter was converted into a viable combat machine with dual Dillon cannons and an MX-15 electro-optic sensor. The dual M134 Dillons were capable of firing three thousand rounds per minute.

At night, with a tracer every fifth round, it looked like a lava waterfall when observing under night-vision goggles. The electro-optic sensor had a target illuminator that was capable of illuminating areas of interest or targets and identifying them from distances well beyond the sound signature of the aircraft. A few years later, a .50-caliber machine gun was also added to the 412 Griffon helicopter, which enabled accurate gunnery to destroy targets from about 2000 meters.

In addition to this, the training plan rapidly unfolded to enable pilots, air engineers, and gunners for close combat attack techniques, overwatch, aerial escort, surveillance for counter IED operations as well as basic infantry ground fighting skills in the event they were making unplanned stops (shot down) outside the wire.

Christmas 2008, the initial cadre of six Chinooks started hauling people and supplies. With them, eight Griffons (four sections) initially armed with C6 machine guns started providing escort, surveillance, and infantry team overwatch. Blowtorch was born of the Chinooks and Shakedown of the Griffons.

As escort duties became proficient and experience in theater built over the next year, combined with the integration of the Dillon M134 cannons with electro-optic sensors, the capability of the Shakedown Flight greatly improved. Higher headquarters soon realized that the Griffon, with door gunnery, was capable of maintaining continual suppressive fire on the enemy as opposed to the limited forward firing guns of the Apache or Kiowa; whose enemies would squirt away after their initial pass.

It wasn't long before the weapon airspace controller's ("Slayer") favorite resource, when ground troops were in a fight and needed help, became the Griffon.

"Shakedown, we got a TIC in progress. Can you respond?"

The eager response was "Go for Shakedown."

Chapter 2

Trapped: Summer in Salavat

As most days, the valley was brown and dusty but had a rustic beauty where the desert met the irrigated fruit, marijuana, and opium fields closer to the wadis—"the green zones." The sun blazed through the bright blue sky, raising the temperatures to a common 40 degrees Celsius. My section had just finished a Chinook escort and was heading out to do overwatch for infantry teams patrolling Panjwaii.

As usual, the greenhouse heat in the cockpit was well over 50 degrees, and sweat poured down from my helmet, filling my ear cups and stinging my eyes. Every now and then, to improve hearing, I pinched my lower ear cup, breaking the sound seal, allowing the fluid to drain.

"Shakedown 25 (Two-five) Flight, this is Slayer TOC," the radio opened, requesting communication with my Canadian Griffon Weapons Team flying over the Tarnac River a few miles west of Kandahar Airfield, KAF. We had been in theater for a half year. It was to be a ten-month tour, one of the longest consecutive overseas tours the Canadian forces had authorized since the Korean conflict. The fliers of 408 Squadron, known as Roto 8 or Task Force Freedom, were well into their routines and had become seasoned theater pilots but not without weathering some operational and personal storms. Shakedown was more than a call sign; it was our role.

"Go for Shakedown," I curiously responded to what Slayer needed. Slayer controlled all the airspace above the Canadian AO – Area of Operations. He monitored the activity of the troops below and helped by allocating fire support such as mortars, artillery, bombers as well as helicopter gunships.

"Shakedown. TIC in progress near Salavat. Two-two (22) in an IED ambush—can you respond?"

An improvised explosive device is a homemade bomb made by skilled explosive manufacturers in rudimentary labs through the country. Sometimes they had enough explosive power to create craters ten meters in diameter across highways. They had been successful killing hundreds, if not thousands, of people over the past several years. 22 was the call sign of the infantry commander needing assistance because his troops were in contact (TIC) with the enemy.

"Romeo Tango," I responded affirmatively, meaning "Roger that."

"Shakedowns have eight thousand rounds, each of seven-six-two dual Dillons and sixty minutes playtime," I added to let Slayer know what weapons and ammunition type (7.62mm ball) I had on board and how much fuel time remaining.

"Contact India 22 for a battle update brief," Slayer directed and continued with critical airspace information. "My ROZ is hot, but the guns are cold. Cleared into my ROZ," he added to advise me that his area was active, but no friendly artillery was going to be threatening us in the ROZ (restricted operating zone). A battle update brief is a summary of situation directly affecting a commander's troops. I would get that directly from the infantry officer I would be supporting.

"Guys, we got troops in contact—near Salavat. They were on patrol when we last checked with operations," I advised my copilot and gunners.

My copilot was new, a first-tour pilot. He was intelligent and inquisitive; however, his enquiries were not always timely appropriate for the situation, and I admit it drove me crazy at times. Likewise, as a grumpy old bugger, I knew I drove him nuts too. Balance! He often asked for positive reinforcement about his flying technique while concurrently flying the next sequence, usually absent-mindedly toward some threat, like the ground or another helicopter coming at us. This often led to an emotional response of "What the fuck are you doing?"

However, after six months, accustomed to mutually working through the stress, we became synced to each other's quirks. So when these situations arose, we seemed to transition into battle in fluid harmony.

"Roger, Haycee," my perky engineer exclaimed from the rear right gun position, acknowledging he understood the situation and was ready. He was always excited about the mission to unfold despite knowing that the area around Salavat usually offered a challenge. He was a perpetually smiling, a keen aboriginal from Labrador. He had a knack of being able to engage in battle yet still find the opportune moment to document the event with the camera permanently strapped around his neck. Of course, interpreting his high-speed accent was a challenge. "Haycee" translated was AC or aircraft captain, which he still calls me to this day.

"Taliban's going down today," Gunny's voice flatly added from the left rear seat. I served with three different army gunners, all of which were outstanding soldiers. These guys were young but wise veterans of Afghanistan, making them reliable ground tactical advisors. As young veterans, the war was more personal to them: Hawk, Gunny and Zorg had already faced the enemy eye-to-eye and had lost comrades in battle.

Gunny had a positive sense of humor blended with a keen professional eye. His marksmanship with the Dillon was remarkable. His accuracy suggests he had an in-brain firing computer figuring the helicopter flight path, winds, and distance so that his first rounds landed on target—reliably. This would be extremely useful later in the war as I was requested to put suppressive fire less than twenty meters from friendly troops—another story.

"26, this is 25. We gotta TIC at Salavat! 22 needs support. Switch to his frequency and monitor," I directed to my wingman on the radio. He was flying in formation behind me to cover me while I researched and choreographed the plan.

"25, this is 26 on frequency," 26 said, indicating he was on the army frequency, listening and ready.

"Infantry 22, this is Shakedown 25 Flight checking in," I radioed to the platoon commander.

"Shakedown, roger," a loud partially gasping voice answered. "We have had an IED explode in grid reference QQ4190. One ANA dead. My troops are cordoned around a grape hut. Suspected enemy is two FAMs (fighting aged males) northwest our location 200 meters. I need you for overwatch and track those dickers," huffed the army commander. Most of these foot patrols consisted of about thirty Canadians and ten Afghan National Army (ANA) soldiers under mentoring of the Canadians. Today one ANA soldier was so far dead.

It was obvious from his pitched and panting voice he had been running while concurrently stabilizing chaos while under fire from the enemy. He needed us to watch for dickers—enemy combatants that observe their targets from fairly close. Dickers watch and pull the trigger using cell phones to detonate IEDs. Sometimes they observe innocently and then give a hand signal to someone far away to pull the trigger. Regardless of technique, they are effective and deadly.

"Roger, 22, we'll be there in three mikes," I replied, acknowledging that I am three minutes away.

"All right, guys, we're looking for dickers," I briefed the crew. "Any strange patterns of life or dickers stalking from compounds, let me know —watch the northeast."

"26, it's 25. Follow me for a high sweep. Then I'll stay high over the friendlies and look around. You go low and poke around." I gave my initial tactical plan to the wingman.

"Check," the radio confirmed bluntly.

I didn't have to direct my crew to the area that was given in the grid. They knew Salavat well. They could see several kilometers ahead and correctly assumed the dust cloud from the explosion was our destination. I didn't have to direct my copilot at this point. He automatically knew how to position the aircraft for everyone's best mutual support and tactical advantage. The streets and compounds below were empty, unusual for the time of day. The pattern of life (POL) felt eerie. When bad things happened, locals stayed off the streets and hid in their compounds.

"POL is quiet. No one outside of compounds," I radioed the ground commander.

Then the radio broke out excitedly between the infantry section leaders.

"22, this is 22 Alpha. I got another IED wire north road. They are setting us up."

"22 Bravo, roger. I got the same on the south road. We got IEDs all around us. We walked into an ambush," another voice flatly reported as if this was a normal day in the job.

"22 Alpha and Bravo, keep it tight. Cordon around the grape hut. Clear that hut and get me observation from the roof." I heard the commander order. "I'm trying to get counter-IED from higher HQ."

Shit was about to fly, and we were above the middle of it. In these situations, you never knew who would win this deadly game of tag. I remember the hairs on my neck tingling as I looked for threats. However, our mentality had shifted by this time in our tour.

Every day, briefings showed us death of ground troops and civilians targeted by the Taliban, rarely via combat, almost always a hit-and-run ambush. We too were shot at, shot down, and had lost brothers. After many months of flying in the area, we had transformed our psyches into warrior hunters instead of the cautious hunted.

"Haycee, gotta guy running tru de field on da nord side. He's dickin' from da trees," my right gunner reported.

"Good eye," I answered then continued onto the radio. "26 contact. FAM northeast running through a field to a tree—come back and put some low pressure on him. I'll observe," I guided to my other helicopter.

"Contact, I got him." My wingman confirmed he was visual with the suspect. I watched him bank his helicopter aggressively below toward the threat.

From high above, my Griffon didn't seem to be a threat to the Taliban soldier below. He did stay covered but was being tracked. My wingman's aircraft aimed toward the man and remained low level, directly flying over him. He was surprised. The low-level chopper was masked by my noise. As soon as they flew over, the insurgent's eyes filled with panic, and he bolted in the opposite direction toward a grape hut. He didn't know he was also being observed with an MX-15, a high-powered optical system that enabled me to see him in what appeared to be him communicating into his collar as he moved.

"He's dicking. He's the fucker that pulled the trigger! But who's he talking to?" I mumbled rhetorically then continued talking with Infantry 22.

"22, contact. One FAM. He's talking into his collar, running toward the Grape hut near grid 416902."

"Roger, Shakedown. That's the FAM that's been tracking us all morning. Continue to track him . . . There is another one. Keep your eyes out," he warned.

"26, this is 25. FAM is now in the grape hut. I'll continue high. You continue to prod—it's working," I further asked my wingman.

Every time 26 flew near the suspect, the suspect ran in an opposite direction and made apparent communications. He continued to move in and out of the grape hut watching for the low Griffon that was interrogating him.

Compounding the excitement on the radio was activity from the headquarters wanting details about the soldier who had just been killed. He seemed to have been a relative of a local municipal leader—an elder; he was recently a teammate that the Canadians had been training. He was dead, physically rearranged from the explosion.

"2, this is 22," the infantry commander was calling his headquarters at Forward Operating Base (FOB), Masum Ghar.

"How's my counter IED team?" he asked. "I got three wires around me and still trapped."

"They are on the way, but it will be awhile," a sympathetic tone replied. Unfortunately, this would take time. The convoy had to move cautiously as typical tactics used by the Taliban was to hit the emergency responders as they moved from the FOBs (forward operating bases where soldiers could have a "relatively" secure area to base from). Unfortunately, the time required to make the trip would be longer than my Shakedown team had fuel to support. The Taliban knew this. They just had to lay low until the helicopters ran out of fuel and then resume the attack.

"Shakedown, how much playtime do you have?" 22 asked.

"Thirty-five minutes," I answered.

"Roger, we are working on getting the counter-IED folks out. It's gonna take a while." He seemed to be calm yet alert. He had to be; several of his troops were ANA. It was personal and traumatic to them. He had to be an example of professional stability, courage, and compassion in this situation where IEDs and machine guns could be going off toward them any moment.

"25, this is 26, contact!" my radio boomed. "One FAM running in toward the other man from a compound 250 meters northeast," my wingman discovered.

"Gunny, he's on your side. Got him?" I asked my left gunner.

"Got him," Gunny responded. I immediately directed my copilot to fly his orbit so that Gunny would always have his eyes on the two Taliban soldiers.

"Guys, I'm staying in the left orbit. I'm not losing PID," I adamantly stated over the radio, so my lower wingman knew my intention. Positive identification (PID) was required to be established and maintained before fire could be directed onto the enemy targets. The crew knew. They understood.

I felt like a dog with a bone in my mouth and wasn't letting go. So many enemy forces had been let go only to kill again because of ROE– (rules of engagement) restrictions. Every nation interpreted the same ROE differently.

As a soldier hunting an enemy, it was paramount to abide by the tightest standard in overlapping regulatory zones. The enemy was smart. Their first priority was to cause us to lose continual contact with them and create doubt in our minds as to their identity. But I had PID. I wasn't letting go!

"They are both dickering from the grape hut," my wingman called. "We have contact on the two guys. They are in the grape hut. That's a suspected weapons cache, possible RPGs. Be careful." He further highlighted from our intelligence brief received earlier in the day. An RPG (rocket-propelled grenade) was a very effective weapon in taking out helicopters, especially at the height and speed we were working at.

"We got PID, we got POL. Shit! We have weapons release criteria," I stated out loud. I realized at that moment that these two Talibans' days were numbered. They had made some critical mistakes in their tactics and revealed their intention. They wouldn't be pulling the trigger anymore.

"26, we have weapons release criteria. Confirm?" I double-checked with my wingman.

"Roger that. I concur," he stated.

"Advising 22, it's his turf," I added.

"22, I got PID on two FAMs at a suspected weapons cache with erratic behavior and POL indicative of enemy activity. We have weapons release authority on target at the grape hut," I stated. "Get your heads down."

There was a pause.

"Shakedown, roger that," the infantry commander answered.

I continued on the other radio to my wingman. "26, fire mission. Friendlies on the grape hut 400 meters west. Enemy is two FAMs at the grape hut below, circle pattern—left gun attack. You hit the building, I'll catch the squirters. No effects directly west—I'm dropping back into behind you from high. Stand by for fire."

"Visual friendlies, tally target," my wingman acknowledged.

I took the controls of the aircraft and assertively dropped in from high above into a trail position behind 26. The target was in view of Gunny only 300 feet below and 75 meters away. The IED days of these two enemy soldiers were about to end. I looked over to the west at the friendly infantry on the ground; they had done just the opposite that I directed to their leader. They all got onto the roof and stood up to watch. I shook my head and muttered over the intercom, "Look at our guys—dumb asses!"

A flashback went through my head. How had we gotten to this point? We were about to remove two more combatants from the planet. It was clean and unemotionally professional. It was a culmination of years of professional duty and practice and over a half of year of looking eye to eye at my potential executioner, often the same guys. There was no hatred, or anger, only respect. He was my adversary, and I was his. I respected him for his devotion to his system, his religion, and his people, but I detest his methods and affect. I took a breath.

"You ready, Gunny?" I asked my left gunner.

"Romeo Tango. Visual friendlies, tally target," he responded.

"26, this is 25. Fire! Left gunner, fire," I ordered over the radio and intercom. The Dillon deafened the entire crew. The smoke from the cannon filled the cockpit window. The rooftop of the grape hut and earth surrounding exploded into a cloud of dust.

Two men came squirting out, one with a bulky silhouette of an AK-47 concealed under his man jammies. One ran under the large solid mud wall trying to hide in the grape rows; the other went toward a compound. However, both were engulfed into an exploding cloud of dust. Then half a flight orbit later, the gunners stopped firing.

Chapter 3

Dust on My Boots

I spent a year in Afghanistan yesterday.

October 2009. It's 5:00 a.m. Roto 8 had arrived from Canada after three days of transit to what seemed to be from all corners of the earth to get to what most would refer to as the dustiest shithole on the planet.

I disembarked the Canadian C-17 Globemaster from our layover in Cyprus and shuffled across the tarmac just as the sun was illuminating a beautiful bright yellow across the blue sky. An orange band topped the yellow where the light met the dust suspended in the air. Everything below was brown, covered in a thin layer of moondust. Even the green trees were covered in dust, making them brown.

As I marched off the concrete, each step resulted in a small explosion of talcumlike powder that engulfed my pants to mid shin. I chuckled in disbelief as my new boots already looked like they had "time in."

After "checking in" to the new resort, my chalk of air soldiers was ushered through numerous stages of orientation. Since no one had slept in the past three days, except for a few winks on an airport floor in "secret" isolation in Germany, most of us were aloof to the detail of material presented. However, coffee and snacks were a welcome provision as we listened to what sounded like Charlie Brown's teacher professing.

Following this reception, we were ushered through the equipment issue process. Side arms, ammunition, administrative forms, and videos on combat first aid techniques were all completed with a focus on the most recent tactical situation to sharpen our purpose.

I retrieved my pistol, a Browning 9-millimeter sidearm and thirty rounds of ammunition. I loaded it, made it safe, and holstered it over my shoulder. Later that night, we would go to the ranges to verify they were working. Then like a flock of sleepy sheep, we were herded onto another bus, which crawled down the dusty labyrinth of roads. The roads were curbed by 20 feet high concrete barriers for protection against rockets. Once the concrete ended, large sea containers continued to outline the roads. Each steel sea container was approximately 40 feet long and 10 feet high—these often double-stacked, forming further channels through Kandahar Air Field –(KAF).

I arrived at my temporary accommodation called BATs (big ass tents), which would be home for the next two days until the crews of 430 Squadron, who we were replacing, departed so we could take their lodgings. The BAT was a huge white (dusty brown) temporary housing for soldiers transiting through KAF. It had numerous rows of bunk beds easily being able to house hundreds of soldiers.

At the BAT, we were granted a couple of hours of personal time. This was very welcome after three days of travel before further orientation started in the afternoon. Most flopped onto a mattress and immediately slept despite the noisy infantry platoon that had also arrived. Anxious to go home, they were all telling their war stories—adding another realistic dimension to the anxiety of our newly arriving aviation team.

I couldn't sleep. My mind was nervous about the unknown. So coupled with my body vibrating in sleep deprivation, I could do nothing other than explore. I needed to look around. I clung to a respected colleague who had already completed a tour in KAF several years earlier—Grumpy.

Grumpy was a fellow Griffon captain and section leader. He was respected for his experience, meticulous work, and detailed planning. A person one could admire for both friendship and advice. However, he had little time for nonsense, which was quite plentiful in a military organization. It was common for him to look wide-eyed at someone who was presenting a ridiculous comment. And with his head sternly tilted forward and forearm held out across his chest, he would slowly raise his fingertips, pivoting about his elbow, vertically representing an analog meter as he sarcastically warned his conversant, "My fun meter is pegged! Conversation over!"

He was proud of this demeanor and often referred to himself as *the* grumpy old man. This in itself was contradictory since he was upbeat and pleasant most of the time. However, at one point in our training for Afghanistan, he comically labeled our entire cadre of captains 'Grumpy Old Men," depicting the gruff attitudes of our group of senior captains—most of us older than our supervising majors and colonels. Unfortunately, the overwhelming majority of young copilots learned to cope with us for eight months of pre-deployment training followed by the year in theater.

Grumpy noticed my perplexed look, an epiphany that we were actually in Afghanistan. Conversely, he looked excited to return and anxious to do some "show and tell."

"You gonna sleep?" he asked.

"Nope," I responded.

"Timmy's for coffee?" He was referring to Tim Hortons, a Canadian coffee company with an outlet to support the troops in KAF, an iconic bit of home away from home.

"You bet. I need something to keep me awake. I'm sleep-fucked and won't be getting any rest with those guys telling war stories," I enthusiastically requested, throwing my gear on a bunk and followed him through the door.

We proceeded down a narrow dusty road walled by sea containers on each side. I was entirely disoriented, but he knew exactly where he was in this labyrinth. I surrendered to my curiosity by plodding along in tow. It all looked the same.

Everything, of course, covered in dust.

I followed along watching the little dust explosions climbing and wrapping around Grumpy's knees as he pointed to landmarks.

"There's the TLS again, front gate, HQ (headquarters), barber, Canadian gym . . ." He toured with his arm pointing out landmarks. I was excited to see all these points but figured I needed a 3-kilometer-long string to find my way back to the BAT.

Tim Hortons was a kilometer away, which was really two thousand dust-exploding steps, making my shiny, virgin, tan-pattern uniform instantly looking experienced.

As vehicles slowly passed by, the intensity of the rising dust forced pedestrians to stop walking until the visibility increased. I coughed the excess dirt, learning quickly to cover my face by raising my undershirt over my nose. Even after reopening my eyes, the sweat from my brow streamed the stinging dirt into them. I couldn't escape the talcum powder invasion.

Additionally, the dust immediately fused with sweaty wet clothes forming a darker brown in those affected areas. It was the typical Kandahar look—a dusty brown frame with a bacon-stripe butt and arm pits. Despite only two hours since arrival, my uniform appeared like everyone else's. The differentiator was the white skin tone and wide but red eyes.

The boardwalk was the social center of KAF. It was a large 150 by 150-meter square market and recreation field. The center courtyard shared a basketball court, a gravel football field, a stage, a memorial garden to remind those inside the wire of the war going on outside the wire, and of course, the Canadian hockey rink.

There were market stores and cafes offering some psychological reprieve from the ruggedness of the operation. It was comfortable in KAF, especially to those soldiers who lived and worked outside the security fence ("outside the wire"). To them, this was a resort.

Our aviation battalion aircrew worked outside the wire but lived inside. We understood and respected what the troops lived (and died) through and never tried to take the "resort" feeling for granted. There was already animosity between soldiers living in the FOBs (forward-operating bases outside the wire) and soldiers that worked entirely inside the wire (KAF).

FOB soldiers patrolled day and night, risking their lives experiencing pain, death, and blood. Yet everyone serving in Afghanistan was on the same danger pay and received the same campaign medal. Aircrew appreciated life in KAF but mindfully respected that one well-placed bullet would make us instant foot soldiers outside the wire. So respect for those living 'outside the wire' was never yielded.

"Steve, check this out," Grumpy directed. "You can go inside or take the walk through. It's like a drive-through for people." He pointed to the little coffee window with twenty people in line outside of the store.

"How's this work?" I inquired, looking at two long lines with several dozen people in each.

"If you have a small order, you go in the walk through line. It's faster. If you want a larger order, go inside," Grumpy explained. "We'll stand in the walk-through outside line. There is a lot to watch from here."

It took ten minutes to serve the twenty people in front, but it gave a chance to greet various people. It wasn't uncommon to meet Australians, Russians, Brits, and especially Americans who quickly fell in love with iced caps and doughnuts.

A designated colleague for orientation escorted newly arriving American soldiers around KAF. Tim Hortons was part of the tour. I felt proud to overhear him telling his colleagues about how Timmy's was a "must" place to go with the best doughnuts, bagels, and iced caps.

"Dude, you just gotta say black, which is black. Or regular, which is one cream and sugar. Or double-double which is two of each. They automatically know," an American with a Southern drawl enthusiastically explained to another.

"Oh, all right. I got this," the new comer replied.

"But you gotta order a Wayne Gretzky," he added.

"What's that? A hockey player?"

"Ya, he was number 99 for Los Angeles Kings, but here, it's a large coffee with nine creams and nine sugar. I recommend it highly," the Southern drawl expertly advised.

Grumpy and I were both astonished we looked at each other silently, repeating in disbelief, "Nine and nine?" It was an extreme Tim's order, but nevertheless, I was proud of our national institution in coming to KAF and influencing others from afar to choose Timmy's over Green Beans, the American choice on the boardwalk.

Timmy's was perched beside a small patio, which overlooked the ball hockey rink and also had the best Canadian Wi-Fi connection on base. Many soldiers had coffee while concurrently Skyping home and watching the game. The hockey games seemed perpetual—even on hot 40-degree days.

Some Canadian night-shift workers were currently playing hockey following their shift; soaked in sweat. I noticed the thermometer anchored above the door at Tim's. It was only 33 degrees on this dusty autumn day. However, it was also only 9:00 a.m.

Grumpy treated me to coffee, and we continued walking. Our home-to-be was 200 meters away. We proceeded that direction. He gave me the change from the coffee at Timmy's, a POG. There were no coins used in theater, only cash. It was too expensive to ship coins into theater, so the task force created temporary paper money. And instead of coins, a paper POG was given representing 5¢, 10¢, and 25¢—my first souvenir.

Our accommodations were beside the Niagara DFAC (dining facility, pronounced as Dee-Feck). This was where the majority of our meals would be for the next year. It was primarily American cuisine, but offered amazing variety. The omelet bar in the morning became my favorite —a four-egg omelet with cheese, ham, and peppers became my routine, potential last supper, prior to mission launch.

I entered the small weather haven, a dusty torn tent about 56 feet long and 16 feet wide with an arched roof. It would soon be home to seventeen pilots.

It was dark. It took several minutes for my eyes to adjust and likewise just the opposite as one returned outside into the bright sunlight. I introduced myself quietly to one of the guys; I recognized him from Canada. Tactical aviation in Canada is a small community. We all cross paths with each other at exercises, courses, or on operations such as Afghanistan.

In a whispering French accent, he excitedly welcomed us. "Bonjour! Bien venue au KAF! I am glad you ayr haiyr. I keen gow howm now," he snickered. "Dees eeze your chamber," he continued. "You can feex it up az you pray furr."

I shook his hand as he directed me to a vacant bedspace. My room was a small 7-by-7 foot square with a sloping roof. It had a bed and some handmade furniture made from scrap wood. It would eventually provide me 6 square feet of living space, which I would occupy with a swivel office chair. This took up all remaining floor space. So to access my bed, desk, and shelf dresser, I had to first sit in the chair and spin to the appropriate furniture desired. However, it would become home and a sanctuary. It even had cable wired beneath the ceiling, providing a motivating but not very reliable Internet service. Air-conditioning seemed to be stable, holding desired temperature, but we were cautioned not to adjust it, or it would fail. This eventually proved true advice.

Since night crews were sleeping, Grumpy quietly exited to continue leading the tour. We proceeded to the laundry facility, and Grumpy demonstrated the routine. As we approached the laundry, my eyes began to sting. A penetrating ammonia odor scoured my sinuses making my eyes water. This, in addition to the dust, causes my eyes and nose to go into sensory overload. I had to take short little breaths to minimize the sharp sting.

"What is that smell?" I asked, half covering my face.

Grumpy was smiling. "Next on the tour, my friend." He smirked, leading me forward. "But first the laundry instructions," he continued. We entered the laundry buildings.

"Okay, stand in line there," he directed, pointing to the start point and continued briefing. "Then zap strap the laundry bag closed with several straps, not just one, or it will open, and you will lose all your clothes. Use at least three. Got it?" He looked sternly at me. This apparently was important information.

"Yup, I got it. Three straps." I nodded.

"Then fill out paperwork and keep that green receipt. You need to have that to claim your clothes, or you may never see them again." He paused, making sure I acknowledged with a nod. "Then pass the bag to that Afghani laundry clerk." He smiled, looking at the young lady and turned back to me, whispering, "Then hope you'll see your laundry in three days. No worries. The only clothes I ever lost was because the bag opened. Three straps!"

I chuckled at the preciseness of the operations and observed the mechanical procedure in progress as several Americans had demonstrated whilst we stood there discussing it.

"I usually jus' puts two straps, but I weaves dem thru the mesh real tite like—ya'll see dis." An America soldier, who overheard our discussion, held up his bag, demonstrating his expert technique in clothes loss prevention.

"And that works well too," Grumpy closed with a nod and smile as we departed the tent into the ammonia stench.

Just around the corner was the poo pond. It was the open pit circular sewage sump that is so large it can be clearly seen on a Google satellite image. It was right behind the laundry. During a westerly wind, the entire camp was infused with the sewage stench. Unbelievably, I did get used to it. However, there were some days the intensity was overbearing. With a west wind, I had to sleep with my nose covered as the fumes easily penetrated our tents.

Grumpy smiled as he showed me the pond and pointed to the "no swimming" sign. We both laughed.

We continued touring around, dusty step by dusty step, getting the first kiss of sunburn on our faces as he showed me the other two DFACS, the NATO, American and Canadian gyms as well as the Canadian barber shop and Canadian lines. We finished at the Niagara DFAC for lunch.

After overfilling my tray to satisfy my starvation from the three-day travelling fast, we sat next to a few young American infantry soldiers. The newest was rapidly stuffing his face with what he thought were french fries while the experienced colleagues smirked and chuckled, hiding the truth. The french fry eater twisted his face and slowed his chewing:

"These fries are awful, kinda rubbery and fishy!" he disgustingly reported in his Southern accent.

"That's not fries, Bob. That's whut theys calls cal-i-mari." His colleagues chuckled.

"Cali whut?" he responded.

"Squid, y'all!" They both broke out in laughter as the novice calamari eater had never been exposed to such flavor and began politely pulling it out of his mouth with his fingers, silently dry-heaving in the process.

Grumpy and I chuckled at the entertainment and finished lunch. Satisfied that KAF had not changed very much, he showed me to our next required location. I do not know how we returned to where we started. I was still geographically confused but a little less anxious.

That afternoon was filled with more administrative paperwork, training, and briefings. The entire team was required to walk through a mock-up IED (improvised explosive device) minefield, reviewing safety drills and IED hazards. By this time, it was 36 degrees. Wearing fighting gear and helmets gave us a taste of what was to come.

"The first group was getting hammered with instruction. "Stop, stop, stop. IED, IED, IED," the sergeant yelled.

"So who's in charge of everyone in this vehicle? What the hell are you gonna do now? Five and twenty drills—do it!" he yelled specific instructions, expecting immediate action of his trainees—also adding graphic detail to what would happen if we did not do it right.

"Some of these IEDs have enough explosive power to rip a tank apart!" He hollered. "Get your shit together, ladies and gentlemen. You two, sweep the front and rear up close. You take up observation.

You sweep the back of the vehicle for potential traps" he kept yelling direction to us sleepy trainees.

We had conducted this training extensively and repeatedly over the past six months, not only the basics but also with respect to being shot down and concurrently being in a firefight while treating casualties. It was called combat first aid. And we briefed it daily in our jobs. It was real, especially if we were shot down.

"Roto 8, you are finished for this afternoon. Next timing is 1930. Bring your pistols to verify they work," a familiar voice bellowed. It was Sergeant Ricky. He was our training noncommissioned officer (NCO). With a vast experience in the army, weapons, and Afghanistan, he led preparatory training for field craft and tactics in Canada; now he was there to help transition us into the war. He was a keen professional soldier, but cross his intent, and you could set his emotions off like a bullet in a steel cage—a ricochet—or Sergeant Ricky for short.

At this time, I don't recall much. I must have slept in the bus, and then I think my head hit the pillow for a quick nap. And what seemed like seconds later, someone woke me. It was dark. It was 1920 hours and time to go to the pistol range.

The drive was unique. The rows of stacked sea cans on either side of the narrow road made it appear like a dust trof to navigate through. The brown fog rose from the vehicles and obscured vision to only a few feet at times. Since the road was barely two cars wide, the driver proceeded at a walking pace in order to veer from the oncoming headlights, which were only visible about 50 feet away. Despite the heat, the windows remained closed to protect from the incapacitating dust.

We arrived at the pistol ranges. It could have been Tarnac Farm, but I don't recall for sure. It was once outside the outskirts of KAF but was now part of the area. Tarnac Farm is significant. In 2002, an American F-16 pilot killed the first four Canadian soldiers here. The pilot had mistaken them as enemy and attacked them. He did not have PID. It served as a reminder to always have positive identification of the enemy prior to shooting. The rule was if any doubt existed, wait for another day.

One public speaker briefed us before deployment that the bottom line on pulling the trigger is whether or not you can sleep with your decision. Appropriately, this affirmation of restraint and patience would come to challenge us on a daily basis. The result leads to many nightmares that some soldiers still have to this day. It's cliché to say damned if you do and damned if you don't, but in Afghanistan, you're sort of damned just by being there.

At the range, I stepped off the bus into another cloud of brown talcum. Dim lights illuminated the 25-meter pistol range at the corners, offering just enough light to function. We marched into rows behind ten targets down range, approximately five persons deep in each row. This wasn't about accuracy; it was about proving your weapon worked—a quick five-round shoot and review of safety drills.

It was an assembly line shoot, a normal indoctrination procedure on arrival. Along with most others, I had not slept for almost four days. I was mechanically reacting like a cow in the herd. Brain activity had shut down; it was all muscle memory. Hell, I was still mostly asleep. Is this safe? What could go wrong?

"First row, at the 10-meter target, on your own time, fire!" commanded Ricky. He was in charge of safety.

Blam, blam, blam.

That seemed to wake me up a little but not that much. My eyes were mechanically open but my brain was shut off. It reminded me of basic training twenty-five years earlier when I actually fell asleep marching. I didn't think it was possible, but I kept stumbling while hiking beside a cliff in the mountains of British Columbia. Then I finally awoke, realizing I was falling asleep on the march, and there was a 200-foot drop beside me.

"Clear, clear, clear!" he bellowed as he inspected the row of shooters in front. I awoke again. "Next row, advance to the firing position!" Ricky yelled. I looked around and slid forward to my firing spot. My turn.

"With a five-round magazine, load," he commanded. I loaded the magazine and placed the safety on.

"Target in front. At your own time, fire!" I cocked the weapon, took it off safe, looked at the target, and fired. *Blam, blam, blam, blam, blam. Shick.* I automatically removed my magazine, double-cocked the slide, aimed, and fired once more, proving it safe. *Click.* Exercise done. And my eyes started to get heavy again.

"Shooters, make safe you weapons!" Ricky yelled. I already did that. Eyes were a bit sleepy. As were everyone's I had observed.

This required removing the magazine, cocking the weapon as many times as required to clear any remaining bullets, and then test firing down range to ensure it clicks but doesn't fire.

Click, click, click. Blam. The gun fired. "Oops," a humble voice embarrassingly called out. I woke up. That was unusual, sort of alarming actually.

"Number 4, check fire. Is your weapon clear?" boomed Ricky, somewhat perturbed.

"Well, it is now, Sergeant" was the sleepy reply, attempting some levity.

"Number 4, clear your weapon and test fire again!"

Shick, shick. Blam. "Fuck!"

Sergeant Ricky approached the individual and took the firearm.

"You need to remove your fuckin' mag first, soldier!" Sarge cleared the weapon, test fired—*click*—and returned it firmly to the candidate with a small shove.

"Against the back wall for remedial drills!" he ordered. "Next line advance!" he continued onto the program without haste.

"With a five-round magazine—load!"

And the progression continued. At the end, everyone loaded onto the bus and waited patiently—sleeping—until the remedial training was complete on the four failures.

I'm not too sure what happened next. The bus stopped, and robotically each of us staggered into the BAT. I do recall my face falling on a rolled-up jacket being a makeshift pillow. I was exhausted and overwhelmed. I never thought I would get to sleep with my mind racing and body buzzing with the huge sleep debt. But obviously I did . . . until about 2:00 a.m.

MMMMMRRRRAAAAWWWWEEERRR!

A deafening siren shook the camp, repeating its oscillating and screaming sound. I sprung out of bed, disoriented. Where was I? What is that noise? I coughed out some dust. Oh ya, it was coming back to me. I covered my ears.

"What the hell is that?" I yelled into the dark.

"Rocket attack!" a voice hollered back.

And so begins day 2.

"Like a lotus flower that grows out of the mud and blossoms above the muddy water's surface, we can rise above our defilements and sufferings of life." —Buddha

Chapter 4

The Devil's Infidels

I thought I would sleep soundly. However, after settling from the rocket attack, my bliss only lasted two hours as my body adjusted to the twelve-hour time change. Then finally I slept. Then up again. It was a rough sleep, and at 5:00 a.m., I couldn't force the slumber any longer and decided to explore the gym. Perhaps some exercise would help loosen up the stiffness of numerous days of sitting. Exiting the tent, through the partially hinged flapping door, I collided into Grumpy.

"Morning. Are you going to the gym too?" I whispered.

He smirked. "Just coming back. I've been there since three thirty," continuing his stumble to his bunk.

I admired his dedication but acknowledged with a nod that it was a disrupted sleep pattern motivating him. I turned, walking slowly to the gym. The road was dimly lit. Combined with the potholes and large cable bundles strewn across, tripping was highly probable without cautious foot placement each step.

I arrived unscathed. Hoping for a peaceful early morning workout, I was surprised. There were about two hundred soldiers varying in size from the bodybuilding gorillas to the lean marathon runners. With nothing else to do in KAF, this congestion became the norm.

After the gym, a shower, and a quick breakfast, I waited for the bus with the other newly arrived and enjoyed the cool 25-degree air, with only a hint of poo pond lingering. The sun was rising over the desert, not a cloud in the bright blue sky. No coughing yet.

The morning air was breathable until about nine. Once the morning traffic started, the dust rolled up and became debilitating. Over the concrete rocket barriers, the sound of the bus could be heard closing. It was prevailed by a tidal wave of moondust. Once the bus stopped, the wave of moondust continued, bathing us.

"What was the point of showering?" I coughed out rhetorically, joined by a few other coughing chuckles.

This was my first trip to the other side of the airfield, a twenty-minute turtle-pace drive, but we enjoyed it like enthusiastic tourists. The accommodation side of the airfield seemed to stretch forever—the entire length of the runway. The rows upon rows of military vehicles and aircraft never seemed to end. Of course the dusty trip was made longer by the slow-moving traffic jam, which was a normal daily event.

Aircraft were taking off and landing every few seconds, roaring just a few feet above the vehicle traffic at the end of the runway. Two F-16s zipped by in afterburner, staying low to the desert floor before popping aggressively upward, banking and shooting off defensive flares as they broke their trajectories. It was an air show every few minutes.

Finally we arrived at work, our new office for the next year. A warm welcome was given by the outgoing 430 Squadron from Valcartier, Quebec. 430 Squadron always had their way of doing things as does 408 Squadron from Edmonton, Alberta. The fundamentals are the same, but the "how to" had always been different; it made for a professional friendly rivalry.

Task Force Faucon (French for Falcon) had just finished a six-month tour and were extremely happy to see Task Force Freedom arrive. They had accomplished a few milestones. One was moving the operation center to a new location on the airfield without affecting flight support to the army. An operations center and it's logistics team comprised of numerous buildings and dozens of people, vehicles, and aircraft support equipment—literally tons of equipment.

Additionally, they had integrated the Dillon cannons (M134) into operations. Sadly, they also lost two members of their squadron in a terrible accident near Qalat, about 100 kilometers northeast of KAF. On top of everything, they were enduring the war-fighting season in Afghanistan, a time of year when the enemy was very strong and active. This led them to being physically and emotionally drained. It was time to go home.

War fighting season: 430's tour was from April through September. Counterinsurgency operations (COIN) occurred with a focus on diplomacy through the winter. During the summer, their tour, Taliban fighters combined with foreign enemy fighters from the north, west from Iran, and south from Pakistan joined to fight against us "infidels."

After the poppy resin was harvested in May, the Taliban sympathizers exchanged their farming tools for AK-47s. As one Canadian general stated, "We have three seasons of COIN followed by one intense season of war." 430 Squadron had just endured the war; they were hardened and seasoned veterans but exhausted.

They had been involved in some serious fights and had been shot at so much they could differentiate between the sounds of a passing 7.62mm bullet and a .51-caliber bullet missing their helicopters. I was awed from their stories and tactical tips. However, it didn't help lower the anxiety. And I wondered how I would ever attain that tactical sharpness.

The focus in their eyes suggested they never truly relaxed and were always ready for a rocket attack or contemplating a counter attack at a TIC. In Canada, the ordinary person seemed to take relaxation and security for granted. Freedom and security was never guaranteed in Afghanistan, especially for a westerner.

After introductions and tactical banter, Grumpy and I were assigned to merge with 430 crews. The aim was to fly with experienced crews for a few days before they departed in order to impart some knowledge. This helped orient us to radio, airspace, ground forces, and tactical realities. Once 430 crews departed, the first officers and gunners from 408 would arrive and be oriented by myself, Grumpy, and the other new Griffon section leaders. (A section is two griffons working together—eight people.)

Despite appreciating the mentorship of the outgoing crew, the feeling was not 100 percent reciprocal. From the 430 Faucon's perspective, a new "green" captain would be in charge making life-and-death decisions for these veteran teams. And what credibility could we possibly offer at this point?

Our tour commenced with the 430 commanding officer introducing himself then referring us to our orientation. I was directed to the Tactical Operations Center (TOC) of the helicopter squadron to meet the aircraft captain I'd be replacing.

"Bonjour, eez nice to finally meet chu encore," a tall slender man stated in a heavy French accent. "Now I kin go howme." I knew him from Canada. I had worked with him at before as instructors at a flight school. He was always professional and cheerful—"chipper." I'll refer to him as Chip because of his upbeat personality.

Chip looked younger than his age. He inquisitively raised his eyebrow, studying me for readiness. He had confidence in me but knew I was green; my education was about to start. But he was happy to finally see me; I was the fruition that the end of his tour had finally come; but he would show me what he could in our limited hand-over.

He showed me the TOC. It resembled the bridge of the Star Trek Enterprise. All the chairs oriented toward the front of the room where numerous map screens and digital text boards displayed conversations of platoon commanders and tactical activity within the Canadian AO (area of operations), mostly Panjwaii. Center stage was a large screen TV showing a live video feed from a surveillance drone in the South Panjwaii District, near Canadian troops at Sperwan Ghar.

A few staff soldiers were tending radios and following the flight paths of the Canadian helicopters currently airborne. They were keenly attentive in order to update the operations officer on a moment's notice if he entered.

A senior shift supervisor, shadowed by Sergeant Ricky, his 408 Squadron replacement, announced "We got a TIC in progress at Howz-e!"

There was an IED explosion and then combat occurring along the main highway, which circled Afghanistan. Each day, it seemed, logistical supply convoys escorted by civilian contracted security companies (usually call sign Compass) were ambushed with IEDs and engaged by small parties of enemy fighters often injuring or killing people. The explosions frequently destroyed vehicles also leaving craters in Highway 1. The remaining unscathed traffic veered around the holes and continued. This was normal. Despite the news, most Canadians in Canada were not aware that it was a daily event.

"We got Shakedown 25 Flight responding for overwatch." I overheard the duty sergeant state.

"Go get the CO (commanding officer)," ordered the duty officer to his radio operator, a corporal.

Wow! This was a firsthand "real life" demonstration of how things were to unfold for my year to come. This was like a training exercise in Wainwright, Alberta, but real. This was day two—already action. My contemplations were interrupted as Chip and I were asked to leave. The commanding officer (CO) arrived and was requesting an update; it would be too disruptive to run an operation and a tour at the same time.

"Sir, Shakedown 25 Flight responding to TIC in progress here. They'll be on target in seven minutes, fully armed, forty-five minutes playtime." I heard him briefing the CO as the door came closed separating us from the action.

"You'll get acquainted to that soon enough. It's daily," Chip advised, leading me upstairs to a lounge and offered me a Diet Pepsi. I hadn't had a soft drink in a week. What a treat! It was ice cold. The room was cool, and I sat back in a recliner and put my feet up. That was the most refreshing Pepsi I think I have ever had. I almost felt like I was on vacation for a second. We bantered, exchanged stories, and listened for any news of the unfolding battle for Shakedown 25 Flight from passersby in the hall.

"They were stood down," someone reported.

"That was quick. Why's that?" I raised my chin toward Chip.

"The Taliban broke contact. Once they hear the helicopters, they stop fighting and hide because they know they will lose when we find them," Chip explained. "They hide, pick up shovels, fake being farmers, and escape in the green zone," he added, pointing to a map of the irrigated treed area along the Arghandhab River.

The Arghandhab valley was filled with canals, tunnels, and grape huts which were great for tactical concealment for the Taliban to either hide or ambush from. Pursuing them by foot was lethal as they often placed explosive traps to protect escape routes. However, it was very difficult to escape from a helicopter once we had PID. Once a bad guy was caught and PID was attained, their life expectancy was minutes. Thus, the Taliban, upon hearing any helicopters, broke away from the fight to hide.

"Let's go back to the TOC," Chip stated.

In the TOC, the situation had already moved forward; the TIC was old news. A black-and-white TV screen was showing three men walking in the mountains near Sperwan Ghar.

"What's going on there?" I asked to the duty sergeant.

"It is a UAV (unmanned aerial vehicle) drone feed," he advised.

"HHQ (higher headquarters) has been covertly tracking these FAMs from a known enemy arms cache near the Reg Desert for several hours, if not days." He pointed to the screen and then the side screen. "If you follow the text on the prompter over there, you'll get the entire story since late last night," he added.

The insurgents had been using explosives from a secret cache to conduct ambushes near Sperwan Ghar, Gundi Ghar, and Howz-e Me Dhad. They had trekked up this particular mountain and placed some new material in a secret stash. It was all captured and recorded on UAV camera. To me, it was very surreal. These guys looked like normal local people. How would I be able to tell the difference? I turned to leave the TOC.

"Dead men walking," the radio operator stated to get my attention.

"Pardon me?" I leaned back in the door.

"You don't wanna leave, sir. There's a Shamus team coming, and these FAMs (fighting aged males) are about to be hit."

Shamus was the call sign for a team of Kiowa warrior helicopters that patrolled the entire area twenty-four hours a day. They were armed with .50-caliber forward-firing machine guns and rockets. They had been in theater over a year and were known for taunting fights with the bad-guys. They knew how the Taliban played ROE (rules of engagement) games and countered with the art of provocation.

Basically, the ROE at that time was that you cannot shoot a suspect, only a proven. But you can always use self-defense and match lethal force with lethal force. So the "art of provocation" is to entice the known bad guys to shoot at you, which included making yourself somewhat vulnerable too. 408 Squadron, Roto 8 pilots and gunners would eventually get some informal mentoring with Shamus and use this technique—effectively.

I watched the video feed. Three men were sauntering casually up the mountain. Moments later, numerous clouds of dust and a white flash exploded around them. The TV screen flashed black and white, and then went blurry and slowly regained focus. There was a massive dust cloud. The camera operator scanned left and right quickly to try and track any movement. It panned out to a wider view angle. It found one person staggering down the hill to the left of the screen. It went to color mode.

A shadow of a Kiowa warrior flew over and disappeared off screen. Seconds later, the ground around this last man exploded like popcorn in what appeared to be a .50-caliber strafing run—then two more rocket explosions. Obviously, the second Kiowa's follow-on attack. The last man standing took a direct hit from a rocket.

I saw something flash in from the right of the screen directly onto the FAM. Then the details became obscured by an exploding cloud of dust that dominated the TV screen. I switched my focus to the text bars rolling information on the other TV screen. It was the factual play by play.

Time XX:XX Shamus: "Shamus contact three times FAM on hill top."

Time XX:XX: TOC: "That's your target, no friendlies in the area, cleared to fire."

Time XX:XX: Shamus: "Shamus tally target—in hot."

Time XX:XX: TOC NOTE: "Shamus engages, standing by for battle damage report."

It was an unemotional account of communications regarding the event. I looked at the TV feed again as the picture started to clear. The camera operator on the UAV was switching camera modes from infrared to color, attaining the sharpest perspective. It then went white hot and held. Pieces of hot metal, presumably rocket shrapnel and heated rocks, illuminated alongside what appeared to be warm pieces of body parts spread around a hundred square yards of mountain ridge.

The text screen reported:

Time XX:XX: Shamus: "Shamus BDA (battle damage assessment), grid reference QQ28298235, three times insurgents destroyed, six rockets, fifty rounds of .50-caliber expended, continuing on patrol with Slayer. (Slayer is the airspace controller who coordinates all the aviation resources in the area.) Shamus out."

That was it. A simple aviation task while patrolling the Panjwaii District resulted in three insurgents being killed. Several small arms (weapons such as rifles) and explosives caches were also discovered. Then the Shamus flight of two Kiowa warriors continued on patrol as if it was normal. Possibly several weeks of intelligence reports, finding the targets for days, and then tracking the hours, all culminating in a ten-minute aviation task at the sharp end.

"Holy shit!" I caught myself muttering. This is reality. I had an epiphany that the last eight months of intensive training was now fruition, with a real purpose. There is a war here in Afghanistan. People died daily. I was at war.

Chip saw my face empathizing with it from his own feelings six months earlier.

"Oui—yes, Steve, that was real. You're not on exercise anymore. Welcome to Kandahar," he affirmed, staring me right in the eye. He saw my novice apprehension.

"Wow. Rocket attack last night, TIC an hour ago, and watching an engagement of what we will be doing—all within twenty-four hours of arriving. I'm a little overwhelmed," I reflected.

"Watch," he stated, focusing me back to the UAV feed.

I looked at the screen as it panned over to the village a few kilometers away from the Kiowa strike. The locals heard the explosions. They knew there were dead. People started to come out of the village and were walking up the hill.

"What's going on?" I inquired.

"There is a speck of humanity. The women and older children will go up the hill and collect the bodies. Apparently they have to be buried before dark," the sergeant guessed. "Those dead insurgents terrorized them. Yet they respect the same religious traditions and ensure they receive the dignity of an appropriate burial."

I nodded my head. The learning never seemed to end.

"Anyway, you have a big day tomorrow, sir," the duty sergeant concluded as he reviewed the schedule. "Might as well get back and settle in for some sleep. You're up tomorrow with the Devil's' Infidels," he advised.

I raised my brow and smirked inquisitively, indicating I wanted more info about the Devil's Infidels. He said nothing. He gestured with his chin to follow Chip out of the room.

Chip guided me to the flight preparation room. This is where the pilots, gunners, and engineers gathered to determine their tasking for the following day. The crews were divided into four sections, a board detailed: names, table time, briefing time, and launch time for the next subsequent task. I was scheduled for a day familiarization and one at night, which was combined with a Blowtorch (Chinook helicopter) escort mission to move some personnel.

"Devil's Infidels?" I queried.

Chip laughed, explaining, "We got into a TIC, an overwatch task suppressing a tree line with a few thousand rounds. The bad guys were engaging our troops from the green zone. The infantry company commander we were supporting (the officer in charge in the battle below) reported that I-comm chatter used that description of us from an enemy conversation he heard. I-comm chatter is the intelligence network that listens to the enemy radio and interprets what the Taliban are saying at the moment. In this particular case, the Afghanistan interpreter reported that the man being shot at was cursing because he could not escape.

Man One: "You must leave now. The helicopters are engaging."

Man Two: "I cannot leave. I am pinned down and getting shot at by those flying Devil's Infidels!"

We chuckled at the story. Chip continued, "This is my section, and they are very proud of this." He unzipped his flight suit to the waist and showed me his T-shirt beneath, further educating me. "Ironically, we are Quebec Catholics who proudly mock the enemy by wearing this." He pointed to a Griffon logo and words stating, "The Devil's Infidels."

Chapter 5

First Flight

"Blowtorch 60 Flight is clear to the north," the radio cracked, advising KAF tower that the two Griffons and one Chinook were proceeding outside the control zone.

My introductory flight was combined with an actual Chinook escort mission. So my first flight in theater was classed as a mission day.

"All right, guys, let's practice some tactical formation turns," Chip announced over the radio.

"Tac right!" the radio announced. The Chinook veered to the right sharply. This led to a sequence of three aircraft doing an organized ballet of twisting through the air. The sequence allowed the Chinook to avoid enemy fire while allowing the Griffons to position for counterattack, all while maintaining collective integrity.

The Chinook then completed some unannounced surprise turns. "Shakedowns shackle," 26 called, asking us to switch sides for better use of space and tactics. I slid over to the right side of the Chinook while Grumpy, being oriented in the second Griffon helicopter, avoided me and crossed under and behind to the left.

We twisted through the desert sky east of Kandahar city for fifteen minutes, practicing tactics to regain our proficiency.

"Shakedowns, hate to break up all your fun, but we have a task to do; time to go into Nathan Smith," Blowtorch announced. Blowtorch had to drop passengers and cargo into the city central FOB (forward operating base) called Nathan Smith, named after one of the first Canadian soldiers killed in Afghanistan.

The scenery en route was surreal—brown ground, brown city, and bright blue sky making for golden reflections off the mud walls. The city was widespread but lacked tall buildings. The tallest and only colorful building was a bright blue domed mosque, which was part of the religious university. The remainder of the city was a series of walls forming a labyrinth of roads, canals, and courtyards, all made of mud sun-hardened into a concrete strength.

Outside of the main city were smaller villages referred to as compounds along the green zones. The Arghandhab River flows toward the south. Hand-built canals veered off the river, which irrigated the vast areas of grapes, watermelons, pomegranates as well as easily seen green marijuana and opium poppy fields. All this was coated brown because of the summer dust.

"Inbound Nathan Smith," Blowtorch advised as he was on final approach.

"Two Five checks," Chip acknowledged. "Two Six you go high and cover me. We take low. Deconflict at 700 feet," he further instructed Grumpy. This allowed each Griffon to individually maneuver. The top griffon was not allowed below 700 feet and the low griffon not above. It allowed us to individually operate in close proximity to each other but focus on the ground. And in case we lost visual separation with each other, the arbitrary altitude gave us a "do not cross" line to prevent collision.

There were numerous tactical methods that could be executed to conduct escort operations and overwatch protection. Sometimes the situation developed that would require a different technique depending on whether the mission was protection, attack, or observation. It varied quickly, and it was worthwhile to do a brief confirmation over the radio. As often, the biggest threat was the risk of colliding with each other— easily preventable with simple communication.

Once the Chinook was on the ground, the Griffon teams either climbed to be quieter and show respect to civilians around the FOB; or we operated in a distracting, aggressive manner to prevent Taliban from positioning for an attack. This depended on the expected threat briefed prior to flight from the intelligence personnel. Shakedown crews also looked for anything strange such as DShK .51-caliber heavy machine guns, POL (pattern of life) changes or rockets (RPG) teams maneuvering to ambush the Chinook. In most cases, just enemy dickers were spotted. Dickers were Taliban positioned to report and/or strike if the conditions were favorable to attack the Chinook. Often, the Griffon presence prevented the attack.

Our Griffon team tailed Blowtorch into the FOB, checking the flanks for any dickers. I saw nothing peculiar, but then again, everything was peculiar. I was so hyped from training and anxious from the past two days of incidents that I could not tell the difference between what was normal and what was not. It was a very overwhelming.

In training, we became conditioned that people with shovels were digging IEDs. But now that we were there, I realized almost everyone had a shovel. They were filling in irrigation holes for the winter so the waters from the river could be trapped in the fields. Additionally, a shovel over the shoulder looks remarkably similar to an RPG from a distance; and RPGs were not uncommon in the ANA (Afghan National Army) or AN Police. So it became evident very soon that an RPG was not necessarily a threat unless pointed at you.

And weapons? Everyone had weapons. Farmers all had Russian AK-47s, usually one per family as a minimum. The question then became what are they doing with them? Are they concealed or open? Are they shoulder slung or aimed? What is the behavior of the person with the weapon?

As the Chinook lowered its speed to land at Camp Nathan Smith, Chip and I peeled away to air-patrol the FOB, looking at anything suspicious outside a quarter mile.

Meanwhile, 26 with Grumpy popped to higher altitude and observed the overall perspective. He maintained a position to both protect us and allow himself to dive in like a hawk to counterattack threats if required. Based on what he saw, he would also advise the Chinook for the safest departure direction.

"Blowtorch lifting in fifteen seconds—southbound," 60 announced. Fifteen seconds gave us time to get quickly organized, assess the departure path, and fly to arrive in a flanked protective position as Blowtorch lifted away. When this was done well, the choreography would impress a crowd at an air show.

"Zat formation rayjoin worked out better zan expected. I guess you gotz a bon demonstration on zis first day," Chip proudly stated in his French accent, admiring his smooth execution.

"Sweet." I was impressed. We accelerated over the city at a low level, escorting the Chinook back to KAF, a short trip for Blowtorch today.

The radio sounded, "Blowtorch is clear to the south. Thanks, we can take it in solo, guys. You can proceed with training."

"Roger dat," Chip replied.

"25, this is 26. Ops authorized us to proceed to the Reg for dust ball landing training and gunnery," Grumpy announced from Shakedown 26's radios. He was monitoring Freedom Operations (the TOC) frequency, and I was monitoring Slayer's air space frequency. We had limited number of radios, so between two helicopters, we had to independently listen and then share information on a private frequency between us. The gunners from the Devil's Infidels in the back of my helicopter were vibrating with excitement, hoping for a TIC every time Slayer talked. However, there was no TIC for us yet.

"It's good to be finished walkin' the dog," a voice stated over the intercom. It was a friendly rivalry between the two helicopter types. The Griffon crews preferred hunting for bad guys over escorting Chinooks, and conversely, Chinooks hated flying slow because of the Griffon's speed limitations. They had superior a speed and power but could not use it if they wanted protection. Our retort to them bragging about speed was that we were "walking the dog." It was just like having a big dumb dog on a leash constantly panting and pulling us along. We had to often remind them to "heel dog" or "slow down 10 knots (buster 10)." They despised our slow speed and limited power. So on hot days, when Griffons were struggling to take off when maximum power was required, it was common to hear cocky comments from the Chinook pilots over the radio in retaliation: "I think I can, I think I can, I think I can . . .".

"Absolutely, time to practice for TICs!" an eager voice replied. "Let's go shoot some shit."

I aimed our section south, then we split into single-ship entities as we approached the Reg Desert. Generally, it is safest in twos, as a team. However, the threat was minimal in the Reg. If an insurgent wanted to shoot at a helicopter, he would have no place to hide, so it would be a suicide mission. And people who kill helicopters are not suicide bombers; they are specialists wanting to collect a bounty. Martyrs in the desert were not a concern.

I aligned the Griffon with the landing spot and slowed my approach.

"On final approach," I called.

The dust began to rise behind like a surfer's tidal wave. It approached the cabin, and the right gunner called, "Dust ball by the door."

About 2–3 feet above the ground, the ball of dark brown talcum dust entirely engulfed the helicopter. The dust rushed in the open cabin doors, up under my visor, burning my eyes, forcing me to close one. I held the controls smoothly as Chip called the radar altimeter and ground speed:

"20 feet, 10 feet, 5 knots . . ." Cough, cough. *Pooof!*

The sky darkened as the Griffon grabbed the ground. The dust matured into a cloud about 300 feet in height, blocking the sunlight. The talcum fine dust was not like anything I had experienced before. I could barely see the pitot tube on the nose of the helicopter. We waited for the dust to clear enough to depart.

I coughed and rubbed my eyes. "I can't see a fuckin' thing."

Chip wiped his chin and cleaned dust from his visor, getting ready for the departure. "Za FOBs are like dees, so we haves to practice. You did okay. Let's do anodder."

I briefed the takeoff plan to the crew. "All right, guys. It's clear right, moving up," I called my actions.

"Clear left, gun ready," the left gunner called.

"Clear right, gun ready, skids free, move up," the right gunner called.

"Standing by," Chip answered, indicating he was ready at the controls in case I lost reference and needed assistance. The dust thickened and swallowed the helicopter again. I held my breath and looked at the instruments and went vertically to clear the obstacles and gently moved the controls forward, pitching the nose gently down to accelerate.

Five seconds later, the helicopter reentered clear air and a bright sky. I climbed and turned around to see a thick ball of dust that resembled an explosion. I exhaled forcefully, clearing the dust from around my mouth. I was shocked by the difference between the dust balls experienced during training in Arizona and here in Afghanistan. It was significant. Arizona was grainy; this was moondust. I looked over a few miles and saw 26's similar dust explosions.

"That was nuts—my eyes are burning!" I announced.

"Yup," Chipper coughed out, clearing dirt from his mouth. "Let's do some more—pfft, pfft," he answered while blowing the dirt out of his microphone, indicating he was also suffering but used to it. The gunners wore full-face shields resembling storm troopers from *Star Wars,* so the dust wasn't as bad to them.

We continued another twenty minutes taking turns at landing until our roles as the pilot flying and the nonflying pilot went smoothly. Once Chip was satisfied, he announced fun time. "Shall we review some gunnery?"

"Yes, pulleese," I hollered excitedly.

"Woo-yea!" the gunners responded. "Finally get to have some fun shooting now that this 'pilot shit' is done."

"26, it's 25. You ready for some gunnery?"

"That's a big Romeo Tango (roger that)," 26 replied. I could sense the eagerness behind his voice.

"Check that—we're going to Texas Helo. Call when you're in position," Chip commanded as our two-ship formation journeyed east to an isolated mountain where many of the coalition helicopters practice aerial gunnery.

I watched the other helicopter aim toward us from the right as we passed eastbound. He climbed and banked sharply over and behind us and then dropped into the left rear about 100 meters away.

"26 is in," Grumpy called, indicating his helicopter had caught up and in tactical formation again.

"Steve, first thing we do is a fly past to look for za people. Zere are Bedouins living in za range, so we will just overfly a few times to makes sure zey get out of za way before we shoot," Chip informed.

"What are you talking about? People live there?" I was perplexed.

Chip pointed to the ridge of mountains oriented southward. There was a deep cut from the sand edge of the desert easily 300 feet deep and 200 meters wide. At the lip where the sand wall levels, the desert continues for 100 miles west and 50 miles south to Pakistan. Often caravans of camels could be seen slowly migrating across the rolling sandy hills just to the west side of Texas Helo.

"Over zere, on za west floor are Bedouin tents." He pointed. "They come out to collect za brass casings after we shoot. They sell it backs to us at za KAF market as brass camel sculptures and stuff," Chip added.

I was astonished. These groups of tents had been set up for several years. Women and children (WACs) were playing among the tents, but they moved out of the way as we circled. It was a brass collection tribe.

The hot brass casings from the helicopter machine guns would fall close to them if not on them. Bedouin children will competitively wrestle to collect more than the other as we fired thousands of rounds from directly above. The brass was sold to artisan merchants who converted them into artifacts.

"Area clear. Bedouins clear. Target brief. Target iz za white marked boulder, one o'clock at 1 kilometer, marked by lead's rounds. Zis will be a single pass, one plus one, right gun attack, 200 meters, 200 feet high, all effects east." Chip gave the fire orders over the radio.

"26, visual friendlies, tally target, check brief," a happy tone responded from Grumpy's radio.

Chipper continued internally, "Right gunner, copy brief and target?"

"Roger dat, sir, tally target, standing by," the right gunner acknowledged professionally.

Chip steered the aircraft to about 200 meters left of the targets and about 200 feet above the valley floor.

As we approached the target, he commanded. "Right gunner, are you visual with 26 and the Bedouins?" Chip asked.

"Roger." It was a last-chance check just to note where the closest friendlies were in order to ensure no one got hurt other than the targeted red rock rapidly approaching.

"Cleared to fire," he commanded

Up until that point, the only weapons I had commanded was the C6 (M240). I knew this wasn't going to be the "chug-chug-chug" that I was accustomed to, but I never expected this. The initial noise spike painfully penetrated my skull through the helmet.

BRAAAAAAAAAP . . . BRAAAAAP . . . BRAAAAAAAAAAAAAAAAAAP.

Fifty rounds per second of 7.62mm tracer volleyed off the painted rock target. It was a lava flow of light and a piercing noise that overcame cockpit communications. The smoke from the rotating barrels spooled out beside my head and filled the cockpit through my window. The gunner stopped every three to four seconds for a quick communication break. If no one was yelling "check fire," then he continued blasting at the target.

Out the left, young Bedouins were running toward the falling casings, fighting each other along the way. I looked right and saw the bullets looking like laser beams ricocheting of the rock from 26 joining our fire stream of bullets.

"Out of arcs," the gunner stated, stopping his gun. This advised the pilot that he couldn't accurately or safely shoot anymore, and it was up to us to adjust our flight path or escape. At times he may yell "kick right or left" to tell us to press the yaw pedals to twist the Griffon in the air, allowing for continued firing time on the target.

"Same attack, left gun south to north," he commanded to 26.

"Roger that," Grumpy acknowledged from 26.

"You have better view, you have control Steve!" Chip stated.

I turned around to realign on the target for the left gunner to fire. I aimed the helicopter just left of the Bedouins to not drop casings directly on them.

"Left gunner, Bedouins WACs right, same target. Fire!" I called.

"Visual WACs, tally target!" he replied.

BRAAAAAAAAAAAAP.

"Out of arcs. Weapon safe," called left gunner as we passed.

"After zis pass, we quit," Chip advised over the radio. "The Bedouin WACs are too close now they're gonna take a ricochet. Let's go to the Reg to finish up." Chip made the safety call.

We proceeded out to the middle of the desert to continue shooting, near an old dead lakebed where the sand was smooth.

"For fun, we're gonna do a double gun, full forward fire to show you—just cause it's cool." He smirked. "Now keep your hands inside the window, or they'll get sawed off!" He grinned but was serious. If I stretched my arm out the open window, it would be sawed off at the elbow in less than a second. With that in mind, I slouched and dipped my body behind my small armor plate on the left of my seat. Chip noticed and shook his head, smiling at my expense.

We overflew the target, a small plant bush easily identifiable to both aircraft.

"Target brief. Reference east-west lying lake bed 2 kilometers south?" he directed to 26.

"Contact lake" was the quick answer.

"Center of lake south side is a prominent bush," Chip further described.

"Contact bush," Grumpy answered.

"That is the target," Chip stated.

"Talllleeee target," Grumpy sang triumphantly.

"Dive attack from 500 feet, left egress!" Chip called over the radio.

"Roger that!" was the acknowledgment.

We raced across the desert floor at maximum speed and pitched up aggressively to 500 feet. 26 was 800 meters behind with Grumpy flying. Then we dove at the target, accelerating.

"Gunners, do you have the target?"

"Roger that, sir," they both replied.

"Left-right gunners, fire!"

The sound was deafening beside my head. Chip flew directly at the target and wiggled the yaw control pedals left and right steering the bullets across the target. The desert floor exploded into a dust cloud with splashes of tracers occasionally bouncing off small rocks. I squeezed my helmet tighter to eliminate some of the noise.

He turned aggressively left at 200 meters away. The left gunner stopped firing, but the right gunner continued suppressing until Grumpy's bullet stream joined on the target.

All I could smell was cordite, and my ears rung.

"That's bloody nuts!" I yelled, overwhelmed with the smoke, the fire, the noise, and the dive attack! "But so cool!" I couldn't help but smile as I wiggled my jaws trying to clear the ringing in my ears.

"Ha-ha-ha!" Chipper was laughing proudly. The other guys followed.

"Woo-hoo, yee-ha. Fuckin' A!" the heavy French accent gleefully cheered from the back left.

"That's why the Taliban call it the breath of Allah!" the gunner on the right proclaimed. He laughed. "Are you okay up there, Steve?" he asked mockingly. I smiled. I knew they were laughing at my shock.

"Dat's why dey call us za Devil's Infidels!" the left gunner proudly stated, referring to the enemy's description of them.

"It's getting dark soon," 26 advised over the radio. His smile could be heard through his voice.

"Roger that. Let's go to the FARP and then head home," Chip agreed as he directed me with his arm pointing in the direction to fly.

The FARP is the fuel and ammo replenishment point. All the helicopters stopped and fueled with the engines running so they could be ready for the next mission immediately without shutting down.

"You can lead us back. We'll take number 2 position and get some formation practice," Chip advised to Grumpy in the other helicopter.

"Roger."

It was my turn to fly protection. I slipped in behind Grumpy and practiced maneuvering to cover lead to KAF. It was an overwhelming orientation so far.

The sun was setting in the west, and the sky was a bright rusty orange. It was beautiful considering the lifelessness. Yet with such a hostile environment, there were villages and Bedouin towns every few miles all throughout the desert. The people here were rugged and able to make life survivable despite the harshness.

"Let's grab some gas, food, and brief. We have a mission later tonight, and we'll do the familiarization again but on NVG (night vision goggles)," Chip concluded and briefed to all over the radio.

"Roger that. 26 out," Grumpy responded.

"Shakedown 25, this is Freedom Ops, over." The squadron TOC was calling.

"Go for 25," I replied.

"Gas up and top your ammo. Ricky will join you at the FARP. You have passengers at X-ray ready to go to Graceland," he informed us of our new tasking.

And this would become normal, a mission came in while we were airborne. No time to plan, just go. My night orientation was just turned into a mission . . . but Graceland meant Special Forces.

"Go for Shakedown," Chip answered.

Chapter 6

Night Flight Orientation

"Freedom Ops, this is Shakedown 25 Flight at the FARP, estimating X-ray in fifteen minutes," Chip advised over the radio.

Hasty mission changes were common. Actually, I preferred the hasty mission over the planned mission. The end state was the same in Afghanistan, but planned missions seemed tiresome and pedantic for a small scale missions. Too much emphasis on formalities and something referred to as "battle procedure"—systematic method of planning to execute a mission when in reality, the plan never seemed to survive first contact with the enemy. Now if the enemy came to the planning sessions, then I am sure all would work out flawlessly.

Hasty missions, on the other hand, were given quick over the radio. "You, go here and do this." Simple. The tactical situations and enemy intelligence briefings were often speculative based on past events. Then intelligence would forecast future events based on their "sources." Despite their efforts, often, they were like a bad weather forecast. Expect sunshine but get shot at or expect dark and gloomy, and nothing happens. So from my experience, I preferred the "giddyap" style. Just give 'er!

Since this was common, our days with only one task usually expanded into three, four, or five tasks as the tactical activity unfolded. To prepare, we took a cooler with food expecting long days. The common load for the crew was Pop-Tarts, water, and Red Bull.

I remember having numerous days in which I was strapped to a cockpit seat for ten hours with a full ballistic vest, tactical weapons vest, pistol, and ammo all on top of dual-layer clothing for fire protection. The cockpit was rarely below 40 degrees Celsius (105 Fahrenheit), leaving us soaked in sweat before we even lifted off the ground. And the only time we stepped out was at a fuel stop when we could pee on the rocket defense berms, snooze in our seats, or stretch while waiting for the next mission, but the rotor never stopped.

"Zis is excellent. We can get za night training done too," Chip stated. "And I can go howme sooner!" he added with a sarcastic giggle.

"All right, guys, let's goggle up while we wait," he told the crew and subsequently hinted to the other aircraft with hand gestures. Each of us prepared our night-vision goggles (NVG) and attached them to our helmets. Ricky joined us at the FARP to refresh his night gunnery. In addition to his operations and training responsibilities, he was also a gunner—tonight he is also conducting his gunnery orientation under the supervision of the 430 Squadron outgoing gunner.

"Welcome aboard Ricky, can you pass forward our NVGs?" Chip stated.

Ricky passed me my goggle bag from behind my armored seat. I clicked the NVGs into their mounts and strung the electrical connection to the battery pack behind my head. When I clicked the goggle tubes forward, the world was illuminated once again in a green haze. I twisted the tubes to clear the haze and sharpen the image. The world became clear, but green.

"On goggles left," I stated, letting the crew know I could see.

"Goggles right. Left gun on goggles. Right gun on goggles," everyone sequentially advised.

"25, after FARP, come to X-ray and pick up two passengers for Graceland," the radio ordered.

"Shakedown 25 flight, roger," Chip responded.

Graceland was a Special Forces base. Apparently, it was the former home of Taliban leader, Mullah Omar, who was ousted during the initial war. It was now home to Coalition Forces conducting special missions and training for local ANA.

"Two full throttles, complete the takeoff check, and let's go," Chip commanded as he rolled the throttles, bringing the rotor to full speed.

"KAF tower Shakedown 25 Flight at the FARP request air taxi to X-ray ramp," I asked over the tower.

"Shakedown 25, winds zero-eight-zero degrees at 5 knots, altimeter two-niner-niner-five, cleared air taxi direct X-ray," Tower answered as we lifted the two helicopters sequentially east for the mile-long flight.

On arrival to the ramp, a couple of civilian-looking guys with beards, long hair, and jeans were waiting for the helicopters. I lifted my goggles to view them in the ambient ramp light, not looking at all like soldiers but obviously Snake Eaters, a slang term for Special Forces. They often lived a harsh life surviving on minimal resources in remote areas doing their "business"; hence, the descriptive nickname. These were most likely Canadians from JTF-2, a special counterterrorist organization that was "apparently" employed in the Afghanistan area. There was no need to ask for a passenger manifest; there wouldn't be one for the team—Snake Eaters travelled incognito.

"What the hell? Is that dude actually wearing sunglasses?" Ricky stated sarcastically. The passenger, like most of us, was wearing ballistic glasses and had probably broken or lost the clear lenses. I myself had gone through several pairs, leaving only my shaded lenses to wear. So I understood the dark sunglasses at night problem. However, it did make an opportunity to poke some fun at the stereotype approaching the chopper.

"No way! Is dat za terminator? Is he getting on hayr or on two-seex?" the right gunner's French accent inquired.

"Here. Go get 'em," Chip stated laughing at the description.

The right gunner hopped out and escorted our passenger onboard. He strapped himself in like he had done it a hundred times. He didn't flinch amidst the apparent jocularity of the Devil's Infidels. He didn't put on a headset, just rose his thumb in the air, converted it to a karate chop which sharply chopped into the direction he wanted to go. I smartly replied with my own thumb up and karate chopped in the proper direction, mumbling over the intercom so only the crew could hear.

"Not that way, Rambo. This way," which was supported by a few chuckles from the infidels. *(Despite the mocking jocularity towards these specialists; nothing but respect is felt. These guys do things that only a rare few are capable of. I'm just glad to drive them to the job; and also that they are on our side.)*

"26 is green to go," Grumpy announced, keying Chip to wind up the throttles.

As we flew past the airfield and cleared the security fence (outside-the-wire) to the north, Chip called, "Fence out."

I replied, "ASE, guns, lights, check." It was a standard checklist to prepare the aircraft for battle. I ensured the antimissile flares were enabled, the gunners' guns were enabled, and the external lights were blacked out. The only way we could be seen was with night-vision devices.

Conversely, it was important to complete this checklist "fence in and fence out" on arrival to a FOB to ensure the flares and guns did not fire off inadvertently. The "fence" drill was a last-chance safety check. The flares are devices designed to fool a heat-seeking missile. Sometimes the flares would fire spontaneously. That was called a false hit.

This was unnerving as the loud bang of the flares going off implied a missile was coming to greet you. If a missile didn't explode near the helicopter within a couple of seconds, it was a false hit, and you could relax. If it did explode? Well, I suppose you would not notice the difference. After several hundred of these events, we became quite desensitized.

"So ze plan is to drop off passengers and zen go to za desert to experience ze flares and zen some night gunnery and dust ball landings. After that, if we have za time, we'll go hunt for IED planters for an hour," Chip radioed the section.

"Roger that" was 26's response. "Hopefully, Slayer will have some work for us tonight," he added.

"Hope so. We'll poke around Panjwaii and try to provoke something," he cockily added.

"What? Provoke?" I responded with naive concern.

Chip coached, "Just about every engagement helicopters have are due to prolonged observation. Ze Taliban are smart; zey are not going to be shooting from obvious locations and make zemselves overt. You have to find zem, watch zem, and zen poke a bit."

"Ohhhh kaaay," I reluctantly replied, hearing some chuckles over the intercom. I was about to get schooled again.

Chip continued, "If you find a suspect, just observe. Let 'em know you see zem and are watching. You'll see. Ze innocent people will go hide, but Taliban will saunter around watching you. Sometimes you have to get 'in zayr face' and make zem draw."

"You got my attention," I responded. "Maybe you gotta show me."

"Yaaa, that's what we're talkin' about! Call Slayer," Ricky cheered over the intercom.

"I will, but we have to get za training done first," Chip stated. I looked towards him, his NVG goggle tubes were staring back at me, shaking left and right at the over enthusiastic gunners.

We approached the city despite having very limited light; it was still brilliant using the night-vision goggles. Chip pointed out the blimp cable. A tethered blimp with a camera attached was moored to Camp Nathan Smith (CNS) and extended vertically to 3,000 feet. It was difficult to see in the day, let alone the night.

Once we located the tether-line, we steered to avoid collision. This had happened to a smaller version spy blimp a few months earlier (to another nation's helicopter). Thankfully, it was only an embarrassment vice, a potentially lethal crash.

"Slayer, this is Shakedown 25 over Kandahar for CNS. Request an airspace update," I stated over the radio.

"Roger that, Shakedown. Shamus One-one is over the city at 5,000 feet going west to east on patrol. Shamus one-two will be following in five minutes. They are escorting a Blackhawk to Camp Nathan Smith. I gotta UAV blocked fifty-five to seventy-five. Stay below five," Slayer advised.

"There's lotsa hardware in the air tonight in this small space." Chip sounded vigilant, referring to seven helicopters spinning in a 6-square-mile corridor. Rightfully so, I was already searching and couldn't see the infrared flashers on the other aircraft because of the city's illumination camouflaging them.

"26, you go in first. We'll overwatch high to the north over the weapons range," Chip briefed to our wingman. We overflew Graceland on a low-approach path and then circled to a reverse direction away from Graceland to see 26 behind us on approach. Then we spiral climbed to a height out of small-arms range toward the north.

"You guys see those Kiowa's?" I asked the crew.

"I got the first set two o'clock, 500 meters by the prison up high," the right gunner answered.

"Visual," Chip called. I could see him stretching his neck around straining to find the other traffic. Then we looked for 26 on approach. He was masked in the town lights.

"26 is down. Lifting in fifteen seconds," Grumpy's crew called stating he had finished his insert.

"Sir, you gotta come north. Those Kiowa's are leaning this way," Ricky called.

"26, it's 25. Lost ya in the lights," Chip called over the radio.

"26, roger. We'll climb north to a thousand," Grumpy stated as he flew the helicopter out of Graceland. Chip was concurrently flying our helicopter onto final approach while avoiding the other semi visible choppers.

After the radio chatter, I advised, "Roger, looking for Kiowa's. Adjust your approach north, Chip."

"Check that," he answered as the helicopter veered right on the westbound track.

"Left gunner, do you have him visual?" Chip injected to Ricky with concern about possible midair collision over the city.

"Yup, but he's going to the left. He should be well above us," he astutely informed.

"Roger. Dropping low onto final approach into the FOB," Chip stated.

I was watching for the other Shamus flight that was still unseen. And where was the Blackhawk? I noticed Shakedown 26 climb out north. He was clear. We were getting close to the FOB.

"Check that. The other Shamus flight is just coming over the ridge now. He's clear—no conflict," I answered.

"26, Shamus 12 is at your six o'clock for 1 mile, same altitude," I advised to Grumpy's aircraft over the radio of the possibly threatening traffic.

"Got 'em, visual. Thanks. Proceeding north. Why aren't they talking on Slayer's frequency?" he answered and rhetorically commented in frustration as Chip had maneuvered us over the large rock barrier entering the FOB.

"Clear the wall and below. Clear below for landing," the right gunner advised as he leaned out scanning for obstacles.

"The Shamus is clear now, and 26 is high in overwatch," the radio informed.

Everyone refocused on landing duties. On touchdown, the stoic passenger raised his thumb and hopped out, adjusting his sunglasses as he disappeared into the compound. He didn't have a clue that there were seven aircraft overhead and a cable tether all competing for the same few miles of airspace.

"All right, that was busy," Chip stated, reflecting comically on the obvious. "Is it clear now?"

"Yup, they are all east. Let's go west," I answered. It was extremely confusing. Everyone was looking out for helicopters among the lights of the city. Everything was a blurry green. The biggest concern was trying to avoid a midair collision—which was realistic.

"Roger, moving up," he announced, queuing us to our takeoff duties.

"25, we check your down and clear. We are maintaining high overwatch," 26 advised.

"Roger that—lifting now," I advised over the radio.

"26, roger. Go north," Grumpy called over the radio.

"Check." We lifted the five and a half tons of helicopter into the air. As he reached the height of the west wall, he tipped the nose gently forward and started accelerating into the green haze.

BANG! BANG! BANG! BANG!

A loud explosive series of shotgun blasts went off just as we lifted over the wall. My eyes enlarged. The side of the cockpit illuminated with bright light. Crap. I couldn't believe this! We were being engaged on takeoff. All this shit within my first few days in Afghanistan. It was logical—an opportune time for the enemy to shoot a helicopter and then follow with a ground attack in the confusion, an expected occurrence, which is a reason the armed griffons were deployed in the first place.

"Is that a contact near Graceland?" I called.

"Ahh, Tabernac, colis," Chip swore. It was not the reaction I expected. His tone immediately aligned me with reality. With the confusion of the aircraft doing the dance of death with other helicopters in the dark sky prior to landing, I forgot to safe the flare dispenser. I forgot my first "fence-in" drill.

On departure, the aircraft sensed a false missile attack that caused it to fire off a salvo of hot flares into the FOB. If they had landed in a fuel supply area, the mistake could have ended in an entirely different outcome.

"Shit, I'm sorry. I could have set off a fireworks show if we hit a POL (petroleum, oil, and lubricants) pit!" I stated as we flew off toward the darkened ridge.

"I guess that's one way to remember the fence drill from now on," Chip added. "No problem. We'll just have a little paperwork to do when we get back," he said, referring to an incident reporting system.

The gunners laughed as it wasn't the first time. "No problem. Notting cot fire," a voice said from the crew. "Let's go find some action."

We immediately refocused on the next mission and didn't dwell on the mistake. I took control and steered the Griffon into formation as we passed the mountain ridge west of Kandahar city. A hushed voice sounded over the radio as we proceeded west, "Shakedown, this is Graceland Zero, appreciate the support, less the flares thanks. Graceland out." I grimaced knowing I screwed up. Chip shrugged it off, "No worries man."

Chip guided the tour over the main routes and FOBs en route to the Reg Desert. The three main routes were Highway 1, Hyena, and Lake Effect. These were east-west roads meandering through the Canadian Area of Operations (AO), Highway 1 being the main ring highway, encircling Afghanistan, and was extensively cratered from IEDs.

"What's that burning along the highway? Is that a blown-up vehicle?" I asked, referring to the bright plume of green light and subsequent specs of green around a dark hole.

"Oui. Look at the crater. You can see za thermal hot spots with ze goggles. All ze traffic is diverting around the highway. Oh, check out that truck!" Chip noticed a transport vehicle was lying on its side, almost cut into two pieces and still smoldering.

As I inspected the carnage from the IED attack of a few hours earlier, blinding plumes of green light a couple of miles to our left distracted me. Balls of light were shooting into the sky, illuminating the mountains. I was startled and started to veer away to the north. "What the hell is that?"

"It's black illumination. Someone is firing infrared flares into ze sky. The friendly troops, possibly Special Forces, are observing with night-vision technology for movement in ze area or along ze mountain ridges," Chip answered. "Look under your goggles."

I lifted my goggles and saw nothing. Black. Dark. Then I looked through my goggles again and saw the IR fireworks show. It was like daylight to anyone on NVG, made it easier for special night missions to happen on the darkest nights.

As we neared the highway, I could see friendly forces on patrols, obviously using the black illumination to their advantage. Also, I watched local people in their compounds going about evening activities, totally unaware of the covert activity occurring among them.

Chip continued the tour as we flew past the fire-works.

"That bright area ahead is FOB Wilson. Further south is Masum Ghar, and way to ze south you can see another bright FOB with a conical hill. Zat's Sper," Chip pointed out.

"Got it," I stated becoming more familiar as we flew.

Chip continued, "If you look west along Highway 1 for another ten clicks, you can see some lights on ze right. Zat is the American FOB near Howz-e Madad. All ze area on ze left is a red zone—very dangerous area. Zis is where ze main fighting has been for our tour. Watch yourself in zayr."

"Check that!' I acknowledged, looking at the apparently quiet area. It looked no different from every other group of compounds we had flown over, yet this area was extra deadly as opposed to regular deadly.

"Eh, let's go low and do some hunting boss." Ricky's voice excitedly rose from the back.

"For sure. Why don't you check in with Slayer and see if zey need some help somewhere?" Chip suggested.

"Slayer TOC, this is Shakedown 25 Flight," I stated over the radio.

"Go for Slayer" was the reply.

"25 Flight of two Griffons, approaching your ROZ (restricted operating zone) for an AO tour near Wilson. We're available for support if required. We have two times dual Dillon door guns, twelve thousand rounds of 7-6-2, request into airspace and an update." I stated proudly for my first real check-in (for action).

"25 flight, roger. Airspace is *hot*. Guns are cold. I got Predator at Angel 20. Shamus operating in airspace currently near Howz-e Madad. Remain below Fifty Five," he cleared over the radio.

"Romeo tango. Approaching Wilson now," I advised as I looked forward to Howz-e to see Shamus. I could see the faint sparkle of the Kiowa warriors infrared anticollision beacons. They were posturing, waiting to swoop in like hawks on a mouse.

"Zere is lots of troops here over ze next few miles," Chip stated. "1 RCHA from Manitoba is moving into Wilson. Zey have artillery support to about as far as Nakhoney."

We continued toward Masum Ghar, a FOB on a ridge that overlooked Bazaare Panjwaii. It was a small town nestled between two mountains. It acted as a strategic choke point for people travelling from Highway 1 south to the lower Tarnac Valley and Reg Desert. It was about a two-minute flight south of Wilson.

"The Lord Strathconas from Edmonton are gonna be here with ze Leopard tanks," he added. Canada was the only country in this war that had armored units in theater. The Leopard 2 tank was one of the only weapons capable of penetrating the mud walls that the Taliban hid behind. Another two minutes south was Sperwan Ghar.

"3 PPLCI (Princess Patricia's Canadian Light Infantry), also from Edmonton with some artillery, are moving zayr," Chip added. "Watch ze tether. It is a mini balloon wis a camera a couple of hundred feet high. A mini version of ze one at CNS. Just don't go directly over ze hill, and you'll be clear."

"Ha. Unlike doze guys last week that hit it, eh?" the right gunner sneered in his French accent, referring to a helicopter collision with the tether cutting the balloon lose and also damaging the aircraft.

"Everyone okay from that?" I asked.

"I think they just shit their pants but otherwise okay," Ricky answered, having knowledge of the incident from his operations job.

"Watch ze west of Sper, dangerous territory and lots of green space right to Howz-e. Stay high or stay aggressive," Chip stated.

Stay aggressive? I pondered that. Those words echoed in my head for the entire tour. And affirmations of the concept developed as I met more aviators in this role. As of now, I did not know what he meant. It was more about attitude and spirit versus tactics and procedures.

We veered east to Salavat and Nakhoney. Unbeknownst to me at this time is that this would be my busy area this year and would leave an impression forever. The First Battalion PPCLI and then eventually in April, the RCR (Royal Canadian Regiment) had the pleasure of working there. It would probably become the deadliest area of the war during 2009 and 2010, easily overtaking Howz-e's reputation and rivaling Helmand Province 150 kilometers to the west.

Everything was dark in Nakhoney; it was a series of unlit mud walls, making it difficult to even see the road ways on a dark night. Ironically, I would eventually know this like the back of my hand: from steel door to cemetery, to wadi west and south, to Three Hills, to the large grape hut that specific Taliban soldiers would taunt me from during the next year. The images of these landmarks are still burnt in my mind. I developed feelings of responsibility to patrol here when I had the chance. I eventually badgered the operations officer to allow me to overwatch whenever my primary Chinook-escort task was done just for a chance to hunt the devil from Nakhoney who conducted despicable acts of terror in these parts. I knew his hiding holes, escape routes, bomb emplacements areas, and dicker spots. I saw Canadian blood spilled and children used as enemy shields here. It was going to get ugly. I didn't know that yet. As right now, it was just a dark, void with a few firelights spread about compounds.

We continued east for 10 kilometers toward Dand, which was only 20 kilometers west of KAF, completing the loop. It was the southern cutoff from the Reg Desert to Kandahar City.

"Contact! Tracer fire ahead—4 kilometers. Should we break?" My heart pounded. This can't be happening. First night in theater and shots fired already.

"Naw, it's okay! It's just a wedding," Chip stated calmly and veered gently out of the way.

"What the fuck?" I exclaimed. "Don't they know there is a war going on?"

"Wedding . . . you're gonna see lots of bullets going into the air when you fly at night. Sometimes it's just a wedding celebration, or other times it could be indiscriminate fire in your general direction. Not necessarily at you but more just up," Chip stated.

"Eez kinda like how dey make za helicopter noise complaint," the intercom added with a cocky giggle. "Kinda let you know dey don't want you deyr, but dey don't wants to fight you eider."

"It's not a threat, just note it and report it to Slayer…you'll get used to it!" Chip explained.

I paused for a moment to digest that info in my brain. This wasn't in the training plan that is all I could think. I shook it off and radioed Slayer.

"Slayer, this is Shakedown 25 Flight."

"Go for Slayer."

"Slayer, we got gun fire shooting into the air, not directive towards us, it's about 3 kilometers west of Dand on Lake Effect. You got anything going on there?" I asked.

"Wait out." Slayer needed a moment to investigate.

"Shakedown, this is Slayer. No friendlies in that area. Civilian advisor stated that it's probably celebratory. Lots of weddings going on in that area this month. We'll note the grid location and get the Heron (UAV or unmanned aerial vehicle high above with a camera) to take a look. Slayer out."

"There ya go," Chip concluded. "Let's hit the desert so you can see the guns at night. You already saw the flares!" he added sarcastically to rub in my embarrassing error.

The difference between night and day gunnery was that with NVGs, every tracer round looked like a laser beam shooting to the target. With every fifth round, a tracer meant that there were ten lasers per second attacking the target. It looked like a combat sequence from a *Star Wars* film. And the ricochets looked like a fireworks starburst.

This time, as we pitched in for the attack, the full forward fire was not as shocking. However, the plume of light from the gun barrels combined with the tracer light blinded my field of view. So in addition to being deaf, I was also totally blind.

"Left gunner, check fire. Right gunner, continue," Chip yelled. "Pull out and break left," he added for me. I could see the ground rushing toward us.

As the left gun stopped shooting, I pulled back on the cyclic and looked back toward the target. Grumpy's aircraft was trailing directly behind me, and once I was clear, he unleashed hell on the sand dune. A lavalike waterfall of bullets joined my right gunner's tracers to bounce off the target. Then I noticed movement in the desert below as I scanned my head left.

"Check fire, guys! I see movement," I called over the radio.

The waterfall of bullets stopped.

"What are you looking at?" Chip asked.

"I got 'em. Bedouins over to the left 500 meters," Ricky stated. "I think they are coming for the casings." Amazing! Even in the darkness, these nomadic people were running across rugged terrain in the hopes of finding little brass pieces, which represented income to their sustenance way of life.

"Well, let's knock it off for now, infidels. I think we've accomplished all we can tonight. Let's head back, check one final time with Slayer, and go home," Chip radioed the team.

"Roger dat. How was Steve's first day?" 26 cockily added.

"I think he's been schooled," Chip replied. I looked over at him through my goggles. An unfocussed green image of big grin looked back at me, and I replied by silently holding up my middle finger. He laughed at me over the intercom.

This time, as we approached the fence of KAF going into the FARP, I called, "Fence in. Don't forget your ASE safe, guns, light!"

Chapter 7

Last Party for 430 Squadron

It was a cool 35 degrees in the shade next to the helicopter maintenance hangar. Our combat gear was kept inside a wall of large walk-in sea cans. The door opened about 2 meters away from the broad side of the aircraft hangar. Often we sat bantering in the shade while cleaning weapons and preparing gear. Today we were preparing our "go bags."

A "go bag" is a backpack to complement our survival vest. It carried the necessities required to fight and survive if we were shot down. The air force mandated that we should carry basic survival equipment in our vests and go bags. Ironically, it was filled with fishing line, snare wire, matches, and survival booklets with a few ounces of bagged water—which mostly just attracted mice. Otherwise, the survival gear was fantastic for the boreal forests in Canada but not so suitable for combat in the 45-degree desert heat. Nor did it acknowledge that one team member would most likely have a combat-related injury. This notion created some sarcastic banter ridiculing the equipment:

> *"If I land in the desert, I'll set up a snare-wire defensive perimeter."*
> *"If the Taliban shoot me down, I'll set up a survival fire. Someone will find me!"*
> *"Maybe catch fish in the wadi? Right next to the IED trap."*
> *"Always stay by the wreckage, and then Search and Rescue will find you! Ya, so will the Taliban!"*

This was opposite to the advice our infantry trained door gunners provided such as to blackout, move to survive, and learn tactical bounding.

"I can't believe they sent us this crap!" Grumpy stated. Grumpy was instrumental in making sure we had the appropriate go bags that would carry what we actually needed.

"Get rid of that shit, Steve! Load it up. I recommend an ammo pack here, here, and here . . . the rest inside." He was pointing to the various belt placements to attach gear.

"How much are you carrying?" Fender stated. Fender was an experienced tactical pilot. His strongest asset was his ability to stay calm. Even in the most trying times, he would pause, breathe, turn his head contemplatively, and then respond even calmer. He decided to learn music while deployed. He brought his guitar and spent a few minutes each evening strumming a few tunes meditatively before he slept.

"Ten mags, all full of ammo," Grumpy instructed. "Four on my chest, two on my holster belt, and the rest in the bag," he stated seriously as he continued loading his magazines.

Big C nodded in agreement. Big C was a large, strong, and stocky Saskatchewan farm boy. He was generally quite stoic. He always had a mischievous smile and a hard work ethic. He had a practical farmer's background that if he couldn't fix a broken tractor in the field, he'd push it back to the barn by himself. He had served in Iraq with the Americans on an exchange tour and offered a depth of knowledge about tactics and the enemy. He also liked to enable, nonmaliciously, situations to humor himself. Stir the shit, so to speak.

"What about these survival books and snare wire?" I asked, holding them up.

"Put it in your locker," Grumpy stated while everyone loaded magazines. "Not required."

"Helmet, water, bullets, and first aid gear. It's all ya need. Emphasis on bullets and water," Big C stated without lifting his head from loading his magazines.

"And the spur-ride carabineer and strap," added Fender. If you were shot down and you needed a quick escape but with no other helicopters available with seats, spur ride was a way to strap onto the outside of an Apache or Kiowa helicopter. Basically, you tied yourself to the weapons pods and rode out.

"Lotsa bullets. If you go down, you may only have your pistol available, so make sure you have three or four mags on your body too," Grumpy further advised while aiming his 9mm at the ground, testing his personal laser-aiming device.

Fender nodded and strapped some extra mag pouches to his pistol holster.

I picked up my first aid gear, which was nothing more than a QuikClot bandage, a triangular bandage, gauze, and some tourniquets. QuikClot is an anti-hemorrhage material. It has kaolin, which instantly cauterizes a severe bleeding wound—like an arm ripped off.

I carried half my first aid kit, including tourniquets and QuikClot in my flight suit at all times; even in KAF, I ensured I had enough bandages to initiate first aid to any rocket attack victim; self included.

"How many tourniquets you guys taking?" I asked.

"You should have at least one," Fender stated.

Big C looked up, listening to the direction of banter.

"I'll take two for sure," Grumpy added as Fender grabbed an extra, placing it in his flight suit pocket and the other in his go bag.

"Ya know if ya get hit in the leg with a .51-caliber DShK round, it'll pretty much rip 'er off," Big C stated monotonously without lifting his eyes. He kept packing mags in his go bag. "How you gonna put one on your leg in the cockpit in all that pain when your shin is blown off?"

"Hmm, you gotta point," I was startled. "I can't even reach my pedals with all that armor on in those plated seats."

"Ya know what the tank drivers do?" Big C offered omnipotently, raising his eyebrows, his smirk beginning to grow across his face.

"What?" I asked naively.

"They wear 'em . . . one on each leg. At least they are on and ready."

"Shit. Maybe I should do that," I stated rhetorically. I wrapped one on each thigh to try it out. My go bag was now packed, and weapons were ready; it was time to try it all on anyway. I loaded all my gear on my back—armored vest, tactical vest with multiple magazines, leg holster with about forty rounds ammo, and my go bag with helmet, camouflage nets, six bottles of water, extra first aid gear, and about two hundred more rounds of ammo. I was an extra 85 pounds with my rifle. Some guys carried over 100 pounds.

I strutted over to the helicopter feeling invincible, like a Mech Warrior. However, my proud swagger was being inhibited as my tourniquets kept sliding down my thighs to around my ankles—like a failed garter belt. I had to put my rifle strap over my neck and walk with each hand holding up a garterlike tourniquet on each leg. The image was destroying my rugged, invincible self-esteem.

"What the fuck are you wearing?" the experienced French-accented gunner asked as I approached the helicopter.

"I gotta tourniquet on each leg in case I take .51-caliber while flying . . . then I'm ready," I spoke confidently.

He shook his head in disbelief but added, "Well, okay, but I bet you won't be wearing those in a week from now."

"I don't know why I wouldn't be," I answered logically. "We're not much different from the Leopard tank drivers who wear 'em," I further parroted Big C's words.

I wobbled back to the sea cans, holding my garter belts up. My 85 pounds of gear was swaying like a turtle partially connected to its shell continually testing my balance.

"I think I can easily work with this," I stated matter of fact to the guys.

Big C just smirked; success in self-entertainment accomplished.

Fender took a glance at my condition, tilted his head, and changed the topic. "All right, we have the 430 commanding officer's departure parade in a couple of minutes. We should lock this gear up."

In the maintenance hangar (which we're just leaning against).

"Tomorrow, the remainder of the crews of 408 will arrive, and we will have our change of command parade," the CO addressed all the 430 staff at a biweekly barbecue in the helicopter hangar.

Every two weeks, we paused operations for an equipment care day (EC day). EC days allowed time to repair equipment, clean weapons, and conduct maintenance on the aircraft. It also allowed for needed recreation time and mindful self-centering.

Another bonus of the EC day was that every second one allowed the Canadian entitlement of two beers. And this one happened to be a beer day. Although this may not appear unique to most Canadians, to the soldiers, technicians, and aircrew working in 30–50-degree heat and coughing up camel dung for a month, an ice-cold Molson Canadian beer was a welcome motivator. Additionally, it was the last day before the 430 Squadron members, Task Force Faucon, would head home.

"We've had a very challenging tour, and I thank you for all the hard work and perseverance you've demonstrated. You can all be extremely proud of the move we accomplished to our current lines (referring to a unit relocation of all equipment on the airport). Roto 8 will be very comfortable now, and the operations center is very functional. And we—you—did this without any pause to the operational delivery for the Canadian Battle Group." He spoke proudly of his team's logistical and tactical accomplishments.

"And we initiated the M134 Dillons and quickly converted to dual-Dillon operations shelving that C-6 crap!" he proudly hollered, referring to the inferior machine gun the aviators had to start Afghanistan with.

"Yaaa! Woo-hoo!" There were a few gung ho cheers from the gunners.

"And we had our share of combat, spread bullets on the enemy, and each have our stories to take home . . . and share."

"Yaaaa, infidels!" a French accent cheered from the crowd followed by a murmur of giggles.

"But most of all, we enabled troops and logistics to be moved quickly and safely with the Chinooks. This allowed the task force to complete more missions—more safely that they would on the roads. But"—he stopped and paused, continuing silently, respectfully—"but this was not without loss." He was emotional, and his eyes swelled with moisture. He took a breath to calm the mist in his eyes. There was silence.

"Every day we walk down this ramp, we see the memorial we left here to remind others of their sacrifice. Master Corporal Pat Audet and Corporal Martin Joannette. We will always remember them." He bowed his head as did everyone for a moment of reflection.

He looked up. "You have been the best team a CO could ever ask for. I wish you safe returns and a healthy time off." Then he looked at everyone and started to applaud them; they returned the applause. He opened a beer. "I salute you. Salute!" And he raised his can. "And I toast our lost brothers, Jo-Pat!"

The crowd stood tall, raising their drinks, and toasted back. "Jo-Pat."

I walked over to the CO when he was finished addressing his troops and said farewell.

"Hey, Steve. These EC days are important to take every couple of weeks. Time to breathe," he counseled me and quickly changed the recent topic of his speech.

"Yes, sir. Nice to have a beer too." I clicked his beer can.

"We made headways in convincing the army that the door guns and Dillons are a very viable asset for continuous time-on target as opposed to forward-firing Apaches and Kiowas," he professed. "You guys are getting the MX-15 next week. That standoff optical capability combined with the dual Dillons will make you one of the most sought-out close combat attack platforms for Slayer. You're going to have a great tour. Fly safe."

I nodded. The MX-15 was brought with very short notice. It was a training nightmare to try and figure out in a couple of weeks, but we had a basic idea of how to get it working. It wouldn't be easy, but I was amazed by its long-range capability at both night and day. It also had a high-powered laser that could easily point to things well beyond 10 kilometers, from a landing spot at night for Chinooks or a target for an Apache to kill. It was capable.

"I will and thanks. Enjoy your time off, sir," I answered as he made his way through his troops to share memories.

Chip came by and gave me his last few words of advice. "Steve, fly your guns. Fly protection—not formation."

"Cheers." I clicked my Molson Canadian against his.

"Salute," he responded.

I nodded and contemplated. I thought about those words over the next few weeks. It became obvious that was going to change the way I flew in Afghanistan—not technically but the attitude. The advice felt like a graduation gift from flying at home to flying in theater—I took it to heart. My crew, some quicker than others, also embraced that philosophy.

I returned to my tent reflecting on the evening. I had my mission for the next day. It was "walkin' the dog" on Montreal route—a canned logistics and personnel transfer route with the numerous stops at various FOBs. It would be my last trips with 430 crew as the remaining 408 crew were arriving later that evening.

"Alonsi!" my French copilot stated to me. It was time to get back to the tent lines. "We have table at 0530 demain."

There was a community table under some army canvass central to our tent line referred to as the Table. "Table Time" was when and where everyone met to depart for work.

I crashed down on top of my bunk and reflected on the day and week while watching the dusty canvass roof waving gently in the sulfury poopy breeze. It would take some time to desensitize to the throat-burning stench of the poo pond. It was our first night in our new tents. The privacy was welcome over the BATs; it was our home. However, the poo-pond would never be a welcome aroma.

Fender was playing a few tunes softly on the other side of the thin fabric wall.

"There's a lady who's sure,
all that glitters is gold.
And she's buying a stairway to heaven . . ."

I would get accustomed to his music over the next year. It was very relaxing, almost putting me to sleep recognizing familiar tunes . . . until he missed a chord and then repeated it a few times before moving to the next bar.

"When she gets (strum) there . . . (strum) there . . . (strum) there . . ."

I nodded my head with each strum, hoping in silent cheer for him to nail the correct chord correctly.

"She knows if the stores are all closed . . ."

Yes. Ahhhh. Silent applause in my head. Regardless of missed chords, I found the music soothing, maybe even more than him at times.

MEEERRRRRAAAARRRROOOOOWWWWWWW.

A long blast of the attack horn pierced through the camp. I couldn't believe it. The first night I was finally getting some sleep, and the horn goes off.

"Is this for real?" I called through the fabric divider to Fender.

"Yup, it's a rocket attack," he stated, annoyed of the disruption to his practice.

"I'm trying to get on the floor, but I don't have enough room, do you?"

"Nope, just slouch a little," he mumbled back.

I grunted in frustration trying to maneuver to the small floor space. It was too small to lay out flat as prescribed. "I'm on my hands and knees, but I can't get flat. My ass is in the air." I chuckled nervously. "If that rocket lands near here, I'm gonna get sent home in a box with my ass blown off."

"I don't fit either. I'm just sitting on the floor—slouched," he called back through the fabric divider.

I surrendered to that idea, flipping my body to a more comfortable posture and then pulled on the light string to see my barrack box for my weapon and helmet.

"Rwokit attack, rwokit attack, rwokit attack," stated the prerecorded sexy female English voice of the emergency alarm system.

After the mandatory two minutes of floor discomfort, I took my protective gear and pistol and proceeded to the rocket bunker to wait for further information. The bunker was a huge concrete Lego-like structure with walls and roof that were about 18 inches thick. Our tent group with about fifty other passers-by amalgamated at the bunker and waited. Most people wore shorts and T-shirts, with rifles slung, drinking their evening Tim Hortons coffee.

"First one?" an American soldier inquired, lifting his eyebrow.

"Second. How can you tell?" I anxiously responded. He smirked at me. My eyes were full open. It was easy to tell. He was cool, relaxed. He was smoking a cigarette. Not me. I was jacked on adrenalin and ready to run somewhere. I kept thinking first aid—heavy bleeding first, then airway, then blood, then circulation.

He raised his chin, exhaling his cigarette smoke: "Number 53 for me. I'm countin' for fun," he then calmly added. "You'll get used to it."

I don't think I could ever get used to it.

"Did you hear it?" He looked in the direction of an explosion that went off a few minutes earlier. "I heard an explosion, but it seemed far off."

"Pretty sure it's outside the wire. Sometimes they miss the camp all together," someone else added rhetorically to the conversation.

"That's good because if no one gets hurt, the 'all clear' will come really fast," he responded.

He was right.

MEEERRRRRAAAAARRRROOOOOWWWWWWW. The siren sounded again.

This time, the English lady voice stated, "All clair, all clair, all clair." People started moving on with their business as if nothing happened. I walked to the mini bunker outside my tent and paused for a moment. I was very awake. I sauntered back to my bed. I laid my clothes on the chair, placed my pistol in the barrack box, and sat on the edge of my bed. I watched the indirect light over the top of the fabric wall go dimmer as each pilot pulled his light bulb strings. *Click, click, click.* It was dark everywhere, except my space.

I lay back staring at the ceiling a few more moments. I couldn't imagine a full life like this.

In a small compound 3 kilometers from my bed, a mother was worrying if she and her daughter would live the night because she took her daughter to school. The Taliban forbid girls to go to school, and death was the punishment. And Canadian soldiers were on night patrol trying to avoid the Taliban-placed roadside bombs.

While in Canada, people were getting kids ready for school, ordering Starbucks and complaining because the first frost hit the ground. However, that didn't stop me from wanting to feel the frost on my face and to breathe clean air with a cup of coffee misting my nose.

How long would it take to desensitize? It wouldn't be tonight; I sat up and dropped my feet to the floor. No way I was going to sleep. I put on my gym shorts.

Chapter 8

Casualties of War

I saw this many times. This situation occurred in the spring, but it represents daily examples of the brutal tactics used by the Taliban. I wondered how it would all transpire. What were the catalysts, and how did it come to fruition? We knew the Taliban were bullies, but bullies that used lethal force, amputations, and washing faces with acid to force compliance. That's appalling. Fear and manipulation; the method.

There are many casualties in war. Perhaps the most damaged veterans are those that don't realize they are in the fight.

The sun was beating down, searing the desert and the mud-walled compounds that lay below. It was well above 40 degrees. The locals kept cool in the afternoon by carrying out light chores or resting in the heat. In some areas, local men were preparing the fields for the grape harvest. Others were tending to the poppies that would be ripe soon for the opium harvest. Some were repairing their compounds from the winter rains of January and February. Many irrigation fields had corner holes to allow water to fill from the Arghandhab aqueducts that were centuries old.

"How's the POL?" I asked my first officer, referring to his awareness of the patterns of life in the compounds below.

"Quiet today," he answered as he looked around.

"Don't see too much . . . too hot," Snapshot, my right gunner, added.

I looked back, and he had his camera up. Occasionally, he would see unique sites that few others had the eye to appreciate.

"I don't know how the ladies in the compounds keep their beautiful blue gowns clean," he observed.

"Ya, interesting. They're shimmering. Look at the dust everywhere," I added, noticing a woman with her child in the shaded corner of a compound.

We flew over at 75 feet above as we crossed Nakhoney toward the Adamz-eye chain of compounds that stretched from Salavat Mountain to the Reg Desert in the south. It was a narrow band of homes but extremely tactical for the insurgents. They commonly attacked the Canadian FOB in Nakhoney and escaped through the mine-filled grape fields to the west, unscathed.

"I only see a few people here—a man, a woman with a little boy," Snapshot noticed.

"Unusual this time of day," I answered skeptically.

Men were usually at the markets in Kandahar or Bazaar e Panjwai selling produce or else working in the fields. Regardless, it was rare to see them together in compounds. They seemed to be dialoguing. The child seemed to be stuck to the mother, not like a child would behave near a father.

"Who knows? Keep your eyes out. This place is crazy," I added. But nothing would "likely" happen today. The opium harvest was the most important activity this month. Fighting us infidels would be secondary. Their prime mission was to sell the drugs, raise money, and then take up arms after harvest in May.

We proceeded west to Sperwan Ghar for an overwatch task, ignoring the events below. It was just another day.

In the Compound Below

"Look at the helicopter," the woman told her son as they worked in the yard. She had a way of keeping her clothes shimmering in the sunlit sky as she tended to her chores.

"Yes. Will they hurt us?" the boy asked.

"No, look at them. They usually wave if they see you," she added, referring to the door gunners, especially Snapshot who was also waving and giving thumbs-up to the ladies.

She was about twenty-five years old. She was taking care of her wifely duties inside her compound—her home—about a kilometer west of the FOB in Nakhoney in the Adamz-eye chain of villages. She wasn't afraid of the foreigners. However, she stayed in her home and tended to the needs of her family. Together, they tended to the yard until some weapons firing commenced in the east toward the Canadian base. She was used to this. It was nothing unusual and occurred almost daily. She knew the difference between the sound of a Taliban AK-47 and a Canadian C7 assault rifle. She recognized the AK-47 shots.

The fighting had been going on long in her country. She had heard tales from her parents about the Russian invasions some thirty years earlier. She had witnessed her own horrors and wondered if the fighting and the hatred would ever end. Now the Taliban and the ANA and more foreigners were in her land.

"Stay close to that wall." She pointed east, knowing it was the safest part of the compound when the fighting started.

She interpreted these shots as a Taliban ambush against a Canadian or ANA patrol. It was no concern of hers. The bullets would not be going toward her. Even if they did, the walls were thick, and bullets could not penetrate them. She was safe as long as she did her duties inside the walls. She and her son continued their work.

A man ran into compound from the east.

"Move inside," he commanded fiercely.

"You cannot be in here. My husband is not home," she said humbly with her eyes to the ground.

"I know where you husband is. Be silent and do as I ask," he firmly stated, moving toward her.

She pulled up her bright blue burka and covered her face as per customs; she grabbed her son and pulled him inside the accommodations portion of the compound.

The man moved into the corner of the open doorway and maintained a watch of the road as he spoke with her. He was well aware of the combat occurring between Taliban and Canadian troops. He scanned in all directions. He held a small cell phone and was talking in short concerned, yet angry bursts into the phone.

"Bring the package. Bring the package now," a faint but panicky voice stated over the phone in Pashtun.

She could hear. She knew. The Afghan mother protected her boy and curled up with him in the corner across the room in terror. She recognized him, but he was not family. He had arrived from Pakistan during the winter. He had been working with her husband in the opium fields. He was an opium buyer and an insurgent.

The young boy whimpered in a shallow cry and leaned into his mother. She stroked his head, holding him tight, covering his ears as the man looked over to him. They rocked together, worried of the situation.

"Tell that boy to be quiet. Allah demands it," he hollered. He was perturbed at the whiney interruptions of the sensitive phone call.

"Now?" the man asked in the phone, looking at the boy.

The mother saw his eyes and pulled her boy tighter.

Gunshots continued to echo a few hundred meters to the east. Then helicopters started to arrive. The sound of AK-47s shot and now those shots were answered with more gunshots. The sound of an occasional bullet zinged overtop of the compound in which they stood.

"I am trapped. The enemy is engaging from the north. I cannot get a clean shot at the infidels. I need the package now!" the voice exclaimed.

"No! You cannot take him. No!" she argued. She held her son tightly. The boy started to cry.

He walked toward her angrily. "You insult me, your husband and Allah. Stop it!" He raised his hand, threatening to strike.

She cried silently as tears fell down her face.

He grabbed the boy and pulled his arm. The boy started to whimper. The voice on the phone continued faintly but persistently yelling demands.

"Yes, I am bringing the package," the man answered into the phone, looking directly at the woman.

The man took a deep breath and calmly kneeled down to the boy.

"Do not be afraid. It is time for you to become a man and stand up against the infidels and what they bring to the land," he preached intently. "This is a great noble task, and Allah will protect you. You will be safe," the man continued as the boy intently listened as he dried the tears from his cheeks. His mother went into a private room to hide her fearful tears.

"Allah will stop all the shooting when you go into the field of battle. You are special. All men will stop fighting. The man on the phone needs you. Allah will protect you," he preached calmly to manipulate the boy.

He pulled the boy out of the compound. The mother looked out from the shadows, tears rolling down her face. The boy went limp with terror. The clenching grip of the man dragged him down the road toward the firefight, his face paralyzed and flushed of all emotion.

The helicopters buzzed above their heads as they walked toward a large grape hut. He heard the bullets zipping above his head. He saw the dust splashes of bullets impacting the grape huts a hundred yards ahead.

"I am bringing the package to you," the man yelled into the phone.

The boy looked up to the helicopters. He saw the masked face of a door gunner looking directly toward him. He was aiming his weapon on the grape hut. The boy knew the gun; it delivered the Breath of Allah. The noise. The dust. The gunshots.

The door gunner was not shooting yet, but the boy could see him taking aim. He felt the painful squeeze of the man yanking him down the road, forcing his legs into a trot. He went numb with terror.

Chapter 9

408 Task Force Freedom

"'All conditioned things are impermanent'—when one sees
this with wisdom, one turns away from suffering."
—The Buddha

Montreal route was a standard logistical resupply route conducted by
Blowtorch. I was in Shakedown 30 and wingman in 31. Our mission
was to keep them from getting shot at. Basic training 101—keep your
fire team partner alive. It was no different in aviation.

My fire team partner was Shakedown 31. The protected helicopter
was Blowtorch 60—he didn't have a fire team partner; he had us. Part
of a Shakedown camaraderie was of course to berate the faster and larger
Chinook. Since Blowtorch did not have a fire team friend, they just
seemed to run away with their tail between their legs, hoping not to get
butt smacked by a Taliban rocket. I say this entirely in jest as part of a
loving rivalry between pilots of varying feather.

I had been in theater a week and remnants of 430 Squadron, a few
gunners, and copilots, were still flying with the new 408 Squadron
captains. Fender and myself, along with a Blowtorch captain, were
commanding the three aircraft for Montreal route today. The operations
officer and commanding officer were having their first day of command
by quarterbacking the missions as the 430 squadron leadership stepped
aside.

The CO (commanding officer), Skipper, had been in theater for a
week. Skip had been meeting with all the major players affecting our

operation. He was a young, keen commanding officer with a dry sense of humor. It was common to see him routinely cycle around the rugged, dusty 10-kilometer route from south side to north side KAF, spitting out the dust on arrival from between the teeth of his grin. He was an astute person, easily recollecting detail from incidents as complicated as battlefield TICs to as simple as which DFAC omelet chef served the best yolk-free breakfast.

Today Skip gave the flight launch authority; he was taking official command. Launch authority was the final step before the mission started. It was a final assessment to make sure as many risks as possible were mitigated.

"Shakedown 30 and 31?" Skip asked, taking roll call.

"Yes, sir, and this is my crew. Fender?" I pointed to the guys and asked Fender to answer the same.

"All here," Fender answered, looking at his team.

"Go ahead, Scrappy," Skip redirected, passing the reigns to his operations officer.

Scrappy was the operations officer. This was his first in-theater dispatch briefing in which he had full control. We called the dispatch briefing an 'Ops Walk.' All crew had to be briefed on the latest information about threat and environment before flying. Scrappy was not a stranger to this, as this was his second tour to Afghanistan. He was stalky and strong, organized and thorough, but feisty—he had a temper. He was both blunt as a manager yet respectful of experience. He did not like to be crossed.

Scrappy was not one to use discussion to resolve an issue. His response to someone frustrating him was usually a covert physical "smarten-up" shot or covert kick to the shins. And if you were fortunate to experience his playful side, it wasn't uncommon for him to force you to join him in his version of UFC athleticism.

"All right. Intelligence . . . go," Scrappy sternly directed to the sergeant who pointed to the "bird table." It was a small table in operations that mapped out the entire AO, showing where the FOBs were located.

"Along Highway 1, several IED attacks occurred overnight here and here," the int sergeant started. "On a positive note, a bicycle bomber was preparing an IED near the prison, and his bomb predetonated, taking only himself out."

The crowd of the a dozen onlookers chuckled. "Poetic justice," Ricky stated rhetorically.

The int sergeant continued, "You have three Canadian patrols in these areas here, here, and here." He pointed to roads near Sperwan Ghar to Wilson. "The guns have been live from Sper to the area here, so I suggest you take the Reg Desert route to avoid conflict with their artillery."

"Roger. Got it," the Blowtorch captain stated. He would lead the formation. Shakedowns would picket the landing zones and protect him en route. Picketing means going ahead to secure it before the Chinook lands.

"You are heading out to FOB Ramrod. It's in the middle of nowhere. Few threats, but you need to watch for infiltration from compounds to the southwest." He continued to point out where previous assaults have occurred. "And stay away from those locations while waiting."

"That's not what happens. Ya know Steve?" my French copilot interrupted, whispering over my shoulder.

"I know. Chip told me the first thing the FOB asks us to do while waiting is to go and probe those areas for POL," I answered. I was now getting the gist of things, and it had only been a few trips. "Forechecking," I summated while the int briefer listened, fully aware of our defiance.

"Yes, forechecking," Fender joined the interruption as he enacted holding up a hockey stick doing a cross-check.

The int sergeant shrugged his shoulders and shook his head.

"I'm just telling you what I have to, guys," he added, raising his brow. He knew we were already keen to start poking and provoking, basically help the soldiers in the FOBs to look at their problem areas, but it included some risk.

"I know you want to help the guys on the ground. Just be careful," Scrappy closed. "We are still getting used to things around here."

Scrappy spoke from experience. He had operated the UAV in previous Afghanistan tour and had seen the ugly escalations. He knew what risks were involved and was appointed this executive position for a reason.

"The threat is real!" he continued. "Out in Bastion earlier today, a Chinook got hit. That's only a few kilometers from where you will be.

Pictures, Sarge." Scrappy raised his eyebrows, suggesting the sergeant add some graphics regarding the threat.

A picture of a clean hole with four razor thin fin marks were displayed. An RPG (rocket-propelled grenade) had hit a Chinook.

"Wow! Did it detonate?" Fender asked.

"No. Brits got lucky. This RPG round went clean through the side of the helicopter and then through the back of a seat and out the other side without exploding," the sergeant briefed.

Eyes in the room were large. He had everyone's attention.

"And check this picture out." He showed a picture of an RPG round lying on the floor in the back of a Chinook, undetonated, and then a subsequent picture of a scraped helmet and a 4-inch-diameter hole in the windscreen.

"Tabernac!" a gunner swore in astonishment.

A second RPG round on the same attack had gone through the front window, glanced off the helmet of the pilot and then spun around in the back of the Chinook like a hot potato.

"What happened?"

"They were on approach to a FOB in Helmand Province (about 100 kilometers west), and they got ambushed. They continued the landing into the FOB, completed an emergency shutdown, and everyone scrambled out racing the possible explosion. Fortunately, it didn't. EOD later secured it," the int sergeant briefed with intonation. (EOD is emergency ordinance disposal. They are specially trained to disarm and destroy explosives, depicted by the film *Hurt Locker).*

"I guess eet sucks to be za dawg (referring to the Chinook). Das why we stay wit za Griffowns en shoots back," the French accent from Fender's gunner cockily added.

The levity added some relief to the anxious crowd but not so much for the Blowtorch crew (Chinook).

"Those guys in that Chinook were extremely lucky. Extremely! Be careful, guys," Scrappy emphasized. "A few Tylenol and a change of shorts is all the pilot required to get back in action; could have been worse."

"All right, gents. Time to get a move on. You're airborne in thirty-five minutes. Just take 'er easy out there," Skip added and left the room.

"Section brief, guys. Come over to the main briefing room," the Chinook lead stated.

The six pilots walked into the next room to have a quick chat.

"Okay, you know the route and the FOBs. The only one new is Ramrod. I will do my approach from the southeast and exit north unless you see anything." He threw his map on a table and pointed near the FOB. "I have a large tractor load to take, so I may be on the ground an extra twenty minutes. You have enough fuel?" he asked.

"Yes. I should be good. But they have gas there, so if there are any delays, let me know, and we'll top up," I added, looking at Fender who nodded at the refuel plan.

"What's gonna really happen since we have extra time is that this American FOB will ask us to look around, especially at these compounds." Fender's copilot pointed at a small village very close on the map toward the southwest. "They get rocket attacks from here often. They also found numerous IEDs in the area and are looking for an explosives factory too, so I expect we'll be requested to investigate overtly while the Chinook loads."

"All right, got it." I nodded.

"How you wanna do it?" I looked at Fender, referring to our tactical plan.

"Well, let's go high and get an overview first and then go into low-trail formation and poke at anything that looks interesting. The rest, we'll coordinate on the radio."

"Sounds good. Radio check-in in twenty minutes?" I looked at my watch.

"Check," the other two captains acknowledged as we walked out the door. As I departed the dimly lit, air-conditioned TOC (tactical operations center), the blast of heat and light shocked me into the Afghanistan environmental intensity.

I could smell the dust in the air again, and a few steps later, beads of sweat started rolling down my forehead. It was only 34 degrees, but with multiple layers of flight clothing on, my body heated up quickly.

I went to the sea cans where my go bag and rifle were prepared. I quickly put on my armor and tactical vest; lifted my bag on my back, picked up my rifle, loaded it, and hoisted two tourniquets around my upper thigh. As I walked toward the helicopter to meet my crew, they slipped and fell around my ankles, so my last 50-yard macho walk was a shuffle so to not lose my tourniquets under my feet.

Ricky, my gunner today, watched me arrive. I was such a novice. I shrugged my shoulders at his expression. "What? What?" I barked as he shook his head in embarrassment. He laughed and continued feeding the ammo link into his Dillon gun.

"Okay, let's brief." I ignored the two gunners comically slandering my appearance.

"If we go down, 31 becomes our overwatch. Immediate drills are to establish a fire base around whatever main gun is functional. You two are the right side fire team." I pointed to the right gunner and right seat copilot. "You and me, Ricky, left," I directed to seriously align everyone on the task.

"Priority review . . . First, we'll establish a fire base, combat first aid, and then we grab gear and bound. The rest, we'll make up as we go. Check your gear, review your escape and evasion codes. Any questions?"

Everyone nodded. Their faces became stoic. Eyes connected. They all knew what to do. A briefing was not required. But it set the tone. It was a reminder. The team was ready, there was a couple of minutes remaining for individual rituals and personal mental transitions.

Everyone went through a transition at some point. Usually between the safe air-conditioned TOC acting with bravado and cocky banter to actually becoming a stoic, aware, and respectful warrior. And it was visible.

Not every trip posed tremendous hazards. But every trip had the potential of turning into a TIC, a casualty evacuation, IED intervention, or responding to an attack on the Chinook or yourself. There was an acceptance of our impermanence that had to occur for a person to get the job done. That is what I felt, and it's what I think I saw in everyone else's eyes as we prepared to start the helicopter. We stopped becoming Grumpys, Fenders, Snapshots, Scrappys and became a focused, unified fire team—Shakedown.

Chapter 10

Ramrod and Back

When pilots are away from flying for a few weeks, it takes a day or two to get past robotic skills and fly smooth again. It's like any skill; it gets rusty without practice. Combine that with war stress, people trying to kill you, poor sleep, and poo pond stench, it takes a little longer to get into the "groove." But today I was feeling the "groove." I was in the aircraft, my scan of performance instruments, and feel of the aircraft had returned to normal, so I started to relax. Vigilant, yes, but relaxed (although my crew may have different opinions).

I was 10 kilometers outside the wire looking ahead to Fender's aircraft. I was enjoying the beauty of the ruggedness. The image of the Griffon helicopter against the jagged peaks of the mountains was surreal. The sky was intensely bright, a piercing blue, captivating.

My glaze over the terrain was broken as shots of smoke were bursting near Fender's aircraft.

"Breaking right, threat ten o'clock!" Fender's aircraft jaunted right following the Chinook who lumbered right while making the call.

Doodle, doodle, doodle, doodle . . . A high-pitched tone and instrument panel light flashed, indicating a missile threat coming from the left.

"Do you see a plume left?" I yelled to Ricky. "I got nothing," I said, referring to the potential missile coming our way. Ricky normally worked in operations. However, as a training sergeant, he augmented the gunners and shifted into the flight line occasionally to keep current. Plus he loved flying and proud of each combat mission he could record in his log book.

"Keep the bank light. I gotta keep my guns on the ground," Ricky commented. "I'm lookin' for plume. It's just a false alert. No worries. But if you bank too hard, my guns are too high, and I can't shoot back. Fly the guns . . . remember?" he added to coach me.

"Roger that. Fly the guns, Rick," I repeated. I looked back to see the maximum range of motion of his Dillon gun. I had to be careful when turning not to limit his arc of fire; I was getting the hang of it.

My training kicked in, and I turned left toward the threat. Realistically, we can't beat the missile, that's why we had flares. We had to be smooth and let the flares trick the missile away from us. However, if we can find the source of plume, we can shoot back and get the bastard before they send the next one.

"Counter left! Ten o'clock. ASE alert! Looking!" I responded over the radio after being coached.

"False alert," the radio cracked with Fender's voice.

"Roger that," I answered.

"Yup, I am really starting to get annoyed by that," Fender's heightened voice transmitted. The veterans chuckled at us new guys again.

"You won't even pay attention to it in a week from now," the desensitized gunner added over the radio with a chuckle inspired by his amusement to my overreaction.

"Check the impact explosions at two o'clock, 5 kilometers," a voice commented over the intercom.

I looked over to the right, and in the distance, explosions of dust were rising near the Salavat Mountains; they were 155mm rounds from the Canadian artillery guns at Sperwan Ghar. They were firing as we expected from our Ops Walk brief earlier in the day, hence the reason for flying the Reg route.

"Damn! Someone's having a bad day!" Ricky commented as he stretched his head forward to look at the explosions.

"It's best stay out of the way and then check in with Slayer on the return route after we get rid of the dog," Fender radioed referring to the Chinook task as the priority.

"Roger that," I replied.

"I think I can. I think I can," a Chinook voice replied sarcastically over the radio, obviously from Blowtorch counterpunching the dog reference.

As we neared Ramrod, our formation of helicopters dove off the high desert plateau into the lower plains along the Tarnac Valley. There wasn't much of a valley, just a dried riverbed scorched from centuries of heat. Most of the water was underground.

Hundreds of miles of tunnels existed deep beneath the desert floor providing access to water springs. They were easily marked by water fetching tripods near holes every few hundred meters stretching for dozens of miles.

"Ramrod is on the nose 5 kilos," Blowtorch called. "Going straight in from here."

"Check that," I answered. "31, you got the base?"

"Check," he answered as he called the FOB on the radio.

"FOB Ramrod, Blowtorch 60 inbound landing in three minutes. Shakedowns will stay airborne and loiter. Got anything for us?" Fender asked.

"Roger that, Blowtorch flight. I got a couple of pallets to load. For the Shakedowns, we had an RPG and SAFIRE from the Southwest earlier today. It seems to have quieted down, but can y'all put a little pressure on over there? Take a poke around."

SAFIRE is small arms fire. It was common for RPG attacks to be accompanied by small enemy teams of Taliban shooting at the soldiers concurrently.

"Blowtorch 60 Flight, roger that, sir. The Chinook is on final now. Shakedowns breaking off to the south. You got any friendlies we need to know about?" Fender responded.

"Roger that. Along Highway 1 to the north, we got an IED team along the highway, maybe just show a little support for them too. Otherwise, no one else is outside the wire," the Alabaman accent responded.

As we finished the conversation, Fender led our two helicopters around the FOB. We watched Blowtorch land and the dust explode, engulfing the FOB. We then focused our vision onto the small village and the highway.

"Blowtorch, wheels down," the radio sounded. It was a confirmation that they were okay. Otherwise, we wouldn't know for several minutes until all the moondust cleared if they had crashed on landing.

"Check that," I answered.

"Got some clutter on the highway. Let's check it out. High then low," Fender stated.

"Roger that," I answered.

"Ramrod, this is Shakedown. Is there an IED ROZ? Any flight restrictions?" Fender asked over the radio to verify all the known IEDs had been safely detonated.

"Negative. It is blown. They are just clearing wreckage right now and want to make sure no one takes any pot shots at 'em," The FOB answered.

"Roger, sir," Fender answered. His aircraft was high above the highway we could see a black scorch mark and vehicle flipped along the road. Local traffic deviated into the desert to bypass while several Afghan National Army and American military vehicles scoured and secured the smoldering truck.

Fender's helicopter subtly dipped a wing, and he began plummeting from the sky, obvious he was going in for a closer look. We followed. Our mission at this point was to protect him. He was looking around for ambush sites that the Americans couldn't see. Our job was to simply protect him, our fire team partner, while he did his job.

"Got nothing," Fender stated as we flew a few orbits around the vehicle. We also looked into the mountains and nearby wadis for any possible dickers.

"Me either. Follow me, and then let's split it up. I'll stay low you go high." I took the lead and veered toward the town.

Fender climbed high out of a rifle's range but stayed close behind to draw attention away from me. I turned toward the north side of the town, low off the desert floor, about 50 feet.

"30, this is 31. You got a couple of guys behind those trees at eleven o'clock, just on the roof of that compound observing the FOB," Fender spotted.

"Check that, eleven o'clock, 1,500 meters?" I asked.

"Roger that."

"Rolling in." I steered the chopper directly toward them, altering my course abruptly. Fender followed but more central over the small compound—he stayed high to watch them from a larger perspective.

As we approached the trees near the compound, a head popped up to look at us. His eyes widened in surprise, then he dove behind the wall.

"Ha! Busted!" the right gunner called out. "Contact FAM, one o'clock," he continued. His voice was calm—this was normal.

"He just dropped off the wall and is scrambling into the compound," Fender stated over the radio from high above.

I popped the helicopter up and banked slightly to give the right gunner freedom to protect us with the gun. A man, maybe a teenager, ran into the compound.

"I'm breaking left down the wall," I called, indicating my left turn.

"Them fuckers use kids to dicker too," the right gunner stated, commenting on the teenage boy being used as an intelligence gatherer or a lethal cell phone, bomb-detonating dicker.

"How's it look up there?" I asked Fender.

"Really quiet. Just that dicker. He's gone. Possibly a WAC (woman and/or child). Can't tell for sure," Fender answered.

"It was possibly a WAC, but no doubt a dicker." I answered. "Let's keep patrolling." We rejoined a tighter formation and circled for more observation.

"Ramrod, this is Shakedown. You got a dick wacker on the wall, northeast corner by two trees," I reported. I chuckled at myself for the tongue-twisted, phonetic error.

"Roger that," he answered dryly. He had obviously heard that before. "They have the kids and WACs spying while the fighters lay low. What's the POL?"

"A dick wacker, eh, cap?" Ricky smartly retorted, interrupting over the intercom.

"I know you miss home, Ricky, but I don't want to hear about your alone time," I stated, managing to find a comeback and instill a bit of laughter.

"Pretty quiet. Don't see anyone out." I quickly jumped back to the radio conversation with the FOB cutting off Ricky's defense.

"Ya, all right. Usually there is more activity than that. Maybe something brewing. Just keep a little overt presence if you can. We'll see if the cell phone I-comm chatter is active. Y'all keep your heads up," the radio responded.

The voice was different, probably the duty officer talking instead of the radio operator suggesting our vigilance was necessary. The I-comm chatter was the intelligence network listening to enemy communications.

"30 flight, this is Blowtorch. We're gonna be a while. They just drove the fuckin' forklift into the side of the chopper. Got some airframe ribs damaged. We're trying to get Scrappy on the sat phone," the Chinook called.

"30, roger. You broke?" I answered.

"Dunno yet, still seeing if we can fly it like this. Stand by."

"Check."

"Fender, how much gas you got?" I asked.

"Maybe twenty minutes to bingo fuel, but no TIC reserve," he answered, stating he would have to go straight back to KAF and wouldn't have any reserve to help in an emergency if the infantry called along the way.

"Okay." I paused. "Give him ten minutes, and then we will go fuel?"

"Roger that. They have a couple of FARP (refuel) points available by the looks of it. Sounds good. I'll advise Ramrod."

Meanwhile in operations . . .

"Sir, we got a TIC in Howz-e Madad. Shakedowns can be there in ten minutes if we leave Blowtorch," the radio operator informed Scrappy.

Scrappy was sitting on the bird table. When it wasn't used for planning, he often placed the chair on the table and looked forward as if he was Captain Kirk on the Enterprise.

Initially it was for humor. But he soon realized he could monitor everything more easily from above all the staff heads. People could still walk around in the crowded floor space, so it became operationally practical. It looked funny but practical.

"Got it. The text board is showing Shamus is responding. They have thirty minutes fuel. I expect our guys will have to swap in when they bingo out of fuel," he pondered. "Get Shakedown to refuel now, and we'll have them available to cover Shamus in thirty minutes when Blowtorch 60 gets back."

The satellite phone rang. Scrappy hopped down and picked it up.

"Blowtorch is damaged in Ramrod. Fuckin' forklift damaged the bird. Get me the squadron aircraft maintenance officer (SAMEO)," he hollered, waving the phone. Things were starting to get complex.

The radio operator (RADOP) picked up his phone and called the SAMEO. After a quick explanation, he hung up.

"On his way, Major," he reported to Scrappy formally and then continued onto the radio, "Shakedown 30 Flight, this is Freedom Ops. I need you guys to FARP up now. Another task possibly coming in."

"Roger that," my voice acknowledged.

"Blowtorch 60, this is the SAMEO. What's the matter?" Scrappy observed the SAMEO chatting on the satellite phone.

"Bulkhead ribs and ramp actuator? Roger. Is anything leaking? Does the ramp work?" he asked.

"Roger that. You guys feel comfortable bringing her home? Is it cracked? If not or if anything structural, we can shut you down and get ya later," he advised over the sat phone. "RPG attack earlier? Roger that! Stand by."

After listening and while rapidly researching a technical manual, he confirmed. "Okay, nothing is structural. Bring 'er back, boys. Okay, Shakedown is fueling. See you in thirty minutes." He looked over to Scrappy to summarize the information.

"Scrappy, just bring Blowtorch back. They described the damage to me, and it appears superficial. The forklift twisted while on the Chinook's ramp, and the load damaged some airframe near the bulkhead. The engineer described the damage, and no systems were wrecked. It seems pretty superficial at this point. They can bring 'er home," the SAMEO coached. "We'll fix 'er back here, so the enemy doesn't rocket us nor Ramrod."

Often, if helicopters sat too long in a FOB, it gave an opportunity for the enemy to fire mortars and rockets at the base with a much higher probability of success. So helicopters in the FOBs acted like mortar magnets, thus increasing the danger to the base personnel as well as the aircrew.

"Roger that. I'll dispatch them," Scrappy answered and pointed to the radio operator who got on the radio.

"Hey, check the text prompter. Our guys just called in some dicker near Ramrod," Scrappy retorted.

Time: XX:XX: Shakedown 31 reports one times dicker at grid PR82590240, 2500m SW RAMROD. Dicker ran into compound. Shakedown continues observing.

"Okay, I'll close the loop with Ottawa," the SAMEO concluded as he went into a side office to call his aircraft maintenance superiors in Ottawa.

"Let me know when they get airborne. I'm going to brief the boss," Scrappy called to his radio operator who was monitoring the satellite tracker on the Chinook. "Hey, how much playtime does Shamus have?" he asked.

"About twenty-five minutes, sir, according to their last check-in with Slayer."

A voice raised, interrupting the office. "What the hell are you talking about?" A muffled and angry voice was yelling in the next room. It was the SAMEO on the phone.

"It's airborne now. I am *not* going to ground it. I know it's not in the minimum equipment dispatch list, but I need it here to fix it." Everyone stopped to listen to the rage.

"Jesus Christ! You want me to send a mobile repair team halfway to Helmand for a dent in the aircraft? Do you have any idea what the fuck is going on around here? Get me your supervisor!" He paused. "I don't give a fuck that it's 11:00 p.m. over there. We're in the middle of a war over here, and shit happens. Right now there's a dicker on a wall ready to fire an RPG round into FOB Ramrod as soon as the Griffon overwatch stops, so the Chinook is fuckin' moving. Put this in your log and have him call me when he wakes." *Slam!* The phone was hung up. He walked out of the room and frowned toward Scrappy, shaking his head.

"I better talk to Skipper. There's gonna be verbal shit storm coming from Ottawa. I'll be damned if some junior duty officer watching TV at midnight with his feet up on a desk downtown Ottawa is gonna screw up my day here!" He stormed out of operations.

At Ramrod . . .

After we refueled, we lifted first out of the FOB then circled to watch Blowtorch depart. As the wounded Chinook began to lift from the FOB, a faint voice was heard over the radio in a French Shakedown accent. "I tink I can. I tink I can . . ."

"Nice one, guys," Blowtorch retorted sarcastically as he blasted the FOB in a nuclear explosion of moondust, and continued on the radio:

"Freedom Ops, this is Blowtorch 60 Flight, wheels up. Back in twenty minutes."

"Roger, Blowtorch out to you. Shakedown 30 Flight, I need you to escort Blowtorch to the KAF Control Zone then get back to Howz-e. TIC in progress. Shamus has two-zero minutes playtime until they have to refuel."

"Shakedown 30, roger that. Retask to Howz-e. We'll break away from Blowtorch near the desert," I called in. "Blowtorch, are you guys okay solo from there?"

"Roger that! The helicopter is solid, just scuffed a little from that forklift, it seems. The damage isn't affecting us at all," Blowtorch 60 responded.

"31 checks," Fender also acknowledged but his voice not as enthused. I empathized with his tone. Howz-e had a bad reputation. Many helicopters came back from there with extra holes. It was one of the centers of battle, the big game in town. There were more bullets flying there every day than the rest of the AO.

"Woo-hoo. All right. Last day in theater and gonna get me some payback," the infidel's gunner called over the intercom. "Yaaaa, go infidels!"

I tried to add my excitement, but at this point of the game, it was more anxiety than excitement. We were going to Howz-e.

I looked out in the direction of Howz-e as we escorted the Chinook toward KAF. It was about 10 kilometers to my left. Smoke was rising from obvious combat. The small silhouettes of the Kiowa warrior choppers were buzzing in circles, diving toward the smoke, Shamus 11 and 12.

My veteran copilot sensed my anxiety, "All right, Cap, no worries. When we get to Howz-e, the shit is all within a few hundred meters of the highway, but north of the highway is safe, desert . . . I suggest getting a tactical talk-on from the north, maybe fly the guns into the threat area, and then . . . well we get into 'er." I nodded and held my thumb up. He was smiling. Obviously he had somehow emotionally transitioned his anxiety to cautious yet excited bravado over the past six months. I couldn't help think if it was bravado or the calm acceptance of impermanence.

The Chinook separated from us as we cleared the desert toward Dand. KAF was a few miles away and visual. He was safe to solo. Fender and I veered away toward Wilson on the north side of the mountains and climbed.

"You guys be careful. Blowtorch 60 switching to KAF tower, out," the Chinook called.

"Roger that, Blowtorch," I answered and then switched to Freedom operations.

"Freedom Ops, Shakedown 30 Flight is breaking off from Blowtorch. You have them now. We are heading to Howz-e," I relayed my actions and intent.

In Operations

"Shakedown, roger that. We're monitoring," the radio operator stated, referring to the text board. As he turned, he looked at the duty officer. "Better get the boss. Shakedown's going to a TIC in progress."

A few moments later, Scrappy and Skip entered the room with the SAMEO in tow. Additionally, in the hallway were a few fresh 408 copilots were being oriented—first day on the job. They watched as the three senior officers walked by dealing with one crisis as yet another rose. It would be the standard routine for the next year.

"Welcome, guys. Good to see you. Wait here. We'll chat when I'm done," Skipper acknowledged the new faces of his team ready for orientation briefings. "But first, Blowtorch 60 is damaged. Shakedown 30 and 31 are going into a TIC, and so I need to be in Ops. Welcome to the war," Skip stated bluntly as he rushed by, leaving their eyes widened in a reality shock.

"Scrappy, mind getting your Enterprise chair off the bird table?" he jested as Scrappy cleaned off the table. The senior officers gathered around watching the UAV feed and text prompter for the play by play.

This complexity of multiple activities would be the daily norm. Both Scrappy and Skipper would occasionally go flying outside the wire about once a week just to relax from operations stress. It was probably mentally easier to go get shot at than deal with the constant bullshit from the varying layers of headquarters and national command.

I am sure there were many frustrated colonels in Ottawa who were trying to get feedback from our CO while enjoying their morning coffee and were only to be greeted by our radio operator who would sarcastically state, "Sorry, sir, he can't come to the phone. He's outside the wire getting shot at right now."

"Update please," Skipper asked as he stepped behind the bird table.

"Roger, sirs," the radio operator started to brief. "We got Blowtorch 3 miles out estimating the ramp within a couple of minutes."

"Any problems reported?" the SAMEO asked, concerned, not knowing how severe the damage may have extended.

"No, sir. All good so far. And Shakedowns are en route to Howz-e to cover for Shamus while they refuel."

"What's the update for Howz-e?" Skip inquired.

The RadOp looked over at the teleprompter screen and summarized, "IED, rocket, and small arms attack from the south. Americans lost a vehicle and a platoon dispatched on foot south. They are moving slow due to the mine traps. Shamus put a few rockets down and pursued some FAMS into some compounds around here." He pointed to an area near the FOB on the bird table.

Skip took a breath. "Who is out there?" he asked as he went over to the manifest list beside the door.

"Steve and Fender's crew. They refueled in Ramrod, should be good to sustain for a while," Scrappy added.

"They haven't checked in with Slayer yet. I expect the text prompter to update shortly, sir." The RadOp looked to the 60-inch TV with the scripted tactical updates.

"Okay, roger that. That's why we're here, guys." He paused, looking at the SAMEO and Scrappy. "SAMEO with me. Scrappy, you have the helm. Call me when things calm or get worse." He left the room and walked through the crowd of new copilots who were in the hallway attentively eavesdropping. The facial expressions revealed polarity from fearful jaw dropping "holy shits" to gritty excited "fuck yahs!

Airborne Near Howz-e

"Slayer TOC, Shakedown 30," I called the airspace weapons controller in charge.

"Shakedown 30, go for Slayer."

"Hey, Slayer. We are two Griffons, eight thousand rounds, seven point six-two dual-Dillon door guns, sixty minutes playtime, ten minutes back from Howz-e, request an airspace update," I replied.

"Roger, Shakedown 30. My ROZ (restricted operating zone built around the combat) is hot. Guns are hot. Gun to target line is two-five-zero degrees from Wilson to Howz-e. Two times Shamus call signs on site. They require bingo fuel now (a word to say they only have enough fuel to get to a fuel cache). Check in with Shamus 12 on frequency four five point eight for your handover. Fires is controlled by my FAC (forward air controller), same frequency Slayer three five," Slayer ordered.

"Roger all that, Slayer. Switching over to Slayer 35 for the battle update brief (BUB)," I responded.

We were just passing FOB Wilson. We had four minutes to go. No one talked on the section radio or the intercom. Everyone just listened.

TICs were very busy with artillery, mortars, infantry movement, and casualty evacuation (casevac). Everyone followed strict protocols. If protocols were nonstandard because of battle, you just listened. Everyone had to know what was exactly happening before engaging with lethal force.

Smoke was rising about 500 meters south of FOB Howz-e due to the 2.75-inch rockets fired from Shamus. An American vehicle was burning on the road from an IED or RPG strike. It was pretty obvious where the fight was happening. Now it was our turn.

"Shamus, this is Shakedown. Inbound two minutes from the north. Ready for your handover brief," I called on the radio.

"Shakedown, roger that. We are visual with you. Egressing south of you to Wilson to refuel. Lotsa shit happening. Head over to the north of Howz-e. Contact Slayer three-five for an update brief. We'll be twenty minutes."

"Roger that, Shamus," I answered as we went to the north about 1,000 feet above the ground. My crew could see the area and quickly oriented to the fight.

"Slayer 35, Shakedown's checking in."

"Roger that, Shakedown. I check your status from Slayer TOC," he stated, knowing how much fuel and ammo we had. He did not require us to repeat that information, nor had he the time. "We got

FOB Howz-e. 200 meters south of Howz-e are twenty-five dismounted friendlies," he stated, orienting us to the battlefield.

I looked frantically for the American troops. The left gunner called it. "By the gas station, down the alley, visual."

"Okay, thanks. Got 'em," I answered as my eyes locked onto the patrol. "Slayer 35, visual friendlies."

"From the friendlies, 200 meters south is smoke. West of smoke, 50 meters, is a compound." He continued to talk my eyes onto the target area. I could see in my peripheral vision my entire crew stretching their neck to follow. Some holding thumbs-up, acknowledging they could see the target area while the radio blared.

"Three times FAMs last seen entering that compound. Shots still being fired toward my infantry. My plan is to advance friendlies on that compound. Mortar fire is under my command shooting from Wilson, it's cold (not shooting currently). Your mission is to set up close observation over my friendlies on that area on an east-west pattern and be prepared to suppress that area while my guys move. All your effects to the south of friendlies . . . how copy?"

I then repeated back to Slayer as I rolled the helicopter and dove out of the sky toward the objective. "Slayer-Shakedown is visual friendlies. Tally target area. All effects south. Rolling in for over-watch."

"31 checks," Fender responded as he followed me, acknowledging he understood the mission and the plan. There was no time to repeat any instructions, so he just went into a default trail position to cover me and was prepared to engage any targets to defend the troops on the ground.

My face and hands tingled, and for a second, I could feel my heartbeat . . . but just for a second.

Chapter 11

Welcome Home, Team

Scrappy observed my exhaustion as I stagger into operations. I was soaked in sweat, my face red from sunburn. I was mentally exhausted. But somehow I felt less anxious about the entire mission and year to come—baptized by fire, so to speak.

Fender was the same. I had an ice-cold unopened can of Diet Pepsi in my hand. I rolled the can across my brow, relieving my hot skin with the cool condensation.

"Stood down, eh?" Scrappy stated.

"Yup, but what a rush." I exhaled. "We rolled in on the target and set up a pattern ready to lay down a blanket of lead on that compound, but there was nothing. Didn't see anyone. They were near-by though; I know it.

Slayer Three-five said all the firing stopped, so we picketed for another twenty minutes before Shamus got back," I continued to explain. "The Taliban just laid low or escaped in our handover, I suppose. There are many compounds and wadis to hide in."

"Did you hear the I-comm chatter?" Scrappy added, asking if I received any real-time intelligence from the intelligence persons listening to enemy communications.

"Nope."

He rewound the text prompter, and it showed.

Time XX:XX: I-comm chatter FOB Howz-e: "Top hat gone. Infidels in. Do we attack?"

Time XX:XX: I-comm chatter FOB Howz-e. Second voice answered: "No. Wait and leave."

"Top Hat?" I asked.

"The Taliban call Shamus 'Top Hat' that because of the EO-IR ball on top. Looks like a top hat," Scrappy answered frankly.

"Oh, yah . . . Huh." It seemed an appropriate description.

"Otherwise pretty mundane day today?" He smirked.

"Mundane?" I exclaimed. "If steering around artillery blowin' the crap out of something near Chalgour, doing overwatch of an IED on Highway 1, scaring dickers off walls near FOBS while the Chinook gets skinned by a loader all followed up with a live TIC in Howz-e is mundane, then yes."

I could see him smirking, knowing his sarcasm caught the best of me.

"And we are gonna go through a lot of flares by the end of the tour. But I'm starting to get used to them firing off," I summed.

He glared at my apparent sense of complacency toward the missile-warning system. "Well, you guys keep doing your counter drills. You never know when one is going to be real." He paused from the lecture. "The dicker was young, I heard? Well, get used to it because that's how the Taliban operate. They could be paying some kid or blackmailing him to report knowing we won't shoot them. Hell, the kid could be the one pulling the cell phone trigger too. Never know. But keep reporting this to intel. That could be a mask for a bigger threat!"

Fender nodded. We left the room and proceeded to int to report the activity.

"Hey, Steve, check this out!" Scrappy called me back to his personal ready room a few doors down the hall.

"Right behind ya, boss," I pivoted on my heel and reversed course in an animated fashion.

Scrappy rounded the corner to his private office and aimed his arms, directing my attention to his bunk.

"A cot? You're gonna sleep here?" I exclaimed. "No, no! You'll burn out, dude!"

He disagreed, shaking his head. "Look, I figure I will be at work for the next 7,368 hours." The math penned onto a white board above his desk. It was below a lined-out number 7,380, indicating a recent recalculation. "I really don't have any extra time for the transit to my bunk on the other side of KAF. This job will be nonstop, and I am always on call. I plan on staying here. If I'm not busy, I'd rather bang off a half-hour sleep then be sitting in a van driving to the other side. I knew it would be like this, so if you need me, I'll be here," Scrappy concluded, flopping onto his bed, crossing his shins with his hands cupped behind his head. "Mind getting the light on the way out?" He smiled and closed his eyes.

"Your call, buddy." I raised my brow, shaking my head and pressed his light out. "I'm heading over to the other side. I heard the rest of the team has arrived. Copilots and gunners."

"Yup, they are just completing their weapons verifications and will be heading over to the tents around 7:00 p.m.," Scrappy informed with his eyes still closed. "They were a bit shocked as they walked in earlier during all the hell breaking loose around here: TIC and a broken Chinook. And some duty officer in Ottawa told the SAMEO that the dents in the Chinook did not meet the criteria for him to release airworthiness. Told him it was to be grounded in Ramrod until Canadian morning when the staff returned to work."

"You're kidding! There were dickers getting ready for something out there," I stated.

"I know, and the SAMEO lost it on the phone at the poor paper-pushing, midnight desk commando in Ottawa. It was quite a show." Scrappy smirked as he rolled onto his side. "Anyway, it would be nice for you guys to meet your crew at the tent." He waved his hand for me to leave so he could have a snooze.

"Roger that. See ya later," I stated sarcastically. I closed the door and then followed Fender and Big C out of the building to the squadron bus stop.

"So how was your flight?" I asked.

"Sounds about the same as yours but we went north. Same shit different pile," Big C answered with his level smile. "Shall we head over to welcome home the rest of our team?"

"Absolutely," I answered as we shuffled out of the TOC.

At the tents

I went into my corner space, which I had decorated with a carpet and makeshift plywood shelving. It was positioned for watching movies on my computer 3 feet away. My shipping boxes had arrived with extra clothes. I used the boxes as leg stands, and across them, I placed a 2-foot-wide piece of plywood; alas, a desk. My spinning office chair parked in the remaining floor space.

I hopped in my chair and spun toward my bed, got out and removed my sweaty tactical clothing, and hung it on a line over my bed along with towels and other clothes. This completely engulfed all the space from 4 feet up. I had to remain sitting in order to see anything. If I stood up, my head entered a field of crisscrossed laundry lines.

Despite the cramped quarters, it was becoming a comfortable sanctuary. Next door, literally 5 feet over on the other side of a privacy sheet, Fender was strumming quietly to his "Hotel California" tune.

"On a dark desert highway,
fuckin' hot wind in the air,
warm smell of the poo pond,
stinging my nostril hair."

I giggled as I whispered, "Nice lick, dude—don't quit your day job!"

"Ha-ha! Whad ya mean? I'm awesome!" he replied, continuing to strum.

The door opened, shining some light over my wall. "Hey, guys, copilots are here," Big C announced.

"Right on," I replied. Despite recently together for intense training for the past nine months, it felt like a family homecoming. It was good to see them.

Irish and Arnie walked in. They were exhausted and did not look impressed. They forced a smile and gave each captain the alpha-male man hug then stopped in shock of the confined space. Irish was an intelligent and technically apt individual but preferred things to be of first-world standard.

"You guys got in a TIC today?" Arnie asked excitedly.

"Not really," Fender responded.

"We got called in, all jacked up, briefed it, and rolled in," I added.

"But nada," Fender sang as he strummed a chord.

"What?" Irish asked, alerted to the situation.

"As soon as we set up on the target area, they broke contact and hid. I-comm chatter showed them pausing for another day, so we hung around until Shamus got back," I briefed. "They were there, and we stayed offensive on the area, just couldn't PID them."

"So cool. Awesome," Arnie whispered.

I nodded. "A little exciting though." I looked over to Irish who was listening intently as I pointed him down the narrow bent hall toward his future home.

"Irish, good to see you, man. You're space is two down on the left, under the Internet repeater wires!" I excitedly welcomed him. I figured this is how Grumpy felt when he showed me around.

"Thanks?" he responded hesitantly. His space did not even have a functioning lightbulb. His bed was tipped up sideways with the mattress leaning against it. There was some broken plywood furniture thrown aside in the space. It looked like a garbage room.

"Hmmm . . ." I patted him on the shoulder as I followed him to his chamber. "Mine was like that a few days ago. It'll be fine. We'll get some lightbulbs from the American PX across the street, sweep the floor, and put a rug down. It'll be like home in no time." I tried to be encouraging yet in a sarcastic manner.

He was unimpressed.

Arnie's voice blurted from down the tent hall. "Ten more months! You gotta be fuckin' kidding me!" He then giggled quickly seeing the potential as he scouted other rooms. I knew it was bad, but I was already over my shock reliving it through their reactions.

Arnie grunted then flexed his Schwarzenegger muscles, moving a massive crate to clear space for his gear. "Aaarrghh!" he exerted. "Perfect. Actually, I think it's gonna be just fine," he retracted his previous displeasure as he looked at the condition of Irish's space.

Hollywood was at the other end of the tent. He was a cheery tall young aviator. As a charismatic storyteller, he was eager to attain hardship stories to share with his infantry buddies for credibility. He felt he was losing respect of his previous combat-arms brothers since he went to the air force. "This is perfect!" he hollered as he gathered evidence with his camera.

He leaned over Irish's shoulder. "Oh, dude! Your room really sucks!" He paused. "Which is totally awesome!" he continued, clicking away with his camera. Excitedly, he went down the hall inspecting everyone's room.

Arnie smiled. "Okay, this is pretty cool!" he stated rhetorically. "But what the hell is that stench?" He had discovered the flora of the poo pond.

Fender smiled while peeking out from his studio. "I'll tell you what it is." He started strumming the same tune again.

"On a dark desert highway,
fuckin' hot wind in the air,
warm smell of the poo pond,
stinging my nostril hair."

Arnie chuckled, peaking into Fender's space.

"Well, you asked," I stated while smiling at Fender's lyrical response.

Fender laughed from behind the canvass wall as he rehearsed his song once again. Big C smiled and explained about the sewage plant a few hundred meters away.

Irish continued complaining. "This dust is burning my eyes out! Oh shit, what the fuck have I got myself into? I have a dust headache."

"They have Claritin at the PX. Already on it, buddy," I barked down the hall, giving a suggestion to relieve the pain.

The door at the other end of the tent opened, interrupting the banter with Grumpy cheerfully entering.

"Welcome home!" He was happy to see the guys but also rejoiced in experiencing their initial discomfort. Having all the copilots around was like a piece of home coming to this God-forsaken place. KAF just became a little more bearable. However, they were not as excited—and still sleep-fucked.

"How'd the weapons shoot go, guys?" Grumpy asked openly.

"That was crazy! Everyone was falling asleep while shooting," Hollywood answered laughing. "I thought I was gonna experience my first casualty of war."

"It was kinda dangerous!" Irish critiqued. "I'm not sure it was thought out properly."

"How many 'do overs' did you get?" Grumpy acknowledged, smiling, looking at Arnie who appeared sleepy.

"Ha-ha," Arnie responded. "How'd you guess?"

"I think we had five on our validation," Grumpy answered, looking around from someone to nod in agreement. Big C dropped his chin twice in agreement. "Mmmm. Hmmm."

"I think we had five or six demonstrating the Mexican unload (unloading by shooting all the rounds until empty but without authority)," Arnie answered. "No one got killed, so I guess that's good."

"The trucks are arriving with your gear, guys. Let's help them unpack and get their quarters all established. Big day tomorrow!" Big C coached with his senior wisdom.

Everyone filed into the dust-ridden street forming an assembly line behind a two-ton flatbed truck filled with kit bags and barrack boxes. Grumpy jumped on the back of the truck and started reading names as he tossed a box to the next in line.

As the evening went on, I lay on my bed listening to the banter of the new guys carve out a home for the year to come. Someone found a lightbulb for Irish, so he was less disgruntled, and Hollywood kept checking other rooms for ideas and taking pictures for his journals. He was excited; his chuckles in finding humor in the collective discomfort could be heard through the tent.

Shorty was another copilot. He lived across the hall. He was quiet, yet he had the driest sense of humor of us.

Irish continued to mumble about little bothersome things and asked other guys to help him, which they did. This was all under the musical umbrella of Fender lightly strumming tunes from songs he knew, often repeating chords and words until he got it right before moving on to the next bar.

Every ten minutes, a pair of jet planes would drown out all sound as they shook the entire camp followed by Hollywood, stating, "That's awesome!" Shorty occasionally blurting out rhetorical facts with timely humor such as, "Apparently the dust we are breathing is 30 percent camel shit." This was usually answered with silence as everyone digested the fact then a snort giggle of acknowledgment before returning to the murmur of business.

I slowly drifted to sleep in the comforting noise of my friends.
MMMMMRRRRAAAAAWWWWWRRRRRR.

"RWOKIT ATTAK, RWOKIT ATTAK, RWOKITT ATTAK."

I rose up immediately, heard the rocket attack warning, and listened. I thought about rolling onto the floor as I heard all the new guys saying, "Get down, get down! Two minutes on the floor and then the bunker!" However, my chair was in the way.

I listened for an impact explosion. I didn't hear any. I smiled at the commotion of the other guys scuffling to find their helmets and weapons. Then I decided to turn my light off and closed my eyes. I heard the guys bitching about trying to find a place to lie down on the floor.

"Fuck, I have no space."

"My ass is in the air."

"Turn on a light. What do we do next again?"

"Two minutes then to the bunker."

"Oh right. Did you hear an explosion?"

Two minutes later, they shuffled by going to the shelter.

The thought of that being number 58 for the American I met calmed me. So this time I hid in silence, falling back to sleep.

Chapter 12

Irish's General Mission: A Typical Day

"In preparing for battle I have always found that plans are
useless, but planning is indispensable."
—Dwight D. Eisenhower

408 Squadron's air crew were now veterans—a month of experience. We were familiar with the AO: the mountains, the marijuana fields, and the smoke-laden valley from the brick factories. And the desensitization had commenced—to the false missile warnings, dust, and TIC calls.

Most missions involved escorting Chinooks to Helmand, the Arghandhab, and even north toward the 17,000 feet mountains of Oruzgan Province. However, occasionally, a TIC would pop up, keeping us sharp.

The normal POL in Afghanistan was preparations for winter. Roofs and walls were being repaired. Canals were being diverted, allowing the winter rains into fields. The fall harvest was finished, and now, the marijuana was ripening for winter sales.

It was November 2009. We had the complicated task of coordinating a milk run around Kandahar Province in conjunction with the task force general requiring a tour to his various FOBs. I asked Irish to plan this one. I was being selfish; plus he wanted it for training. I expected frustrating delays at the FARP, possible TICs, and Special Forces restrictions en route inevitably causing the detailed timings to fail. So why would I want to plan something that will have to be changed anyway? I'd let Irish do it. Anyway, he was meticulous and loved these challenges.

So Irish spent the previous day diligently preparing. The result was a massive complex booklet of spreadsheets with landing zones, timings and our action required. He built it; he briefed it, and we flew it.

Professor was my immediate boss, but tactically, he was my subordinate. It meant he had more rank and administratively was my commander. However, since I had more experience on the aircraft, I was his mission lead during flight. Basically, Professor gave me orders to get the job done, and then I returned orders on how to do it.

Professor was an energetic, intelligent man with some eccentricities stereotypical of an old English university professor. Since he couldn't smoke his pipe in the building, he used chewing tobacco and carried a styro coffee cup as a spittoon. Between sentences in conversation, he'd lift his cup to his lip and release a black gob of spit.

On this particular day, while occupied with planning, he placed his spittoon among the other styro coffee cups, making it undistinguished. Unbeknownst to Grumpy, his attention also directed toward flight planning, he picked up what he thought was his coffee and placed it against his lips.

"STOP!" yelled Irish.

"What?" Grumpy retorted angrily as his pleasant sip was being interrupted.

Irish pointed at Professor and gestured spitting into the cup and then pointed to Grumpy's cup. Grumpy looked into the cup. His eyes enlarged, and he started convulsing. His cheeks puffed out, holding air of what could have been vomit. His content-working smile vanished into rage. He put the cup down and raised his arm to the level position, slowly raising it about the elbow—a signal of his temper rising. Professor was oblivious to all this and walked out the door with Grumpy five steps behind.

"Is this yours?" His voice could be heard down the hall.

"Yes, why thank you, almost forgot that," Professor replied cheerfully, aloof to Grumpy's disposition and took the cup.

Grumpy's voice was low and upset. "When you place it amongst the other coffee cups in the room, there may be a risk of confusion. Would you refrain from spitting in here, sir, at least do not let your spittoon out of your hands?" he angrily directed to Professor.

Professor stood erect, raised his nose, and looked down toward Grumpy. "Well, I suggest you need pay a bit more attention." He placed his lips against the cup and released.

Grumpy froze his face with rage as his eyes exploded out of his head. He wasn't sure whether to scream or throw up. He exhaled and exited himself from the room.

Professor started to show some remorse but then smiled as he realized how funny the situation would appear from the room of giggling pilots.

"All right, Section 1, let's brief," Irish called out, interjecting. He was ready. Professor, Arnie, Hawk, Gunny, Snapshot, Zorg, and myself all gathered to listen to the brief.

Hawk was the lead gunner, an experienced infantry sergeant with previous tours in Afghanistan. He was an earthy Newfoundlander with a practical approach to problem solving—if it doesn't work, get a bigger hammer; and if that doesn't work, time to go to the pub. And being a large, muscled, and tattooed man, he had little resistance when he solved problems. Despite this, he was about the people, a compassionate leader with great sense of humor.

Snapshot was my right gunner and technical expert on the helicopter. He was also an avid photographer; almost every descent Afghanistan helicopter picture in the media was taken by him. He was a cheerful Labradorean man. He talked fast, and his Inuit accent made him almost impossible to understand. He manned his Dillon with pride, but he was much prouder of the Canon camera perpetually hanging around his neck. He was often in trouble for taking pictures instead of manning the gun, yet the senior brass loved and encouraged the photos—he was caught in the cross fire. Despite this, the captured images will be his legacy.

Zorg was a quiet infantry-experienced gunner. Despite being a young man, he had already completed a couple of Afghanistan tours. He was practical and loved to provoke those that weren't.

Irish completed his mission coordination brief. It was very thorough—extensive. Despite the exact detail on the prepared maps and time tables, it was too much for information for me. He briefed every action for every contingency.

"Irish, I'm dazzled by your work," I stated as I perused the maps and charts. "But I'm gonna need a binder to contain it all. It's pretty, but can it fight?" I critically continued. "I'm on the controls, but you're on the MX (camera). You're listening to five different stations on three different radios and watching for threats, friendly troops, and other aircraft. When the hell do you have time to pull out and read all this shit? I just need a one-page list of frequencies, FOBs, and timings" I pleaded. "Plus the doors are open, and the wind is gonna make this stuff fly everywhere."

He was less than happy with my lack of appreciation.

"I have it very well organized. You'll see. You just do the flying, and I'll coordinate it—page to page. I got this," he retorted, defending his plan.

"All great plans never survive first contact," I argued, quoting a statement I heard.

"Ha-ha. Okay, let's just get our int brief," he directed.

"Well, I think it looks great," Professor interjected with his supervisory support, adding encouragement. "You did a lot of work." Irish's head perked a little higher.

The int op gave a standard brief depicting the hot spots of enemy activity in the area. It was similar—green, yellow, and red spots further to the west. The same patterns of color seemed to stay consistent throughout the war, sometimes changing depending on how active they were. It was like a traffic light of combat activity, which shifted around the map like a lethal whack-a-mole game.

"All right, Scrappy, what is everyone doing today?" I asked, referring to the battle group's patrol activities.

"You got First Battalion out here and Third Battalion here. Their patrol route will be about three hours to the south and back," Scrappy continued, pointing to his bird table map to show what all the Canadians were doing in the AO. This was the most important thing to me. If I had extra fuel, I was going there to show support by flying overwatch for the patrols.

"You guys got the general on board today. He has a robust schedule. Make sure you keep your timings," Scrappy continued.

I looked at Irish and gestured. "He's got 'the' plan," I stated sarcastically.

Scrappy continued, "The route south from FOB Wilson is hot right now. Taliban have been acting up with shoot 'n' scoots. Our soldiers and Americans are also patrolling south from Wilson. Make sure your approaches are all from the north and coordinate with Slayer and the

FOB before you arrive!" he further advised. "Shamus is fighting right now and will need to rearm and fuel. They have refueling priority at the FOB, so you may have to hold over the desert."

I felt a little vindicated already. A hold would screw up Irish's timing.

Irish looked at me. "I got it covered. I planned for these contingencies," he stated proudly.

"Hmmm," I grunted; my skepticism was losing.

"Any chance they'll need us while the general is on the ground visiting?" I asked.

"I think they'll be fine. But if they get shot up, you're on deck," Scrappy advised.

Irish looked concerned. Not so much about the combat, more about how the Taliban were gonna fuck up his detailed schedule.

"Okay, Irish is running the section today. Talk at him." I winked and nodded my head toward Irish.

"What the fuck you got there?" Scrappy stated as Irish handed him the detailed booklet.

"It's our timings and locations for all the stops. It also has my detailed routes," Irish briefed.

"It's a fantastic coordination plan!" Professor encouraged, very impressed with the scholastic production—well above tactical school standards.

Scrappy held it, speechless. It was massive. "All right, it looks impressive. Very pretty. Safe flying," he summed up as he aloofly tossed the booklet over to the Radio Op to track.

"Yes, sir," Irish acknowledged and then redirected his focus to the team. "All right, check in on the radio in forty minutes."

All the team members dispersed to complete their individual preparation and rituals. I realized mine after a few trips. I always walked around the aircraft with one hand in contact the entire time, a blessing or a circle of power. I don't know, but it worked. Or maybe it didn't. It may have been someone else's ritual that worked, but I couldn't take that risk.

Irish was always quiet. He had a pillow that he placed on his seat to help with the hours of ass pain on a bullet-resistant steel seat. He fluffed it like a cat would claw at his bed before sleeping. Of course he received teasing. But we all did.

"Snapshot, do you think we should fill his pillow with baby powder?" I stated out loud behind Irish's back.

He laughed. "Powder his ass."

"At least it would smell good. Help reduce that SWASS (sweaty ass) odor in here," Zorg added.

"Especially when he jumps in hard. There would be an explosion of flowery smelling white," I added.

"I heard that! No one is gonna powder my ass!" Irish answered adamantly.

Snapshot got into his corner behind the right gun. He checked his sites, checked his weapon, checked his cameras, and then lay back, putting his feet up on the gun—ritual complete. He quietly meditated for his private last minute and then bounced back to his eccentric, smiling self.

Zorg disappeared from the team and went behind the gun on the left. It was the only place he could find isolation. He only needed thirty seconds, and then he lay on the ground under his gun and stared up at the sky. Sometimes, he needed an extra prod. He got stuck at times, almost like he had seen a few too many things from previous tours; either that, or he was sleeping.

"Final brief," I called the team together. Irish led the charge this time.

"Guns all loaded and ready?" he asked.

"Three-quarter bomb, ASE full, codes loaded . . . and camera has a new data card," informed Snapshot, smiling with his camera dangling from his neck as he pointed to the can of six thousand bullets, only enough ammo for about one minute of continuous fire from both guns.

"Shanique and Genevive are ready to go, sir," reported Zorg. All the guns had lady names. His responsibility was ensuring the guns were prepared. Snapshot made sure the aircraft was prepared and loaded with anti-missile flares.

Irish had briefed all the details, again, very thoroughly.

"Snapshot, when the general is on board, please minimize your camera exposure," I added with a grin.

"Roger dat, Haycee!" He held up his thumb, not being offended by the motherhood statement.

Zorg didn't talk very much. It took several weeks just to get him to say "clear left." I couldn't see past that portion of the aircraft because of the armored seats, so I needed his eyes to make sure the area was safe and clear. I also had to encourage him to speak up.

"And Zorg?" I looked at him with eyebrows raised.

"Clear left!" He sarcastically answered.

"We ready?" Irish asked.

I looked over at Professor's aircraft. He was onboard. The gunners were ready but no Arnie. He was running late from across the ramp.

I yelled toward him, "Let's go!"

"Fuck, I gotta piss!" he yelled back.

"No time. We're late! Hold it until first refuel."

He looked toward the flight line for observers as he danced on the spot. He then shuffled to the back of the helicopter under the tail rotor and opened his zipper. With his back toward us and with no one else around, he let out the stream of piss under the tail boom. Professor never noticed, and only the right gunner could see. He wouldn't say anything. Alas, another ritual would be borne.

He held his thumb up and shuffled to his position. "Good to go!"

Chapter 13

Stone, Rocket, TIC: Day Continues

"So much shit happens here in a day that it takes a long time to reflect, contemplate, and try to organize it into something that makes sense, even if it isn't acceptable or understandable from a Western cultural perspective. Some will never make sense of it, and it will linger."

On X-Ray Ramp

The two PT6 engines wound up, stirring the main rotor in the air. We started the tactical checklist. The preparations Irish made were ready to be executed.

Another clear day in the Arghandhab Valley but already hot; sweat was dripping down my nose and filling my helmet ear cups.

"Enable ASE and load guns," Irish commanded over the intercom system.

"Coke can in, ASE enabled, and right gun loaded . . . left gun loaded," the two gunners reported. The Coke can is slang for an external shutoff safety switch, preventing the flares from firing inadvertently. It looked like a mini Coke can, especially since it was also red.

"Shakedown two-six, this is two-five. We are ready. Call green," I radioed.

Professor was still going through the checklist.

"Give us three minutes," Professor responded pleasantly.

"He's gonna put you behind your detailed schedule." I smirked to Irish.

"I planned for his pedantic checklist procedures," he defended.

"You gotta be kidding! You included his specific pace in your timings?" I responded, surprised.

"Yup." He proudly smiled.

I looked out toward Professor's helicopter. Arnie was in the seat closest to me. His hand was out the window, and he looked back at me with his palm up and head tilted back, indicating his impatience with Professor programming of the MX-15. Although it wasn't required for this mission, Professor disciplined himself in learning it proficiently at every opportunity. After a minute, Arnie held his thumb up and pulled it inside the window.

"26 is green and good to go, up on tower frequency," Professor called.

We attained our takeoff clearance to air taxi to the south side of the airport to meet the general. The general boarded, and his entourage walked over to Professor's chopper behind us.

"Shakedown 25, this is KAF tower. You are cleared to depart parallel to runway zero five along the taxiway, parallel the Predator UAV, and pass behind it at the departure end."

"A Pred? Where is it?" Irish called as we accelerated through 60 knots along the taxiway.

"It's not clear left, sir. Pred coming abeam," Zorg stated while he tapped the general to see.

"I got it," I answered, viewing the UAV. "Hold this speed and heading. It will pass soon."

The general held up his thumb and smiled, pleased with the multilayers of activity.

We were flying in formation with a Predator drone. There was no pilot on board—unmanned. We slowed slightly to allow it to pass us and then formed up on its wing.

"Fuckin' cool," Zorg stated. "We are in formation with a drone."

"I wish I could get a picture of that," Snapshot stated frustratingly because of the restriction of having the general on board. The Predator continued climbing above us.

As we passed the end of Runway 05, we turned north.

"Visual Pred, passing behind and proceeding on course," I called to KAF tower.

We climbed above the Arghandhab valley and checked in with Slayer.

"Slayer, this is Shakedown 25 Flight of two Griffons en route through the ROZ to Wilson, request an airspace update," Irish asked.

"Shakedown 25, this is Slayer TOC. ROZ is hot. Guns are hot from Wilson to the southeast. The gun line is onto grid QQ30759572. I've got two Shamus flights supporting a TIC in progress near Wilson. Area south of Wilson is restricted. Stay north and contact Wilson landing zone controller to coordinate your approach." Slayer already knew our task. With a high-profile guest on board the helicopter, all the controllers attempted to expedite our flight path.

"Romeo Tango, Slayer," Irish replied, understanding the instructions.

"Roger that. 26 checks," Arnie replied, indicating they heard the information.

I looked at Irish, challenging him to stay ahead of the game. "So what's the landing plan?"

"Let's talk to Shamus, deconflict with them, and go straight in from the north," he suggested.

"Roger, I'll get that coordinated for you," I acknowledged and then called Shamus.

They responded, "Roger, Shakedown. This is Shamus Two-one. One-one is currently engaging east-west patterns, 400 meters south of Wilson. Reference smoke. I am Shamus Two-one, and I am in the FOB now reloading. Gunsmoke is at 2,000 feet—no conflict. (Gunsmoke is an Apache attack helicopter with weapons and optics, allowing him to stay far away). Y'all come straight in from the north desert—it's clear," the Southern accent reported in a friendly manner despite the heightened activity.

"Roger that," I responded.

"Shakedown Two-six checks," Arnie's voice acknowledged as he tightened the formation by moving his helicopter within a couple of hundred meters of mine.

We landed the helicopters by the south end of the large landing zone; Professor and Arnie abeam us. The passengers were quickly met with FOB staff.

"Thanks for the ride, guys," said the general. "I know there is some activity going on here I don't think you'll be able to get back, but I'll stay with the RCHA (Royal Canadian Horse Artillery) if need be."

"Okay, sir," Irish stated, holding his thumb up.

"No sweat, sir. We'll be back as per your schedule. I think Shamus has things pretty much in control," I injected, looking forward at the rocket explosions about 600 meters to our south.

"Roger that boys, woulda been nice to have a pic of that Pred…next time," the general stated raising his thumb as he hopped out.

"Aaarghh," Snapshot called after the general departed.

"What's next?" I asked Irish ignoring Snapshot for the moment.

Irish shuffled through his detailed planning book. "Over to FOB Tarnac for a shuttle."

"Roger, dodger. Let's go," I answered happily.

"Roger, I am lifting. We are on time, and on target," Irish advised.

Irish continued to orchestrate the milk run. And despite delays from extremely dusty landing sites, navigating around IED ROZs and delays at the FARP, he managed to keep the schedule accurate to my dismay. We even had time for a few minute break at the KAF FARP.

As we sat at the FARP refreshing with Red Bull and a pee break, Irish looked at his watch. He noticed a possible time compression in his plan. He jumped in and spun his finger in the air, demanding me to wind up the engines to keep on schedule.

"Winding up," I announced, twisting the throttles open and further passing the information to my wingman, Professor, to do the same.

"Shakedown Flight cleared takeoff X-ray east river, altimeter is two-nine-nine-eight," the tower instructed, responding to our request. We departed from the FARP.

On the north side of Threemile Mountain between KAF and Kandahar was a large Bedouin village. It was mostly canvass with various mud huts dug into the ground. The occasional brick factory chimney added smoke to the dusty air.

Today there was a gathering of about fifty people in a circle near mid-camp; I veered away not to disturb them. Zorg was watching from his side. As a gunner, he observed the detail in activities of the local people, screening for strange behaviors or weapons that could harm us.

"What the hell is going on down there?" Zorg inquired.

"I didn't notice. A circle of people? Are they kids playing?" I queried.

"Oh my god, sir, it's a fuckin' stoning!" Zorg sounded distressed. "They are stoning her!"

"What?" I challenged.

"About a kilometer back, they were stoning a woman—a girl—like a teenage girl!" he continued his rant.

"You're kidding me!" I asked.

"We gotta do something! We gotta go back." Zorg was adamant.

"Two-six, this is two-five. Did you see a stoning back there left side?" There was a pause, apparently a similar discussion going on in their aircraft.

"Roger that. Continue, Steve! We can't interfere." Professor's tone was different. Professor knew my crew would be discussing possible methods of intervention. He knew it would be a huge mistake. I knew it would be mistake too, but I couldn't help trying to think it through.

I paused for about three seconds. In those three seconds, my mind raced through scenarios. We could turn back, force an interdiction, and extract the young girl. There would be anger, possible fighting, and bloodshed. If we got away with it, shame would be brought to the family for us escalating the situation, causing Westerners to be involved. Great shame. There would be further stupid punishments to her family. Yet we had the power to disperse it—temporarily. And what they were doing was legal, a normal custom. And our prevailing orders were to report and not interfere. I felt helpless.

In Canada, we take so many simple freedoms for granted. One of the reasons a stoning occurs is if a person, which usually seems to be a woman, brings shame upon a family. The expected community response is to punish her, stone her. She is half buried, and everyone must throw a stone. If she lives, she lives. If she dies, she dies. It is justified by the will of God. I couldn't imagine without my stomach turning what it would be like to experience that in downtown Edmonton, in Churchill Square.

"Roger," I replied. Professor was right.

"We have to continue with our primary mission, guys. All I can do is report it." My voice was heightened, heavy. I didn't know what to do. It was deathly quiet as I went out on the radio to Slayer.

"That ain't right. That ain't right—we can help!" Zorg stated.

"Zorg, we gotta carry on with our task. We'll talk later!" I was concerned because of his tone.

"Too many people dying for stupid reasons here," he stated quietly.

"Shakedown 25, this is Slayer TOC. I copy your report, and it has been passed up to the chain." His tone was the same. To him, it was a routine report to file and pass. I was amazed by the lack of intonation. He had probably received so many inhumane reports that he was numb to the lack of compassion witnessed each day.

"Airspace update report," Slayer continued seamlessly. "No change to the airspace, but Wilson is hot. TIC in progress. Two times enemy mortars have been shot into Wilson. Shamus helicopters are continuing operations south of Wilson with rockets and .50-cal. All effects are east-west, approach from north and contact LZ (landing zone) controller in Wilson to deconflict your arrival. I say again, Wilson recently under mortar fire."

"25, roger, copy that. Are you in need of our support at this time?" I asked.

Irish's eyes got big. He realized I was asking to get into the fight. Zorg yelled a huge battle cheer from the back.

"We gotta straighten these fuckers out!" Zorg hollered.

"The general has to be picked up. He's expecting us," Irish stated.

"Yes, you're right. But I'm sure the general will tell the FOB commander that he can use us if they need extra helicopter gunship support," I added. "He won't mind waiting."

"Well, boys, be prepared for anything," I said in nervous anticipation of Slayer's fire mission, directing us into battle.

"Negative. Shamus has got it. They have too many choppers in that location as it is. Thanks, but proceed on task," Slayer responded after a short delay.

There was silence the cockpit. I'm not sure if it was relief or disappointment.

"I guess I can put my gun away and pick up my camera again," Snapshot joked.

"Do you think that girl is okay?" Zorg dwelled in a concerned tone. He seemed only half engaged in the current situation.

"What did you see?" I asked, hoping he would quickly dump the past and return forward to the present.

"She took a bunch of stones to the body, hunched, then a big one directly to the head and tipped over, limp." His voice stated flatly. "I didn't see her move after that. It was hard to see."

Everyone was quiet. We were about to go into Wilson; it was under attack.

"Focus, Zorg." I raised my voice. "We'll talk after."

The crew was quiet listening only to the radio filled with combat activity near Wilson. Again, the landing zone was jammed. We were able to approach into the same place where the general was dropped.

There was a medevac. Dustoff, a Blackhawk CASEVAC helicopter, was inbound five minutes after us to extract casualties. This was being orchestrated while four Kiowa Warriors were rotating in and out of battle only 400 meters away.

Gunsmoke, the Apache helicopter, was also still high above using 30mm cannon to augment the Shamus teams. The radios were blaring with activity to the point that our crew couldn't even talk on the intercom. It was confusion, and the air was congested with choppers all within a 1-kilometer radius.

We were landing in the FOB when a plume of smoke rose a few hundred meters in front of us on the south edge of Wilson.

"All call signs. Rocket attack. Rocket attack," the Wilson LZ coordinator called. "A mortar just landed on the south wall of Wilson."

This was all happening as the general was approaching the helicopter. He was poised and taking the appropriate time to share handshakes with the persons he was visiting, slightly ducking as he heard mortars explode a few hundred meters south. His pause, taking the time to "grip and grin," was aggravating both myself and Irish. He looked over his shoulder to watch the rising black smoke of the Taliban attack and turned to watch the Kiowas release their rockets, adding to the smoke in the valley. He seemed to be enjoying the stroll—all while we impatiently waited to expedite into the air where we felt less vulnerable.

He boarded, smiled from the back seat, and gave us the thumbs-up. He yelled to communicate over the noise of the helicopters, mortars, and rocket war just a quarter mile south.

"Got ourselves a bit of a war going on here. Didn't think you'd make it!" He smiled.

"No problem, sir. That's what we're here for," I yelled back, faking my extreme confidence. "We'll be off in a second."

"Ahh, we should go now. The general's on board," Irish directed.

"We'll stay together as a section. It's best," I trumped. "Wait for Prof. We'll go together."

Professor's aircraft was still loading the general's entourage: a chief warrant officer, a staff officer, and a guard. They were shaking hands, doing their final good-byes. They were almost ready to go.

Nevertheless, our section couldn't split up and go independently with all the other helicopters in the air. It would have added too much confusion. All the players expected two helicopters to move for one radio call. There was always higher risk of crashing from confusion than from the enemy.

Another plume rose across the base from our location, 400 meters away. A few moments later, a light shock wave was felt from the explosion. Our eyes mutually enlarged, pausing to look at each other's nonverbal response to the excitement.

"Those mortars are getting a bit close, don't ya think? We gotta get going!" Irish insisted in a slightly elevated voice of concern.

"Yup. I agree. I think we are starting to attract indirect fire. What the fuck's taking them so long out there?" I looked as they shook hands and jocularly smiled, aloof to the plume of rising mortar smoke due to the chopper noise.

Irish looked out toward them, eyes grew enlarged with palms up, gesturing the "let's get the hell moving, people" signal. They moved toward Professor's helicopter.

"We're good. They are aboard. We'll be outta here right away," I encouraged, faking a smile. Moments later, 26 called ready, and we departed as the Dustoff medevac arrived.

The general put his headset on. "Thanks for coming back and getting me, guys," he said cheerfully. "It's getting a bit exciting down there, but the RCHA (artillery) are doing well and getting some business today—it was a good visit." He paused, reviewing his notes with his travel partner. "I have a bit of change, gents. You can take me over to the Lord Strathconas now at Masum Ghar," he informed.

"No problem, sir. I told you we'd be back. Have you over there in a jiffy," I answered.

Irish was quiet, sorting through his paperwork as there was now a change in timings and location.

"Shakedown, this is Freedom Ops," Scrappy's voice came over the radio, breaking our silent tension.

"Go for Shakedown 25," I answered.

"After you drop off the general, escort Blowtorch to Senjeray. He's loading at KAF and will go solo over the mountains. He will meet you north of Senjeray in twenty-five minutes for landing protection," Scrappy stated.

This was the norm: changes, add-ons, and rerouting. This is what I liked. No paper, no extensive, wasted planning. Just fill with gas, bullets, and Red Bull and make it up as you go along.

"Roger that. We are taking the general to Masum Ghar," I responded and continued on the intercom. "Guys, we're walking the dog into Senjeray." It was followed by the normal acknowledgments. I smiled. I knew this was the straw to break the camel's back of Irish's timetable.

As we approached Masum Ghar, Irish shook his head and threw his papers beside his seat, surrendering to the changes. He smiled, shook his head, and crossed his arms while mouthing silently the familiar words: "What the fuck." I felt vindicated—for now.

Chapter 14

Senjeray PID RPG: Irish's Day Continues

Next to Senjeray was an American FOB along Highway 1 to the west of Kandahar along IED Alley. IED Alley is named for a several mile section of highway in the green zone of the Arghandhab River. Tactically, it was a kill zone, an ideal place to ambush your enemy and destroy them.

NATO decided to maintain the highway in the middle of the kill zone, and the Taliban decided to kill us there—daily. Senjeray was a built-up town in the "green" zone. Its threat level was constantly switching from code yellow to code red.

We arrived over Senjeray and saw the Chinook orbiting high to the north, waiting for us.

"Shakedown, it's Blowtorch. We're going in from the north. It is the safest direction and away from the town. Need you guys to watch that south flank," Butch, the Blowtorch captain, stated. He was the CO's backup and one of the senior Chinook advisors on the squadron. He was a good doggie to walk because as soon as he was in a safe zone, he would go solo and release us to work with the infantry. As opposed to other Chinook drivers that would not release us as they wanted the security of our guns from takeoff to shutdown.

"Roger that," I answered.

Once Butch maneuvered in the FOB, he would still be exposed to an attack from the south side. Our task was to sweep and clear the approach and then provide a presence on the southern flank, hopefully to prevent an attack.

"Prof, go low along the road. I'll go high and overwatch behind you."

"Roger that," he responded. Professor would apply low-level pressure wherever we found potential threats, and I would protect him.

The lumbering Chinook was almost on the ground, very little dust ball because of gravel they hauled into the helicopter landing sites to cover the moondust. I was on the right flank of the Chinook. Once it was in the FOBs protective fire arcs, I broke off and followed Professor.

"Prof, go check out the road. I see some slow traffic 500 meters east," I passed the observation.

"Roger that," Professor responded as his Griffon steered in the direction. I popped up high to observe. A vehicle surged around the roadblock rapidly approaching the FOB.

"Hay, Cap, gotta high-speed vehicle moving up to the FOB," Snapshot called.

"Roger that," I acknowledged.

"Prof, check incoming vehicle east side." I passed to my low-flying wingman.

"Roger that," Professor announced.

I rolled out and detailed the vehicle, a pickup truck coming down Highway 1 at a much higher speed than usual. Dust was rising behind the wheels. It was almost as if he was racing the helicopters to get to the FOB.

"Something's not right," Irish commented.

"Circle right around the vehicle to keep Snapshot's eyes on," I directed Irish's flying.

"There's a guy in the back with an RPG! He's getting out and running toward the FOB," Snapshot called.

"Fuck!" I called. "Keep your eyes on. If he shoulders and aims it, fire! Irish, get into better position, high trail on 26," I ordered then called out on the radio.

"Prof, I gotta contact. One man with an RPG running down the road toward the FOB. He's on the south side of the road in the shadowed area against the wall. He has *not* shouldered the weapon. Advising the FOB. Go investigate," I ordered.

"Roger, looking," Professor answered back. I noticed my wingman aggressively turn toward the man.

"Contact FAM (fighting aged male) with one times RPG (rocket-propelled grenade) and AK-47 (assault rifle)," Professor called excitedly over the radio. His helicopter closed in from the higher orbit onto the potentially lethal target.

Was it a single RPG shooter? Where was his support team? There could be others in the immediate area with AK-47s to join into the attack against the Chinook as it departed. Those insurgents would be deeper into the green zone a few hundred meters, covertly hiding and ready to attack. They usually ambushed in multiple teams from different locations, all focusing their fires onto the airborne target. Like a fly into the spider's web, everywhere you turned there would be more havoc to get tangled into.

Professor's crew made himself vulnerable in order to defend the Chinook. As we teamed into battle formation, we became much more lethal, accepting certain risks to place our gunners into optimum position to defend—or attack.

The FAM was now partially hidden from the observation of FOB Senjeray. He was under some trees in a cutout in a wall along a road. His RPG could be seen moving, but he didn't seem to be aiming it. It went from over shoulder to under shoulder, then held, and then disappeared as he leered from behind the concrete hard, thick compound, only the shape of the warhead tip occasionally emerging.

"I'm tracking him with my gun—if he pulls any shit, he's done," Snapshot called. "Can we get in lower?"

"Roger that. Coming in behind, Prof! Cover his ass and watch that green zone for support shooters!" I yelled over the intercom. I was concerned about what we couldn't see. I then pressed my radio foot switch to talk to Professor on the radio. "Professor, you got him?"

"Roger, I got him," Professor answered, his voice alert and focused. The FAM had bunker like walls all around him. It was an ideal place to shoot from and stay somewhat concealed.

"Stand by. He is still not a legal target. I am coordinating through the FOB. It will be your shot. I'm on high cover dropping into your trail," I further directed. I looked out to the Chinook on the ground in the FOB. The last passengers were loaded. He would be lifting right into an ambush. I had to warn him.

"Blowtorch, this is Shakedown. Stay on the ground. Possible RPG threat to your southeast," I called to Butch. "Man with RPG about 250 meters on your nose in a compound."

Professor interrupted with a report. "I'm in position to fire. He seems to be hiding behind the wall. He looks suspicious—spying."

"Check that. Stand by," I answered. I had to get more intelligence. I hoped the FOB had a sniper also viewing. I may have to call him onto the target or smoke it to mark it for identifying him as a target, but that would take time—and time was fleeting.

"Shakedown 25, this is Blowtorch. We are ready to lift. Holding position. Holding position," Butch answered impatiently.

He wanted out, but he had to stay for the time being. It was a time crunch from his perspective. The longer he sat there, the more likely he would draw indirect enemy mortar fire into the FOB. But if he departed right now, he could be flying into an ambush.

The Chinook had enough power to depart the opposite direction against the wind and uphill—it was an option but because of the semi-overt presentation of the RPG holder, he could be a decoy trying to encourage the Chinook to fly away from him for a possible ambush. All these defensive options raced through Butch's mind—yet inevitably, if he delayed much longer, the mortars would definitely come.

"Roger that, Butch. Stand by. We're in firing position. FOB also investigating. Stand by!" I cautioned him. I could feel his impatience. Everyone's vigilance was heightened. It could be felt and heard in the tone of voice.

We reversed course, aggressively following Professor about 200 feet over the ground. The gunner's both intently scanning the RPG man and the surrounding wadi and compounds for any other unusual activity or persons with weapons. I looked over to the higher terrain to the north side of the FOB. It seemed normal, I hoped.

"Shakedowns, this is Senjeray. Do nawt fire! Do nawt fire! He's an ANA soldier! He is friendly!" an American accent announced over the radio. "The son of a bitch was layt for his guard duty that's whay he wuz runnin' and not proply drayssed. That's his nawrmal pawsition," he continued.

"Holy shit! Check fire, Snapshot," I yelled over the intercom and then replied on the radio, "Roger that—visual friendly—visual friendly."

"Stand down, Prof! Stand down, gunners! ANA soldier—friendly. Resume normal orbit," I advised.

"Roger, it's a friendly. Check that," Professor answered to me. He was pissed off. He continued onto the other radio. "FOB Senjeray, this is 26. You tell that son of a bitch he almost got his ass shot off—26 out!"

"Rawger that, Shakedown 26," the American accent answered cautiously. "We gawt this." There would be a scolding debrief to the ANA security team.

"Check, it's friendly." Snapshot stated and raised his gun level.

"Okay," Butch's voice intruded into the tactical conversation. "We are outta here! Lifting in fifteen seconds eastbound," he announced in relief from his Chinook. He had had enough time sitting on the ground being a potential mortar magnet.

The dust began to erupt around him as he lifted. Our two Griffons aggressively split apart and circled around to the flanks and rear the departing heavy helicopter, protecting his flight path.

"Well, that would have been a bit of paperwork, sir," Zorg added sarcastically, proud of his calm yet cheeky retort.

I wiped the sweat out of my eyes and drained the perspiration from my ear cup as I looked at Irish and shook my head in disbelief. He looked relieved as he sank into his pillow about an inch. He let out a nervous chuckle toward me, laughing as my eyes were bigger than my head.

As we relaxed, we started joking about the situation, laughing at the ridiculous intensity and bantering possible comical outcomes while finishing our morning escort missions.

"So the ANA platoon sergeant yells to the other soldiers, 'Achmed has fifty holes in him.' Why? He was late! The rest of you guards take note."

"Guards, how many times do I have to say, don't take your RPG home at night after work!"

Operations

It had been an exhausting day. But this was normal—change and reaction; emotionally, digesting appalling trauma would not be a stranger. After six continuous flying hours, we walked into operations for our debriefing with Scrappy.

He looked at our frazzled team of Shakedown 25 Flight. It had been a month first arriving. In his opinion, we needed to maintain vigilance but also accept the realities that existed here. Scrappy needed to put some perspective on it.

"So in summary, you flew in a war zone, had the potential to get shot in a mortar attack, saw a medieval stoning that we were all briefed could be part of our experience here, and almost perforated a friendly ANA soldier?" Scrappy sternly lectured our physically and emotionally drained crowd.

"Yup, pretty much!" Professor stated as a matter of fact, looking at me, and then spit chew tobacco in his cup.

"This is my second time here. This is normal. But you did a good job. You didn't get killed, and you didn't kill a good guy," Scrappy summed, paused, and then curtly left the room.

There was no discussion. No sympathy. Just an acceptance of the way life was in Afghanistan. All these events affected everyone. We can accept shooting, being shot at, mortars and rockets landing around us, but the stoning? It affected everyone. Those people weren't even the threat, but the act of stoning a young girl was deplorable. Or is it deplorable for me to judge her judges? Some things just never sit right.

"Why the fuck are we here if we can't help the innocent?" I heard Zorg quietly mention to Hawk. "And these are the people we are liberating from the Taliban?"

I looked over and saw Hawk shrug as he glanced back at me. I was stoic. I got up to leave the room. I paused and looked back at the other seven.

"Irish, your mission was well planned, and the timings worked out flawlessly! Well, for a while anyway." I smiled. "Good job!" I stated in front of the team and departed. He was happy to be acknowledged, but there were now more significant things being processed in his mind than the exactness of his complex planning sheet.

In operations, Grumpy's team had just come back from their mission toward Helmand Province. Helmand was one of the most brutal areas in Southern Afghanistan. The Brits were losing soldiers weekly just like the Canadians and Americans were losing people here in Panjwaii. We had similar grim expressions on our faces.

"How'd it go?" I asked, recognizing a look of exhaustion on his face.

"Let's see." He looked up, reflecting on his day. "Craters, TICS, burning vehicles, arguing with copilot, suicide bombers, medevacs, IEDs."

"Huh. Pretty standard day, I guess," I said.

"I heard you saw a stoning. It's medieval times! I guess that's pretty normal for this place," he summarized, twisting his face. He held his arm up at a vertical angle about the elbow. He had enough bullshit for the day—not from his colleagues but from the mission.

I nodded. "I heard you got called to a TIC?" I inquired.

"Yup, but the Taliban put down their RPGs and picked up shovels by the time we got there." Grumpy shook his head. "Can't kill a sand farmer, can I?"

"SNAFU?" I asked.

"Yup." Grumpy smirked, turned, and walked away. "SNAFU."

(Situation normal—all fucked up!)

Again, so much shit happens in a day here that it takes a long time to reflect, contemplate, and try to organize it into something that makes sense, even if it isn't acceptable or understandable from a Western cultural perspective. Some will never make sense of it, and it will linger. Even as I write and edit this for over the past five years, new revelations still come to me.

Chapter 15

Nakhoney: A Response to: "Casualties of War"

> "I hate war as only a soldier who has lived it can, only as
> one who has seen its brutality, its futility, its stupidity."
> —Dwight D. Eisenhower

Nakhoney is a small village about an hour drive south of Kandahar, ten minutes by helicopter. It was the hotspot for my section. We had been responding to attacks on FOB Madras (school), where a small unit of Canadian Infantry was based. It held many memories, and the area became personal to my crew.

All the landmarks were close together—basically within the effective range of an RPG round. To the south of the FOB was Three Hills; the west was a north-south creek called West Wadi, and immediately on the other side of the wadi was Steel Door. Steel Door was a three-story grape hut with a steel door facing east and a solid roof as opposed to most grape huts that were open. To the northwest was Bell Grave cemetery; from the air it looks just like its name. To the west, another 200 meters from Steel Door, was a group of compounds known as the Adamz-eye chain.

The overwatch in Nakhoney was my favorite mission. It involved directly supporting the patrol commander on the ground: for observation, fire power, lifting injured soldiers, or whatever they wanted. Scrappy knew this, and he tried to arrange it so I could fly overwatch when the opportunity arose. And by this time, my crew preferred it too. Every day I would meet our team at the table, bringing back scheduling news for our next mission.

"Guys, we got Nakhoney overwatch at 5:00 a.m.!" This was usually responded to with "Awesome. Woohoo!" or I could present the normal mission: "We're walking the dog all morning." The reaction to this was usually a whiney "Oh man, can you get some overwatch after they're done? When are they done?"

Ironically, the infantry on patrol liked to have Shakedowns. But in the FOBs, to the soldiers, a Chinook usually represented new cargo, mail, crew change, visitors, or best of all, a ride out.

Flying overwatch in Nakhoney also offered the advantage of being central to respond to any other TIC or IED activity in Panjwaii. All the Canadian FOBs were within five minutes and almost visible from above Nakhoney. And if they were in a TIC, we wanted to be there too.

At the KAF FARP (Fuel and Ammo Replenishment Point)

Skipper was flying on my wing today. It was a chance for him to attain reprieve from his administrative duties of running the squadron while also allowing him to keep his skills and knowledge fresh regarding the challenges the flight crews had on the front lines. Conversely, it allowed Professor a chance to get off the front line and work his desk to deal with the administration required for commanding all the Griffon crews.

After refueling, our section was waiting, with the engines idling, for our next mission to come over the radio. The guys got out to stretch their legs, take a piss, drink a Red Bull, and eat Pop-Tart—the standard food supplement. Some even slept lying on the jagged rocks in the shade of the helicopter while still connected to the intercom system. The ballistic vest and helmet helped the protruding rocks from piercing our skin.

I enjoyed the silence, or rather the loud white noise of the engines and rotor turning drowning out all other sounds—pseudo silence. I had again managed to find the most comfortable position in the discomfort. I shifted my hips forward, causing my ballistic Kevlar chest plate to surge up under my chin. The two magazines of bullets lifted just high enough that I could rest my chin on them. I would lock my harness in position and sleep like a baby to the droning noise and vibrations of the helicopter.

I was often disoriented from a dream when waking in my seat. No, it wasn't a warm tropical breeze I was feeling or a bartender asking me if I wanted a shaken martini. It was the downwash air from the rotor blades washing down my neck and Scrappy yelling "Shakedown" over the radio.

"Shakedown 25, this is Ops. TIC in progress at Madras," the radio broke the sound of the helicopter engines, waking us from our short nap in the shade. I snapped awake and recalibrated my location.

Once I was semi-alert, I responded, "Roger. Go for Shakedown." I looked around at the guys who sat up and started prepping their Dillons, also coming out of their routine FARP slumber.

"25, they have shots fired from the west, platoon of forty friendlies dismounted and under fire. Contact Slayer for an update. Call when airborne," Scrappy ordered.

"Roger that," I responded.

I held my hand out the door and spun my fingers in the air, signaling it was time to go. Skipper was already boarding his crew as he heard the call and returned the thumbs-up.

Irish wound up the throttles. Everyone was quiet: the silence conveyed either cautious anxiety or more likely, residual slumber.

Irish pulled the collective control lifting the helicopter and departed west; Skipper flew into the wingman position slightly behind and right. As we flew west, I contacted Slayer.

"Slayer, this is 25, checking in."

"Shakedown 25, this is Slayer. The ROZ is hot. The guns are hot at Wilson. Gun line is southeast. TIC in progress at Nakhoney. Contact India 21 for tactical check-in and battle update brief," he advised.

"This is Shakedown. Copy that. Switching India 21," I confirmed before talking to Skipper.

"26, how copy?" I stated.

"Romeo Tango," Skipper acknowledged.

We had about six minutes further to fly. In these six minutes, we needed to build a complete picture of the battle on the ground as well as visually identify all friendly and enemy targets. There were no explosions of dust to mark the objective, so pinpointing the area would be more challenging; I had to locate the Canadians first.

"India 21, this is Shakedown checking in," I called to the infantry unit getting shot at.

"Shakedown, this is 21. We have shots being fired toward us from one or two insurgents. They are in the vicinity of Steel Door. We are on a foot patrol in a north-south line 300 meters northwest of Madras near Bell-Grave. Possible RPG and IED west of our locations. We are thirty Canadians and ten ANA soldiers in a line 250 meters long at grid QQ42618880. From my location, enemy fire is coming from one of the grape huts near Steel Door, approximately 200 meters west. We do not have PID (positive identification) on enemy. I say again. No PID. Request assistance to PID and suppress."

We could hear the occasional snap of gunfire in the communication. My crew became excited as the helicopter got closer; we expected the shooting to stop and the insurgents to hide. However, the Taliban would most likely take several shots toward us if they were in a position to conceal the muzzle flashes from their AK-47 rifles. And since the Canadians had no PID, the enemy would feel comfortable in doing that.

"26, this is 25. Did you copy all that?" I asked Skipper to ensure I didn't have to repeat the battlefield report. I was programming the GPS while he replied.

"Roger that." Skip understood everything.

"You guys copy?" I asked over the intercom.

"Roger that, Haycee. Romeo Tango, Cap," the gunners replied calmly.

"Irish, just head straight there. I put their position in our GPS (global positioning system). Follow the navigation needle and offset right, so first turn is left over the friendlies. Guys, I am planning a north-south figure eight, low level down the road to identify them. Got it?" I directed.

"Got it." Irish knew exactly what was going to happen.

"Snapshot, your side will be exposed first. Get ready!" I cautioned.

"Check," he responded. The camera was put away. He was tuned in. Everyone was vigilant. We were about to get shot at.

"Skipper, my plan is left base. North to south figure eight to PID friendly and enemy, fly along the friendly line. If we engage, all effects west," I ordered to my wingman. He didn't need to respond. He would just follow along since he knew I would be busy coordinating. We were two minutes back.

"India 21, smoke the target area," I requested of the ground commander. I wanted him to identify exactly which hut the shots were coming from or suspected to come from.

"Roger that, red smoke," he answered. "This is the target area. I cannot confirm exact spot yet." Five seconds later, a stream of red smoke landed near Steel Door.

Zorg called out when he saw the Canadian foot soldiers. He was enthusiastic about overwatch. The guys on the ground were from his Regiment, his army family.

"Visual friendly troops on the nose, slightly left, behind the wadi wall! 'Bout forty of them!" he called, bringing our attention to the line of troops.

"26, I've got a visual on the friendly patrol at twelve o'clock about 1,000 meters. Call when you are visual. Red smoke is target area."

"Visual friendlies and contact smoke," he responded. *Contact* was a key word. It meant he knew that was the area but not an enemy target yet. *Tally* meant enemy target.

"Irish, left gunner, right gunner. Friendlies are a line of troops 40 long on our nose 800 meters. They are taking cover along the road wall," I formalized the situation as per our procedures.

The two gunners stretched their necks out of the helicopter door and took a verifying look.

"Visual friendlies, contact smoke!" they each called in sequence.

We were turning onto the north-south line. I could see the soldiers leaning up against the wall. Princess Patricia's soldiers. They would take turns leaning over the wall to try to locate the enemy fire. However, most were sitting in the shade taking a break now that the helicopter would take over observation. They were pretty casual about getting shot at; it was daily for them.

Five minutes waiting for us was an opportunity for them to have a short break. They carried over a hundred pounds of combat gear on their backs in 40-degree temperatures and would take a break whenever they could get one, even in the fight. If they spotted the enemy, it was difficult to chase them because of the weight combined with possible IEDs waiting. The Taliban often baited our soldiers, hoping for them to pursuit. Sort of like the way we provoke. It was a deadly game of tag.

A few days earlier . . .

A few days earlier, I worked with the same platoon in Chalgour. The instructions from India 21 were a little different than today.

"India 21, Shakedown's checking in."

"Roger that, Shakedown. I need you guys to stay about 8 kilometers back."

"What?" Irish stated rhetorically over the intercom.

"Confirm 8 kilometers?" I answered on the radio. I was confused why he didn't want me there.

"Ya, we got some dickers in sight, but they ain't pulling the trigger yet. We trying to get him to shoot at us so we can chase the fuckers down. If you guys get too close, you'll scare 'em away. So pretend you're looking at something about 8–10 kilometers south, and I'll call as soon as they engage . . . then you can chase 'em down," he requested.

"Copy your plan, India two-one. Proceeding south," I acknowledged in reservation.

It wasn't a typical battle plan. We didn't practice that in Wainwright, Alberta, on exercise, but it seemed like a good idea. It followed the triple *F* philosophy of soldiering: find 'em, fix 'em, and then fuck 'em up. How you found them was the creative side of being a soldier, and sometimes it required you to hang your ass out a little.

Back in Nakhoney

"Snapshot, to the right of the friendlies 150 meters is a grape hut with a steel door, closed roof," I directed.

"Contact hut, contact red smoke," they both responded.

"That is the target area. No PID yet. Do not shoot unless self-defense—observe only—all effects west but mind the village on the other side."

"Roger that!" they acknowledged.

All our interplane communications were being conducted on the Freedom Ops frequency. Scrappy would not interject as he respected our busy battle focus. However, it allowed him to listen to the situation and make plans such as casevac (casualty evacuation) or other helicopter support without asking.

Operations

"You asked me to come and get you when they arrived to position boss," Ricky advised Scrappy in his office next to the operations center.

"Roger that. Coming," Scrappy acknowledged, placing the phone down and followed. He reviewed the text information on the TV screens to orient himself with the situation. However, the text prompter was a little behind.

"What's up?" he stated to his duty sergeant.

"They've been give a target area brief by India 21, and it seems shots are being fired at them," Ricky explained. "No damage reports so far."

"Seems so," he breathed some relief. "All right—so Skipper is number 2 and Butch is not back yet correct?"

"Yes, sir. He switched out Professor this morning before you were here. You were at the Task Force Kandahar meeting. He's 26," the radio operator summated. Scrappy walked over the manifest to check the crew names.

"Yes, they both passed me the reigns earlier!" Scrappy affirmed. He was now in charge of the Squadron.

"Well, let's get busy. Contact the HQ and see if they have a UAV feed coming, also find out the status of Dustoff, the medevac chopper. We may require to provide information to them, and coordinate medevac if this goes south. I also need to know where Grumpy and Big C are in case we have to RIP in for Steve and Skip. Questions?"

"Nope. Roger that sir," Ricky picked up the phone and directed the RadOp to do the same to find the back-up crews.

Scrappy paused, looked at each of his staff, reviewed the screen, grabbed his chair, placed it up on the bird table. He sat up high, and smirked.

"I'm it, lads! I'm in command. Let's watch and listen to the show, boys!" He confidently stated as he leaned back, hands behind his head, crossing his legs. "I need a coffee." He snapped his fingers in jest toward Ricky, laughing to lift the stress.

Nakhoney

Inside my aircraft, all eyes were on the grape hut near the red smoke.

"26, keep your eyes near the red smoke. Go trail and be prepared to counter. I'll stay low." I kept shooting out commands as thoughts came into my head. I figured I'd be in best position to draw fire, identify the source, and then Skipper could release hell on the target.

Skipper acknowledged. He slid from the right into an astern position, climbing slightly. Irish flew the aircraft cognizant of the guns, low enough to observe and engage if required. My aim was to visually look into that hut to see any persons, muzzle flashes, or fire arms. Additionally, I checked the fields to see if any Taliban would pop out of a grape row. But they stayed in the shadows.

We flew by Steel Door at 50 feet above the ground and close. Small explosions of dust from bullets were impacting the walls beneath me.

"Who the fuck is shooting?" I retorted over the intercom.

"India two-one, this is Shakedown. Are you shooting? I got impact strikes on the hut," I called.

"Negative," 21 answered after a brief investigative pause. "Wait, the ANA are firing on the smoke." I could hear the snaps of the ANA AK-47 assault rifles through the radio.

"Do you have PID?" I radioed back.

"Negative. It's the ANA. No Canadian PID. We still cannot verify the target," he cautioned.

Despite our rules of engagement, the ANA interpreted them differently. They were great soldiers, just not all that savvy with NATO protocols. It was their land, their rules. They saw red smoke, so their section commander started shooting at it, even though our helicopter was almost directly in front of them.

However, the Canadians still did not have the legal criteria to fire simply because there was no positive target yet. Restraint. The smoke was an indicator to investigate the area, not shoot at it.

"I can't even suppress yet?" I questioned, rhetorically thinking out loud.

"Nope," Irish answered, reinforcing my interpretation of the rules.

"Skipper, it's the ANA. They are shooting on the target area. Canadians do *not* have PID yet. Do you have PID?" I asked, hoping he might see a target.

"Not yet, still looking," Skipper stated inquisitively, "…but I hear the odd bullet zippin' by!"

"They might not even be in the hut. They could be anywhere. But they are shooting at us. Keep looking, guys," I stated.

We continued in the pattern while observing as the ANA continued to shoot. Everyone, including the ground troops, was trying to find the spot. The ANA didn't care; they just fired at the sound and the smoke.

After a couple of threatening patterns from the Griffons, the enemy revealed themselves.

"Shakedown, I've got I-comm chatter. Do you want it?" the ground commander radioed, signifying relevant intelligence was available.

"Roger that," I answered. Everyone in the cockpit was quiet, ready to hear the message.

"Bring the package!" India 21 answered. "The TERP says the voice on I-comm chat sounds anxious," he added. A local Pashtun interpreter was assigned to the Canadian unit to assist in communicating with the ANA and listen on enemy radio frequencies. He also advised on the emotional state of the voices he heard.

Bring the package? I pondered on what that could mean. He must be bringing a heavier weapon—RPG maybe?

"Guys, keep eyes out for anything suspicious. Watch for an RPG plume. I-comm states bring the package," I cautioned my section. RPGs were a weapon of choice for the Taliban. They had been firing RPGs at India 21 almost daily during the past month.

Operations

Scrappy jumped to his feet, almost banging his head off the ceiling. He caught his chair before it slid off the back of the bird table. He read the screen showing the I-comm chatter. He was concerned about what it read. "Bring the package." Could it be something that would harm the helicopter? He needed more information.

"Go get the int briefer now!" Scrappy told Ricky as he jumped down.

The intelligence briefer arrived. Scrappy update him with the situation. He outlined his concern and asked for a threat analysis.

"Sir, it is most likely an RPG or possibly a DShK .51-caliber weapon system. But if the DShK isn't in position already, they wouldn't be moving it while in contact with us," he reported.

"What about SAMs?" Scrappy was asking if there was any change to the surface to air missiles threat from his understanding. He needed all the info to pass to our team should we need it.

"No change, sir. Yes, there are SAM possibilities but no recent reported activity—the chance of them using these limited resources on a small helicopter is low. They'd be saving it for one of our Hercs or C-17s." he advised.

"Thanks, that'll be all." Scrappy released him as he picked up the radio's microphone.

"25 Flight, Freedom OPS, do you have the I-comm chatter?" he blurted.

"Roger that. Do you mean the package?" I responded.

"Roger, we can't make out. Just keep safe. No change to the Int from this morning," Scrappy quickly reported. He said no more. He knew we were busy, but he was also concerned.

"25, 26 checks all from Ops," Skipper called to acknowledge he heard the report from Scrappy.

"Actually, watch out for the fuckin' ANA friendly fire. It's more likely to hit us!" Zorg practically hollered.

The bullets from the ANA rifles continued to splash bullets off the walls of both Steel Door and the next grape hut south despite us flying directly between the target and the friendlies. It was only 30 meters away at times. I tucked my head and shoulders a little more inside my armored seat on subsequent passes, fearing both enemy and friendly fire.

"Shakedowns, I've got PID!" announced India 21. "Are you ready for a five-liner?" he asked. Holy shit! This was it! We are going hot. This was our authority to fire on his command.

"Go for Shakedown," I responded.

"Five-liner, friendlies are patrol north-south line west of Madras. Enemy is one times FAM with AK-47 rifle in Steel Door. My plan is advance upon that target from east. Required you to provide continual suppression for five minutes, all effects west. Maintain fire line over the friendlies to cover my advance," India 21 ordered.

I read it back quickly. "Visual friendlies. Tally target. All effects west."

"Roger," he stated. "I-comm chatter still repeating to bring the package."

"26, this is 25. Did you copy five-liner?" I radioed to Skipper.

"26 is in," he acknowledged curtly.

"Attack plan, next southbound pass, start with right gun attack, figure-eight pattern," I commanded to my wingman.

"Roger that," Skip responded.

Irish started his turn toward the south as I indicated with my hand to roll in hot. We were going to rain down pieces of led for the next five minutes in short blast of fire. The Breath of Allah, as the enemy had been heard to say, would be echoing through the Panjwaii Valley, raining down on the building and the FAM inside to finally finish his days of killing Canadians and ANA soldiers. We had to be careful to cover the attack of the Canadians yet protect them. Everyone was focused. We had a clear target, PID and permission.

"26, 25 is rolling in *hot,*" I stated to Skip. No response was required.

Operations

In operations, Scrappy heard the attack brief and read the teleprompter on the TV:

Time XX:XX: Shakedowns hot at FOB Madrass, grid QQ42618880. Supporting I-21.

"Well, they're going hot!" Scrappy exclaimed upon hearing the news. Butch had just walked into the room still in his flight gear from the mission we were previously on.

"Shakedown is rolling in hot in Nakhoney right now. You're just in time. They've been getting shot at and are in overwatch for India 21 patrolling," he reported while pointing at the battle map on the table between his feet.

Butch smiled, raised his eyebrows, and looked at the screen while tilting his head in contemplation. That was his initial body language response for everything.

Back in Nakhoney.

"India 21, Shakedowns in *hot*. Get your heads down," I advised to Princess Patricia's infantry below. I watched them; they didn't take cover but instead leaned up to watch. The shots would be about 150 meters from friendlies, and we were about 75 meters from the target at the closest point. Hot shell casings would be raining down on the heads of the Pats. We dove to get low to shoot inside the narrow windows and cracks of the grape hut.

"Right gunner, confirm visual and tally?" I asked Snapshot before releasing the fire command.

"Roger, Haycee. Visual troops and tally target!" He took aim at the openings in the grape hut.

As the Griffon crossed over the friendly troops, I ordered, "Fire."

There was a pause. Was it jammed? Why does the Dillon not deafening me?

"It's no good! It's no good! Checking fire. Checking fire," Snapshot yelled back just as I was covering my ears from the anticipated intense blast of the Dillon.

"I got a WAC (woman and or child) 75 meters other side of Steel Door in my arcs. No, it's a man! He's dragging a child toward the grape hut," Snapshot called.

I immediately shifted my eyes onto the jogging Taliban soldier dragging a child by the arm.

"Check fire, check fire. Child west of Steel Door," I called to 26 and then repeated it to the army commander.

"Fuckin' bastards. Cowards," I swore profusely over the intercom, drowned out by the sound of the rotor blades. We passed the target but continued in the pattern to observe, firing no shots.

The man dragged the stunned boy to the other side of Steel Door. The boy's face was pale with fear. A man came out of the west end; he grabbed the boy's other arm, and he glared directly at me over his shoulder. We made eye contact. They jogged over toward the compound. He knew the helicopters wouldn't shoot if children were around. He used that child as a human shield.

"India 21, it's the package! A small boy. A human shield, check fire," I reported.

"Continue to monitor. Tell me where they go," he requested, frustrated.

We overflew the corner of the road they rushed up. The Taliban men went into a compound, left the boy with a woman who collapsed onto her young child, embracing him. She was distressed. The two men then disappeared into the labyrinth of mud walls. They were not seen again.

"I almost pulled the trigger. That kid was in the back line of my aim. They would have taken rounds for sure." Snapshot sounded somewhat distressed.

This could have been the worst nightmare for my crew. The act of accidentally killing an innocent weighed heavily on everyone's thoughts. No one wanted to have to deal with that. The Taliban won this battle today but hopefully not against that family.

How does this happen? Perhaps atrocities occur in combat all over the world. However, I like to think that all honorable soldiers—Canadians and our allies—have a code of conduct and ethics—a soldier's code. It's a soldier's duty to protect noncombatants from harm, not put them in harm's way. I have not seen anything in my fight against the Taliban that would grant such honor.

Chapter 16

Just a Quick Recce for Devil Strike

The history of Afghanistan is very unique. It is a land filled with thousands of years of invaders attempting to dominate the trade passage from Europe and Arabia to India and the Orient. The mountains are relentless; water is scarce, and the desert is deadly. However, the nomadic people and traders of the past learned to adapt finding sustenance in these hostile environments.

One such passage is Qalat, 150 kilometers northeast of Kandahar. This village is marked by a massive castle built of mud and stone by Alexander the Great 1,700 years ago. It still exists today and has been occupied by every conqueror to this day, including the Persians, the Soviets, the Mujahedeen, the Taliban, and now the Western-backed Afghan National Army (ANA). Task Force Freedom occasionally conducted logistic resupply missions to Qalat following this long, rising valley to the north.

A short flight northwest from Qalat was a high mountain FOB. The site elevation was at 8,000 feet inside a large mountain cirque rising to nearly 14,000 feet; at the base was a village in the pristine bowl. Since the Griffons did not have enough power at their combat weight to land, we circled, waiting for the powerful Chinook to conduct its business. A helicopter behaves like an airplane in forward flight, requiring less power than at hover speed. The Griffon did not have the required power at those altitudes to hover.

Another thirty-minute west of Qalat and north of Kandahar was a location controlled by the Dutch, Tarin Kowt. It had a long runway on a steep hill, which was too muddy during the winter for fixed wing aircraft to land. Thus, the massive Russian Mi-26 helicopter would frequently bring in supplies from KAF.

The Mi-26 was comparable to a C-130 Hercules transport plane but with a rotor on top. It weighed close to 120,000 pounds when carrying roughly 50,000 pounds of cargo. It is the world's largest helicopter, ten times larger than the Griffon and almost three times that of the Chinook. Despite the massiveness of the Mi-26, it too was vulnerable. In 2009, one was ambushed and destroyed in Sangin, Helmand Province, killing six Ukrainian crew and a local child crushed in the falling debris.

Along the massive mountain ridges, some snow capped at well higher than any mountains found in the Canada were isolated small family villages. They were unique, there were no villages at similar altitudes in Canada. The family groups took advantage of the steep V-shape valleys of the mountain to catch water and then direct the runoff into irrigation ditches to nourish their communities.

Over decades, terraces forming food gardens and orchards were built. Once the water saturated this ground, it spilled over, continuing further downhill to accumulate in storage ponds where numerous families groups lived.

The next level of overflow filled terraces containing livestock. This system provided thousands of years of simple sustenance in an inhospitable place. Despite the harsh surroundings, these communities were beautiful, civilized patches of terraced greenery.

And despite the beauty, it was deadly. Neither NATO forces nor the ANA had control in these northern mountains; the Taliban and seasonal insurgents were free to maneuver as they pleased.

TOC

I walked past Scrappy's office. It was midafternoon; my section had a late-evening and night patrol mission. I looked in his door; I hadn't seen it open in a while. He was sitting at his desk. His cot obviously used as the sleeping bag was ruffled. There was a head dent in his pillow.

"Actually using it?" I inquired.

"Ya, but I never get a chance to sleep," he sleepily responded. "I don't have time to go to the other side for food. The operations here are running twenty-four hours a day, and I gotta be on top of it."

"By the way," he continued, "I had some good discussions with the Task Force Headquarters regarding the area immediately around the FOBs. They are going to clear kids and people from the walls and secure the first 200–300 meter radius. You guys shouldn't have to worry about it. You can relax on the tight security pressure."

"Awesome. Thanks," I replied. "Dand District is really bad. Hundreds of people rush the walls when the Chinook arrives. We were going nuts thinking a grenade thrower could easily wander in with that crowd."

"It'll be taken care of. The civil-military (CIMIC) staff will be discussing our concerns in a shura for everyone's benefit," Scrappy finished. "And the FOB soldiers have some plans to mitigate that risk as well."

"Everyone will be happy to hear that," I exclaimed and then redirected my attention to his cot.

"I guess it's better for us that you not sleep. That way more FOB coordination can be done; and we can have a safer overwatch," I smartly added. "But you are gonna go stir crazy. Go out and get some cycling or running in," I preached.

Scrappy smirked. He was a physically strong individual and proudly kept fit. He was always too busy for personal time and was envious that I, Arnie, and Hollywood always had some time to get exercise. As opposed to his schedule, or lack thereof, he barely had time to sleep.

"All right then!" Scrappy's brow raised as he glared at me. "Let's go! Pull-ups!"

"What? I'm beat. No."

"It's not a request. It's a challenge." He nudged his chin, directing me toward the door.

"All right, shit," I sighed in submission. I followed him behind the operations center. Between the buildings was a set of weights, a bench, and a pull-up bar roughly manufactured of a steel bar sandwiched between a wood two-by-four vertical stand. These mini-fitness centers were common all over KAF. The rule of thumb is that you never walked by a stand without stopping to do as many pull-ups as possible.

In the corner outside the blast walls was a small covered patio and trailer, respectively a smoking area and convenience store: cigarettes, pop, chips, Red Bull, Claritin, and Tylenol—the necessities. I noticed Hawk and Zorg were sharing a smoke, having a serious talk as I sauntered by.

"What's going on over there?" Scrappy said quietly, pointing his chin in Hawks' direction.

"Dunno. Zorg was a little frazzled by something recently. The stoning maybe?" I answered.

"He also went to a ramp ceremony for an old friend the other day?" Scrappy informed, referring to a memorial service for another recent dead Canadian soldier.

"Ya, I'm sure that's bugging him too," I replied.

"Worth checking it out. He's a pretty passionate guy. Lost a couple of buddies on his first tour here with the Pats. Now another? Combined with the stoning? What did he see anyway?" Scrappy added rhetorically. "Just talk with Hawk. Find out if you can help him. Padre is just down the hall," he concluded as he pushed away from leaning against the pull-up stand.

"Now get your ass on the bar. You first!" he commanded, changing the subject abruptly.

I shrugged, jumped up, and started doing pull-ups.

"One, two, no kipping," Scrappy counted and critiqued me for pumping my legs for upward momentum. "Three, four, keep them honest, six, seven . . . fowwwwwerrrr—teen." I fell off the bar and huffed a few times catching my breath.

"Remember my flight suit has fifteen pounds of extra crap in the pockets!" I tried to make an excuse. Scrappy scowled.

"I know. Your pockets are full of tourniquets!" He laughed at me and hopped up. "I'm up!"

"One, two, three . . ." I scowled and then counted for him. He did straight arm, no swing motion pull-ups. "Twelve, thirteen." He struggled, popping a vein out the side of his head, but he was competitive and would not be beat. "Fourteen." He fell.

"I would have beat you if you hadn't of kipped," he argued, smiling. "Excellent, we're gonna do that every time I see you this from now on." He knew I was always up to a challenge.

I nodded. Scrappy started walking toward his office and directed me with his arm on my back.

"I need to tell to you about the mountains, the Devil's Belly button, and your mission coming up," he stated seriously.

We walked inside the operations room and pulled out a map.

"You guys have been flying in this area for a month, transiting without problem." He pointed to the map as he glared in my eyes. "I worked here as a UAV operator two years ago and this area"—he pointed to the map—"is the Devil's Belly Button. It is a major transit route for insurgents." He paused. "Right now, they are transiting out of battle for the winter. However, there will most likely be enemy strongholds here, observing us, waiting for an opportunity to strike." He sat down in his chair and raised his brow. "Remember, if you go down here, you're done! No one, not even the ANA are in that area to assist you. Take that in consideration, and I further suggest you plan flights along this route." He returned to the map, drawing his finger along a safer route, circling around the Belly Button.

"This is at least occasionally patrolled by ANA and is a logistics route for vehicles going north. This means you may have a chance of getting some support if you get shot down," he advised.

I exhaled, absorbing all the information. My eyes widened from the knowledge. "All right." I pointed to some FOB locations marked on an old map. "Are these still active?"

"They are former patrol bases. They were when I was here a couple of years ago, but I have spent the last two days trying to contact other nations and our headquarters to find out. They are probably closed now, so let's just say no," he stated adamantly. "Like I said, you're on your own. I'll brief the other pilots but make sure you pass it along as well," he warned. "We are starting to do more work up north."

"Now about your Operation." He switched subjects.

"Whatcha got for me?" I asked enthusiastically.

"Operation Devil Strike. Your job is to insert a sniper detachment onto this mountain at 0200 hours in two days. The snipers will spend a few days there providing observation for the battle group over Chalgour. There is lots of activity including some suspected IED manufacturing. They figure they need to watch everything covertly and watch for any HVTs (people designated as high-value targets) that may be transiting into the IED factory." He set the stage sternly.

"Snipers? But the Taliban will hear us landing," I said with concern.

"Yes, but there is a deception plan. The battle group commander will be putting in some sort of noise screen to mask or detract from your landings," Scrappy briefed.

"Noise screen? What the fuck is a noise screen?" I reeled back.

"Your landing will be coincidental with a tank and APC road move, or maybe even artillery—not sure yet. It may be covert. You just have a specific timing and LZ—that's all," he informed.

"Cool. We'll get 'er done."

"Your job is to land the team at the darkest hour of the month in red illum (indicating no moon), blacked out," he ordered. It was more of a question as to whether I wanted to accept it rather than an order. He knew it would be very challenging, almost offering me to decline if I preferred.

"Professor is your wingman with Arnie. He has already gone to int (the intelligence section) to request a terrain analysis of the mountain to find the most ideal landing spot. On your next task, I suggest you covertly fly by and look at the recommended landing spots to see what you think."

"Good idea. I'll go chat with Professor." I started to depart.

"Remember what I said about the predictability and the mountains. It applies. The Taliban aren't stupid. Look for any caves or hidey holes near there as well!" He closed with concerned sincerity but maintained professional stoicism. "This is a high-risk mission. Skipper and the wing commander will want to be personally briefed before they allow launch authority."

"Okay, thanks." I paused as I departed the room. "Oh, by the way, I purposely stopped at fourteen," I said, referring to the pull-up competition. Scrappy's necked tightened, and his eyes enlarged. I expedited my departure, smiling.

Professor had already acquired a detailed terrain analysis and had chatted with Skipper about the task. I was excited about it. I never cared for planning the big large-scale operations, but I loved planning the small specialist missions. I met Professor to review the maps.

"The terrain looks like shit!" Professor snarled while looking down my nose. He had an enlarged lower lip, indicating he was enjoying the flavors of red chief tobacco between his lips and gums. He spit into his coffee cup. I was disgusted.

"Fuck, that's disgusting," I retorted, ignoring his map comments. He smiled; he seemed to like to put people off balance with his gobby black spit.

He continued. "But I think we can fly by and check out these two locations on the ledges. What do you think?" he asked, spitting again into his coffee cup.

I nodded to his advice but reeled back to his habit. "That's gross boss," I said, twisting my face. "I think you need to get a new vice."

He smiled. "Yup, but it's 'my' vice, so suck it up! Enjoy your coffee, Red Bull, and pull-ups. I'm chewin'. Why don't we check 'em out while en route to the west?"

"Okay, let's look from both directions to be ready for a wind shift. Let's not slow down though," I answered. "Just zip by, nonchalantly."

Professor nodded and then spat again.

I continued, while holding back a dry heave, "I want to head here as well and practice some night mountain landings to get refreshed." I pointed to an entirely different area on the map. "I want us to get comfortable before we execute the Op. Practice single skid-on work too. I anticipate that will be our only option."

"Good idea. I'll get the CO to approve," Professor acknowledged. We had a plan.

Our remaining crew arrived for briefing later that afternoon. Hawk came into the operations center. As the senior gunner, he wasn't allocated a specific crew; he rotated into any crew, giving each his gunners a break not to mention that he also loved his job and flying with the Dillon gun. He liked being involved directly with his infantry brothers while on overwatch, a helping Hawk if needed.

"Sirs, Zorg's taking the night off," Hawk advised Professor and me.

"He all right?" I inquired.

"Lotta shit on his mind right now. He's all right. He's gonna chat with the padre and let off a bit of steam," Hawk informed. "I'm with you for now."

I nodded and gave him a quick outline of the task. "Pretty simple mission, guys. Just go look at possible landing spots here." I pointed to the map as Professor showed pictures. "Then refuel and look for Taliban insurgents planting bombs in the dark. We are also going to practice mountain landings."

Scrappy interrupted, hollering down the hall, "I have an add-on for you, guys. You'll be heading out a few hours earlier than you thought. Simple task. Get your guys ready for this afternoon, 1500 hours brief."

I nodded. As expected, a day never seemed to go as planned.

Chapter 17

Crappy for Scrappy

It was 1500 hours; we sat ready for our update briefing. "Bit of a change to the plan, guys," Scrappy stated, laughing in order to maintain his sense of humor despite the dynamic barrage of changes.

"A high-ranking Polish officer is in charge of many aspects of the defense of this base. Quick reaction force, guards, screening, fences, etcetera—you're taking him for a perimeter recce," he directed toward Irish and me.

"I rearranged the schedule. Fender and Big C are going to escort the Chinook to the desert and conduct night training." He looked at Fender who nodded back. "Steve, you guys will do the base recce and then check out your landing sites for Op Devil Strike. Pause for an hour, eat, refuel, and then do a night practice. Got it?"

"Got 'er, boss," I answered. "What time is the passenger here?"

"About sixteen thirty." Scrappy looked at his watch.

"Where are you guys headed?" I asked Fender in order to be aware of his location—in case we needed each other.

"We're heading to the Reg Desert with the Chinook. We'll practice some mountain approach techniques and do a little gunnery practice," Fender stated, pointing to the map to show the specifics. "Got the MX, so we'll try some single ship shoots via laser designation. Should be fun."

"Sounds pretty cool. We have an MX as well. We'll be taking some imagery for our mission tomorrow night. We'll be working over toward Sperwan Ghar." I pointed to the map. If either of us went down, the other section would hopefully be the first to respond.

"Take 'er easy. Fly safe!" Big C stated as he walked out of the room with his level smile. Big C only had two facial expressions. It didn't matter what emotion he was feeling; it was a big smile or a level smile—binary. He was contemplating and focused right now. Level smile.

Engines Running on X-Ray Ramp

A stalky Polish officer and his crew approached our helicopters. He resembled a beardless Santa with his girth, twinkly eye, and pleasant smile. In his broken English, he pointed to a map and circled specific areas he needed to view. I briefed the plan to Professor on the radio, and then we departed. I flew the path, circled KAF a few times, chatted with him, and forty-five minutes later, landed him back at the ramp. He disembarked with a big smile, shook my hand through the side window, and off he shuffled, ducking to maintain clearance from my main rotor. I laughed in spite of myself thinking about Santa wobbling off to protect the base.

"Pretty simple task," I stated over the radio in conclusion.

"Yes, it's nice to be a tour guide now and then," Professor answered as our engines wound down.

"Meet you guys at the sea cans, and we'll zip over to north DFAC for a quick dinner."

"Roger that."

Sitting in the Griffons on X-Ray

After a leisurely afternoon flight and some dinner as a family team, we departed to complete our counter-IED scouting task and mountain landing site inspection. We suited up with night-vision goggles and checked our equipment.

"26, this is 25. My MX-15 is good, calibrated, green, and ready to go. You ready?" I asked on the radio.

"Green to go. Switching to tower frequency," he answered.

The halos of bright green light at the airfield were particularly blinding through the night-vision goggles (NVG). Through experience, we learned scanning techniques to look around the blurred halos, even glance underneath the goggle tubes in the blackness to overcome being blinded.

"Fence out," Irish called.

"ASE armed, lights NVG, MX camera is forward, and gunners?" I answered as I selected various switches in the cockpit. It was an automatic reflex now; I never worried about setting flares off inside the wire since my first flight with Chip many months earlier.

"Right gun enabled—26 on the right," Snapshot answered, also adding in Professor's location in the formation.

"Left gun enabled," Hawk replied.

Hawk replaced Zorg who needed a little time to organize his emotions.

As part of the recce, we also conducted counter-IED surveillance. We scanned for thermal changes in the roads because of digging: Highway 1, Hyena, and Lake Effect. We flew high to be somewhat covert, using the MX-15's thermal imagery for any strange sites or suspicious behavior.

As the team proceeded down route Hyena toward Masum Ghar, a flare shot up in front of us about 5 kilometers ahead.

"Contact flare," Arnie called out over the radio.

"Contact," I answered.

"Wonder what's going on?" I asked openly.

"Dickers," Hawk answered. "When I was here last time, they have dickers in place several kilometers away from where they are putting in bombs. As soon as they hear a helicopter or suspect getting caught, the Taliban sympathizers shoot up a warning. The IED planters will disperse immediately and stay covert. We'll never find them. However, we should report it. Maybe Slayer has a UAV available."

"Thanks. I'll do that," I replied while absorbing the information.

"26, this is 25. Let's back off and climb, and maybe you can get some eyes on that area," I radioed.

"On it!" Professor replied.

We continued on the task, poking the MX-15 optics onto all the roads and villages for about forty-five minutes. Concurrently, listening to Shakedown 30 and Blowtorch make radio calls indicating their departure to the Reg Desert for training.

"Got it!' Professor stated ecstatically on the radio. "I got a lollipop on Hyena about 1,000 meters from Bazar-e Panjwaii. Keep this orbit.

I am getting some video evidence and passing the grid reference to Slayer TOC.

A lollipop is a thermal change in the road made by digging a wire and planting explosives into the dirt. It's narrow where the wire is buried then flares wider for the explosive hole, so on thermal camera, it looks like a lollipop.

"Got any PID on people?" I asked.

"Negative. I think they hid when the flares went off," he stated.

"Slayer TOC, this is Shakedown 26. I have a possible IED at grid PQ90953132 on Hyena east of Bazar-e Panjwaii," Professor reported.

"Okay, roger that, Shakedown. I'll pass that to the Battle Group. We have a patrol heading out there tonight. I'm sure they'll appreciate not stepping in that shit," Slayer responded. It was just one more suspected IED site on the pin board map in the valley. However, with a thermal camera and a lollipop, this was pretty much a sure thing.

"I wish we coulda caught the bastards! That would be awesome setting up that attack," Hawk exclaimed. "A little payback for my buddies."

"In time, someone will expose themselves," Irish stated.

We had a new capability with the laser pointer that Canadian Forward Air Controllers were not used to. It would take some time to show that we would be effective. Finding lollipops was the first step in preventing deaths. The next step will be to use it like a big invisible flashlight to reveal the enemy. (A FAC is a Forward Air Controller; embedded with infantry units, they call in bombs, artillery, mortars, and guide aircraft and helicopters onto targets.)

We neared the mountains south of Sperwan Ghar. There was a mountain range perfect for rehearsing for Devil Strike, steep brittle cliffs, brownout landings, and razor ridges to place a skid on. We would have to be light on fuel to successfully land. The light weight would leave extra power that would be needed to hold a hover on a razor edge landing.

"Prof, you take that east ridge, and I'll practice on this one," I directed over the radio. The two ridges were about 2 miles apart and allowed us to practice individually while keeping our eyes on each other.

"All right, there is a spot at ten o'clock that we can practice on," I stated to Irish as I flew close to the ledge to assess its suitability. I positioned the aircraft on a shallow-approach angle. As I arrived, I slowly increased power, spewing grainy dust through the open cabin.

"Loading 'er up," I commented, referring to the power demands. The rotor blades slapped the air more violently, lifting dust through the cabin. I hovered near a ledge, and Snapshot directed me on. We placed one skid on a knife-edge ridge and held it for a moment duplicating the next night.

"Good enough. Lifting and moving forward," I advised. As the helicopter gained speed, I passed control to Irish.

"You practice on a different spot," I suggested.

As Irish piloted the aircraft around looking for a spot, Slayer opened up with some activity on the radio.

"Shakedown 30, this is Slayer. Possible IED emplacement activity in progress. Are you able to observe and report?" There was a pause on the radio. In that pause, my crew let out their disgruntled moans.

"Oh man, why not us?" Snapshot answered.

"Stand by, guys. I'll program the coordinates just in case they can't. Irish just hold the orbit for now," I stated interrupting Snapshot. Slayer was about to task the other Shakedown crew to investigate some IED planters in action. If they caught them in time, it would definitely become an engagement with the Dillons.

"Slayer three-zero, go for Shakedown." I heard Big C call back.

"30, Slayer, suspected three FAMs (fighting aged males) implanting IED on main route 5 kilometers north of Dand at grid QQ53999724. UAV is observing. I need you to move in covertly and establish PID prior entering."

"30, roger that. We'll be in location in five minutes," Big C acknowledged.

"Professor, did you get the coordinates in the MX camera?" I asked my wingman.

"Roger that," Professor acknowledged smartly, always prepared. He plotted the GPS coordinates into his MX-15 and the aircraft navigation system and called back. "It's twenty minutes away."

"Figured that. Slayer knows we're too far. 30 Flight is closer. Keep the practice going, but let's keep an extra half hour of fuel just in case we have to RIP in (Relieve them In Place). Let me know when you're at a thousand pounds," I briefed.

"Romeo Tango," Professor acknowledged.

"All right, Irish, continue onto that spot you picked. Looks like a nice little ridge line—dusty." I switched our focus back to the mountain practice.

"Roger that, guys. I'm on final approach to that ridge. Hawk, it'll be on your side," Irish answered.

"Roger, I'll shoot the PEC laser at it," Hawk stated to verify the location. "Is that it?" He pointed the laser attached to his Dillon gun onto the intended landing spot.

"A little right . . . that's it. Contact spot. We're going there," Irish directed. Everyone could see the infrared beam with the NVG goggles. Everyone was now oriented.

Irish activated the infrared search light, which was invisible to the naked eye but acted as a floodlight to the goggled team. He steered the beam, increasing illumination on the ledge.

"That's it Irish. It's clear left; another 20 feet to go," Hawk advised. "Shit, what's that?" Hawk exclaimed. "I got wires! A box! Fuck! Overshoot! Overshoot! Possible IED," Hawk yelled.

"Roger! I see it," I exclaimed. "Abort! Break right. Let's get away from it now, Irish!"

"Check that!" Irish tipped the helicopter right and added maximum power to accelerate. The device was barely visible—even on the goggles. Of all the areas I could pick for practice, I selected the one with a bomb on it.

The Taliban had skills in placing anti-helicopter explosives. Some were activated by contact and others detonated by remote. We assumed the worst and needed distance.

"Professor, we got a device located where we are landing—possible IED. When you finish, I need you to come and get some MX photography of it, and we'll take it to Int," I called over.

"Check that. Whatcha got?" Professor answered.

"It's a metal box and wires. Dunno, but I don't wanna get close and personal to it either," I stated sarcastically; my heart still racing.

Professor rejoined us in trail position. Irish flew them around within a few hundred meters of the ridge, and Hawk pointed out the area to Professor with his gun laser—the PEC.

A beam from Prof's helicopter joined Hawk's laser on the site. "I got the area. I'll scan it," Professor stated.

Irish and I pulled up high and stayed out of the way. We monitored Professor from above. He was doing circles at a safe distance, scanning and taking pictures.

"Ya, I got it. We have the grids and video footage for the intelligence section. Approaching a thousand pounds of fuel now," Professor informed.

"Roger that. Let's start heading back. Your lead," I stated. Irish turned and dove in from above onto Professor's tail, following him toward KAF.

"Listen on Slayer's freq. Something's going on for Fender and Big C," Professor told me as he was monitoring their frequency.

I switched the frequency to monitor Slayer. Big C and Fender had been tracking the insurgents digging an IED into the road. I caught the last few radio transmissions as the situation unfolded.

"Shakedown 30, fire mission. No friendlies in the area. Enemy are three FAMs emplacing IED on the road at grid QQ53999724. Cleared to engage," Slayer stated over the radio.

"Shakedown 30, tally targets, rolling in hot," Big C's voice read back his instructions.

"Holy shit!" Irish stated.

"Awesome! Payback!" called Hawk. "Maybe we can get in there if they run out of fuel."

The radios went quiet. Everyone in the cockpit was waiting for updates as we flew across the desert toward KAF. We switched the frequencies to coordinate our arrival with KAF tower while monitoring the hunt as it unfolded. There was action, but it was quiet, waiting for Big C's report.

"Freedom Ops, Shakedown 25 is FARPing. We'll check in when we finish," I advised Scrappy. We had to refuel and rearm in case we had to RIP in for Big C's section.

"Roger, out," the radio operator stated.

Professor and I sat at the FARP waiting.

"Freedom Ops, battle damage assessment. Three times insurgents engaged. Approximately three thousand rounds, seven - six - two expended. Two KIA (killed in action). One escaped southeast. Remaining on station to observe," Big C reported.

"Freedom Ops, roger. When are you bingo fuel?" Scrappy stated. We were excitedly hoping they were out of gas and need to be replaced.

"Thirty minutes playtime," Big C answered.

"Check that. I'll phone Slayer and get an update if you need replacing."

"Roger, out."

"Oh man." A disappointing moan came from the back. "They got lotsa gas."

I was getting excited to tag in and continue the hunt. I looked out my window at Professor and held my thumb up. Professor responded with the thumb indicating he was ready too.

"Freedom Ops, this is Blowtorch," Butch's voice interrupted. "We got an emergency in progress. One of the gunners is seriously injured. We're proceeding direct to Role 3."

Role 3 was the largest medical facility in Southern Afghanistan, parked right next to the runway in KAF.

"What the fuck is going on tonight?" I stated. "Did you hear that Irish?"

Irish looked at me and nodded. We completed fueling and hover taxied to the gravel fifty meters behind to wait for further orders. As we were hovering, flashes of light dazzled our NVGs briefly, explosions. I felt the concussion of the blast over the helicopters vibration.

KAWUMP KAWUMP KAWUMP.

"Shit, what was that?" I exclaimed.

"Explosions toward Threemile Mountain," Hawk called.

"Yup, everything seems okay in here. I saw it too," Irish reported. Threemile Mountain, as it's named, is 3 miles north of KAF separating the airport from Kandahar City. Many of the rocket attacks aimed at KAF originated from the Tarnac riverbed that lay at the base of Threemile Mountain.

"All traffic, this is the control tower. KAF is under a rocket attack. KAF is under rocket attack," reported tower and soon to be echoed by Freedom Ops over the radio.

"We have to land here and wait it out," I stated to my team.

"All call signs, this is Freedom Ops." It was Scrappy, and his tone was elevated. He was trying to coordinate the various helicopters all low on fuel. One returning from battle and one with critically injured crewman—all while under a rocket attack. "We are having a rocket attack. One rocket landed on south camp, one north of the wire. Steve and Prof, return to X-ray once tower clears you. Butch, you continue as a medevac priority direct to Role 3 (hospital). Big C, Slayer is moving you off IED task now. Coordinate return with tower. Freedom Ops out."

His transmission ended abruptly. As expected, he still had to coordinate with the hospital, report to intelligence on the helicopter IED trap as well as with the headquarters regarding the battle at Dand.

As for us, the buzz of excitement was filling the air, but we sat contemplatively in the droning noise of the running Griffon until tower cleared us to lift.

"South camp?" Irish queried. "I hope everyone is okay. That's where we live," he reflected, referring to almost the entire thirty thousand people on base. Not only was it the life center of the base; it was also our home.

"All stations, this is tower – all clear. Break break. Shakedown two-five flight, you're cleared to take off from the FARP and air taxi direct to X-ray. Caution Blowtorch on final approach Role 3," Tower gave us our movement instructions.

"Shakedown two five, roger. I'm visual with with Blowtorch," Irish replied, indicating he would remain clear of Butch expediting to the hospital.

I looked out the window and received a thumbs-up from Professor. We lifted into the hover and flew over to the parking area. The team was quiet.

After shutting down, our eight-team members loitered between the Griffons—waiting for Blowtorch to return. We watched across the airfield toward Role 3 as the Chinook lifted and flew toward us. It landed and was followed moments later by Fender and Big C returning from the hunt. There was both victory and despair permeating the air; it was difficult to process, surreal—there was tangible death tonight.

The body language was somber from the Chinook crew as they disembarked the rear ramp. And the Shakedown crew, they were distressed. Big C and Fender were pale and exhausted.

"Let's just go into the briefing room and wait," Professor mentioned to our section. "Give them space. We'll find out more in a few minutes." We walked over to the sea cans and removed our combat gear.

"Sounds good, boss, but I gotta go see. Be there in a moment," Snapshot replied quietly. The injured Flight Engineer was more than a colleague; he was like a brother. Was he injured? Dead? All the engineers shared a kinship. It was a small community, and they had trained and worked together closely, some for decades. The worry showed on his face.

Hawk patted him on the back. "I'll get your gun. You go see." Snapshot nodded, leaving his Dillon and gear and walked over to the Chinook team. The rest of us went to Ops.

We all met at the TOC. Our faces soaked in sweat, and our flight suits decorated in white salt stains. My face was sunburned below the helmet visor line, and my forehead imprinted with a line from the helmet's liner as it seemed to fuse to my head in the heat and sweat; even at night.

I looked at Scrappy. His face was white with stress.

He glared at me. "During my evaluation as the operations officer on our predeployment exercise, in Maple Guardian, they gave me a test to see how I would respond to three entirely different situations." He set the stage, looking intense.

"I thought bullshit. That would never happen! Tonight, I've been corrected. While you guys were searching for Taliban IEDs and potentially finding a target, 30 was redirected onto an IED planter. Then you almost stumble onto a helicopter trap while Gil is getting crushed to death in the back of a Chinook. He's not dead. He's in critical condition now at Role 3. And finally, this all occurs during a rocket attack which, by the way, I've heard may have killed some people on the south side."

He shook his head, obviously venting to organize his stress, then he switched back to his duties.

"Get your team together, and I'll debrief everyone together. I don't want to keep going over this with everyone who passes by," he ordered.

All twenty airmen plus a few extras sat in the debrief room. Professor had concurrently downloaded the data from the MX-15 and submitted it into intelligence for an assessment. Scrappy walked in about fifteen minutes later.

"Shakedown 30 got two kills tonight." We nodded, but the victory was suppressed. "That's the good news."

"There will be two less IED bombers on the planet. From the reports, the remaining FAM most likely shit his pants when he was evading the breath of Allah, so he'll be easy for the dogs to find. The UAV tracked him to a building where he is fixed for the night. He'll soon have visitors," he reported, implying a quick reaction force was being deployed from FOB Dand to arrest him.

"There were four rockets fired at us tonight. A couple landed inside the wire and one into a tent of European soldiers playing cards," he paused to breath away some emotional stress as moisture gathered into his eyes. "Apparently that Polish brass you flew around the base earlier. They got hit with a rocket; heard one was dead; and definitely some injured."

I paused. It shouldn't feel personal, but it did. That was the beardless Santa, and he could be dead. I was just shaking his hand what seemed to be moments ago, visualizing his Santa smile and posture. I couldn't help to consider the irony that the man in charge of security is the one who has a rocket land on his lap.

Scrappy continued, "Gil? Well, —he's in critical condition at Role 3. The Chinook was doing a heels low pinnacle landing in the Reg Desert. Gil was lying in the ramp door over the edge. He was directing the pilot down but didn't see a rock under the other side of the ramp door; he was almost cut in half from the ramp being forced up as the Chinook lowered it's weight down.

"His ballistic vest prevented penetration, so he basically got squeezed. The other engineer and gunner couldn't see but heard his voice change. Tiny ran to the back and saw his face growing like balloon about to pop. He yelled to the pilot to pull up immediately. Gil couldn't talk during the flight to KAF, so they knew it was bad and went to Role 3."

It was quiet in the room.

"Tiny saved his life. You are all dismissed. Go get some sleep." Scrappy calmly exhaled.

"Steve, you're up tomorrow night," he directed as people rose to their feet. The murmur of discussion started while we all shuffled out of the room. Irish and I went to the crew vehicle. We passed Big C and Fender on the way, giving them a pat on the back.

"Good job, guys," Irish added.

"It was a bit confusing out there. We'll tell you about it at tomorrow's post-engagement briefing," Big C answered. His tone was different, a little more stoic.

"It was a helluva day for just a recce." I tried to be sarcastic.

"Yah, it sure was," Big C answered flatly, and for the first time, I noticed his binary smile actually was bent a little down.

Sunset of KAF Tower

Sunrise Griffon and KAF Tower

Canadian C-17 Globemaster bring troops to work.

Timmy's on the Boardwalk.

KAF hockey rink at the Boardwalk – Wi Fi corner

Thermometer Outside Tim Hortons in the Shade

Home Sweet Home for 2009/2010.

Kandahar looking East at Sunset

Dillon Silhouette

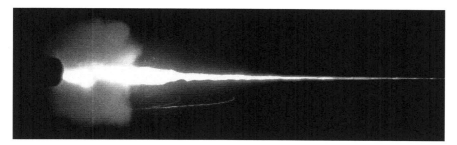

Time Lapse Dillon shots at Night

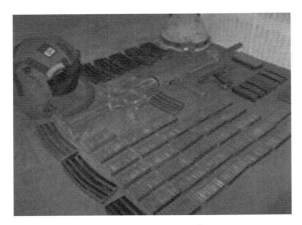

Go Bag Basic Supplies

Table Time – The Table

30 seconds of Ammo.

Camel Train in the Reg Desert

Over-watch of Blowtorch departing a FOB Ghundi Ghar

My personal AO - Nakhoney Area.

Fun at the FARP, Pee, Red Bull and a Pop-tart.

Alexander the Great's Castle near Qalat

Chinook enroute to the Monster Mash

Marijuana Fields

Opium Season – Pretty - Deadly.

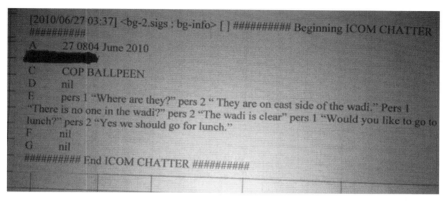

Lunchtime? – Hit them later.

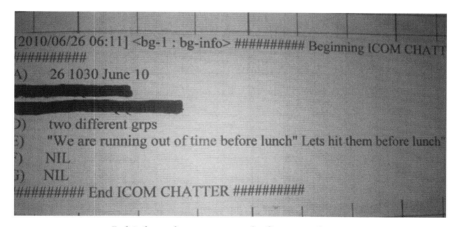

I think we better get ready for something.

Day Off? Panic - Where is my pistol? Why don't you speak Spanish?

Griffons Stacked.

Internet file photo, RIP Jo-Pat

Standard Loading

My Office

Traffic holdup near RAMROD – again. IEDs

Girlz taking a rest.

Sunrise over the Reg

Christmas at the TOC – Scrappy's Pullup bar just inside.

Typical grape-rows and walls.

Going by the Elephant west end Kandahar city

Mountain Training Daylight – Careful Ramp engineers.

Mantra at the Table

Sunset Over Jelewar – Arghandhab River towards Frontenac

Stormtrooper? Nope just Snapshot.

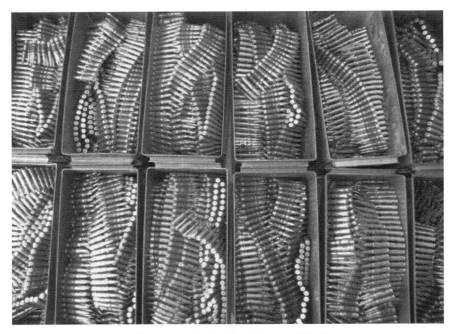

A few rounds for the Monster Mash

Overwatch near Masum Ghar in July 2010.

Firing at Texas Helo

Ramp Ceremony – 6 years later this still makes
my eyes swell while writing this caption.

The edge of a Green Zone

Going Home. Canadian C17 in the Sun over Blowtorch.

Chapter 18

OP Devil Strike

"One minute, hustle! We're waiting." I stretched my head through the flapping door of Arnie's room, splashing my MOAC yelling. MOAC stood for mother of all coffees. It was a Green Bean special that was available twenty-four hours a day on the boardwalk, the ideal motivational drink for missions at strange hours. It was a twenty-eight-ounce dark roast coffee boosted with four espresso shots—my staple when Timmy's wasn't open.

A few minutes later, Arnie stumbled out to the van, the other seven waiting patiently for him as usual. He was never early nor late—perfectly timed to the second and still half asleep from an early evening nap.

"Arnie, how many times I gotta tell you, if you're not ten minutes early—" I was interrupted by everyone else in the van who finished my sentence in mocking chorus.

"You're late!"

"Gotta relax, man. You're too uptight. Ease off the coffee." Irish took the opportunity to critique my vice.

I glared back, tired and stressed. Zorg was flying with the team today; he was refreshed and ready to add levity.

"Oooow . . . clear left, boss. I'm going to the back row!" He crawled through the van from the front to the rear, over three rows of seats to be annoyingly funny. It was his attempt to smartly deflate tension as his feet flailed past our heads, each person retaliating by grabbing and twisting his flesh or bag-tagging him for punishment, answered only by his laughs of defiance.

I liked being early. The guys did not, but they tolerated me. The seemed to respect my need for an extra half hour on X-ray ramp to psychologically prepare. Conversely, they accommodated by sleeping for the twenty-minute transit as I drove.

I reported to the TOC and started completing the preflight risk assessment, a protocol required for each mission to attain launch authority. It was a pitch-black night and thus a high-risk mission, not from enemy fire but from the combination of precision landings using NVGs combined with brownout obscured conditions. More aircraft crashed in Afghanistan from the environment than to Taliban fire, so the threat was duly noted. Skipper was overseeing the mission.

"Hi, boss." I forced a greeting through my fatigue, the MOAC not quite active yet.

"You guys ready?" he asked.

"Yes, sir."

"Well, let's hear it. Over to the briefing room."

In the briefing room, the mission coordination team was present as well as the operations officer, Scrappy. They went through an organized sequence of briefings starting with weather.

The briefer talked about the winds expected and illumination levels. Skipper immediately asked me how I was applying this information on every aspect of the mission. We discussed the timings, terrain, wind, and lack of lunar illumination and how it would affect the mountain landing. The winds were light; this would increase the intensity of the dust ball, decreasing visibility.

The int op briefed recent enemy activity within the AO and then focused on the applicable FOB reports. Special maps were produced, depicting the angle and jaggedness of the terrain based on satellite imagery at our intended landing areas.

"So where are you landing?" Skipper inquired as he looked at the entire map which showed no suitable landing spot available.

"I'm not, sir. I'm putting one skid on and holding it right here. Prof will follow once I clear." I pointed to the map. "This spot is my primary. It's closer to the top. This is our backup." I pointed to a ledge about 100 meters away and 100 feet lower on the jagged cliffs. "It'll be a right skid landing, and we'll hold 'er there until the snipers deplane. I checked it out yesterday, and the references looked adequate."

"All right," he agreed, raising a brow of concern, but he had confidence in me. "Please continue." He gestured to the briefers.

Scrappy and Ricky finished briefing all aspects that could affect the mission: enemy, friendlies, lighting, timings, ammo, known activity, artillery, and all other aviation flying in the area. They covered it all. Overall, it was a simple task—pick up some snipers and drop them off.

"Sir, the Lord Strats are running a concurrent deception plan to mask the noise of the helicopter." Ricky pointed to the map. "They'll be running their tank logistics convoy along this route at precisely the same time as the intended landing sequence of Shakedown 25. The intent is to create a sound screen to prevent anyone from the area from noticing the landings," he concluded.

"Very well. It won't be easy. Fly safe," Skipper stated. "It will be tricky, so take it slow out there."

I nodded, picked up my maps, and proceeded to the flight line. My mind was full of various contingencies plans and potential emergencies, firefights that could occur. I looked up at sky which was clear and pin-pricked with stars. No moon. It was dark. The air was still. The dust had subsided, so the air was breathable. I loaded my 85 pounds of go-gear on my back and wobbled toward the helicopter as silhouettes of my team members moved in their rituals.

I noticed a figure stealthily disappeared behind the tail boom of my wingman's chopper—Arnie. He was continuing with his urination ritual. Shortly after the first time he urinated under the tail boom, he went on an overwatch mission. The infantry reported shots being fired at the helicopters. He and the right gunner heard the crack of the bullets passing by, fortunately missing. Ever since then, he hasn't changed a single action prior to his departure. He figured the freaky universal magic associated with that piss routine was somehow associated with redirecting the bullet from hitting him. He was not about to change fate and screw with the gods.

Snapshot noticed. He liked to make little rhymes to add cheer:

"If you gotta go, pee in the snow, but there's no snow, so just go, go, go."

"Poetry is not your forte. Stick with the photography," Zorg critiqued then went back to his rest position, seated with legs draping over Betty, his gun.

I subtly walked around the Griffon, rubbing the helicopter's nose in contemplation. The gunners were in their seats as I walked my ritualistic path. As I walked by the gunners, I rubbed their foreheads too in jest. I reviewed the entire mission in my head.

We departed proceeding to the Reg Desert to test fire weapons and lasers. I looked far ahead across the valley. I could see the mountain we were to land on, Masum Ghar, where the sniper team was and the towns where the high-value target was to be observed. I rehearsed it in my head as I monitored the silence beyond the engines and rotor noise.

"Prof, is your test fire green?" I radioed.

"26 is green. Good to go," Professor replied.

"Going to Slayer," I stated so he could follow on the radios.

"Shakedown 25, you're cleared into the ROZ (restricted operating zone). Guns are cold tonight. Heron UAV is overhead Chalgour monitoring. There is a special operations ROZ established centered on grid reference QQ4593. It has an 8-kilometer radius. Controller is Snakebite on frequency 234.4," Slayer responded.

I punched the grid into the navigation system and figured out the circumference, and of course, it encompassed my entire mission area. The Special Forces never told anyone what they were doing.

It was probably a ROZ for the mission I was on, but they never told us. So perhaps it could be someone else's mission of higher priority; the tanks perhaps? However, because it was a restricted operating zone, I wasn't allowed to conduct operations inside without permission.

"What the fuck! It's right in the middle of our mission area," I radioed to Professor. "Stand by. I'll contact Snakebite. It may be for us," I stated reluctantly. They never answered the radio.

"Check that," Professor answered.

"Snakebite, this is Shakedown, over," I called three times.

No answer. This was usual. Frustrating.

"Let's veer around it for now, and I'll try on the return trip to establish contact," I stated to Irish. Irish extended his course along the Reg Desert for spacing from the ROZ. The last thing we needed was to get shot down by friendlies or fly into a firefight without knowledge.

We flew to Masum Ghar. While Professor landed in the base, we orbited. There was only enough room for only one helicopter in the landing zone, so we scouted for potential threats since Professor was vulnerable on takeoff to RPGs.

"Contact, by the bridge north. I see movement underneath," Snapshot blurted breaking the silence.

Immediately Irish steered the helicopter toward the bridge, and our heads snapped toward the direction of the movement. Irish flew low so the gunners could look underneath.

"Right on, Irish!" I was happy he was flying as I wanted.

"Looking, looking," Irish stated. "Going a bit lower and slower."

Irish informed the gunners so Snapshot could get a better look. Snapshot activated the laser pointer on his gun and with the infrared beam pointed to where the movement was.

"Right in there," I announced. If anyone popped out and started shooting at the Griffons, Snapshot would only have to pull the trigger, and fifty rounds a second of lethal saturation would land on that laser spot.

"I think I see what you're looking at. If that's a person, he's staying still and hiding. He knows he's been spotted," Irish stated.

"Probably a dicker," I speculated.

A dicker or an IED planter. He would be armed with communications and a shovel, maybe explosives. The only way to prove it was a dicker is to actually watch them for hours and track communications. We did not have that liberty, but the FOB might.

"FOB Masum Ghar, this is Shakedown 25. We've got a possible dicker under the bridge 600 meters north of you. Can you put observation on that?" I reported to the base.

"Roger, Shakedown. We're looking for him. Thanks," they responded.

If there was someone under there, it would probably be an all-night project for the sniper teams to track him and prove if he was a dicker. But the FOB could call on a UAV or other helicopter teams flying by as they monitored to see if it was a threat. But who else hangs out under a strategic bridge at two o'clock in the morning in a war zone?

"26 is lifting in fifteen seconds," Arnie stated.

"Romeo Tango," I acknowledged.

Irish swooped down and picked up Professor's tail to cover his egress. Professor climbed high, turned slowly left, allowing us to pass inside his turning radius and lead into the FOB. Professor slowly assumed the tail position and protected my ingress, especially since a suspected dicker was noticed.

Irish flared the helicopter's nose up over the fence, decelerating, and then descended to land. A small explosion of dust rose, obscuring our vision. Flying into Masum Ghar was a one-way trip. There was no overshoot option because the landing zone was in a bowl, and a mountain was directly in front. Once crossing the fence, we were committed to the landing regardless of the situation.

"Three feet, 2, 1 . . ." Snapshot was calling the heights since us pilots couldn't see because of the dust. "Steady right. You're drifting!"

"I'm losing references," Irish stated, a normal call to request support if I was able to. I was. I found a reference on the left side and added some cyclic pressure to stop the drift. It wasn't anything serious, but the extra assistance helped for safety. Irish settled the aircraft onto the ground.

"Good job," I stated. "Go get 'em Snapshot."

Snapshot hopped out and walked through the cloud and returned with two heavily packed soldiers. I was in awe as to how these men climb mountains and trekked through the dark while carrying an extra 150 pounds of equipment. The two soldiers lumbered aboard and strapped themselves in.

"Lifting in fifteen," I called to Professor. Irish pulled the chopper into the air. It climbed slowly forward. The extra 700 pounds was a significant load for the Griffon in these conditions. It was high and hot; the helicopter felt it.

"Torque, watch the torque! Engine temperatures at 825 degrees," I called as the little yellow advisory light came on, indicating that we were using every ounce of available power.

"Check!" Irish froze the controls and allowed the airspeed to increase to help the helicopter climb out of the pick-up zone.

"Airspeed alive and through 40 knots, set cruise power," I stated, indicating it was safe to reduce power. "I gotta sort out that ROZ with the snake eaters now. We still don't have entry clearance."

"Back to cruise," he answered indicating he was lowering the collective safely below take-off power.

"Haycee? These guys want me to test fire. They haven't seen the Dillon shoot?" Snapshot asked for the snipers who were showing interest in his weapon.

"Roger that. Mountains twelve o'clock. That's your target area. We'll turn left, and you can fire into them," I complied.

"The mountain straight ahead is clear. Clear to fire," I stated.

I heard him yell to the guys in the back. "Test firing."

BBBRRRRAAAAPP.

"Haycee, she's as good as can be," he stated, proud of his show 'n' tell. I could hear them hollering and bantering in the back over the helicopter noise. The sniper team was obviously hyped and enthusiastic to get to work. Test firing was more than for a cool fire-power demonstration; it was also about enhancing their knowledge regarding the spread and effect of the Dillon's bullets. It was not uncommon for snipers to become FACs in their role and it was educational to them to have knowledge of the effects of this new weapon.

"Wow! Nice rate and tight spread." A voice yelled to Snapshot, who returned the comment with a thumb up and a pat on the shoulder.

"I think we just added sniper's to our client list," Snapshot added over the intercom.

"I'm sure they will find us some descent targets someday, they like to stay covert if they can help it," I replied. "We're two minutes back," I switched focus. Everyone knew the plan; it was briefed and rehearsed. "Calling the ROZ."

I hoped they would answer. And if they didn't, I was going anyway. It was very likely the ROZ was for the mission we were on; we just weren't advised. If it wasn't? Well, I figured they would call us.

"Snakebite, this is Shakedown 25, over," I radioed.

No response. My frustration rose. I decided to tell instead of ask. It was always our backup plan with the Snake Eaters. The old adage seemed to apply: "Sometimes it's better to ask forgiveness than permission."

"Snakebite, this is Shakedown 25 flight. We are inbound to the ROZ and will be overflying Hyena and landing near grid QQ494963. Out!" I asserted blindly on the radio, not expecting a response.

But this time there was a response. "Snakebite, roger, out." It was a quick and emotionless acknowledgment. That was Snakebite's typical way of saying, "It's not an issue. Quit bothering me. I'm busy. Now just shut the fuck up and get on with it."

"I guess that's that!" I retorted. Irish laughed at the level of nonrequired stress that I had exerted.

"26, this is 25. Snakebite has been advised, continue," I stated.

We were closing on the landing spot. Irish was on the controls. The depth perception was lacking, making it very challenging. I helped fly the last portion of the approach.

As I arrived over the spot, Snapshot directed me to a razor's edge to place a skid on. I had no visual references to hold a hover. I had misjudged the closest obstacle; the vertical cliff wall was only 20 feet away from my rotor disk. We were 300 feet up a cliff face sitting on a small ledge, and I was staring into nothing but dusty green air.

"Fuck! I got nothing for references. Irish, I need your help. Can you see references?" I asked.

"Yes," Irish stated. "I have control. I got the cliff visual on my right."

"You have control. Get us on that ledge," I stressed.

"Roger." His voice was nervous. Mine was elevated.

I watched across the cockpit over my right shoulder through Irish's door. I could see the mountain face. The rotor was only meters away from the vertical cliffs. I felt the cyclic start to shake back and forth indicating Irish's difficulty finding good contrasting references to use for hovering. I followed him on the controls, reducing and stabilizing his movements.

"Steady!" I called to Irish while holding the cyclic from moving.

"You still have control. I'm just steadying your movement!" He could hardly see, and the rock face was intimidating. "Snapshot, we're steady. Get us in there now!"

"Steady forward, Haycee. Move right 3 feet, two, one, steady right," directed Snapshot. "Move down 2 feet, one, 6 inches, contact! Hold 'er there!"

"Hold 'er here," I called rhetorically to Irish. "Are you good?"

"Yup, but I don't want to spend a lot of time here!" he exclaimed nervously.

"Snapshot, unload quick," I commanded.

"You're doing fine, boss. They didn't put their night devices on. They can't see—it'll take a minute to get them going," Snapshot casually advised.

Fuck! I thought I should have had them do that. I knew there was something I overlooked. The snipers were blind. They had their night-vision gear, but it should have been donned for the flight so they could get out for the black ops task. They didn't. They slowly moved onto the skid and then stepped onto the ledge, feeling the ground with their hands to prevent going over the side.

This all took about two minutes as they slowly used brail techniques to move around in the dark—two minutes longer than expected! Snapshot was helping the snipers out of the aircraft. He could see. If they fell off the cliff or twisted an ankle, then OP Devil Strike would be turned into a medevac, which I did not want.

"Hurry up, Snapshot. I don't know how long we can hold it here!" I stated in a heightened tone.

The aircraft was rocking; all my effort was to help stabilize the aircraft. I had visions of tumbling down the hill into a fireball and didn't want to wake from my unconscious state with a burnt face and broken legs while being fucked up the ass by a Taliban interrogator.

I recalled our training stating that that was common for interrogators to sodomize their captives. This was better than being beheaded apparently. The interrogation trainers concluded their briefing to us, stating to not take it personally, just "take it like a man."

"Just a few more seconds, Haycee!" Snapshot stated happily. His tone was happy like he was having a coffee break and sharing stories with the sniper team.

In my stress from being perched on a fragile inch of rock, inches from my death, I envisioned him casually visiting. "Hey, guys. Big mission. How 'bout a selfie?"

"Would you fuckin' hurry before we tumble down the goddamned mountain?" I finally blurted.

"Roger that. They're out. Cabin is secure and the teams in position. Move up 2 feet to clear some rock, one. Skid's clear, clear to fly," Snapshot guided.

The helicopter punctured out of the dust cloud into the clear air again.

"Well, that was entertaining. Clear left!" Zorg chuckled, being able to observe everything objectively.

"26, you're up. We're out," I called.

Our sniper team's job was to crack the infrared marker sticks. I watched across the valley looking for the mark. They needed a little time to get organized.

Meanwhile, 26 rolled onto the same flight path that we had just flown. They were arriving too early. I was observing from across the valley. There were no markers.

Professor started his arrival to touchdown. Something wasn't right. I was disoriented and trying to locate the snipers through the dust. We watched Professor's helicopter add additional dust. His helicopter disappeared into a mushroom cloud of green which obscured the mountain ridge.

"You guys okay?" I radioed.

"Wait out," Professor radioed back. He was busy.

As the dust settled, the IR marker beacons lit, but there was no helicopter.

"What the fuck? He missed! The guys are lighting up the beacons behind him," I exclaimed.

"I don't think he's in the same spot as you were," Zorg observed.

"Shit," I said. I glared out the window studying the spot intently.

"You guys are in the wrong spot!" I radioed. "You're at the alternate."

"I couldn't see any IR markers. The dust was too intense," Professor answered.

"Tell them to get back in!" I ordered.

"They're out, and I'm off the ground!" Professor stated. He was stressed; also facing a cliff a few meters away and wobbling on the edge of death with minimal visibility. A voice bellowing over the radio was the last thing he needed at that point.

"I'm going back in. Stand by. I gotta call from Ops. You go top cover," I answered to 26, telling him to climb above me as I was on my way into the landing zone to reposition the snipers. Ops was calling at the same time on the other radio.

In Freedom Operations

Back in operations, from the live TV feed off the Heron UAV, Scrappy had observed the second helicopter go to a different LZ.

"They're in the wrong spot," Skipper sighed calmly. It was the only possible flaw that I assured would not happen.

"Talk to HQ Scrappy," he directed Scrappy to call the Brigade Tactical Operations Center who was also watching.

Scrappy picked up the phone. "Yup. He'll go back and fix it. No? Okay. Bye."

"Task Force HQ says leave 'em in that spot," Scrappy stated. At the same time, I radioed him.

"Freedom Ops, it's 25. We got the guys in the wrong spot. I'm going back to extract and move them."

"Negative. Knock it off. Go refuel and then check back in," Scrappy ordered as he looked at the Skipper. Skipper smirked, shook his head, and left the room. "Sometimes it's the shit! And sometimes shit happens," he stated in a disappointed rhetoric.

"I got them on different spots," I stated defiantly on the radio. "I'm going back in to relocate them. It'll only take a sec."

"Roger. I know that. Knock it off! Knock it off!" Scrappy reordered and listened to the pause.

"Roger, out," I obeyed. I failed.

Over Chalgour.

"26, rejoin on me. We're FARPing," I stated over the radio.

I flew back with my tail between my legs. Irish was excited. He was so happy to have completed that complicated landing as a team that he was high-fiving me in the cockpit. But the mission was not a success. I was quiet. We refueled, returned to X-ray ramp, and shut down.

"Put 'er to bed, guys," I asked, referring to the helicopter. I was disappointed in myself. "I'm going to Ops. Meet you there."

Scrappy looked at me and saw my disappointment. He nodded and invited me for the update. I looked at the UAV feed on the TV screen of four of the snipers, 50 meters apart.

"They are going to try to link up tonight. They are only 50 meters apart and 50 feet vertically separated, but they only have three hours before first light, so they don't have much time. The mountain has a potential for IEDs. Searching for them will slow them down. I'll brief you tomorrow. Report in at 1400 hours for a follow-up." Scrappy briefed sympathetically.

The rest of the section arrived. I looked at them and shrugged my shoulders. "They may or may not be able to link up by first light. Let's go. We're done for now."

"Guys, look at the text chatter board," Scrappy stated, directing me to the text prompter play by play.

We all stopped at the Ops door and turned to look.

It was a text readout from the Task Force Kandahar.

Time: XX:XX: "Snipers inserted, different locations, attempting rejoin."

Several lines earlier:

"Time: XX:XX: FOB Masum Ghar, contact one times FAM dicker IED implanter at bridge 500 meters north of FOB at QQ31529291, engaged with one round .50-caliber, target destroyed."

I raised my eyebrows. "Snapshot. Good eye tonight. One for you."

We departed the TOC. I looked behind me expecting Snapshot to follow; he wasn't there. He was still in the TOC, staring emotionlessly at the text prompter.

"You comin'?" I prompted. He ignored me; deep in reflection. "Hey!" I prompted his attention.

He looked at me somewhat stunned, "Oh. Ya. I'm comin', I'm just trying to put it all together."

Chapter 19

Switch-Up Day

It was a switch-up day. We never had a day off, just a few extra hours to switch schedules from nights to mornings. I was asleep around 6:00 a.m. And table time was 3:30 a.m., twenty hours later. That was considered a day off.

However, a day off usually meant cleaning weapons, tending to personal gear, and mission planning for the following event. Professor had to manage the administration of forty subordinates, so he perpetually worked. Irish and I went to lunch together prior my 1400 hours debrief with Scrappy.

"You did awesome last night," I told him. "That was nuts. The landing was a little more difficult than I anticipated on that ledge."

He smiled and tried to humble away the compliment. We had our interpersonal differences from the beginning but were consolidating as a very effective team. He was a smart academic pilot, but tactically, experience wasn't on his side.

"As for the mission, I don't know what happened," I reflected. "It should have been a straightforward landing on the same spot. Maybe the snipers didn't get the IR markers out, or maybe the dust was too bad to see the IR on time. I should have ensured they had their NVGs on," I vented my frustration to him.

"I suppose Prof could have delayed his approach?" Irish suggested.

"Yes, but still my responsibility," I closed.

"It's ironic because the only thing the wing commander queried was the possibility of not landing on the same spot, and I brushed that off as an impossibility—yet it happened," I said in disappointment. "Aside from that, you seem to be getting comfortable with the helicopter in this environment." I noted his improvement. "This is tense situation. There will be worse situations. More bullets will be flying. I need to be count on you when I ask, Irish." I looked at him in the eyes.

Irish nodded. He wanted to discuss and defend as usual, but I raised my brow and held up my hand to signal "stop." His shoulders dropped. He sighed and held it in.

"Just take the compliment, man," I bluntly stated.

"Thanks?" he reeled back.

"Well, I'm heading over to Ops to get an update for tomorrow's job and find out what happened last night. Three thirty table time tonight. Pass that around to the team." I patted him on the shoulder and departed.

"No problem. Thanks for the chat. We rocked that landing!" Irish sincerely added.

"Yes, we did," I returned with a smile.

Operations

"Scrappy, have you slept yet since arriving to this war?" I asked jokingly.

He glared at me. I never knew if he was happy, angry, fatigued, or sarcastic. He made everyone guess. He obviously had news to share about the night before and the following mission.

"Pull-ups!" he ordered.

"Awe, crap, I am beat. I couldn't sleep last night, so I've already been to the gym. And I just had a heart to heart with Irish," I whined.

He brushed off the heart-to-heart comment and led me out of his office.

"I don't wanna talk about your shit. Pull-ups! Follow me." I went out back following the gloating major. "You first," he said.

I started. I felt stronger, not sure if it was exercise every day or leaving five pounds of sweat in the cockpit every mission, but my count was increasing.

"Fourteen, fifteen, sixteeeeeeen," Scrappy counted before I let go of the bar.

"You're done. I'm up," Scrappy said excitingly.

He'd been practicing. I don't know if he ever slept, but Scrappy was getting stronger and fitter.

"Fifteeeeeen, sixteeeeen, seventeeeeeen," I counted. He jumped down.

"Kicked your ass! Coulda done more! Work on it!" he proudly exclaimed. "Let's go in and chat."

"Oh, it's on now!" I challenged by bumping my shoulder against his back as I passed him through the door. He nodded, accepting as we strolled into the TOC.

"All right, the mission failed," he stated bluntly.

"I asked you guys if I could return. You said no," I defended.

"Don't sweat it. The guys tried until light to link up, but they said the risk was too high on the mountain to climb that last 50 yards. It looks like nothing on a map, but it was pretty vertical, and there was evidence of possible IEDs, so it slowed them down," he reported.

"I'll go pick them up then?" I asked.

"It's done. They walked off the mountain, down to the road, and got picked up already by their own guys," Scrappy advised. "But there may be hope. The top two guys are still up there. They apparently are going to try to continue the mission."

"That's good, right?" I hesitantly asked.

"I guess so, but what's done is done. I knew you wanted to know, so now you know. Let me brief you on the next few days," he continued as if it was no big deal. No dwelling. Move forward.

"Get your head into the next game!" Scrappy observed me overthinking the last mission. "You got guests in the next room."

"Huh? What?" I squinted wondering who was here. I wandered into the next office where two gruff looking soldiers stood.

"Hey! Nice to meet ya," one shook my hand. "I'm John and this is Chris. Thanks for the lift last night. Dillons are pretty awesome."

"You guys the snipers?" I queried.

"Well, half the team anyway," he added sarcastically. "Our brothers are still up there. We are pretty sure they are still covert so they should be able to put some observation on the HVT for the next few days."

I thought they were coming to give me hell; but that wasn't the case at all. "How did you guys get back so quick?" I questioned.

"Walked out. We couldn't link up so figured it was best to walk off and get extracted from the vehicles early while they were there and before sunrise."

"I'm sorry we got the LZ mixed up…I shoulda made sure everyone was goggled first and planned a bigger time-gap in the insert."

"No worries. Shit happens. This is common for us."

"How do you mean?"

"We have lots of failed inserts and get busted; have to bug out. It's part of the gig. Fuckin' kids are the worse. I swear they are all free-range. We spend hours covertly securing a position thinking we are totally covert by 3 am, then along comes some kid and finds us. Yes! At 3:00 in the fricken morning."

"No shit! So what then?" they had my attention.

"They run into their compounds, the lights come on, then of course, we gotta exfil…part of the deal. One time we were in a livestock compound and an old man came and discovered us. But fuck! We had PID on our HVT so we had to capture the poor guy. Chris here, he had to detain him and explain nicely that we had to keep him prisoner for the next 6 hours. He wasn't happy but we re-assured him and shared our rations."

"Ya that was fucked. Had to show him how to play Black-jack! But it turned out okay. He relaxed; won a few rounds too, lost my beef jerky rations to him," Chris added. I laughed.

"That's nuts. Hats off to ya guys. Why are you here?" I asked.

"Actually just coming down to see Hawk and Zorg; get a little more acquainted with the Dillons too. We may have some use for those. Also thought to stop by and say no hard feelings," John stated.

"Well I appreciate it. Hawk is down the ramp most likely," I smiled and shook their hands. They left the TOC. We'd probably meet again without knowing it. I followed Scrappy back into Ops as he led into the next sequence of events.

"We got a doubleheader tomorrow—two Chinook escorts, one north to Tarin Kowt. Grumpy is escorting Butch, and you and Prof are heading to Qalat following Droopy. They should be relaxed trips, but look at the altitudes. They're high. You won't have much of a power reserve," Scrappy cautioned.

Cool, I thought. It'll be nice to get out of the AO and go on a "cross-country" so to speak. In Canada a "cross country" was a chance to practice flight skills while touring the region. Sometimes it even allowed the crew to show off the helicopter to friends and family that may live nearby to gain grassroots support for our air-soldiering. They were rare but sought-after events.

However, this situation was in unsupported territory, meaning there were no friendly troops, no family, and no one on the ground to rely on for help. But it was new and interesting. Alexander's Castle was en route in the valley to Qalat. Therefore, it was the closest thing to a "cross-country" we would have.

Grumpy's crew, on the other hand, had the Devil's Belly Button to navigate, but the reward was Dutch meatballs for lunch in Tarin Kowt. Yes, meatballs! The perk of navigating successfully through the valley of death was a meatball. These delicacies were combination of various meats, finely ground and seasoned perfectly—and the size of baseballs—so delicious and worth flying over the enemy to attain. Aside from overwatch, these missions were the envy of the fleet.

I went to the map room and saw Big C's team. He was scheduling while his first officer, Shorty, was flight planning for a mission. His other crew was designated for maintenance test flights today.

The normal routine was based on a three-day rotation: two flying days followed by a maintenance test flying and mission-planning day. Big C's crew was mission planning, and his wingman was maintenance flying. Test flying occurred every day.

Task Force Freedom had eight Griffon helicopters, and we kept a minimum of six serviceable to fill the three sections (six helicopters) for daily missions. The technicians worked two shifts of twelve hours each twenty-four hours a day for a year to make it happen. They changed from nights to days every two weeks. Everyone worked nonstop. I, overall, had three days off (switch-up days) in theater for the entire year in Afghanistan.

"Where you off to, C?" I asked.

"I'm just trying to figure out this software for mapping," he replied, looking rather perplexed—he had a level smile. His copilot was a technology wiz. Big C was old school. His brow was furrowed, but he tried.

"We're off to Helmand in a few days," he advised. "We're gonna do a few preparatory missions with the Brits. Apparently there is a big 'to do' coming up in the next few months."

"Shania is coming," he added.

"What? Awesome! Is she coming in with the USO?" I asked.

So far the boardwalk had Anna Kournikova and Billy Ray Cyrus—celebrities who came to entertain troops. I was pumped. I love Shania Twain; my family loved her. I had recollections of my family dancing to her music back home as I repeated the moves to Big C. I bracketed my bosom with my hands, wiggled my hips and sang:

"Man, I feel like a women . . . Da da da da da da da."

Hollywood slid in behind me unnoticed, placing his hands on my hips and joined, adding, "Well, I'm going out tonight—I'm feelin' all right.

Da da da da da da da."

Grumpy walked through the door, coffee cup in hand, and stopped, paused—without flinching—turned, and left.

Shorty shook his head at the spectacle and returned to planning.

I was excited, but that's not what Big C meant. He was being Big C again, giving enough information, just hoping the ambiguity would entertain him. It did; his smile curved up. He was referring to an operation that was named Operation Stargai Kwang. However, no one could pronounce the Pashtun word, so it was referred to as Shania Twain.

"No," he stated to our assumptions.

"Huh?" I asked him.

"It's an operation, not a country-rock show," he informed.

"Oh, that sucks." I was a bit disappointed but curious. "Well, whatever you're doing, have a good trip. I haven't been out to Helmand yet. Looking forward to your stories," I stated as I left the room. Big C nodded to my comment, continuing his planning work.

I departed Ops and boarded a transport van to the south side. I needed some decompression time: gym, dinner, movie, and a Skype call home before some sleep—standard routine. I Skype called home and talked with my kids as my daughter was preparing for school. My daughter's ringette team was playing that night, and she was getting her music ready: "Tonight's Gonna Be a Good Night" by the Black-Eyed Peas.

I reflected to a ringette game I had watched when I was recently in Canada for a short home break. I was at the arena, and I watched my daughter win her first ever ringette tournament. The girls played "pump-up" music in the locker room before the game to get motivated. All the parents could hear the music from the stands as the nine-year-old girls proudly tried to out party the other team as they entered the ice.

My boys sat with me on the cold bench also enjoying the pregame show—a family event. Although, I was smiling and happy outside, I was stoic inside. My focus was on Afghanistan, outside the wire, and Afghanistan wouldn't release my soul to fully connect in the moment.

"I got a feelin' . . . that tonight's gonna be a good night."

There was the song. The Black-Eyed Peas began to dominate the rink as the doors from the change room opened, allowing a stream of young warrior princesses out to rally, some stumbling on their skates, others tripping onto the ice as they forgot to take their blade guards off. Parents chuckled, and big smiles could be seen clearly through the face guards of the young girls' helmets.

"Tonight's gonna be a good night."

"Sure is nice that you could get some time off at Christmas," I remembered one of the parents stating.

"Yes, I'm glad to be home," I answered.

"Your daughter has really improved this year. You'll be surprised when she starts skating!" he added.

I hadn't seen her skate since the summer. She was pushing with one leg; the other was stiff. Only one blade was used for braking.

"There she is," my wife pointed.

"Wow! She's skating normally now, and she stopped sideways." I was amazed. "Oops, she just fell!" I laughed. She smiled back at me proud to show off her new accomplishment.

"She can only stop one direction so far, but she's getting better," the other parent said.

"Did you notice her helmet?" my wife asked.

"Hey, she's got a yellow ribbon sticker on it from the military base," I noted.

"They all do," she added.

I looked around and noticed all the girls had yellow ribbons. I straightened up and took a proud breath.

"Why do they have those? Does the league have the girls wearing them for the soldiers?" I asked.

"No." She looked in my eyes seriously. "It's for you. The team put them on for you."

My body tripped over the next breath I took, shaking a tear from my eye. I froze my face and could feel myself losing emotional control. I quickly got up. I needed an excuse to leave.

"I'm gonna grab a coffee. Anyone want one?"

I was overwhelmed by the support from the team and parents. However, my mind couldn't leave KAF. I couldn't allow the emotions to cut through my focus. It may have been psychologically naive, trivial, but it was the "war-face" that had to maintain despite wanting to be home.

I was so grateful at the freedoms my family had, and how the young girls could play, yet I couldn't help thinking about a few days prior to coming home for this break, a bomber blew up a school 2 miles from KAF. It was a girls' school. Three girls died. Girls my daughter's age. Why? The souls of numerous families were fractured. Would there yellow ribbons on the compounds for those families? I had to stay this way.

"Tonight's gonna be a good night . . ."

"Tonight's gonna be a good, good night . . . feelin'."

The music brought me away but also reminded me I was here. I was in KAF. I hit play and repeat on my computer. At two forty-five in the morning, my alarm went off. I woke as a different person, turned off the music, which was still faintly playing in my ears, and started my job.

This was my routine during this war. Table time was 3:30 a.m. I had to focus and get moving. I got up a little earlier than others as I needed my MOAC—again. I had a shower, got dressed, and walked over to the boardwalk to Green Beans. Green Beans hired local Afghan employees; they smiled and ineffectively prepared the beverage. However, they were friendly, thus making the beverage all that more pleasing.

"Your coffee is free today, sir," the Afghani barista informed.

I was perplexed. "Why is it free?"

In his heavy Pashtun accent, he explained, "In United States, someone at a Green Beans store pay for you coffee. It says here on my computer, 'Thank you, this is a treat from a patriot.' Right here. See, sir." He pointed, proudly showing me.

"Thank you!" I said gratefully. Some American bought me a coffee. Not just any coffee but a MOAC, the mother of all coffees. At three o'clock in the morning! Great timing! I appreciated it very much. This should last until about 10:00 a.m. when Red Bull would take the next shift.

I showed up at the table at three twenty; I was always early. I had an obligation to set an example. But that didn't matter. The copilot generation always shows up "just in time." Ten minutes early meant ten minutes of lost sleep to them. They slept in until five minutes prior to table time and then bitched because they were hungry and tired. The grumpy old captains grimaced with this attitude daily. Grumpy was already there, MOAC in hand. His eyes enlarged with frustration at the lack of movement from his copilots.

Zorg showed up. His army background showed discipline with making timings. He forced a smile at the ridiculousness of the mutually shared exhaustion and then climbed into the van over the seats vice around them to find sleep again.

Then Snapshot bounced over. Professor had his own vehicle, but he always drove by to make sure everyone was moving; he waited inside his vehicle a few feet away, occasionally spitting into a cup.

"Who's missing?" he called.

"The usual two fine young officers," I answered sarcastically.

"Sort those two out!" he ordered and drove off in disdain. He wasn't too happy today.

Hawk arrived, also MOAC in hand, and then the other engineer. We sat at the "table" and slowly migrated into the van with Zorg, fast asleep, and then waited for the "special ones."

Arnie came staggering out at 3:29 a.m. and Irish too. However, Irish was going to the bathroom, toothbrush in hand. Arnie quickly pointed out how Irish was late. Hypocrite. I slapped my forehead in submission. At 3:30 a.m., Irish briskly walked to his tent and then immediately returned to the van. He got in as the digital clock switch to 3:31 a.m.

"See, I'm on time," he proudly announced of his precision.

"If you're not ten minutes early," I started to say.

"You're late!" Zorg sleepily interjected in a cocky tone from the back, gaining laughing support from the gang. I shook my head and drove off.

3:32 a.m.: The vehicle departed.

4:00 a.m.: Scrappy's operations briefing.

4:20 a.m.: Scrappy's final mission launch authorization.

4:40 a.m.: The section coordination briefing.

5:00 a.m.: Breakfast at DFAC (highlight of the day)

5:30 a.m.: Aircraft crew final brief by the aircraft.

5:35 a.m.: Rituals. I circled the aircraft and rubbed the nose. Snapshot photographed the sunrise. Irish fluffed his ass pillow. Zorg sat in the shadows and across the ramp at Professor's helicopter. Arnie secretly peed under the tail boom.

6:00 a.m.: Lift off, escorting Blowtorch 62 to Qalat.

Chapter 20

A Short Grumpy Day

The air at FOB Qalat was cool compared to Kandahar—high 20s, clear skies, calm winds, a lighter dust than Kandahar, breathable, and refreshing in comparison. However, it was warm enough for a nap on the rocks in the shade of the helicopters.

Thirteen crewmembers lay alongside the Chinook, snoozing and waiting for our passengers to return from their business in the early afternoon. Most of us had Tilley hats with the brim tilted forward to shade the eyes from the dust of the helicopters arriving and departing.

"Here we go," a voice hollered out. I looked up from my brim watching Blowtorch's passengers return and ready to go.

I yawned and stretched. "All right, guys, saddle up," I stated in my best John Wayne voice trying to be funny. I wasn't. Snapshot smiled. Everyone else focused on forcing their semi-paralyzed bodies to move.

Our Griffons departed first ahead of the Chinook since the air was thin, and power was limited at the 8,500 feet density altitude. The Chinook easily trailed.

Irish lifted up smoothly with the collective and eased forward with the cyclic.

"800, 810, torque is matching," I called as I tweaked the switch to balance the engine's power, Irish straining to focus on smooth movements. "815, 820 . . . 40 knots, back to cruise power." I relaxed my attention as the helicopter's power was reduced when it burbled into forward flight.

"I think I can. I think I can" was sounding over the radio.

"Fence out!" Irish called, reminding each of us to complete our battle preparation checks, ignoring the slander from Blowtorch.

Once in formation, our three helicopters loosened spacing. The Chinook at times was surging ahead and then drooping back, obviously making the point of its superior speed as we bantered over the radio.

"Check this out!" Blowtorch led. The massive aircraft descended low over the fine dust of the desert floor. At approximately 25 feet and plowing along at 100 knots, the massive airflow from the huge blades made a rooster tail in the dust of the desert floor, just like a wake from a speedboat going across a smooth lake.

"You look like a slow-motion Firefox," a voice called, referring to an old Clint Eastwood movie.

"Bit low there, Blowtorch. Cool—yes, but maybe move 'er up a smidge!" Professor called over the radio. Professor was the ranking officer. The Chinook moved up to its legal limit. No answer, just action. The rooster tail was still there, not as pronounced but still cool.

"Looks like a flaming dog fart," a voice called over the radio to point fun.

"Nice," another supported.

"Ha-ha! Funny," a sarcastic tone responded, obviously from the Chinook.

"Shakedown 25 Flight, this is Blowtorch. Satellite call from Ops Freedom Ops . . . wait out." There was a pause while the message came through. The Griffons did not have Satcom, but the Chinook did.

"We are diverting the formation to FOB Frontenac. Shakedown 30 has taken hits around Tarin Kowt and is attempting to get to the FOB," the Chinook announced. "Once we get over the ridge, you should be able to directly contact operations."

"Roger that," I answered.

"Check that," Professor also acknowledged.

"Crap! Who was 30? Grumpy? They have taken hits, guys," I voiced to my crew.

"Ya, 30 is Grumpy's crew," Snapshot responded. "If they are attempting to get to Frontenac, that would suggest they should be okay. That's good news so far," he added logically to inspire hope.

The lumbering Chinook steered right, climbing over the jagged ridge of mountains diverting our formation toward Frontenac. We had to cross two large mountain ranges and the Dalah Lake, a half hour away.

"Ops, this Shakedown two-five," I called to establish communications.

"Wait out!" Scrappy responded. It was barely audible because of the distance. He was busy sorting out the emergency. As we climbed higher, the story started to unfold on the radio as communications could be heard between Butch in Blowtorch 60 and Grumpy's section.

"Ops, this is Blowtorch 60. Shakedown 30 has taken hits. No communications are available with him at this time. No status on crews. The helicopter is flying toward FOB Frontenac. We have no other news. They appear to be in control. We are in trail. 31 and myself are okay. ETA ten minutes. 60, out!" Butch intensely stated. *Out* not only meant he was finished talking, but his tone also meant he wanted silence on the radio for the time being. He was busy sorting shit out.

Freedom Operations

"All right, everyone, listen up!" Scrappy called, continuing to make his commands to his staff.

"Advise Task Force HQ and the wing commander." He looked at his duty officer and then aimed his attention to Ricky and continued, "Get Frontenac on the phone and tell them to get ready. I have no idea how many casualties are on board, but it's possible all four could have injuries. Make sure they have medics ready." They stared back at him, waiting for more. "Do it!" They all started making phone calls.

"Operations, this is 60. 30 is on final approach crossing the wire at Frontenac," Butch's voice sounded.

"Butch, are you hit?" Scrappy radioed in return.

"Nope, I think we're good," he replied.

Scrappy continued to direct us now that he had awareness on Grumpy's section. "62, be prepared to conduct medevac to Role 3, until we know for sure. I'm advising TFK to get Dustoff medevac chopper on standby for any casualties," Scrappy's voice commanded. "However, I think you are closest."

"62, roger. Ten minutes out." Our formation was approaching the headwaters of the Arghandhab River near Shawali Cott.

"Butch, this is Ops," Scrappy called. "When Grumpy is safely on the ground, you and 31 (Fender) get back here for a battle damage assessment," he ordered. "62 is inbound with Steve and Prof to support 30 (Grumpy)."

"Roger, out," he bluntly responded, somewhat stressed. Anxiety could be sensed in the tone of the voices on each radio, yet everyone maintained professional discipline. We had no idea who was hit, bleeding out, or dead.

In Our Aircraft

"Fuck. I hope everyone's okay," Zorg stated with concern.

"They are flying. That's a good sign," Snapshot reaffirmed.

I looked at Irish. We both were expressionless. Worried.

Five minutes later, Blowtorch 60 broke the radio silence, announcing, "Shakedown 30 is on the ground, and everyone is walking around outside with thumbs-up. We got four thumbs-up! They are okay!" Butch's voice rejoiced.

"Roger that. Confirmation coming on the phone now from the FOB." Scrappy's tone relaxed as he also received a confirmatory phone call from the American FOB commander. Now he had to reorganize the lifts and get the passengers where they needed to be. "All right, 60 and Shakedown 31, you guys finish that drop to Nathan Smith and then bring your helicopters back to KAF."

"Blowtorch 60, roger, out."

"31, roger, out," they both responded consecutively.

We arrived over Frontenac just as the two helicopters climbed south toward Kandahar city. I could see the one downed Griffon and the four guys looking around the aircraft.

"Oh man, I can breathe again," Snapshot exhaled.

"62 Flight, this is Ops. The Griffon is staying in Frontenac. However, load Grumpy's team and bring them back. 25 and 26, remain in escort," Scrappy continued, announcing his plan.

"Roger that. I'm descending in for pickup," 62 called over his radio.

The large tandem rotor helicopter spiraled down to pick up Grumpy, Hollywood, and the team. Professor and I orbited the sky watching the activity below, everyone speculating on the story.

"62, how's it going down there?" I asked as he sat on the ground loading the downed airmen.

"I don't have too much detail right now. The chopper is intact. No one is injured; but Grumpy's white!" he exclaimed over the radio. "We'll chat back in KAF."

They lifted, and we trailed for the twenty-minute flight. Speculation began about Grumpy's situation. They had just been tasked for Tarin Kowt and were near the Devil's Belly Button. Was it a TIC? Perhaps an IED?

As soon as we shut down at the ramp in KAF, we joined the massive rush of squadron members meeting Grumpy's crew who were strolling down the back ramp off the Chinook.

The four chopperless crew sauntered across X-ray ramp facing the inquiry of concerned colleagues. Hollywood first.

"We got shot down! It was awesome! About 6 inches from my foot!" exclaimed Hollywood. "The blade took some hits too but just a few tiny holes—and there was dust and shit bouncing off the dashboard. Our comms went out—*khersshhhhh!*" he simulated the radio's static sound. "You could hear the bullets whipping by the door—*snap, snap, snap!*" His eyes were big, excited.

"I am gonna get so much street cred for this," he continued, referring to his former infantry buddies. "Fuck yeah." He punched my shoulder and walked on to share his story, still vibrating in excitement.

Grumpy was not as enthused. Pale and shocked, he shook his head at Hollywood's enthusiasm. "Dumb fuck doesn't realize what just happened, but at least he's positive about the whole thing." He smiled lightly, still shaking his head.

"Is everything okay? What happened?" I asked.

"We got a bit too separated, and I was too low over the ridge. It was like they were waiting for the opportunity, and I gave it to them," he explained, lecturing himself and me. He wanted us to take notice of the wake-up call; we all relaxed a little too much perhaps.

"You could hear the rounds zipping by, and then the nose had a huge smacking sound. Some bullets hit the wiring harness and the entire intercom system went white noise. I couldn't talk to anyone. Fender realized something was wrong as I turned around to the FOB. He figured it out and directed the rest of the formation to escort me to Frontenac. We steered clear of the belly button, the Taliban pretty much own those hills."

"Holy shit! Did Fender get hit?" I asked.

"Fender and Butch are fine, I think. They were flying much higher. They (Taliban) picked out the low bird, me, and concentrated fire."

"Ya, but you're okay, man." I tried to be encouraging as I shoved his arm.

"That was a lot of stress just for a Tarin Kowt meatball, but damn, that lunch was good!" Grumpy exclaimed, forcing a smile, trying to find something bright about the day. I returned laughter.

The sound of the remaining Chinook and Griffon could be heard coming into X-ray ramp. Fender led. In order to accommodate departing UAV traffic, they elected to come in downwind—a more complicated maneuver with less available power remaining to stop and hover.

There was a UAV and another fighter lining up on the taxiway, and it forced him to stay high and fast. He appeared to be aiming right toward his landing spot, a few feet in front of the aircraft hangars, but was coming in fast—too fast.

It seemed half the squadron staff were on the tarmac as they wanted to see the crews and inspect the aircraft for bullet holes.

"Jees, he's coming in pretty hot," Hollywood observed. "It's fuckin' downwind. He's high and hot!"

"He's trying to stay ahead of the Chinook and away from the UAV," Irish stated.

"Oh, that's not looking good," Arnie added. The three of them were observing, being distracted from the other drama.

Fender and Shorty were still contemplating the previous event. They were more concerned about Grumpy's crew than their own situation.

In Shakedown 31

"We're high over the jets and clear. Descend," Fender directed Shorty at the controls. "Shorty, you're coming in too hot. Get low and into some ground effect," he stated.

Shorty was quiet, still contemplating and flying mechanically. He was exhausted, dehydrated, and a bit stressed from the day's events.

"Yup, I got 'er," Shorty responded as he lowered the power. But the rate of closure was too high. He flared to stop and pulled power to slow, but they were at the top end of the power the Griffon could give. The inertia was winning. They flew past the landing spot and were going to crash into the hangar.

"Holy shit! He's going to crash into the hangar!" someone blurted.

It rapidly passed the landing spot and shot up into the sky, climbing over the hangar just like it had hit an invisible ski jump.

"I have control!" Fender yelled as he pulled harshly up on the collective and pulled the cyclic stick back to jump over the hangar.

"Fuck, fuck, fuck!" Shorty hollered.

The righter gunner was yelling. "Move up! Move up!"

They hopped over the hangar and dropped, disappearing on the other side. I could still hear it making noise. No crash sound. He was still flying—a good sign.

Skipper was out watching the entire show. He looked at Professor; he was pissed off and pointing to the senior people in the crowd, indicating he wanted a meeting soon. It was time to slow the boys down. He departed the ramp toward his office. He had his own war to diffuse.

A few moments later, Fender's helicopter reappeared from the opposite direction. It slowly taxied in shame to the far parking lines almost like it had its tail boom between its legs.

"You think anyone noticed?" Shorty smiled at Fender.

"Absolutely not," Fender answered sarcastically as he touched the chopper down on the far landing spot, shying from the crowds.

I couldn't decide whom to query first. I still had my flight gear on and tourniquets around my ankles, which is where my jaw was too. The calmest people in this entire collection of craziness were Grumpy and Butch. And they were the ones that you'd expect to be heightened.

Off in the distance, Shorty and Fender were having a discussion. The remaining people, about forty, joined in the bullet hole search while discussing the air show over the hangar. I decided to join the search.

I saw Butch as others scoured for holes.

"You all right?" I asked.

"Yeah, quite an air show today!" he giggled.

"Did you get hit?"

"No, I don't think so. I heard a big clang, but I looked back at the side door gunner. He appeared to have dropped his ammo box—so we continued to drop off our payload," he explained.

"I found a hole!" someone yelled, pointing at the Chinook's external fuel tank.

Butch's eyebrows rose. "Hmmm," he moaned, turned his head to the side, and twisted his face, as usual. "Well, I'll be damned. Let's go see!" he said.

Hordes of people trotted over to the massive Chinook to spot the tiny small hole in the external fuel tank. The one tiny hole had closed in on itself, sealing it from external oxygen to prevent explosion. The technicians went to the other side looking for an exit hole. However, there was no exit hole. They removed the ammunition box that had fell, hoping to find a hole.

"Huh, I thought that was the ammo box I heard fall in flight," Butch observed.

"Yes, sir, it did fall," the right gunner stated as he explored for damage with the technician. "I heard that thump in flight as well. I watched it tip." A technician began to remove equipment from around the gunner's position.

"There doesn't seem to be an exit hole, but this bulk head is a bit crimpled," he noted as he inspected the inside structure of the helicopter. He looked at the other side to compare. ""Yes, it's lifted and pushed out. Were you empty?" the technician asked.

"Yes, external fuel tanks were empty," Butch answered.

"The bullet ignited the fumes. That bang you heard was an explosion. That's why the ribs are bent," he added. This added volume to the murmur of the dozens of helping people around the helicopter.

Butch went white. "Everyone, settle down. Get back to your primary jobs. Supervisors to the CO's briefing room in ten minutes. The remainder of you, if you don't have anything to do, don't do it here," he yelled, taking control of the frenzy. "I know you want answers. You will be briefed once we wrap up this fiasco. Let maintenance do their jobs!" Everyone dispersed.

After quick debriefs, our crewmembers, less supervisors, drove back to the south side. Everyone was quiet—reflecting on the day. Grumpy was upset with himself. Irish looked scared. Arnie just wanted to get to the gym. Hollywood couldn't wait to tell his friends. Fender looked embarrassed, and Shorty was extremely fatigued and unusually quiet. Everyone dispersed into their rooms. I lay in my bunk contemplating. It's nothing like life in Canada or training could ever match; it's not normal, but here it was normal.

A few hours later, after some gym decompression and food, I flipped back the piece of canvass separating my dusky room from the hallway. I listened to Fender plucking his guitar, relaxing.

Arnie was listening to Hollywood at the other end of the tent rewinding the day, using hands to illustrate. They made bullet sounds describing the assault on their choppers.

Professor was absent. He would be in meetings late with Skipper discussing the critical events over the past few days. Shorty was still quiet; he shuffled into his room, embarrassed. He hadn't had his usual wit about him today or especially during the past couple of weeks; usually he stayed up late and was the person with the lights out last. This time, the lights seemed to dim.

"Plink, plink, plink, plink, plink." I recognized the familiar tune of "Stairway to Heaven" being plucked out through the canvas that separated my chamber from Fender's.

BLAM!

"Holy shit! Shots fired!" I called out. There was a gunshot in the tent. I could smell the cordite. What the fuck? It sounded like Shorty's space. Oh no, did the pressure get to him? Did he snap? I thought the worst.

I looked out of my flapping door and across the hall. Grumpy's head peaked out at the other end of the hall looking toward me with the same freaked-out expression. Fender also joined the inquiry.

"I'm afraid to look," I said.

"Did he off himself? Fuck." Grumpy started to lunge forward.

"Fender, you go see," I stated.

"Ya, right. Me? Fuck. He's my copilot." He surrendered, leaning forward.

Shorty's flap calmly opened. His head popped out of the canvass flap, and he stared back at the hallway of eyes. "What?" he said angrily. "No, assholes. I wasn't gonna off myself. I just accidentally assassinated my fuckin' barrack box while cleaning my pistol. Sheesh!" he stated matter-of-factly. He started to shove by to the exit.

"Now, if you'll excuse me, I'm going to call the MPs (military police) and have myself arrested." He walked by. Everyone was expressionless until he exited the tent and then burst out laughing.

We raced into his room to inspect the carnage. Sure enough, there was a bullet hole through the top of his barrack box and then the back and then cleanly out the lower tent wall and into the sand bag directly behind.

"Well, at least he aimed low when he cleared it." Grumpy smiled. "If he had it raised, he would have put a round into the Dutch Oven Night Club next door. I'm going to bed." We all began laughing and rolled back into our respective tent spaces.

"I survive a Taliban attack and then almost get killed by a copilot cleaning his pistol. Fuck!" Grumpy mumbled to himself as he walked back down the hallway.

"G'nite, guys. It was a good day. We are all on this side of the sod," I hollered as I lay on my bed. "Glad you're okay, Grumpy." I stared at the clothes dangling from the rod above my bed and listened to Fender resume "Stairway to Heaven."

Chapter 21

Fog of Battle

"It's serviceable enough to fly. You have got to be bloody joking!" The SAMEO was on the phone from the Ottawa Headquarters Bureaucrats. "The test pilot, an engineer, and two technicians are in Frontenac with the bird and says they are ready. There are only two tiny bullet holes in the blades. It's safe to fly back from Frontenac."

He was discussing with Ottawa how to get Grumpy's aircraft back to KAF. Grumpy's team was in Frontenac ready to make the fifteen-minute flight back to KAF, where repairs could be made in a safer environment. However, they needed authority from maintenance headquarters in Ottawa for the short flight. No one in Ottawa wanted to stick their career neck out and make the unusual decision.

I walked into the TOC. "Good day, guys. How's the war?" I asked Scrappy as I arrived for my preflight briefings.

"Great! Shhhh . . . just listen to the entertainment. He'll be done in a sec, and then we can brief," Scrappy whispered and pointed to the open door the SAMEO was behind. "Ottawa," he added to clue me in.

"Ahhh, right!" I quietly stated, smirking, and listened.

"You guys don't have a goddamned clue what's going on here!" The SAMEO's voice began to get louder. "The aircraft is fine, and every hour it remains in Frontenac, it brings higher risk of drawing enemy mortars in possibly getting itself destroyed, not to mention injuring the Americans on that base. It's gotta come out now!"

"You what? You want me to take two rotor blades out, change them, and test fly it over there until it's serviceable?" He was yelling now. The staff in the TOC started to remove themselves for coffee, all pointing to the most junior member to remain behind to keep it manned.

"That's asinine! For the time it takes to test fly new blades, I could have it back here and fixed safely!" he continued. "Maintenance protocols? You're policies are putting my guys at risk! What? Goddammit! This conversation is over." *Slam.*

The phone was hung up. He walked into the TOC seeing us eavesdropping. His face was red and brow crumpled with ferocity. He looked at Scrappy. "You have maintenance authority to move the aircraft here with an escort! Get my machine back here please. I going to see Skipper then the wing commander," he flatly stated and continued walking toward the commanding officers' office.

Scrappy nodded and picked up another phone. "Grumpy, yep, you guys are authorized to fly. Bring 'er home." He hung up and looked toward me, stating rhetorically. "I think there is going to be another shit storm from Ottawa today. Steer clear of the Skipper and the wing commander today. Better lay low," he concluded. I nodded and left. I looked at the schedule. "But Skipper is my wingman today."

An Hour Later on X-Ray Ramp

Skipper and Arnie flew together on my wing today. He was not in a great mood. Regardless, he was going to the frontlines today to escape the harsher battles of the bureaucratic frontlines. We briefed, met by the aircraft, and commenced rituals. No one was sure what the Skipper's ritual was. Perhaps it was the dusty 10-kilometer bike ride through the obstacle course of potholes and military vehicles from the south side of KAF. If he could survive the bike ride, he could easily survive the Taliban—but could he survive HQ Ottawa?

On the ramp, I was conducting a quick preflight rub of my Griffon, checking the flares, gun mounts, and MX-15 before climbing in. I looked over to Skipper's chopper—he seemed to be doing something similar.

"What the hell is this?" I heard a loud holler and turned my attention to Skipper. He wasn't aware of Arnie's ritual. He was bent down behind the aircraft under the tail end. He smeared his fingers along a puddle on the ground and then lifted them under his nose. He was suspecting an oil leak but instead discovered Arnie's ritualistic piss puddle.

"This smells like . . . piss. Who the hell is pissing on my tarmac?" He was furious.

I looked at my crew in panic. There would be an inquiry. And I definitely couldn't look at anyone else for fear of breaking out in laughter, revealing my knowledge.

"Start it, start it!" I called to my crew. "Before he comes over and asks." Irish held his index finger up, signaling Snapshot to start number 1 engine. Irish hit the starter just as Skipper started to walk toward them.

The engine igniters snapped, and then the turbine lit and whined to life. The rotor started to turn. Skipper stopped. He lowered and clenched his jaw. He knew something was up and retreated to his own chopper.

Arnie's eyes were big. He slid his visor down, covering them, and then tucked his chin low, hiding his expression.

"I think Skipper tasted it!" Zorg stated, laughing over the intercom. Everyone broke out laughing.

"Ohhh, Arnie is so busted!" Zorg stated.

We continued the start procedure, glancing occasionally toward Skipper to speculate on the interrogation. From the look of the crew, Arnie was already getting a lecture.

Irish completed the system's checks as I prepared the GPS and MX-15, ensuring the infrared camera was calibrated. The mission today was patrol overwatch in Nakhoney. Our team was highly motivated.

Recently, we noticed a change in the Taliban tactics, making it even more necessary to be vigilant. The usual small team IED attacks were increasing in size and frequency. We needed to be alert and aggressive.

"Shakedown 25 Flight, this is Slayer TOC. I have an observation task for you."

"Go for Shakedown," I replied.

"Proceed to FOB Madras, Nakhoney area. There was an RPG attack earlier. There is an unexploded RPG warhead and possible Taliban recovery operations in effect. Contact 21," Slayer informed.

"You heard 'em, Skipper. Off to Nakhoney," I radioed my wingman.

"Check that. Taliban recovering an unexploded RPG round," he acknowledged.

"Yes, this should be a fun search mission. I'm so excited I could pee," I radioed. My crew started laughing.

"Very funny," Arnie dryly acknowledged, indicating he had been reprimanded.

I transmitted to Madras. "21, this is Shakedown, checking in."

"Morning, Shakedown. Area is clear. FOB is secure. We just had a small arms and RPG attack an hour ago. I-comm chatter is indicating that someone is going to recover the RPG round about 1,500 meters south in the grape rows. It is unexploded, and we want to intercept before it is reused."

"Roger that. Shakedowns copy. We'll orbit and get some optics on the field," I responded.

"Roger that, Shakedown. Otherwise, it is pretty quiet right now. Let me know of any POL changes. 21, out."

"Roger, out." I switch radios to direct Skipper. "My plan is to go high overwatch and scan the area with the MX-15. Stay on my wing for now. I'll send you lower if we find anything."

"Roger that," he acknowledged. He did not have the MX-15 today. So my role was find and fix. His role would be to 'finish.'

We established a large orbit scanning the grape fields. The grape leaves were budding, making it difficult to see into the rows. However, we spotted a bicycle and focused in that area. Someone was spotted scouring through the rows obviously searching for something.

"Contact, FAM, white clothes, north edge of the field," I called.

"Contact, FAM," Skipper acknowledged.

"Okay, Irish, hold the orbit. I'm on him with the camera. He's digging under the plants . . . wait. He's got something. Damn, he's putting his back toward us. He just lifted something about a foot long under his man jammies, and it's slung over his neck."

Zorg was leaning up front watching the MX-15 monitor. "Oh, that's an RPG warhead. Look at the shape of the cone. His clothes aren't hiding anything," Zorg stated.

"I agree. Irish?" I asked for confirmation.

"Yup, definitely." He leaned over to look at the monitor.

"Skip, camera is on and recording," I radioed. "He has an RPG-shaped projectile under his clothes. He is getting on his bike heading north. Stand by," I advised.

"21, this is Shakedown. The FAM has a projectile-shaped round under his jammies. He is proceeding north to the southwest corner of Nakhoney by bicycle," I further reported to the infantry company.

"Roger, continue tracking," 21 replied.

"We are gonna lose him if he gets to town, sir," Zorg stated.

"I know. Stand by," I stated. Time was slipping away. That RPG had to be captured or the target destroyed, otherwise it would be used again against the Canadians and ANA. I called Slayer and reported the same.

"Slayer, TOC. Roger, we acknowledge. Did you physically see the projectile?" Slayer stated.

"Negative, only the shape under the jammies. I have it on MX-15 feed," I answered.

"Roger, stand by," Slayer responded.

"The FAM is getting closer to the village. We're gonna lose him," Irish exclaimed.

"I know. I know. We gotta wait," I answered.

"Skipper, get lower and in position to anticipate a fire order," I directed.

"Roger, but I don't see any weapon." He had doubt. He did not have the MX-15 camera and couldn't see what I saw. He needed to see a threat.

I watched the FAM looking toward us as he rode his bike toward the town. He was 150 meters from town and stopped. I zoomed in until his face filled a quarter of the TV monitor. He looked toward me and started to talk into his collar.

"I-comm chatter," India 21 reported.

"Go for Shakedown," I answered.

"I-comm chatter reads, Voice 1: I have the package. I am coming into town to you. Voice 2: Good, bring it to town. Voice 1: The helicopter is above me. Voice 2: Bring the package."

"Wow! I'm watching his lips move seconds before the I-comm chatter as he looks at me. He's a target! That's all we need. We are good to go. Getting fire orders from Slayer," I reported.

"Slayer, TOC, did you receive the I-comm chatter? I got it on the camera as he was speaking. I got him actually looking at me as I-comm chatter called in," I requested.

"This is Slayer. Roger that. I copy all. You are cleared to fire on that target. Cleared to fire," Slayer ordered.

"26, this is 25. We are cleared to engage that target," I ordered to Skipper. "Your shot. Be quick. He is almost in town."

Skipper was a little too far to engage at the moment the orders lined up, but his helicopter banked aggressively to align the guns with the target.

"Roger, I check we are cleared hot. Inbound hot!" Skipper answered.

"He's gonna miss the shot. Target is too close to town!" Zorg yelled. "We can get in there from here. Let's get in there."

"Steady, Zorg! He's got it."

"Shakedowns, check fire, check fire. Do not shoot. We want to intercept," India 21 announced just as Skipper was to pull the trigger.

"We have fire orders. Cleared hot by Slayer," I argued.

"Negative, we want him," 21 countercommanded.

"Fuck!" I yelled over the intercom. I was frustrated. The moment was surreal. It all formulated so easily yet was falling apart in the execution. I was out of position for a shot. Skip was in position but did not see what I saw, so he was hesitant. Slayer authorized the shot; India 21 said not to shoot.

The FAM was quickly approaching town, and the shot would be lost. The warhead would be used again on a Canadians, and there would be death if he wasn't stopped. I couldn't believe I was making life-and-death decisions on the fly. Investigator, police, prosecutor, judge, and jury—all in a day's job—not even a day, a half a tank of gas actually.

"I'm out. Checking fire," Skipper announced.

"Roger that, come back on my wing and we'll track him," I sighed, confused and frustrated.

"He is too close to the village anyway. There are people in the compound that he is approaching," I stated.

"That goddammed FAM is gonna getting away—again!" Zorg was angry. It was personal. Those were his brother's getting shot at down there in Nakhoney every day. He had a chance to remove a fighter but was denied.

We orbited the town. The FAM was proceeding toward north entrance of the FOB. The road was getting busier, about a dozen people walking around. Normal POL. He pulled his hat off. He couldn't have been more than seventeen years old—a kid. Was he a fighter or being manipulated to extract the RPG? I didn't have time to contemplate that—right now, he was a combatant.

"21, this is Shakedown. The FAM is approaching your armored vehicle, north gate, about 100 meters straight in front of you. There are about four people. He is briskly walking by the front gate road," I reported as the FAM approached. He was now on foot. He ditched his bicycle.

"Looking. I don't see him," 21 answered.

"He was wearing white. The sling under his arm is carrying the RPG warhead." I was agitated; he was getting away.

"Negative contact."

"Get out there. He's right in front," I exclaimed.

The FAM moved quickly and timed it, so a few other people also crisscrossed his path. He passed the front gate. He eluded the infantry that were about fifty yards away. He made a quick left turn around a corner and then a right turn and then entered a compound.

"Okay, I got him. He's in a compound. Stand by for coordinates," I stated, looking at my MX-15 GPS readout.

"Send . . ."

"Grid QQ43058800, a compound with the door facing south to the road. It's approximately 150 meters from the FOB entrance," I reported.

"Roger. I copy that, Shakedown," India 21 reported.

"You need us for anything else?" I asked. My adrenalin was peaked. I was psychologically crashing. I needed a break. He was a kid.

"Negative, Shakedown. Cleared off task. Thanks. We're preparing for a hard knock shortly. We'll find something." India 21 released us.

"I coulda had that shot," Zorg vented his frustration at the process, which ignited my frustration.

"It's done now!" I exclaimed. "There was too much confusion. I had clarity. Skip didn't. Slayer did. India 21 didn't. It was fucked up!" I bellowed, justifying the abort. "Plus, he was a fuckin' kid."

"Kid? I joined when I was seventeen, sir," Zorg stated very calmly.

"So did I," Irish added.

I paused. I was silent. So did I. We flew home quietly.

In my dreams, I relive the event. And I can easily justify shooting the target, a FAM, a kid.

During a psychological briefing before deploying, we were coached that whether legally right or wrong, we have to be able to sleep at night and live with the decision of pulling the trigger. And I can sleep. When

I relive the situation to a different outcome, I can still sleep. However, those are in my dreams.

The drawbridge between dreams and nightmares is up, separating them. However, if the bridge falls, the battle between the angels and demons will start, and I fear for what lay in my sleep at night. It takes great energy to keep the bridge up and stay on top of the fog of battle.

Chapter 22

Stargai Kwan

It was many months into my tour. By this time, I had unintentionally removed both tourniquets and was getting use to the TIC support, rocket attacks, area of operations, and the 2:45 a.m. wake-up routines.

Many of the members of Roto 8, Task Force Freedom, had been home to Canada for their first of two fourteen-day breaks from theater. For those of us exposed to "outside the wire" operations daily, trying to calm down for two weeks was mentally challenging. Although friends would see the relaxed attitude on the faces of the warrior, family members could recognize that our minds and souls were not relaxed— that they were still in KAF.

For me, it was surreal. What was my first break like? It was a few months earlier than now, I remember going through airport security in KAF at the TLS. I took out my combat knife and handed it in for security clearing. My knife had to be secured so I wouldn't have access to it on the flight, normal protocols. I remember the irony of watching the infantry machine gunner in front of me put his C9 machine gun through the X-ray machine just to pick it up on the other side of security – yet I couldn't have my knife.

I arrived in Dubai at Camp Mirage on Christmas Day. In Mirage, there was green grass, clean buildings, and civilized happy Canadian soldiers supporting the daily airlift into Afghanistan. It was nothing like KAF. There was an outdoor entertainment stage that played evening movies.

Tonight was Christmas Eve. A pastor gave a sermon, and people sang carols. It was delightful, yet I couldn't release my thoughts from colleagues who at that moment were tracking IED planters or providing overwatch.

On return, I was to participate in a large-scale mission that would use a large percentage of the NATO helicopters in Southern Afghanistan, but no information was passed at this point. Only that it could be really messy.

I spent Christmas Day at the beaches in Dubai and touring the malls and world's largest skyscraper. I had to return to Camp Mirage in the afternoon to catch my evening flight to Canada. A man dressed as Santa Claus was entertaining the Christian families at a resort in town that I walked through. It was ironic how a primarily Muslim country would offer the respect to indulge the Western traditions, yet in Afghanistan, Taliban would execute the same behavior and claim it justified under Sharia law.

I arrived in Canada the next day. It took time to relax over the holidays. I met my family in Victoria, on the west coast of Canada. For the first time in my life, I truly embraced the early morning walk in the cold drizzly west coast weather. No dust. No poo pond.

I went to a local coffee shop early in the morning just prior to New Year and pulled up a seat with a newspaper. I read the first page: "4 Canadian Soldiers and One Reporter Killed." I started to shake as I read the article. A twenty-one-year-old soldier, a young man from my home town was dead. He was just a kid. It hit me hard I can't explain why. Maybe it was that he wasn't much older than my recent target, or that I was on a break from the war, but the war brought death into my home.

My eyes swelled up, and I turned to the window in the coffee shop to hide my tears, sipping coffee to cover up and gain composure. I couldn't stop thinking about his family. I walked back to be with mine. I visited relatives for a few more days and then proceeded back to my hometown to reintegrate into regular family lifestyle for the second half of my time off.

I loved being with my family: daily routine, sports games. I couldn't help to think of how much we took for granted as a civilized society. This is worth protecting, even if I have to die for it.

My break vanished quickly. I wanted to be home, but I needed to get back to KAF and get it done. My soul was locked up until this year in Afghanistan was complete. I wasn't sure if I was guarding my soul or just accepting mortality in order to quit worrying about it. How could one tell the difference?

KAF

I arrived, pseudo-refreshed and ready. My first visit was Freedom Operations. I knew I wouldn't fly since the Canadian Headquarters wouldn't allow flights within three days in order to allow acclimatization and eleven hours of jet lag to catch up.

"How was your time off?" Scrappy asked.

"Great, went to the west coast, experienced this thing called rain," I sarcastically responded. "It was nice to have dust-free breathing for a couple of weeks."

Scrappy chuckled.

"How's the family?"

"Good, busy. School keeps them occupied. Sports. My daughter's team won gold in a tournament a few days ago, and one of the parents treated my family to breakfast as a thank-you for my service. It was very nice, touching." I smiled reflectively. "So what's up?"

"Shania right away," Scrappy informed. "But you can't go out for a couple of days until your jet lag is over."

"Isn't that a night op?" I queried.

"Yup," Scrappy answered bluntly, knowing where I was leading.

"I'm already switched to nights due to the twelve-hour time change, so why not get into the program now?" I retorted at the ridiculous policy.

"I know. It's ridiculous. You have to switch your body clock to days, just so we can switch you back to nights in two days, and then after that, we can do whatever we want with your schedule—it's the rules from HQ Canada." Scrappy rolled his eyes. "Just keep your body on nights—then the show is on."

I nodded begrudgingly. I went to the flight planning room and started reviewing intelligence reports, maps, and the battle text feed on the TV to catch up.

"It's Groundhog Day," Grumpy commented, referring to the Bill Murray film when he saw me reviewing the information. "Nothing has changed. They plant bombs at night, blow up schools and vehicles on the highway in the morning, patrol at day, exchange fire, rocket attack at 7:00 p.m., up at 2:45 a.m. Then do it again. So now you're caught up." His arm pivoted already to the vertical to show his GAFF (give a fuck factor) had peaked.

I stared back at him. "You need a break to go home, don't you?"

"Yup, next week after Shania," Grumpy responded with a twisted smile.

Shania was in Helmand, home of two large bases: American Marine Base Leatherneck and British Base Bastion. They weren't as large as KAF, but they were powerful. Over the next few weeks, the Canadians would be part of numerous missions to assist the Brits in stabilizing and gaining a foothold in Southern Helmand Province, especially Nad Ali and Marjeh.

Since I would be away from my routine phone call home, I made an effort to make Skype calls, but I couldn't tell my wife why I wouldn't be calling. After several months of these calls, she started to recognize the difference between a Tornado jet fighter and an F-16 as they blasted over my tent, drowning out the calls.

"How's everything at home?" I yelled into the microphone.

"Good, the kids have dental appointments this week," she responded.

"I wish I could help you out, sorry." That's all I could think of saying. That all I ever seemed to say: sorry I'm not there to help; sorry I missed that birthday; sorry you're not feeling well, and I am here, blah, blah, blah. It was the life of a soldier, one more piece of guilt we carried around.

"Everything okay there?" She asked.

"Yes, I won't be able to call for a few—" I started.

Varoosh! A jet roared over my tent. I plugged my ears. Our tents were directly under the circuit pattern of the fighters.

"Just a sec," I yelled.

As the noise dissipated in the distance, I continued, "Yes, I am going—"

"Wait for his wingman," she interrupted. She learned they always travelled in pairs.

Varoosh!

"You're getting to know the fighter jet patterns better than me!" I chuckled.

"You were saying?" She laughed.

"I'm going on a, ah, ah, a cross-country trainer. Won't be around for a while," I fibbed.

"Okay, better go, love you," she stated. She knew I was doing something out of the ordinary. However, she didn't even know in the ordinary but assumed there were risks. This made her nervous. She was guarding her heart.

We finished our conversation. I rolled over on my bunk and fell asleep listening to the Black-Eyed Peas in my headphones, reflecting on the ringette game.

"Tonight's gonna be a good night . . ."

Stargai Kwan

The next evening, I departed with a significant portion of the Canadian Aviation Battalion composed of a five-helicopter formation of two Chinooks and three Griffons to FOB Bastion. OP Stargai Kwan was going to be simple, night insertion. The Brits would use the two Canadian Chinooks to insert a company of Polish infantry into a hot area. It would be controlled by British Apache helicopters. Task Force Freedom was one of the prongs on the advancing multinational fork including British, Americans, and other NATO nations.

Many of these missions were semi-invasive to gain intelligence by assessing the enemy response. Every action has a reaction. So the NATO forces poked and then observed the result, which then shaped ideas of how to execute subsequent missions.

Working with multinationals was an education. The command and control made things more complicated. Different interpretations of the rules of engagement had to be mutually agreed upon prior to starting. For example, if Americans were working on British-controlled ground with Canadian officers in charge, which nation's ROE was used?

The Brits were focused on respecting the process. The Americans focused on the outcome. The Canadians were somewhere in the middle. I personally enjoyed the American style, simple to follow. The Brits were more rigid.

We arrived at midnight for our mission orders. The execution was the following night. I was to escort two Chinooks into a landing zone and then orbit south. Unfortunately, between the Griffons and the

Chinooks was an RFL (restrictive fire line). It is a control measure placed upon the Griffon gunners that prevented us from shooting anything across that line. However, the line separated us from our Chinook, the very entity we were to protect. Any suspected targets were to be passed to the Apache lead (call sign Ugly) to prosecute.

After orders, we took our sleeping bags and meandered through the dark streets of Bastion to a smaller version of a BAT (big ass tent). The tent was empty except for several aircraft technicians that had already settled into get some sleep. It was about 4:00 a.m. I stumbled around some people with my head mounted flashlight guiding the way. There wasn't much space, but I found an empty cot along a wall near the back of the dust-covered canvass. I heard snores of people sleeping nearby. I sighed knowing it would be a sleepless night. I closed my eyes and counted a few snore patterns and fell asleep until what seemed to be a few moments later, Big C was shoving my cot in the morning.

"Better get up if you want to get some lunch," he stated.

It took a minute to orient myself. Victoria? Dubai? KAF? Edmonton? Nope—definitely not Edmonton. Ah, Bastion. "Thanks, man!" I answered, wiping the crusty dust out of my eyes. I could see the intense sunlight piercing through the door flap and various other holes in the large BAT.

"Arnie, you getting up?" I asked.

"Uuunggh. Not hungry. I'll wait for dinner." He rolled over and went back to sleep.

I stretched. I wasn't in my sleeping bag. I must have climbed on top during my sleep to escape the heat. The morning sun heated the BAT like a sauna. Most of the captains were walking over to the shower tent. Copilots, as usual, slumbered away.

"How are we going to work around an RFL?" I asked Fender regarding the mission.

"I know. It sucks. If the Chinooks are engaged. We can't do anything immediately. Why are we even here if they won't let us protect them?" he stated rhetorically.

"Skipper told them that if they want Canadian Chinooks, they'll get Canadian escort too. We are a package deal," I repeated.

"So this will be fucked up if shit goes down?" Fender stated. "Ugly (the Apache), better be ready."

"Let's just hope intel is right," Big C interjected. "There's not supposed to be any threat in that LZ. It's been watched for two days by UAV. So relax. I saw this sort of stuff all the time in Iraq. No sweat. Just call it if you see it."

"Yea, but weren't you an Apache pilot for that?" I countered.

Big C smiled, curved up smile, threw a towel over his shoulder, and walked out of the tent. He was calm.

Stargai was a go. It was a red illumination night. It was dark with no moon; it would be challenging even with the NVGs. We had two Chinooks to protect. Fender was the lead navigator. All the crews were in their respective helicopters with the engines idling, gun checks complete, and standing by for our turn. Dozens of helicopters departed in order as per the timing chart.

"You guys ready to roll?" I asked the crew.

"Roger that, Haycee," Snapshot answered.

"Check," Gunny stated. "There are the passengers!" He noted a huge line of Polish soldiers slowly walking toward the back of the Chinooks. They were probably at least sixty altogether. They disappeared into the back of the helicopter and positioned themselves for a quick egress into a possible fight.

"Should be any second now, and the air show will begin. Remember, we have that fuckin' RFL, so don't shoot anyone without advising me," I ordered in jest. They chuckled.

"Blowtorch formation—check-in," ordered the lead Chinook.

"61, 25, 26, 30" were the sequential answers. The call was exactly as per the X-check (the timeline). This one was quite simple.

At the designated departure time, the five Canadian helicopters would fly into the target area, make sure the Chinooks landed safely, climb to altitude, and observe with the MX-15. The third Griffon would climb even higher and observe all. Skipper was on that with Big C; he was 30.

The first wave of troops lifted off. I was getting excited. It was a very dangerous area, but the intelligence reports indicated no activity. It should be straightforward.

The second wave lifted to go toward the east. We were next in one minute. Blowtorch prepared everyone by lifting into the hover and maneuvering away from the Griffons, so it didn't blast us with the powerful downwash. Arnie then lifted into the hover, a nonradio signal indicating we were ready.

"Bastion Tower, Blowtorch departing." Butch's voice came over the radio. It would be one call for all five choppers.

The thundering sounds of the small Canadian contingent lifted down the short runway and over the large defensive wall toward the south. We raced across the desert floor toward the green zone, Nad Ali. It was dark and featureless. Up ahead, the edge of Nad Ali could be seen. There were no lights like you'd expect in a big city, just the occasional dim bulb or fire.

We crossed the navigational lead-in feature to our objective, a well-defined bend in a wadi. 26 and 30 pulled away from the formation, climbing across the RFL to illuminate the landing zone for the Chinook with the MX-15 laser beam.

"Sparkle," Butch called, asking to identify the landing zone. Fender activated his laser illuminator from several kilometers away. A big invisible infrared beam illuminated the landing zone.

"Contact sparkle. Stop sparkle," Butch confirmed. He slowed the lumbering Chinook onto the landing spot as the laser beam shut off.

I flew past to take a low last look for any possible hostiles as they touched the ground. It was clear. I climbed to rejoin Fender, allowing Ugly to continue monitoring inside the RFL.

Once in position behind Fender, I focused my camera on the Chinooks and updated my crew. "The soldiers are deplaning into their defensive posture behind the Chinook. The second Chinook is just crossing the compound and about to land."

I watched the little television showing the Polish infantry egressing into the field. I scanned the area, looking for movement.

"What the hell is that?" I studied the screen. "Keep coming around in circles!" I directed Irish.

"Wholly crap! Contact! They have weapons. One, two, three, four . . . five guys with AKs. They're dispersing around the compound!" My worst nightmare was happening.

I immediately and instinctively wanted to grab control and dive into battle, but I couldn't—RFL. Fuck. I watched the FAMs disperse to specific locations. Were they about to assault the Chinooks from behind the thick wall? They would have an advantage in the short term. I couldn't cross the line.

"Blowtorch 60, contact. You have five armed FAMs directly behind you on the other side of the compound wall. When you egress, go north, go north . . . Enemy is getting organized, not firing yet," I called into the radio.

I quickly jumped onto the fire control radio net where Ugly 14 was to be ready.

"Ugly 14, this is Shakedown, contact," I called to the one Apache overwatching the entire mission. "Fifty meters behind the Canadian Chinooks are five times FAMs with AK-47s. They are reorganizing in a compound," I advised.

"Rawga that," he informed in his high English accent. He was about 4 kilometers away at 3,000 feet above the area, but the optics with Apache was superior, and its guns were coordinated with their camera site.

"Do you have them?" I radioed.

"Negative contact, Shakedown. Looking," replied the heavy English accent.

"Fuuucccckkkk!" I drew out a long frustrated curse over the intercom. "This RFL is bullshit. I need some fire on those assholes before they kill someone!" If they engaged, they could wreck a Chinook and kill some Polish initially, but hopefully the retaliation from the Polish platoon would be overwhelming.

"Ugly 14! I'm sparkling the target now," I called, pressing my laser and held it on the Taliban. Two of them were approaching the wall on opposite side of the compound in what appeared to be preparing to fire.

"Tally targets, tally targets, tracking!" responded Ugly 14 in an excited English accent.

The Chinooks started lifting and progressing away from the Taliban. Lead was up, and the second lifted shortly thereafter. The dust ball on departure helped mask both the troops and their aircraft. Two of the Taliban were in position observing less than fifty meters away. The Polish were aiming their weapons toward the wall. They had received word from the "fire control" network of the "enemy contact" across the wall. The two Chinooks turned north once they were about 500 meters away. They were out of harm's way, but what about the Polish troops?

"You're clear now!" I called to Blowtorch.

"60, roger!" I heard Butch respond in a very relieved voice as he had been listening to my conversation with Ugly 14. His hope was to get out of the LZ before the firefight commenced. He did not like sitting vulnerable. Time probably stopped for him as he sat on that LZ knowing enemy forces were circling around to get a shot on him.

"Ugly, this is Shakedown. My Blowtorch are off the LZ. Polish friendlies east of the wall. We're egressing this time," I radioed.

"Roger that, Shakedown. Visual friendlies. Tally FAMS." Ugly responded.

And that was it! We switched off the fire control net as we cleared the ROZ to the north. We returned to FOB Bastion following the Chinooks, unsure of what happened to the threat. Ugly 14 had the capability to engage those Taliban accurately from his position, but the Polish troops were very close, perhaps too close for his 30 mm canon.

We landed, and I went over to talk with Skipper as he was chatting with Butch. The sky was light pink; the sun was just starting to rise.

"Boss?" I was pissed off. "That was fucked."

Skipper held up his hand gesturing to stop. "I got it. Just calm down. I was monitoring the entire situation with HiCom (higher command's frequency) while you were sorting it out with Ugly 14," he advised to disperse my tension. He nodded at Butch. Butch's eyes were big, and his face was whiter than usual.

"I'm starting to feel like a goddamned bullet magnet, sir!" Butch exclaimed, comparing this mission intensity to his events in Senjeray and flying over the mountains from Tarin Kowt months earlier.

Skipper raised both hands, palms up, his face gaining composure. "Butch, come with me. Steve, go get some breakfast with your guys! We will debrief in an hour."

"Yes, sir," I responded, looking at my watch.

Butch and Skipper went to the debrief representing the team. He knew my emotions were high. If I went, there would have been an international incident with the RFL discussion. Skipper would not allow me in.

I walked over to my crew. "Breakfast, guys. Skipper's got it!" I stated with confidence to my team. They accepted that. Skipper was a diplomat and warrior. They had confidence in him sorting this out.

"This food sucks!" Gunny stated, looking over at Arnie. Arnie was trying to beg the cook to let him have more food. He skipped one meal and was starving now; as a body builder, he usually consumed a fair amount of food.

"I'm gonna get puny with the two-egg limit," Arnie responded in his best Schwarzenegger impersonation while flexing his biceps.

Fender looked at me. I was stuck replaying the event in my head; it showed on my face. "No one got hurt. Let it go. We'll get it right next time," Fender stated. He picked up his coffee and sipped it.

I put my coffee down. "That's not the point!" I looked back to Fender who was sitting across the table. Fender's eyes glanced up to redirect me to someone else coming from behind me.

"The point is that we will never again be restricted from being immediately available to protect our own guys," Skipper interrupted adamantly.

"Eat up, pack up, and let's go back home. I want to be airborne in ninety minutes," Skipper stated.

Butch was smiling. He held his thumb up behind Skipper. He was still a little white in the face. "It was an interesting meeting. I don't think we'll ever have an RFL between you and me again," he added with relief. He turned to follow Skipper out and then paused.

"By the way, guys, Ugly 14 took out two of your FAMs after we left," Butch added. "It took them about twenty minutes of tracking before the weapons release authority was granted from higher. I don't know how high it had to go. The queen maybe?" he chuckled.

"You're kidding?" I stated. "If it was us, could I have given that release myself? Immediately?" I was perplexed.

"Yes—but you know the ROE. This is British. We have to play by their rules," Butch concluded. Skipper stopped to listen.

"I really don't like being in that position. You guys could have all been hit, and my job is to prevent it, but some imaginary line was stopping me," I grunted in disdain.

"It's done!" Skipper interjected. He didn't want to discuss it anymore. From his perspective, he had been forced into accepting those conditions. He was in charge and feeling pressure from his troops as well as his superiors. He was sandwiched.

"It won't be an issue anymore," he concluded sternly and walked away.

Butch was still pale but leaned forward and whispered, "This is a much bigger deal to him than it is to you." He stated quietly, smiled, and left, following the boss.

Chapter 23

Third Battalion

"All right, gents, here's the update," Scrappy started his formal Ops walk brief while pointing to the map. "Steve and Prof, you guys are with the Third Battalion this morning. I just got off the phone with the company commander. They have a patrol going out here and another in the north halfway to Masum Ghar right here."

"They want you on site. Checked in by 5:00 a.m. The guns from Sperwan Ghar will be shooting today, but all coordination will be done with call sign 3, the FOB. The commander will be orchestrating from the top of the ghar," he directed.

"Roger that, boss." I smiled. I loved these missions. Often nothing happened, and we would just fly in circles, but everyone in the crew was engaged, looking for threats, monitoring POL, and hunting bad guys.

"Any questions?" Scrappy asked.

"Negatory." I looked around at everyone receiving affirmative head nods.

"If no one has any questions, then I'll see you all between the machines at 4:00 a.m.," I concluded as the team slowly dispersed toward the flight line, some still barely awake.

The coffee was slowly activating my senses as I departed on another early mission. I appreciated this time of day more than any other. The air was cool and fresh; the pink sky slowly greeted the sun in the east. Everything was still, concealing death, fear, and hate with a false cloak of peace.

Doodle, doodle, doodle, doodle. Poof, poof, poof. I was quickly brought out of contemplation by a volley of flares shooting from my aircraft.

"Counter left!" Irish called flatly as he steered gently toward the direction of the potential missile. "Plumes?" he asked.

The flare dispenser fired a salvo of protection alerting my still sleepy crew. To the villagers below, it sounded like a volley of gun shots. However, it was not unique to them.

"Nope." Snapshot yawned. "It's clear."

"Check that. False hit," I acknowledged without flinching. This was as normal as coffee in the morning. We were desensitized. I called Slayer.

"Slayer, this Shakedown 25, en route to Sper. Checking in for an airspace update," I radioed.

"Roger that, Shakedown. ROZ is hot, guns are cold for now. There is target gun line from Sperwan Ghar westbound laid in for later today. Remain east of Sper and coordinate directly with Golf Three, the artillery. You're cleared into the ROZ." (Golf means artillery guns.)

"Okay, perfect," I echoed to the crew. "This should be simple to coordinate today. Everyone is on one frequency," I mentioned, referring to the artillery, infantry patrols, and their company commander all on the same frequency. It meant I did not have to spend half my time with my head down changing channels and coordinating with Professor.

"One stop, radio shop," rhymed Snapshot. I acknowledged his contemplation with a raised thumb.

"Roger that, Slayer. We're approaching Nakhoney now and switching to India 3 for coordination. We'll be here for the next two hours," I reported.

"Slayer out."

"Prof, put one radio on 39's frequency. The other we'll use privately between us," I directed him; coordination should be easy today.

"I'm up," he answered.

"India Three-nine, Shakedown's checking in," I called.

"Go for 39," the company commander answered.

"Shakedowns have dual MX-15, dual Dillons, sixteen thousand rounds of 7.62 and two hours playtime," I reported.

"Roger that, Shakedown. Battle update brief. I have two patrols in the AO today. India 32 is deploying through the south gate, going east along the main route, scouting a village 400 meters from the FOB. India 31 is already established in the north approximately 500 meters west of

Observation Post Brown. I need you to check in with 31 to start, and then I'll call you over to 32 once they move," India 39, the boss, stated.

"Roger, copy that," I answered.

"Prof, go trail loose and high. We'll set up a wide orbit and scout the entire area first, then focus close up for 32 after," I directed the observation plan to my wingman.

"Shakedown, this is 31. I am on patrol, line of forty troops on an east-west road along the main wadi. PID me, and then I'll tell you my plan," the platoon commander below called.

"Roger that," I responded. Irish had already started flying toward the area that Scrappy had briefed earlier. We had a rough idea of their location, but they were difficult to see until directly overhead. All the eyes were looking to find the good guys.

"Visual friendlies," Zorg called, directing everyone's eyes upon the soldiers. There was a sense of pride in Zorg's voice. He was awake now. He was thinking like a patrol soldier more than a gunner. What did the patrol need? What could they not see? Where are the hazards? Zorg was the bridge crossing the gap between the air and the land perspectives.

"Visual," I called, answering, followed shortly thereafter by Irish. Irish reversed course so Snapshot could get acquainted with the troops.

"Thanks, Irish. I got 'em," Snapshot called.

"31, this is Shakedown, visual on ya. Send your BUB," I called.

"Roger that, Shakedown. My plan is to proceed west for 1,000 meters. There is a north-south road, and we'll turn north at that point and circle back along the wadi that is approximately 400 meters to my north. I need you to check out my choke points, culverts, and compounds for the next few hundred meters and report on POL," 31 briefed.

"Roger that," I stated. "So far, the POL is normal. Compound at your twelve o'clock on the right has a several WACs (women and children) doing normal morning chores, regular movement of people on the roads ahead," I reported. Basically everything seemed normal for a peaceful day. I hoped.

"Roger, out," 31 called proceeding, feeling safer to commence their patrol. We could see the leader make a hand signal, and the patrol subsequently rose up from their kneeling position moving forward slowly.

We continued several patterns. Professor looked through his MX-15 ball, looking specifically at people and into doors and hidden areas to check for potential threats. He scanned the roads with the infrared cameras looking for any evidence of IEDs implanted into the roads.

"Shakedown, this is 32. We are starting to move. Can you scout the initial compound and grape rows to my east?" a fresh voice called. The other platoon was departing the FOB a few kilometers south, one minute away for us.

"Roger that," I called. Irish held his thumbs-up to acknowledge the request and rolled toward the FOB. He planned a left turn to go down the road over the troops and scout the area. Professor followed behind a few hundred feet higher.

We could see the soldiers winding out of the FOB, snaking down a well-travelled path and circling slowly to the east. Every step cautious. Every nook in the road and walls a potential IED. Searching for signs of tampering, wires, fresh digging, and potential ambushes made the political aim of "touching the hearts and minds" of locals a long, slow process.

"Shakedown, I gotta dicker north, 800 meters. One FAM, black pajamas. He's been tracking us since we left the FOB," 39 called, observing from the high point of the Ghar.

"Roger that," I answered.

"Prof, stay high and scan it. I'll stay low with troops along the road," I relayed.

"You got 'er." Professor popped into a high overwatch to protect us while also enabled him to scan for the FAM.

"I got him," Professor stated on our private frequency. "He's moving now, going east. I see another man in white 200 meters over. Looks like he's going to meet him."

I relayed the information to the platoon commander below.

"Thanks, Shakedown. I have contact on both. Continue to monitor." Both 32, in the patrol, and 39, stationary on the hill, acknowledged.

I continued looking into the grape rows and compounds within a thousand meters of the troops. It was quiet, except for a couple of men walking. The POL should have had more activity. However, 1,500 meters east were a dozen people laying bricks, repairing a building. But the immediate area was quiet, giving an unusual sense of security.

Poof, poof, poof, poof. The flares fired again.

"Counter right!" I casually called, looking at the missile warning system. There was nothing. It was another false hit coming from the direction of the FOB. But we were somewhat anxious knowing there were dickers in the area. I looked below, and all the infantry took defensive positions on one knee, also taking precautions.

"Shakedown, contact shots fired! Coming from your direction," 32 called.

"Did they sound like shotgun blasts?" I responded.

"Roger that."

"It was my aircraft defense systems. False hit. No worries. Area still clear."

"Can you turn that damn thing off?" 32 asked in frustration. "It's a little unnerving."

Irish looked at me with big eyes, realizing that meant turning our only protection against a surface-to-air missile off. "Fuck that! I haven't desensitized that much."

I laughed and answered, "Negative, 32, I gotta leave it on," I answered in a relaxed voice then talked to Prof.

"Prof, I got false hits," I reported just to let him know that everything was fine.

"Check that—I saw your fireworks and wondered. I'm still monitoring these two FAMs. They are chatting and observing the troops," Professor reported.

I swept over the Canadians a hundred feet below and proceeded down the road. They started advancing again. I completed a track reversal and started eastbound about 200 meters north of the infantry patrol looking into some grape huts that I felt would be advantageous firing positions from the Taliban enemy.

I felt some turbulence.

"Hang on guys, we have a few bumps starting; probably just morning sun thermals." I advised my crew.

"Contact, IED, IED, IED!" a voice alerted on the radio. I looked left toward the infantry. I expected to see a brown explosive cloud. They were back into their defensive posture looking over the walls for any snipers, but no cloud.

"32, this is Shakedown. I'm looking, where?" I asked.

"Did you guys see the explosion?" I hollered to my crew.

"Nope. Nothing." Irish and Zorg frantically looked.

"Shakedown, this is 39. Report your status. You okay?" the company commander's voice interjected over the radio.

"What the hell are they talking about?" I retorted to my crew. I was confused.

"Roger that, 39," I responded in a perplexed tone. "Why?"

"That IED went off under you and slightly behind," the voice reported. "You had to have taken shrapnel."

"Got 'er, Haycee," Snapshot called as he leaned out the door. "Come around right. It's directly behind us. Probably that bump we felt."

Irish banked the helicopter around. The explosion of dust was clearly visible and climbed halfway up the height of the helicopter.

"I guess that was our turbulence. That was nowhere near the infantry. Fuckers were trying to take us out!" I laughed nervously to relieve the stress. "I guess we're hunting now," I continued, somewhat pissed off.

"Oh, fuck ya!" Zorg added to my sentiment.

"Prof, did you see that?" I asked.

"Roger, got it now. It went off just behind you. You all right?"

"All good, a speed bump from the shock wave, but no rock shrapnel bounced off us—all good. We're continuing," I reported. "Join me, it's hunting time."

"Shakedowns, this is Three-niner. Approximately 800 meters directly east of the explosion is a man. It's your dicker! We've been tracking him. The other one is no threat. He's popping in and out of the grape rows. My sniper can't get the shot," the commander stated from the observation position in the FOB.

"Roger that. We going to check it out," I stated.

"High overwatch, Prof." I climbed the helicopter out of effective weapons range where all the crew could get a good look at the movements in the area. We saw over a dozen people working in the fields as well as the dozen working near the brick wall.

"Three-nine, I got at least a dozen people working in that area. Which one?"

"Black pajamas, moving north. He's jumping over a wall now! Directly west of you 200 meters," the voice yelled. Our heads swiveled, looking.

There were three people on wall from my perspective. Bricklayers. Some were moving around getting water and cement, but all were contributing to the wall construction.

"Prof, I got nothing. Too many fitting that description. Whatcha got?"

"Same, Steve. I don't see anyone in particular."

"Shakedowns, he's right there, right there! He's the trigger. Take him out, take him out," 39 continued yelling.

I was frustrated. I could not differentiate anyone that would be a viable target. The commander had PID. However, the FAM was out of range for the sniper; and I could not see anyone unusual.

"Looking, no PID!" I responded.

"Fuck, guys. Do you have anything?" I yelled to my gunners.

"No. I got the kids on the wall. A man walking on top of the grape row toward another man northeast. And a half dozen people near the construction project. No one specific," Zorg stated.

"Prof?" I hollered out on the radio.

"Nothing. I got nothing. We got fire orders but no target. We gotta relax," he advised.

"Roger that," I agreed and took a deep breath.

"He's getting away to the north. Losing PID!" the commander's voice was frustrated. They had been engaged every day from the west; the troops were constantly being hit. Now they had PID; the target was out of range for the snipers, and the target transfer to me wasn't happening. It wasn't often there was a clean PID. But from my perspective, there were too many people in the target area that could easily be confused. The only wall that had people on it was a wall construction project. It was a no-go.

"Shakedowns, I lost him. Go support 31 for a while. Three - nine out." The voice surrendered to frustration.

"Sheesh, der's an unhappy cust'mer," Snapshot retorted on the intercom.

"Prof, let's go north with 31, hi-lo. I'm going downstairs," I radioed. It was time to go help the other team and shake that experience off.

"Roger that." Professor observed from a high orbit, noting choke points with the MX-15. He was also able to continue monitoring India 32 with the camera. We were close enough.

I stayed low. My gunners observed eye to eye with the people in various compounds. We overflew the troops and waived at the platoon below. Snapshot liked to interact with the troops with hand signals directing attention toward people in compounds that the patrol could not otherwise see. It gave the troops on the ground a little more information. They encouraged him returning a thumbs-up.

Over the following hour, Irish flew the chopper to the various compounds as both the platoon commanders requested. All the eyes were focused on the possible ambush sites. The man in the black jammies never resurfaced.

"Contact, shots fired," a voice came over the radio. "Shakedown, there shooting at you!"

I was confused. Usually snaps of bullets could be heard as they whipped by, but nothing. Irish jerked the helicopter slightly as a defensive evasive maneuver.

"Guys, you see or hear any shots toward us?" I asked, receiving negative response.

"31, this is Shakedown Lead. I'm the low bird. Anything coming toward us," I responded.

"No, your high bird is getting shot at in the west," he answered.

"Guys, where the fuck is Prof?" I called to my gunners to look behind. They immediately looked up, taking the attention off the ground.

"He's way over west, Cap," Zorg stated.

"Prof, you're getting shot at! What the fuck are you doing over there? You're supposed to be covering my ass!" I was pissed off.

"Yah, I saw a possible IED lollipop and was checking it out. Then we heard the bullets zipping by. We're okay and on our way back," Professor responded.

"I'm coming your way, and I'll join on you. Lead us to where the shots came from," I answered, implying it was time to hunt.

"I think about 200 meters southwest of OP Brown."

Our two helicopters pressed toward a compound along a wadi where the shots would have most likely originated. But again, we saw nothing. The Taliban would often take potshots at aircraft that were single ship, but when we paired together, they were conservative. We made several circles around the area but saw nothing.

"India 31, any more shots being fired?" I asked.

"Negative."

"Roger that."

"Prof, let's go back to 31. Stay with me this time. You got any holes in you?" I asked.

"I didn't hear any hits, just misses," Professor answered.

"Roger, how's your fuel? Ten minutes to bingo," Professor answered.

"Let's do a few more sweeps for call sign 3 then go to the FARP," I stated. I was mad at Professor for going solo and also mad at myself for not keeping track of him.

"Three Nine, been a wonderful morning, but we have ten minutes playtime then back to the FARP. Any specific requests?" I asked.

"Negative, Shakedown, just a general POL check, then we'll chat later. Better check for holes when you get back," Three niner stated.

"Roger that. Shakedown out." I finished a few more circles and passed on the information as requested. I checked in with Slayer for the route home.

"Shakedown, this is Freedom Ops. Negative on the FARP. You may have holes. Just bring 'er back home for inspection," Scrappy commanded on the radio. He had been watching the texted version of the mission on the TOC TV. "We'll refuel you after inspecting the choppers."

"Roger that, Ops," I acknowledged.

When I got out of the aircraft, I wanted to talk to Professor. I was pissed at him for veering on his own. I was upset at myself for not tightly monitoring. We were getting complacent. We needed to change our methods. The remainder of our crews combed over each aircraft looking for damage, with assistance from technicians that met us after hearing the news from Scrappy and the SAMEO.

I held my palms up, eyebrows raised. "Why the fuck were you over there? How am I supposed to protect you? And why were you at mid altitude? You weren't even high."

"We saw some movement along the river behind Brown that was suspicious. We thought we were safe over the riverbed," he exhaled. "I shoulda had you come with me."

"Mid-level altitude?" I got angrier. "We either fly the guns low, stay up high, or stay together."

Professor knew I was right but also that I was being hypocritical. He paused, looking at me to allow me time to calm and reflect. I had been taking too many complacent risks as well. It was time to rethink and change some tactics. War fighting season was also upon us.

I noticed Scrappy walking toward us.

"I know what you guys are talking about," Scrappy said. "You both almost got hit today on the same mission. It's not even fighting season yet! We gotta fuckin' adjust and get our shit straight." He walked away without allowing retort.

Chapter 24

Man by the River

Senjeray after the Poppy Harvest

The Obama administration promised thirty thousand more troops to Afghanistan. The region was tactically subdivided as these troops arrived.

Longknife was the new Kiowa patrol replacing Shamus. The American Stryker Brigade had taken the responsibility away from the Canadians, allowing Canada to focus on Nakhoney and Panjwaii. The U.S. Army concentrated security on Highway 1 and Kandahar City. Part of their role was logistics convoy escort. Of course, near Senjeray, the long, deep wadi on the south side of the highway, provided excellent cover for Taliban ambushes. Previously known as IED alley, the new brigade was quickly being initiated into the war by the Taliban.

As always, and ironic to the region, the sunrise was astonishingly beautiful. Despite the ugliness of terror, it reliably cast its orange light on the Afghanistan lands below. The sky was bright blue and crystal clear.

A local man had just completed his morning prayers and went to deliver fruits to market. His farm lay against the mountains on the north slope shadows south of Senjeray.

Later that morning, his wife commenced her routine following the prayer that played over the community public announcement system. She paused to admire the beautiful grape and pomegranate fields looking toward the large trees outlining the wadi a kilometer north. It provided a dust and sound barrier from Highway 1, which was a few hundred meters on the other side.

Since her husband had left for market, it was time for her to tend to chores with her children. She had a large basket of clothes, which she was taking to a water well when she was visited by a familiar, but unwanted man robed in dark clothes. She froze in fear. Nothing good would come from this visit.

"No, please leave us alone!" she begged of a man who had come into her compound. She began to tear.

"Stop your wailing, woman. It is disgraceful," he ordered.

He looked over at her children who were tending to chores in the yard. One was a twelve-year-old boy, old enough to be a man in this culture, and two other young children. He called to the boy, "Come here."

The boy and his younger siblings were patching holes in the mud walls.

"Yes, sir," he responded respectfully and advanced toward the stranger. He noticed his mother was distraught and became cautious.

"You are a strong young man now," the intruder complimented. "Allah has asked me for your assistance."

The boy stood with his eyes lowered in front of the man. The intruder reached and gently lifted his chin to make eye contact.

"Please stop," the mother quietly begged. It was answered with a silent glare. He refocused on the boy.

"You will bring your siblings to the edge of the grape field after noon prayer today. You will wait for my signal and stay there until I call you," the stranger commanded and pointed north toward the wadi. "There may be infidel forces, but do not fear. Allah is with you."

"I should not be doing such things. My father will take care of this," the boy responded bravely. He realized what the stranger wanted and what he represented.

"Your father has been selling his grapes, watermelon, and pomegranates to the people who support the infidels." The man lectured angrily.

"We need to make money to survive." His mother stepped forward and answered.

"Silence, woman. I am talking to the man of the house!" he yelled at her. She lowered her eyes and stepped back. "Your behavior is intolerable.

Your husband has brought disrespect to this community. He was offered a chance to serve Allah and grow opium crops that we requested, but he has not done so," the man lectured.

Small crops of marijuana and poppy were often planted between the grape rows. These were cash crops that many farmers were forced to grow. If not forced, then the logistics to get their legitimate produce to market was ambushed, giving them no choice but to supply opium and marijuana. This was the only crop, which was guaranteed to provide income.

Legitimate crops were subjected to interruption en route to market. The result was that many of the legal crops were left to die, but the opium poppies and marijuana fields bloomed, untouched by the authorities and protected by the insurgency.

"Then please take this up with my father when he returns from market," the boy requested. He was shaking.

"Your father will not be returning from market unless you assist me," the man added threateningly. "He is with the Mullah being disciplined for his ways. Allah has told the Mullah that your father will be shown compassion if you do this small task."

He had the boy and the family captive. She knew that many other husbands have come back severally beaten. Some never returned. Her only chance to have him back would be to comply and hope.

"Very well," she conceded, crying loudly. "After the noon prayer, my children will be over there by the grape rows." She pointed for confirmation as she rocked in terror.

"Allah be with you, young man," the man blessed the young boy as he departed. He glared at the woman who would not lift her eyes.

Chapter 25

Hello from Home

"Hi, glad to hear your voice," my wife said over a broken video Skype call from my tent.

"How have things been going?"

"Fine, business as usual, walking the dog and buzzin' the troops," I answered. I couldn't tell her anything more. I could reveal that I had just conducted a counter-IED operation that resulted in people dying, that rockets were falling into camp almost daily, that I had been shot at, almost blown up, and that some guys had been shot down. I wanted to vent but wouldn't. She wanted to listen but really didn't want to know the truth. So we were left with pleasantries.

"How are the kids doing?" I asked. "Fine, grades are good. The ringette games are a hoot, and the tae kwon do competition went very well," she lied.

She told me what I needed to hear to stay focused on the job. She couldn't tell me about the trials the kids had at school because Dad was at war. She couldn't vent the stresses she had in doing all the duties of Mom and Dad alone, without help. That stress at my job adversely affected her job. She wanted to vent but wouldn't. She knew it was better to let me focus on my job and not family issues. This way I could focus, increasing my chance of returning to my life. She was a good army wife. It was all about hearing the voice, not the content that mattered. There would soon be time to reconnect. We hoped.

"I won't be able to talk to you for a few days," I told her over a Skype call from my tent.

"Oh, what's up?" she responded.

"Well, let's just say I'm going on a cross-country trainer," I stated. She laughed to relieve some tension. Again, she knew it was more than that. She remembered Op Shania.

I heard some fighters approaching the tent. This led to a deafening noise blanking out any ability to hear someone over the Skype network. "Just a sec, fighters," I said. It passed. "So how is everything?" I continued.

"Wait for the wingman," she interrupted. She remembered.

Vvvrrrrroooosssshhhh!

The sound cleared. "What were you saying?"

Rrrrrooooooooowwwwwrrrrr.

The rocket alarm sounded.

Oh great! I thought. I dropped my butt to the floor and continued chatting nonchalantly. She hadn't heard this yet, and it would be just one more thing to worry about.

I didn't do the drills as I didn't want to panic her. The chance of the rocket coming close was unlikely anyway. "Oh, I am heading away, and I'll call you in a few days."

Kaaarrrumpft.

An explosion echoed from the rocket impacting nearby.

"What was that? I don't like that!" she exclaimed over the Skype anxiously.

I tried to calm her. "Oh, nothing, dear. It's just a routine rocket attack."

"That didn't sound routine!" she exclaimed.

"Well, I'm fine, but I should go check it out." I tried to patronize her. She was not stupid. I tried to calm her, but I also needed to go. It wasn't routine; it had hit close. I felt the shock wave but tried to ignore it. I only thought, crap, how would I fake being uninjured if I did get injured during a rocket attack?

We said quick good-byes, and I investigated. I grabbed my holster, shouldered it, and ran toward the shelter. After the "all clayer," I hustled over to the boardwalk where the rocket hit—about 200 meters away. I bypassed the bunker. When rockets were close, most ignored the bunker and became First Aiders. People were injured. No fatalities. We were lucky!

The boardwalk is usually very busy this time of night. It could have been much worse. Thank God they didn't hit Tim Hortons.

Nevertheless, they would be closed the remainder of the night, so my evening coffee plans were wrecked—an effective psychological warfare win by the Taliban.

I walked back toward my tent, and the military police stopped me and several other people.

"Where is your reflective device?" the MP asked.

"Oh shit, I left it in my tent with all the commotion," I answered.

"That's unacceptable, sir. I have to citation you."

All personnel had to have safety reflective vests or flashlight indicators while walking around KAF at night because of the reduced visibility in dust combined with low lighting levels.

"Seriously, you gotta be kidding?" I answered. "My tent is right around the corner."

"No, sir." He wrote up the ticket.

It was like getting a speeding ticket in Canada, a misdemeanor. However, there was no money involved. It was a piece of paper, recorded, that had to be taken to your commanding officer and signed. Then it had to be returned to the military police to show that discipline had taken place for the unlawful behavior. It was an administrative pain in the ass. Arguing with the military police would have been worse, so I begrudgingly accepted it. I took my piece of paper and went back to my tent to prepare for "table time."

Chapter 26

The Monster Mash

In the TOC

Almost the entire detachment of Task Force Freedom met at operations for the preliminary briefing. It was a large-scale mission being led by the Brits. Canada had a major part. This was going to be a doubleheader, a follow-on from Stargai Kwan (Shania).

The Americans were going to tackle Marjeh and the Brits, Nad Ali, in a combined ground and airmobile assault, the largest helicopter airmobile operation Canada had ever taken part of. By the end of the operation, the Brits, with the Canadians, will have moved over one thousand one hundred troops in an hour; the Americans, about three thousand; and a huge ground assault would be added to that.

In the British insertion, there would be over forty-three helicopters including four Chinooks and five Griffons from Canada, all being coordinated in over one hundred execution task lines. Further supporting this mission were UAVs, fighter bombers and Hercules aircraft providing night illumination in a time-sequenced drop across the Helmand sky during the darkest part of the month. However, the operation was so big it was becoming a monster. Hence, Operation Mosteruk became referred to as the Monster Mash!

Scrappy organized rehearsals several days prior. He sent Chinooks and Griffons to practice multiship landings similar to how the night operation was to unveil. It was done in a safe enemy-free part of

Afghanistan, which offered Snapshot opportune moments to take hundreds of photos.

Following practice, our detachment of pilots, engineers, gunners, technicians, and operations staff boarded the Chinooks and Griffons and deployed in formation to Camp Bastion, the main British base in Helmand Province to commence the Monster Mash.

The nine helicopters from Canada arrived to Camp Bastion. Everyone was instructed to meet Scrappy in a corner of the fenced dirt patch for further orders.

"All right, gents, we got a major operation happening as early as tonight. Those Chinooks over there," he said, pointing to the furthest Chinook. "They have the tents, tables, computers, ammo all on board. I need to build an operations center right here. Now. Go form a line and pass the parts over," he bluntly directed the detachment.

"Chief! I want the door opening right here facing that way," he ordered to the most senior noncommissioned officer, imparting on him to get it done. "Everyone in the detachment, including the officers, you are now working for the chief. He needs laborers." We all worked like ants to get it done.

"Generators, computers, over here!" yelled the chief. "Bullets and weaponry, over to you, Hawk, find a spot for it all."

"Gunners, after the tents up, rally on me. We are linking ammo!" yelled Hawk. People obeyed the chief, but people feared the Hawk.

"All right, I need the electricity soon. Get those generators up ASAP," Scrappy yelled.

"Do we really need electricity right now, sir?" someone blurted out.

"No, but I really need power for the coffee machine—now!" Scrappy hollered, cracking his exhausted smile.

Those in earshot laughed but continued working hard. There was a strong camaraderie. So despite the deliberate annoying commands, everyone knew the yelling was in jest. The commands weren't even required. Everyone was seasoned in field craft; we knew what to do and how to get it done. So the commands were to mock military process and add levity.

"All right, guys, after you set up, then go to the tent lines. Your personal gear goes on that bus over there." Scrappy pointed. "We are all sharing a weather haven! The aircraft may launch tonight, so set up, get some sleep, and keep it quiet," Scrappy concluded. "Aircrew, back here for preliminary orders at 1900 hours."

The five sections of canvass modular tent went up quickly. Most aircrew had to prepare maps with the most current tactical information in order to understand the area of operations. Tables were set up for workspace but quickly became overrun with computer printers and coffee pots. Canadian media were also setting up equipment in one end of the tent. They were documenting everything for articles they were preparing for the Monster Mash.

"Steve, JW is flying with you tonight. Go find him and introduce yourself—brief him accordingly," Scrappy added.

Shit, I thought. I had media in my aircraft, and I would be going into a serious, potentially violent battle? I went over and met JW and his team. He was a young, accomplished journalist and very pleasant to be around. He immediately made a person feel comfortable, and we discussed the Griffon's role in the overall mission.

I showed him the aircraft and acquainted him with his ballistic vest and basic survival equipment. Media never carried weapons, but he was trained.

"JW, this is my nine mil pistol, if I am incapacitated, take it. Load it like this." I demonstrated. "Safety here, fire. If it jams, cock it again like this. Aim and fire until there is no longer a threat." I was serious.

"I won't be using a weapon," JW stated.

"You know what'll happen to you, don't you—if you're captured?" I eyed him seriously. JW knew what I meant.

"I'm listening—I'm not carrying one, but go on." JW was convinced to be refreshed on the pistol. I obliged. When I finished, he asked, "Shouldn't I get trained on the C7 rifle as well?" I smiled and continued his education.

I told him where I kept my tourniquets in case he needed them and showed him the communication system on board the aircraft. He was given some NVGs and a quick orientation on how to use them. After his orientation, we exchanged pleasantries and departed. We would meet again at the mission briefing.

I walked over with Hollywood and Fender to the BAT. It was the same tent as the Shania cross-country. We found the gymnasium and the kitchen first.

Bastion was more rustic than KAF. It didn't have equivalent amenities. Nevertheless, the soldiers seemed content despite the limited resources. They did not have a boardwalk. The dining facility was always full as they were supporting more troops than they had logistics to support. So food rationing was in effect.

Our accommodations held our sixty-five personnel who slept on cots within 2 feet of each other. There wasn't enough room to store personal gear without affecting the next person over. The shape of the haven seemed to amplify the sound of snoring, making sleep difficult. I lay down for a nap but gave up after five minutes and decided to go to the gym. The gym was very small with two treadmills as opposed to the several hundred that could be found at KAF, even those two treadmills were difficult to run on as the floor was uneven.

I first burnt out my anxiety on the off-level treadmill, which wobbled while I ran and then hit the weights.

"Hey, Hollywood, you can't sleep either?" I called over to my colleague. He was busy trying to charm some lovely British lady soldiers. I rolled my eyes, finished my workout.

He nodded and grinned. "Gotcha." I smirked.

"Later, buddy," he winked and then continued moving his hands around, sharing his impressive stories with his gruff movie-star smile.

I quietly entered the sleep haven, aiming to get a half hour of sleep before the mission orders. Big C, Fender, and Grumpy all seemed to be sleeping . . . or at least appeared to be. I set my alarm for a twenty-minute snooze but just ended up counting the seconds down until it was time to go.

"It's dark. You know how to get there?" I mentioned to Fender.

"Ya, it's wherever Big C goes. He's got a built in GPS in his skull." He laughed.

Everyone followed Big C through the dark streets of Bastion trying to remember the way to Scrappy's new operations tent.

Skipper and Scrappy had received mission orders from the air marshal. The mission could be at any time now.

Scrappy greeted the arriving crews. "Grab a coffee. The CO will be along shortly."

Skipper arrived and looked at everyone. "Well, the mission isn't tonight, guys. But I am giving preliminary orders, and we will have a practice drill," Skipper announced.

There were sighs of both relief and annoyance. Another day to stay on edge, but at least we could get some sleep.

There was a collective anxiety. There were rumors from HQ in Canada that they had been forecasting dozens of body bags because of the size of this liberation mission. And these body bags were for us. About eight thousand plus soldiers would be involved. These rumors did not go ignored. We were embarking on a Goliath assault against the largest stronghold of Taliban in Southern Afghanistan; we were expecting damage; it showed on our faces.

Skipper continued. "Gentlemen, these are you orders. Situation. Int Op, brief the enemy situation," he commanded.

The intelligence briefer updated the known enemy facts. Then he briefed the threats on the landing zone using current live imagery from UAVs. After adding the effects of the weather, winds, the illumination, he was done.

Then Scrappy briefed all intended actions of all the NATO and ANA units who we would be participating.

"On landing, the intended line of departure for the troops are here, here, and here. They plan on establishing foothold through these areas and link up the Belgians, Polish, and Brits here," he detailed, tracing his fingers over various control lines on the map. He showed the borders of responsibility that each nation maneuvered within. The magnitude of this was becoming realistic; this was it.

Skipper took over and continued briefing the specific tasks of the various Griffons and Chinooks.

"Steve, your section will lead to the landing zone here." Skip pointed to the map. "I'll laze the LZ from above. Once Butch calls contact, your section will go into overwatch in a battle position here. If shit hits the fan, Butch, you'll either stay or egress north. I'll call it. Steve, I'll choreograph the defensive counterassault from overwatch. You and Fender will be the guns."

I nodded. There would be between four and eight large helicopters lifting every two minutes from the Bastion for over an hour. There would be no unnecessary communications. The only person talking to higher command would be Skipper. Everyone was given an execution checklist, a detailed schedule that each aircraft had to abide by to the second. It dictated exactly when to take off, when to land, what route to take, and who was on board.

"Droopy, you'll stay running and be the bump aircraft for the Chinooks. If any Griffon goes down, I'll fill that spot. If I go unserviceable, I am bumping the first copilot I come across—you, Irish." He nodded to Irish and continued adding more detail to the task.

"Gents, suit up, arm up, and start your machines. This is a live on ground rehearsal. All aircraft will start the X check-in." He looked at his watch. "Fifty-three minutes from now, Hack."

We all dispersed with the coordination table in hand. Everyone stumbled over the dark rock field and did exactly what the boss wanted. The helicopters started one by one. Irish started loading all the data into the flight computer, and I prepared the MX-15 database. It was an opportunity to check all the systems, frequencies, grids, maps, and it was done—on schedule.

"All call signs, this is Zero (Freedom Ops)," Scrappy's voice sounded. "End ex, end ex. Shut down and meet in twenty minutes for wrap-up."

The last of the crews arrived at the operations tent shortly following the aircraft shut downs. The CO and Scrappy were waiting. "Gentlemen, there will be a detailed coordination brief, tomorrow afternoon, here after lunch. Irish and Hollywood, you'll coordinate the construction of a massive *rock* drill map outside. We will all walk through and practice our duties until everyone knows them cold." Skipper eyed everyone as he finished.

A *rock* drill map used rocks, twigs, paper, and whatever other material one could find to create a massive map on the ground. It was the stage for a dress rehearsal without the helicopters.

"Questions?" he concluded. No one said anything.

"Everyone has the X checklist. See you at 1400 hours tomorrow. Dismissed."

Next Morning . . .

The operations tent was busy. Grumpy and the other captains were memorizing the navigation route and reviewing the timings. Skip and Scrappy were pouring a cup of coffee, murmuring over the details, and the copilots were busy creating the stage.

Irish, Hollywood, and Arnie, with the help of some gunners, had carved an impressive huge twenty-by-twenty-meter 2D map into the hard-packed dirt next to the tent. String and ribbons were used to mark grid lines as well as rocks, cardboard, and anything they could find to represent wadis, compounds, and coordination lines representing each nation's area of responsibility.

"All right! Listen up, everyone!" Skip called. All the crews gathered in a semicircle. Irish arranged them chronologically in order of flight.

"This is the shit! We have trained, some for twenty years to be involved in an operation of this magnitude. We are ready for this!" He was excited. "This is not an invasion into Nad Ali and Marjeh. It's a liberation! The Taliban have embedded themselves into this area without any resistance from the Allied Forces. They are strong in numbers and are manipulating locals to comply. It is time for them to leave—by force. All the peace shuras have been ineffective." He looked around at each of us in the eye.

"Scrappy, run the rock drill."

"Gents, look at your execution checklist. It's L-hour minus forty-five minutes. (L-hour is time the first aviation unit is to land.) Tell me where you are, what you're doing!" Scrappy looked at Chinook lead.

Butch looked at his paperwork, walked over to a position on the ground map, and answered. "I'm running right here," he said, pointing to the ground and then to his real aircraft. "I should be loading troops and then calling you with the code word to indicate that I am loaded and ready."

"Roger that," Scrappy stated.

Scrappy continued around until me. "Steve, bring your crew. Where will you be when Butch lands here?" I walked over to my position with not only my crew but with JW as well, the reporter. Everyone knew JW by now. He scribbled notes on his pad as I marched him over to our map position.

"What if you go down?" he asked me. "You got JW with you. Did you consider that?"

I looked at JW. "I'll trade him for my freedom," I stated matter-of-factly. Everyone laughed, except JW who didn't know if I was serious or not. Scrappy raised his brow for the serious answer. "We have refreshed his training with our weapons, first aid, and survival gear. He'll stick with our team—as a noncombatant."

"I'm ready to go," JW added enthusiastically. "This is gonna be 'the shit' to quote Skipper."

"Awesome," I answered. Skip smiled.

"All right then!" Scrappy interrupted and then continued through everyone in turn. After that, we rehearsed various contingencies: getting shot at, ground fight, shot down, to a broken aircraft on start.

"A shoot-out commences. Our Chinooks are on the ground, and your gunner is unconscious and bleeding out. What do you do?" He aimed his question toward Fender.

He promptly responded, "Left gunner is trained for combat first aid. He will abandon gun and assist. I'll pop to safe zone and expedite back to the casualty collection point here at Bastion. Skipper will *rip* in if I am in contact with enemy. If not, my section escorts me back, making radio calls." JW took more notes.

Skipper was happy. He ran the drill for an hour, adjusting and confirming as required.

"All right, everyone, go get some supper and then some sleep. Be back here for confirmatory orders at 0100 hours!" He finished his rock drill. Everyone was exhausted. There were so many details, yet the job was simple. The timings would be the most important aspect with so many aircraft airborne. However, in combat, the enemy can entirely screw up a good plan with one bullet, hence, the need to have contingencies.

At the BAT

I couldn't sleep; I listened quietly to some music with headphones on: "Tonight's gonna be a good, good night, feelin'." It calmed me; I thought of my kids.

I heard Fender's alarm; it was a rooster crowing. But it was 11:00 p.m. instead of the morning. I had only slept an hour. Another alarm sounded; it was an Islamic-chanting alarm. Someone brought it for levity. It was dark and cold; shadows moved with defiant moans as sleep was disturbed.

Everyone slowly prepared their gear for the mission assisted by beams from flashlights. Once ready, the crews mustered outside by a dim lamppost. It was a kilometer across camp to the aircraft—again; we followed Big C's mental GPS and his flat smile.

The aircraft started on queue. A full checklist procedure and radio checks were executed.

"Preliminary hydraulics?" I called.

"Check," Irish answered.

"Governors?" I continued.

"Check completed," Irish answered.

"Hey, I don't see your tourniquets on," the voice of JW stated from the back over the intercom. "I heard you wore tourniquets."

"Huh?" I sleepily responded. "I don't think I've worn them for months, JW," I pondered, answering his inquiry. I sat quietly, contemplating why.

"We're desensitized to it?" Snapshot stated. "We jus' keep movin' forward, and don't worry about it. No sense dwellin'—tourniquets make ya dwell."

"I suppose. I haven't though too much about this anymore. Just get up, go to work, go to the gym, eat, movie, sleep," I said flatly. "That's all I do."

"Here come the troops," Snapshot observed. Numerous ANA were embedded with the Belgians and the Polish troops.

In the back of Blowtorch 61, Tiny, a Chinook engineer, scoured over the forty boarding troops. He carefully looked at every soldier. Near the ramp door at the back, he noticed something suspicious. He saw an ANA soldier leaning against his hand, keeping his back toward other soldiers. He rushed toward him despite the limited space.

"I gotta cell phone!" he called over the intercom. "I got him!" he yelled.

"Niner, this is Blowtorch 61. We got a cell phone, escorting him off the back now." We heard Butch called over the radio to the boss.

"Poor bastard is fucked now," Snapshot called. My team all watched across the dim pick-up zone as a huge shadow of Tiny dragged a small ANA soldier half his size out of the Chinook. He handed him over to the military police. He was going for interrogation.

I monitored the radio following the cell phone event. Over forty helicopters were running, and there were several other similar events. Several Afghan locals were captured that night. They were suspected of using cell phones to give sensitive mission information to Taliban, such as "the invasion is starting now." These were not ANA; they had infiltrated the ANA and were tasked or coerced by the enemy to give critical information. This would be their last intelligence-gathering mission.

"All aircraft, stand down. I say again, stand down," the air marshall directed over the radio. The mission was aborted for tonight. All the helicopters shut down.

We met at the Ops tent. Scrappy was waiting. "Good job, gents. Excellent work, Tiny!" He smiled toward the large man. "All the aircraft are in good shape. The technicians will double-check for faults or tampering tonight." He looked at the maintenance leader receiving a nod and continued.

"Tomorrow is the same as today: Rock drill at 1400 hours and maybe another fake mission. At least we flushed out some perpetrators tonight. Get some sleep."

Next Night . . .

The following night was clear with just enough dust to make the stars dim. No moon. Irish and I sat in the aircraft with the rotors turning— déjà vu. All the checks complete, listening for the executive order.

The hour of departure was close, yet still no word. Concurrently, the UAV predator drones were scouring the landing areas looking for threats prior to lift off. Hercules aircraft were overhead ready with a black illumination bombardment of parachutes that would turn night into day for anyone using night-vision devices. The strike fighters were holding high above on standby. Hundreds of helicopters from both the U.S. Marine base and the British base were all postured to commence the Monster Mash. We were all waiting for one word on the radio. My crew was quiet. I remember looking at the sky.

"It's gonna be a dark one," I said rhetorically. "You ready, Irish?"

"Yup."

"Snapshot, Zorg?"

"Gootago" and "Clear left, boss" were their respective comments. It would be any moment now for the launch.

"I gotta go pee," Zorg stated, breaking the silence.

"Seriously?" I answered. "Stay near the skid on comms," I ordered, expecting a call any second.

"Raawggeer." He gave the cocky response as he walked toward the back of the helicopter, still attached to his communication cable.

"Ready, JW?" I asked.

"Yes, this is surreal. Good to go," he answered quietly, his microphone a bit too far away from his mouth, a novice mistake.

"Pull your mic closer," I stated. I needed to say something, even if it was criticism; I was stressed, I just needed to alter the silence.

"How's that?" he answered loudly, obviously fixing the mistake. He put his notepad away. It was too dark, and we were lights out.

"Loud and clear," I answered. "You know any jokes?"

"Yes, but for some reason, I can't think of any at this moment," he answered.

"Good one," Zorg yelled, forcing a giggle from behind the chopper.

"Radios cracking, guys!" I stated.

"It's a go! L-hour is zero two four five local time," commanded Skipper over the radio. Blowtorch 60, 61, 62, Shakedown 25, 26, 30, 31, acknowledge," he commanded. Each captain responded in order.

I looked as my execution checklist and did the L-hour math. "We're lifting in two minutes.

"Wind up the engines, Irish. Get in here, Zorg!" I ordered.

"Coming. Dammit! I pissed on myself," Zorg yelled.

Weeeerrrrrrrrr. The rotor increased in speed to take off RPM. "I got two full throttles for takeoff. Check complete," Irish stated and completed his checks. "Cabin area?" he asked.

"Cabin secure, right gun ready, ASE enabled," Snapshot called.

"Left gun ready," Zorg added.

This was it. The largest airmobile operation I would ever participate in. I was lead escort, first into the zone, feeling sort of proud yet anxious. Skipper would laser mark the LZ. This could be one of the hugest fights of my life. I would immediately have to provide assistance to the infantry and the Chinooks if they were engaged. This was a Taliban stronghold; combat was real. Everyone knew that; everyone was vigilant.

"Tower, this is Blowtorch flight, ready for takeoff," Butch called. He made one call for all eight helicopters; one stayed behind as a back-up. I led out to the end of the runway and turned to watch the entire formation line up behind me. It was dark, and blooms of lights around the airfield masked some helicopters. I managed to count them as they departed ahead. The last Griffon hovering called "chuck wagon," meaning the entire formation was ready to go. I turned the aircraft and lifted into the black.

As we proceeded a few minutes south, I looked into the sky. The Hercules was dropping huge balls of infrared light, like fire balls, sequentially across the sky. The black darkness north of Nad Ali switched brighter with each flare. There was a definitive line on the ground separating the black and the light, like a tide of green light washing north, providing illumination to the entire objective.

I watched for tracers as the thunder of helicopters rolled into the area. No lights were seen. We came quickly upon the landing zone and overflew it. It looked empty and safe. Skipper's aircraft was orbiting above and illuminated the landing zone with his MX-15 illuminator.

"Sparkle on," Skipper called.

"Contact sparkle. Contact LZ. Sparkle off," Butch answered as he slowed his Chinook onto the LZ.

The laser light shut off.

I led the two Griffons into a high orbit searching for any enemy activity with our respective MX-15s. I reflected on the OP Stargai Kwan mission. In my mind, that would not happen again. If five insurgents popped out, armed with weapons, my team was ready to take them out immediately. Skipper had already arranged that; the Shakedowns had full authority to protect Canadian assets. There were no restrictive lines to cross this time.

A cloud of green dust exploded as the first Chinook approached into the landing zone. I scanned out from the dust ball several hundred meters looking for any movement near walls or compounds—nothing. I listened for any contact reports on the radio—nothing.

The Chinooks unloaded all the soldiers. They kneeled in their defensive semicircle outside the back of the Chinook. The dust began to rise again as Butch immediately lifted and veered to the north, the remaining Chinooks in trail. I dove in to escort the departure while maintaining the camera on the troops to ensure they were unengaged. Still no sign of enemy activity.

"Where the hell is everyone?" Zorg asked.

"The Taliban knew there was going to be a large assault," Irish stated.

"Yup, I think any enemy with any sense left the area tonight," I concluded as Irish resumed the escort position for the Chinooks.

We listened to the radios. There were no TIC reports. No rockets. No RPGs or IEDs. It was quiet, despite the thousands of troops being inserted.

We returned to Bastion for the second and then a third lift. During the third lift, I spotted someone on the MX-15 toward eastern Nad Ali.

"I gotta contact 1,000 meters south of the LZ, investigating," I called to my wingman while continuing in a high orbit. The Chinooks were landing. "One times FAM, moving toward a small shack" I called.

I zoomed in with my high-powered sensor, finely detailing the actions of the only human image in the battle field.

"He's kneeling or sitting behind that wall. What's he doing?" I stated rhetorically.

"Fender, I'm sparkling the shack." I put my IR spotlight on the area near the man. Fender matched it with his beam. Our two huge lightsabers met on the ground.

"Contact, I got it!" Fender stated. Both sparkles went out.

"I can't make it out. Whatcha got?" I called to Fender. There was a pause.

"Steve . . ." Fender paused. "It's just a guy having a shit!"

"What?" Zorg left his gun and jumped forward to look at the picture. "Ha-ha-ha! Awesome! Like Skipper said, this is the shit!" he reflected and went back to his gun.

JW chuckled and leaned forward to observe the camera, making mental notes for his memoires. The situation broke the tension, giving us something to banter about. We returned to Bastion without a shot fired. Ironically, the Canadian military estimated that dozens of body bags would be required—just for the aviators. Thankfully, it was uneventful . . . so far.

The Monster Mash concluded. Op Mosteruk was a success—for the air move. However, there would be casualties. As the weeks progressed following our insertion into Nad Ali and Marjeh, there was some very harsh fighting. Some troops lost their lives as the Taliban fought where they could.

However, to the success of the government of Afghanistan, many local farmers met the Allied troops and guided them safely through fields and roads, showing them where IED traps had been set up to kill them—this was a small sign of success but gave hope that the people, the normal people of Afghanistan, did want peace, change, and stability.

Chapter 27

Lunchtime

"Blowtorch flight," the int op started his briefing. "Additionally, today we have some good news. An IED exploded near Kandahar City. Good news is that no one got hurt except the bomber. As he was putting an IED in a dead donkey on the road, it detonated, turning both the asses inside out." He smiled at his own joke.

"Hey, you made a joke," Hollywood poked fun at the usually overly serious briefer.

"Poetic justice," Grumpy added, smiling.

The irony was a little relieving. The Taliban often triggered dead animals with explosives. They knew someone would eventually try to move it—and boom!

"That's it. If no questions, let's go?" Butch concluded. He was Chinook lead today.

Airborne Near the Fence

Our team joined with Butch enroute towards the northwest; we completed fence out drills departing KAF.

"Right gun ready," called Snapshot.

"Left gun ready. Wait . . . Shit, sir! I think Prof has been hit!" Zorg exclaimed. "He's on fire or something!"

I looked out the left to the other side of the formation and saw a huge trail of smoke coming out of Professor's Griffon; it stretched for a quarter mile. I immediately looked around for enemy fire.

"26, you all right? You got a smoke stream a quarter mile long behind you?" I radioed in concern.

There was a pause. "Negative," he stated. "I got lights and no gearbox pressure, turning back," he bellowed.

"Check that. Butch, turn around and follow us back. 26 is broken," I called out as Professor was reversing course. This was serious; if his main gearbox ran out of oil, it could seize. He could crash, so he had a choice: land outside the wire and hope the insurgents didn't start a fight or push it for five minutes to get to KAF, hoping the helicopter would hold out. The latter was the better choice.

"Blowtorch, can you take care of the control tower while I alert Ops," I asked, sharing the radio calls among the aircraft. Butch complied.

The next three minutes were intense. A tingle radiated up my spine, hoping for their safety. An eerie silence was in the cockpit. The gunners were simultaneously looking for threats while wondering what happened.

The Taliban would already know there was a disabled helicopter because of the smoke and course reversal and ready to react. As Professor cross the outer fence of KAF, a massive relief overcame the crew. He could land safely anywhere now. He proceeded safely to X-ray ramp. Home. I landed beside him.

"26, report!" Scrappy asked over the radio now that Professor was secure.

"We're okay. We just lost all our gearbox pressure. Engineer says the vent got stuck open and dumped all the pressurized fluid into the exhaust. We are shutting down before it seizes," he answered, a sense of relief on his voice.

"Roger." Scrappy voice lightened. It was just another day followed by a sleepless night and more crisis. It was normal, and the mission had to continue. Grumpy had just returned from a full-day mission. His team was told to not shut down, as was I; Scrappy was formulating a new plan.

The radio cracked open. "Roger. Here's the situation," Scrappy started. "Wilson is a green FOB, minimal threat. Fender, you escort Butch there. Steve and Grumpy, go work with Slayer 14 in Nakhoney.

Things are heating up over there," he ordered as everyone acknowledged their new roles.

"Awesome!" Zorg whispered.

We knew Nakhoney. India 22 was patrolling. We knew what to anticipate. With Slayer 14 embedded, it meant they anticipated air and artillery support for the work. I had to quickly brief Grumpy.

"Grumpy, I'll lead. You talk with the FOB, and I'll coordinate with Slayer. Call when green to go and come up on tower frequency," I called.

"Roger that. Green," he acknowledged.

Slayer 14 was patrolling with India 22. This gave 22 a capability to have a FAC (forward air controller) with them. He had special training enabling him to control artillery, gunships, and fighters to support friendly troops on the ground.

Grumpy was now my wingman. This was unusual to have two section leads flying together. Every section works slightly different. We get used to each other's position, techniques, and preferences without having to coordinate on the radio. That is the reason sections were always the same; it was called "combat crewing." It was effective.

I quickly briefed Grumpy over the radio as we cleared KAF airspace and pressed into the battle area.

"Grumpy, let's use a low-high trail for a baseline overwatch. I'll lead-low." I briefed. Grumpy knew exactly what I meant. However, unbeknownst to me, in other sections, applications of spacing were slightly different.

"Roger that," Grumpy answered.

Five minutes from Nakhoney, we switched the radios as briefed and contacted Slayer 14.

"14, Shakedown checking in."

"Go for Slayer."

"Shakedowns, flight of two Griffons, eight thousand rounds—dual Dillons each, sixty minutes playtime, send your battle update brief (BUB)," I reported.

"Roger that, Shakedown. ROZ is 3-kilometer diameter centered on me. It's cold. My guns are cold. I am at grid QQ42328845, 1,000 meters northwest of FOB Madras. Friendlies are twenty-two Canadian soldiers on patrol. No enemy contact. How copy?" he radioed.

I acknowledged his location and composition but added that I did not see him yet.

"Shakedown, that's a good copy. My BP (battle plan) is to bring you in overhead to do an area search of POL and identify any personnel on roof tops. Acknowledge when you are visual with me," he ordered. His method was mechanical, dry, professional.

My crew acknowledged, and Grumpy acknowledged. We had been cruising across the desert high, and it was time to get low and PID everything we were tasked to find.

"Switch to trail low formation," I briefed to Grumpy over the radio.

Our two aircraft plummeted toward the earth. Irish maneuvered for tactical protection, reducing our risk of getting shot, abruptly rocking the helicopter. Grumpy, with Hollywood, shackled back and forth behind me, maneuvering similarly.

We flew into Nakhoney toward the area briefed by Slayer 14. I saw the troops patrolling. We circled around the area randomly searching.

"Visual friendlies," each crewmember called in turn.

"Slayer 14, Shakedown is visual," I advised, seeing the soldiers moving slowly through the maze of hardened mud walls.

"Roger that, Shakedown. We have intelligence reporting of dickers on roofs southwest of us. Check it out," he radioed.

"Roger." We steered in that direction looked for the dickers.

"We are looking," Grumpy reported over the radio slightly behind me.

"Contact dicker. I got a guy over here, Haycee., two o'clock, 400 meters! He's peeking over the roof," Snapshot called.

"Roger that." I noted the grid down from the aircraft GPS as I directed Irish to go investigate. He steered aggressively toward the target.

"Slayer 14, contact possible dicker at grid reference QQ42088756. He's behind a ledge. He pops up now and then looking in your direction," I reported.

"Roger that," he replied.

"22 Charlie, copy," a faint, eerie whisper came over the radio.

"Who's 22 Charlie?" I stated rhetorically over the intercom.

The radio sounded again, "Roger that. I have eyes on the dicker, clean shot, tracking . . . 22 Charlie out."

"Sniper," Irish stated in epiphany. "It's a sniper team allocated to the company," he informed.

A sniper had covertly positioned himself somewhere out there to help overwatch the patrol. He had probably been in location all day, just lying under camouflage in the same position, neither talking nor moving, just watching and listening—at most times, not even answering the radio to prevent being detected. He would reveal himself to us. He had a heat signature and didn't want to be mistaken as enemy, so there would be a marker by him that would only be visible from the air. If we saw the marker, obviously, we would not shoot it.

"Slayer, where is 22C?" I asked. He responded with the grid and "marked by orange panel."

"Shakedown, I know your voice," the radio whispered. I pondered the comment.

"Haha. That's John our sniper from Devil Strike," I stated over the intercom.

"Cool," Irish added as we looked for his marker.

"That you Johnny?" I replied.

"Romeo-Tango, out." Johnny whispered then hushed to resume his covert posture.

I plotted the coordinates; he was about 800 meters south of the patrol on a compound roof, a few trees. I briefed all the guys.

"I think I got him, Haycee," Snapshot called. "He won't be in the way if we have to shoot. The dicker is a long way from him."

"Roger that. Thanks."

"Visual with 22C," Grumpy called over the radio, acknowledging the radio communications.

Since we were all aware of the location of the friendlies, it was bad-guy hunting time.

"Contact, I got a guy diggin' at head height in a wall along a road. He's watching us and the area of the troops but hiding, 500 meters south down this road," Zorg reported.

"Check that. Where's Grumpy?" I asked. I wanted to know if Grumpy was trailing okay. "He is high like you said, boss," Zorg stated sarcastically.

"What do ya mean?" I asked.

"He's way the fuck up there!" Zorg answered.

I banked and stretched my neck, looking through the helicopter roof window.

"Shit! What the fuck is he doing up there?" I exclaimed.

"That's the way they do it in their section, sir," Zorg stated.

"Grumpy, you look like a homesick angle. You're so damn high!" I joked at him on the radio.

"Nope, I got your back and can see fine. If shit happens, I'll be on it in a jiff. And my bullets can reach the ground fine from here," Grumpy adamantly replied, restating he didn't like getting blown up or shot down and more than he already had.

"Do you want to switch positions?" I responded sarcastically.

"Nope, I'm good!" he replied. Grumpy observed from high and attacked from low—not in between. Smart. Unlike my IED attack, he was attacked a few weeks earlier, and his aircraft actually received a little damage from debris from a well-timed explosion.

"Check out a FAM digging on the road 500 meters south of my location," I stated.

"Got it. I'll call it in," Grumpy stated. "He's not placing the IED, just making the hole," Grumpy reported. "He has his kids with him. They are under a tree by the wadi about 5 meters away. Probably a decoy." He then passed the information on India 22.

I wasn't surprised. It was another human shield situation. All they could do is mark where the potential IEDs would be and not try to kill any innocents in the process of patrolling. And try not to get killed themselves.

I reflect on this now and consider it a losing situation. Putting children in the middle of the battle was routine. Centuries of war must have conditioned generations of Afghan people to be fighters and numb to peace.

War would continue propagating itself as a realistic answer to problems. How would these children know any different? NATO has since pulled out, but these kids, in twenty years, have already been conditioned to hate us, and fighting will start again. Afghanistan has had centuries of being the pearl of Asia, central to trade routes, and individual human freedoms with education for all. Where have these days gone?

I watched the troops meander over a short wadi to the northwest. I flew over the friendlies to get eye to eye with them. Snapshot noticed one soldier helping another one out of the wadi. He was limping.

"22, you gotta guy injured down there?" I asked.

"Roger, he's rolled his ankle. Maybe broke. He says he can continue on," the platoon commander radioed back.

"Roger that," I answered.

"He's gotta be kidding!" Irish stated. "Guys got a hundred pounds on his back, being dicked, and hobbling through the desert."

"You don't get it, sir," Zorg interrupted. "That's the way it is. He won't ask. He has a fire team partner to protect. He'll suck it up—that's what we do, but if you offered?"

As we patrolled the area, Nakhoney, Adamz-eye, and the main roads seemed quiet. Not normal. The one dicker still watched from the roof, and the IED hole digger had disappeared. Our sniper, 22C, had them covered.

"Slayer, this is 25. There is only one dicker spotted in the area. The remainder of the POL is quiet. No one in the streets, only in their compounds," I reported. "That soldier of yours seems to be slowing you down. Need a lift?"

"Copy that, Shakedown," 22 interjected. "He is. We have to head back. Can you pick him up?"

The aircraft would be very vulnerable and underpowered for extraction. The POL was signifying possible attack. We knew it.

"Guys, I'm sure we can do this. Let's find a suitable spot to extract from." I looked around.

"A hundred meters to their east. They can make a stronghold there with overwatch positions on the walls." Zorg immediately pointed to a defendable compound. He had anticipated this.

"Yes, they can observe from those walls," I agreed as I circled the spot.

"I'm in," Snapshot stated, followed by Irish.

"Freedom Ops, we gotta soldier injured. He is noncritical but needs a lift back to Madras. He slowing down the patrol. Dickers in the area," I radioed. "I plan on picking him up, Grumpy on overwatch. Request approval."

Scrappy received the request. All the helicopters were to land in FOBs only. However, there had to be some flexibility. Was this life or death? Possibly. Landing was a risk, but the troops having to march over a thousand meters in 40-degree heat with a hundred pounds of operations gear on a broken ankle, with a looming firefight, put more than just the injured soldier at risk.

"If you are good with it, go for it," Scrappy stated neutrally. He really didn't know the exact situation and always left judgment for the pilots.

"Roger. Out to you," I answered and redirected the chat to Grumpy. "Two-six, I'm going into extract."

"India 22, there is a compound 100 meters east. On the east side of the wall is an area large enough to extract. Can you secure, cordon, and get some overwatch on the walls? We'll pull him out there," I asked the infantry commander.

"Roger that. Give me five mikes," he responded.

"22 Charlie, copy that, all clear," Johnny whispered. It was a very reassuring whisper to hear; even our overwatchers were being overwatched.

I looked below and watched the platoon commander point to his troops, obviously detailing his security plan. The troops moved quickly. Combat engineers quickly surveyed a landing zone for any signs of IED; a few troops went up on the walls in fire teams and secured all the arcs for defense. Anything that moved within 500 meters would be seen. The injured soldier was being assisted toward the LZ.

"Grumpy, I need you low. Escort and then put some pressure on that dicker. Then I need some noise down low while I get that guy out," I radioed.

"Roger that. Grumpy dove in rapidly and joined on my side as I approached to land. The dust exploded. All visibility was lost, and the helicopter grabbed the ground and surged to a stop.

Grumpy broke away from my flank over the dust ball and proceeded south over the compound roof toward the dicker. His left gunner pretended to aim but without intent to activate the weapon. The dicker dropped low on the roof in a passive posture. He yielded. He knew he was identified and now only hoped he wasn't going to be shot. Grumpy continued his low-level noise masking and forechecking.

The injured soldier hobbled forward with assistance. Zorg leaned out, grabbing the arm of his comrade. He unmasked his face shield and revealed himself while showing his PPCLI patch to the soldier. I could hear them yelling over the sound of the helicopter. The soldier punched him in the arm and smiled. They knew each other from the regiment. They punched knuckles; Zorg masked up and climbed back on his gun.

Snapshot threw an impromptu seatbelt over his legs and called, "He's secure. Good to go, Haycee."

"Roger, lifting." I was at the controls. And Irish followed by reporting our takeoff over the radio to Grumpy.

"Romeo Tango," Grumpy responded, getting his helicopter into position.

"Over to Madras, but let's pretend we're departing to KAF, and then I'll break hard for FOB and dive in," I stated for a deception plan.

I flew as briefed and then aggressively turned the griffon directly into the center of FOB Madras into an even larger explosion of dust.

A medic and another soldier came over, squinting the dust from their eyes, and helped the injured soldier. The wounded soldier gave me the thumbs up and signaled for me to leave. My presence there was an invitation for rockets and mortars. They wanted us gone ASAP.

Irish took control, and we went back onto overwatch for India 22. We felt like we helped out significantly. But the POL was still abnormally quiet, so we resumed vigilance and proceeded toward the dicker on the wall. He was gone.

"Where the hell did he go?" we pondered.

"Got I-comm chatter coming through," Slayer 14 stated.

"Shakedown, you guys did something," India 22 said. "I-comm chatter quote: Voice 1: It's no good—we hit them after lunch. Voice 2: Okay, let's go for lunch first then hit them. Voice 1: Okay, go for lunch. I-comm chatter ends," he continued.

I was bewildered. The intensity of last forty-five minutes with troops, injuries, IEDs, and human shields was appearing to be second in priority to the requirement for a meal. I suppose that is something we have in common with the enemy.

"Okay, I guess we should go for lunch too then?" I questioned in jest.

Laughter echoed over the intercom. "Sounds like a plan," Snapshot stated.

Grumpy was listening, and his voice showed amusement. "25, this is 26. I guess it's time to have lunch too."

"Roger that—we'll come back and hit them after lunch," I answered.

"India 22, this is Shakedown. We're going for lunch too!" I reported in a jocular tone.

"Good job, guys. Thanks for the lift. Your observations will give Johnny something to scout out tonight. Out," India 22 responded.

Our two helicopters departed the Nakhoney area toward the east, low level.

"Hey, captain, clear left for a threat band transition," Zorg shouted, requesting an aggressive climbing maneuver similar to an amusement park, five-coupon ride.

I nodded, smiling to Irish who pulled hard climbing and twisting into the sky.

"Woo-hoo, yee-ha!" Zorg loved this.

However, the smiles were not lasting. We arrived at the FARP thinking the day was over and checked in with OPS. We'd either go back after lunch or be released.

"Shakedown 25 Flight, we got a TIC in progress, RPG, and SAFIRE, multiple casualties on Highway 1. Fuel up and respond. Details will be with the Stryker Brigade. Prof will rejoin you. Grumpy, come back. Your duty day is over." He paused. "Are you good to go?" Scrappy always asked.

I paused for just a moment. The laughing and banter stopped. Thumbs popped up all around the cockpit.

"Go for Shakedown," I replied.

Chapter 28

Man by the River 2

An American Kiowa helicopter attack team had fired at some Taliban IED planters. One of the men escaped into a compound 25 meters away, the other not so lucky. The Kiowas postured to reattack but aborted since they didn't know who else was in the compound.

The explosives were still intact on the road; the remaining Taliban soldier wanted to retrieve them. Within a few moments, a woman came outside. She looked behind her, obviously to the Taliban; his arm was seen waving through the door signifying to expedite and extract the device. The Kiowa pilot adjusted his course to advantage an attack angle onto the door but clear of the woman. However, another obstacle prevented shooting; the man had her child.

KAF FARP

I refueled at the FARP while waiting for Professor to fly over from X-ray ramp. We rejoined and departed for Senjeray. Grumpy was released to join his section and finally get some sleep. But no rest for our section; there was TIC in progress, multiple injuries.

The Stryker Brigade was escorting a logistic supply convoy and was hit—hard. An APC was burning, and casualties were being treated and evacuated while under enemy fire. Longknife, an American Kiowa team, was on station supporting but running out of fuel.

"Tower, Shakedown 25 Flight has rejoined, requesting the northwest road departure," I stated, letting him know we were a complete section once again.

"Shakedown Flight is cleared the 'road' departure. Longknife 16 inbound and Paciderm 60 behind. Give way to Dustoff on your left over the runway," the air traffic controller stated. It was normal. There were always four to six helicopters to dodge on every departure and landing.

"Shakedown 25, roger. Visual the traffic." Our Griffons continued along the departure route looking for the other helicopters as we started to climb over the mountains to Senjeray, wondering what our mission would involve.

The height at the ridge tops gave us a bird's-eye view of the fight along the highway. The ridge was about 2 kilometers south of the highway, the area we were going to work in.

"Slayer, this is Shakedown checking in. We are en route to Senjeray to support Stryker, requesting through your ROZ," I asked over the radio.

"Shakedown, this is Slayer TOC. I have nothing to report for you up in that corner of my ROZ. There is an IED strike with Stryker. Switch over to them on 42.5. Good hunting!" he reported enthusiastically.

"Romeo Tango, Slayer. Shakedown out," I answered.

"I'm up," Professor called, ready on the new frequency.

"Stryker, Stryker, this is Shakedown checking in," I called.

"Shakedown, this is Stryker 1. ROZ is hot. Guns target line from FOB Wilson to my location, cold this time. Dustoff Casevac helicopter is inbound in ten minutes to evacuate another load of casualties. Longknife 12 has control of the airspace above the IED. Situation, IED ambush has destroyed two APCs. Small arms fire continues from the wadi south of my location. I have eight casualties still to EEE-vac. I need security so Dustoff can get in. Contact Longknife for further on this frequency," his Southern U.S. accent reported.

"Roger that, out to you. Break, break, Longknife. This is Shakedown checking in. I have dual Dillon door guns, sixteen thousand rounds 7-6-2 and one times MX-15, EOIR," I reported.

"Y'all got EOIR, Shakedown?" he responded.

"Roger that," I answered.

"All right then. I got five minutes to bingo fuel. Need you to cover me for twenty minutes so we can load up. We had an ambush from the wadi about fifty yards south of the most easterly burning Stryker. Y'all all got that?" Longknife asked.

I could see to burning APCs on the highway. Troops dismounted. Some treating casualties on the north side of the road, behind the armored vehicles. "Roger that. Visual on the Stryker and looking at the AO—now," I responded.

"Uh-huh, I need ya ta hold a battle position over that ridge while we hunt for that son of a bitch. He's down in that wadi somewhere. No PID yet. Can you get your EOIR camera in that area and try to get PID? We'll bug out in about three mikes," he requested with a frustrated tone.

"Wilco. Out to you. You on it, 26?" I asked Professor on the same frequency.

"Roger. I'm scanning," Professor answered. He was busy.

"Prof, I'm staying trail on you. Keep hunting. When they clear, I'm going low bird. You direct," I stated my plan. Professor was good with the MX-15. And my crew preferred eye-to-eye hunting. It worked well.

"You betcha, boss," Professor answered ironically.

"Contact, shots fires, wadi 100 meters southeast," a voice came over the radio.

"I'm looking for the shooter," Professor interjected, pointing his camera in the reported direction.

Ops

The radio operator just picked up his coffee from the microwave again. It was the same cup of coffee he had been working on for the past five hours. Every time he started to sip it, something would happen, or he would have to do paperwork to document what had happened. He placed his coffee down, again, and ran next door to Scrappy's office.

"Sir, it's going live. Shots are being fired by the enemy," he reported.

"Okay. Thanks. I'm just reheating my coffee. Be right there," Scrappy answered, not understanding the RADOP's sigh; he really needed his coffee.

Senjeray

"Shakedown, this is Longknife. We're out. Back in twenty. Your airspace. I have no PID on the shooter. He's near or south of that large tree line by the wadi . . . in the grape fields," Longknife reported as they turned west toward FOB Wilson.

"Roger that," I acknowledged.

"All right, Prof, move in closer. Let's draw him out. I'm going low level and searching that wadi. Cover me at about 700 feet, 200 feet and below is mine, you can have above," I stated. Professor continued in big circles but lower, using the high-powered camera to scan the wadi for thermal images in the vicinity of the Longknife report.

I dropped low level and prodded east to west low and slow at about 50 feet looking directly into the wadi. The gunners scanned the wadi with their weapons looking for someone.

"Contact, I got him. He's fifty meters south of the wadi underneath the grape row greenery. I got a thermal image." Professor was excited.

"Roger, direct me into him and report to Stryker," I stated and then heard him call in the coordinates to the Stryker convoy leader. Professor then directed me.

"Your seven o'clock now! Fifty meters. I see an AK slung."

Zorg's eyes immediately locked on that spot when he heard the radio. "I got him, Cap. Come left. I got two targets," he called while aiming slightly beside the potential threat—ready. "I'm ready."

"Wait for it," I yelled, implying not to shoot yet. I took control from Irish. I banked the aircraft hard left, well beyond the allowed limits. The Griffon's blades slapped the air violently.

"More, more, more!" Zorg yelled. "Roll out now!"

"I got him!" I yelled. I steered to a slow-speed circular orbit around the white clothes of an apparent man under the greenery in the grape vines. Prof covered me from above.

The man knew he was targeted. He tried not to reveal more of himself. I needed to PID him before giving the fire order.

"Is this the guy?" I asked Professor. "I'm circling around him."

"Roger. I got more movement—it seems to be someone coming out of the ground near him. Careful!" he reported, observing possible multiple targets on the MX camera.

"Zorg, get ready! Those fuckers killing days are over," I yelled.

I came into a very slow speed pass. We knew the man had a weapon, but Zorg would annihilate him before he could draw.

Zorg took careful aim, removed the safety, and slowly found the trigger switch.

"There's a kid, two kids, three kids down there," I yelled. "Check fire, Zorg. Check fire!"

Zorg pointed it away and then burst out in a rage. "You fuckin' cowardly son of a bitch. How dare you use kids as a shield. I'm gonna come down there and rip your fuckin' throat out with my bare hands." Zorg continued yelling at the man, he could be heard without the intercom.

I looked down and saw the man looking directly up at us, directly at me. He held three children down under his arms. Two of them he held firmly with his boney fingers, gripping tightly over his arm. A boy about twelve years old stood beside him stoically, frozen. No expression. I memorized his beard, his white man jammies, and his leathery creased face. He had a black shoulder strap or sash holding the shape of a concealed rifle beneath his loose clothes. And I couldn't shoot.

I zoned to deafness as I hovered merely feet away from my enemy, glaring at him with the sound of Zorg's fury fading behind me. I could only hear my heart beat. If it wasn't just three seconds, it was a year I sat there. I pondered about landing and capturing him. Is there another shooter? Is there IED, most likely? There was no place to land. He's deep in the grapevines.

I had been in theater over half a year; I was jaded. I pondered about the Shamus pilots who landed on the road and killed the three insurgents in the culvert after the aircraft ran out of ammo. They used their personal weapons. Initially I thought they were idiots, but now I understood.

After a year, a person could easily cross the line of self-preservation for the mission. It became personal. Where is that faint line between going to the next level and resuming cautious professionalism?

"Get some speed on, Steve!" a voice broke up my thoughts. "Get some speed on." It was Professor bringing me back to reality. I was practically hovering next to the man, 50 feet from him, staring eye to eye, and I couldn't take action.

"Don't even think about it. Get back on my wing. I'll track him." Professor's voice rang over the radio.

He was right. I was setting myself up, my crew up for disaster. I had to get some speed and be more evasive.

"Roger that," I submitted coldly.

I flew up and joined on the wing of Professor. We tracked the man for another ten minutes as he proceeded carefully toward the compound south about 400 meters away. There was a woman observing by the entry of the compound. The man never let go of at least one of the children, holding the child firmly in his grip.

"Shakedown, this is Longknife. Back on station, request a handover," Longknife reported.

"Roger," I responded. "Dustoff medevac chopper is on the ground now loading casualties. PID man in a white shirt with kids approaching the compound about a half mile south of the wadi. Call tally," I stated.

There was a pause. The Kiowas had to get their optical cameras onto the target and commence tracking.

"Tally target," Longknife reported.

"Do not fire. He has WACs. Call visual on the children."

"Awe shit! Visual the WACs. All right, thanks, Shakedown. We'll take it from here," Longknife reported back.

"Roger out." I was defeated.

I took a silent moment to center my emotions as we climbed above the ridge to the south. I had to leave it behind and focus on the next task. The intensity of the event, not to mention the entire day was more than most people have to deal with in their entire lives. However, I had to soldier on; my team had to refocus.

I called back to Scrappy asking if there was anything else as we crossed the ridgeline toward KAF.

"Roger that, Shakedown. We got another task coming in. Go FARP and stand by," Scrappy announced.

Ops

"Boss, we got another overwatch task back in Nakhoney for 25 and 26," Scrappy told Skipper who had just came in to review the day's events. "They have been going pretty solid with some high-intensity stuff. Just review the logs," Scrappy continued. Skipper looked at the log and reviewed the text screen and then looked back at Scrappy.

Scrappy shook his head lightly in silence.

"I agree. They're done for today. Bring 'em home," Skip stated and then looked at Ricky who made the radio call.

"Shakedown 25, negative. You're done for today. Just fuel and return to X-ray. Ops out," he stated.

Operations Postflight

Scrappy looked at me. He had followed the text prompter, which reported the events.

"How'd it go? You all right?" he asked.

"Humans shields again, three children," I sighed.

"Longknife is still tracking. He is having a hard time keeping PID with the hidey-holes and underground tunnels. He'll get away," Scrappy reported.

"Yup."

"How's your team?" Scrappy continued.

"Prof called me out for being vulnerable, and Zorg almost jumped out to take him on one-on-one," I confessed.

Scrappy giggled empathetically. "I think Skipper is taking your spot tomorrow. You need a day off! Take it," Scrappy stated and smiled.

"Awesome," I sighed. "My second day off in over eight months!" I smirked sarcastically, rolling my eyes. "Oh, what shall I do?"

Chapter 29

A Day Off

It was my second day off in theater—a real, complete day off. No test flying, no flight planning, no flights. I was ecstatic yet didn't know what to do. My original plan was to sleep in. However, that failed. Since my sleep cycle was synchronized with a 2:45 a.m. wake-up, I only managed to sleep in until five o'clock.

I stirred and kept looking at my watch then gave up trying to sleep. Most of the guys were up, so I wouldn't risk waking anyone. I heard them moving around a few hours earlier. I got up too. I stretched, wiped the burning crusty dust out of my eyes, placed my outdoor shoes on, and proceeded to the showers where I'd plan out my day. It was as a GTL day: gym, tan, laundry with a coffee inserted somewhere.

To the laundry. I raised my nose but did not find the smell of the poo pond for a change. The poo pond was an eight hundred and ninety five-step walk directly west into the stench. However, today's lovely northwest breeze gave the Canadians a break from the ooze.

I got into line and exchanged pleasantries with some other soldiers for the next few minutes before receiving my laundry tag. Most of the conversation revolved around the poo pond stench and time remaining in theater.

With tag in hand, I walked toward Tim Horton's for a coffee. However, because it was a day off, I thought I'd reward myself and switch to the French cafe for a latte.

I stopped briefly at my tent, dropped off my laundry tag, and had a momentary latrine stop. In addition to being the latrine, it doubled as the local art gallery with unique displays of evolving graffiti. Some was crude yet entertaining.

For the last few months of my tour, there was a mystery grammar teacher that had been correcting all the grammatical errors made by the latrine poets. Another different artist used the stall as a countdown board. The numbers were close to my time, making it appreciable. I had finally reached the two hundreds upward and decided to count down for the rest. There were less than a hundred days to go from the original 308 I started with.

I continued my leisurely stroll toward the boardwalk, navigating through a path of sea cans. I found a shortcut that saved about a hundred meters of walking distance. At the boardwalk, there was an early morning Canadian hockey game and some Americans playing football on the gravel field. Some of these soldiers had never nor would ever see a day outside the wire. It was a bit of contention since they received the same operational pay as an infantry soldier that walked through the valley of death every day dodging dickers, RPGs, and sniper fire.

The French coffee house had a wood picket fence around a small dusty courtyard. Fake plants added ambience. Several wooden picnic tables added to the relaxation and promoted conversation. Sometimes the entire base felt like a thirty-thousand-member armed family; anyone could talk with anyone—comfortably.

I ordered a large, double shot latte. It smelled divine and transported me back to the patio at Starbucks near 124th Street in Edmonton—my favorite coffee shop where I could also enjoy some treats from the candy shop next door. I sipped, held a newspaper, and imagined a massive elm tree stretching over me providing the shade. In reality, the shade was from a defensively positioned concrete rocket wall.

I reached down to adjust my pistol to relieve the pressure point, as it always slipped in behind my back,.

"Holy shit!" I called out, snapping my mind back into reality. I was in the middle of a war. And my pistol was gone, not just the pistol, the entire holster and three magazines of ammunition. Where did I leave it?

I sprung to my feet, looked around the picnic table, and then started sprinting, splashing scalding latte all over my arm.

"Fuck," I whispered as I wiped the hot coffee off my arm. I knew where I left it. It was on the hang-up hooks in the shitter. I retraced my steps, running through the middle of the football field. Players stopped and watched me like a panicky idiot sprinting through the field, splashing coffee up my arm. I ran into the latrines and checked the stall—gone! Oh no! Okay, maybe it was the next stall—gone! I checked every stall and all the latrine houses. Then I double-checked to no success.

I saw the Afghani construction workers next door fixing a latrine that had been hit by a rocket. I spoke in my best panicky Spanish to try to find my weapon. I realized I stupidly defaulted to either French or Spanish whenever I met someone of a different language. My message wasn't getting through to the Pashtun-speaking worker. I shook my head and moved on.

Rationalizing, I thought I forgot the holster on my bed and continued my search there. Nope! I sat defeated. My chillaxing day off was just destroyed. After realizing I had lost it, and most likely in the latrine, I submitted and stopped my search and phoned the operations center to report it.

"So what's the procedure?" I asked.

"You have to go to the Canadian Military Police and report it." I was advised.

"Okay, can you call the weapons techs and find out my serial number? Have them forward it to the MPs. I'm on my way."

I arrived to a friendly bunch of military police corporals who were more than hospitable. A young lady cop offered me some water and took my particulars. Under her breath she was laughing at me for leaving my weapon in the shitter. However, they were extremely professional despite the occasional hidden smirk.

"Sir, it's part of procedure, but we need you to sign this interrogation consent form," the MP requested.

"What? I just told you everything. Why do I need to sign an interrogation form?" I asked, perplexed.

"It's standard procedure. Then we'll take you to the questioning room to get the facts," the police officer continued. "While we question you, we'll send out a squad car to search the area you described in your testimony," the officer continued.

"Testimony? Facts? I just told you everything. What's next?" I inquired.

Ignoring my questions, they continued the pedantic procedure. The lady cop pulled out the map and pointed to the area where I resided. "Is this where the alleged situation transpired, sir?" she asked politely.

"Alleged? I lost it in this stall right here!" I pointed exactly to the map.

"Fine, sir. I'll go check it out." She departed to investigate.

"Okay, sir, if you'll step into this room, we'll continue our questioning," the junior MP stated as he pointed to the room in the back.

I stepped into the all-white room. There was a camera in the upper corner over my right shoulder. It was definitely an interrogation room. Why was I being interrogated? I thought I had already told them what happened.

The MP continued to ask me questions to repeat the history of the event. I was getting frustrated. What? Did they think I was selling my personal weapons to the insurgency? What was all this about? It was simply a lost weapon. There are thirty thousand handguns on that camp all being carried openly on holsters, not to mention the automatic weapons that the soldiers carry all day long; even the occasional heavy machine gun can be seen at Timmy's.

"Let's take it from the top," the policeman questioned.

I sighed and started my testimony. "I pooped, I went for coffee, and I discovered it missing. I ran back. It was gone," I answered bluntly.

"Can you be more detailed?"

"Not without being disgusting."

"The timeline, it doesn't seem to work. It took an awful long time from the alleged poop to the time you arrived here," he stated.

Alleged poop? He's right; I can't really prove that.

"Okay, let me fill you in more. I pooped. I wiped. I pulled my pants up. I walked slowly across the boardwalk. I waited ten minutes in line at the French Cafe. I sat. I read two sentences of an article. I ran back. I searched. I called my ops center. I walked here. Yes, a good hour," I snapped back sarcastically.

The police officer reeled back. "I'm just following procedure. Give me a break, sir."

"I'm sorry. I'm just frustrated and the 'procedure'—it isn't making things any easier," I responded respectfully.

Another police officer interrupted, "The case is closed. We found your pistol, sir. Serial numbers matched. Someone turned your weapon into the IMP—the International Military Police. You're lucky. Here's one pistol, one holster, three magazines, and thirty-nine rounds. Does that sound about right? Not forty?"

I did some math in my head, multiplying bullets by magazines. "Yup, thanks. I don't keep one in the chamber."

They walked me out from interrogation room, gave the weapon back, and started counting rounds out of the various magazines, totally unloading it.

"One, two, three . . . thirty-nine. Yup, I guess this is yours," the officer concluded.

"Yea, my name's on the holster too," I pointed out sarcastically.

The officer gave a sneer back.

I grabbed my bullets and weapon and walked to the door. I still had time to enjoy my afternoon but not without a reminder of my offence.

"You're aware, sir, that this will be reported to your superior officer. It is a chargeable offence. You'll probably be fined."

"Yes, I am aware that my negligence will be corrected. Thank you, ladies and gentleman." I departed. I felt unnecessarily snarky.

The remainder of my day was stable. I enjoyed an afternoon movie on my computer, tanned, and went to the gym. At the gym, I looked through a small window in the door of the spin class room. Hollywood was pedaling directly behind an attractive, fit lady soldier. He was eye-locked onto the tattoo above her yoga pant waist band (a.k.a. the tramp stamp), which was clearly visible below her fitness halter top. Hollywood, being eye-locked on the artwork, swayed in sync with her hip movements on each bicycle stroke. He noticed me watching him and paused to give the thumbs-up. I rolled my eyes, smiled, and quickly diverted from the window to not get busted.

Arnie was at the bench press pushing two and a half plates, 275 pounds. I was impressed.

"Hey, Steve. I'm just warming up. Want to join in?" He raised his chin to invite.

"Warm up? Cardio first for me," I stated. "And that weight will crush me Arnie, 175 not 275!" Arnie lifted his chin and chuckled, admiring his lifting superiority.

I like to run. I hopped on the treadmill or sometimes ran around the KAF airport. I was as crazy as Skipper when it came to enduring the dust to get the fitness complete. The KAF circle was about 14 kilometers but often too dusty to breath.

Arnie didn't like cardio. He did not believe in sweating, and somehow he didn't despite the heat. He would do a set, wait five minutes for a full recovery, and then do another set. He would spend three hours in the gym, but it worked; he was huge.

Snapshot and Grumpy were in the gym too. We all shared the same motivation, endorphin therapy. An easy hour on the treadmill allowed time to metabolize the stress of the day and enter into the next day focused with a calm warrior spirit, once catalyzed by a MOAC anyway. However, I would need about an hour and a half today.

"So I didn't realize the Taliban took sophisticated lunch breaks in the killing fields?" Grumpy announced.

"That was pretty surreal," I retorted. "Ta-ta, gentlemen, let's break for lunch and reengage in mortal combat. At one-ish, shall we say?" I mocked in my best hi-English aristocratic accent.

Grumpy laughed. "So how is Irish?" he asked about my copilot's performance.

"Good, but every now and then, he gets the front and back of the Chinook mixed up and tries to rejoin head-on." I smirked, reflecting on the deadly error.

"Ha-ha! I heard he was playin' chicken with Droopy the other day. Nice!" Grumpy smiled. Droopy was already stressed enough and didn't need Griffons also threatening his life.

"He's getting stronger, but every now and then he wants to kill me doing stuff like that and I don't have the mental energy to teach over here." I responded with concern.

"I get it. I have the same shit, different pile with Hollywood. Very strong hands and feet—but brain focused on the story." Grumpy shook his head. "If it's worth anything, I've had similar days myself. I don't get this generation," Grumpy empathized, referring to our age gap with the first officers. "Brilliance coupled with situational cluelessness."

"Yes, but what's the difference between us and them?" I queried.

"I guess just experience." Grumpy shrugged.

"But it's not like we've experienced anything like this before," I retorted.

"I know, but imagine our experience being reported in terms of a weather forecast. A grumpy old captain's prevailing condition is caution and awareness with temporary conditions of confusion. However, the forecast for a copilots is fearless confusion with temporary episodes of awareness," Grumpy professed, smiling.

I laughed hard, stumbled, and grabbed onto the treadmill rails to prevent from falling and being shot off the back.

Grumpy laughed. "You're starting to act like a copilot. Pay attention!"

"You haven't heard the last part," I added once regaining balance. "I am so exhausted and discombobulated that I lost my pistol in the shitter a couple of hours ago."

Grumpy laughed. I explained the entire story to him.

"So what's in gonna cost? Shorty got tagged for $1,200 for his barrack box assassination," Grumpy added.

"Haven't seen Skipper yet. Dunno. I'm sure Irish is thinking of it as poetic justice." We both chuckled.

I finished my workout and meandered around the gym. I passed the word about the next day mission to those in my crew that were there. Table time at eleven thirty.

I walked the 1-kilometer hike back to my tent, cooling off along the way despite the 37-degree heat. I realized that not being in the daily intense routine was worse for me than maintaining a war momentum. I didn't want any more days off—just work straight through until I could go home.

Chapter 30

Tap Dancing through a Field of Bullets

Infantry Unit 22A, Chalgour

"Two Two (22), this is two-two- alpha (22A)," the young infantry officer called his boss. "Proceeding down route bravo toward Chalgour," he continued. His orders were to lead a typical route patrol. This time the company was out with two LAVs (light armored vehicles) and a platoon of dismounted infantry—Canadian. They were conducting a presence and counter-IED patrol along a main route east of Salavat toward Nakhoney.

"Two two alpha (22A) send over," 22 answered.

"We gotta culvert with some funny markings, stopping to investigate, possible IED," he answered.

"Roger that. You all know the drills!" the boss's voice interjected over the radio, a major, 29.

The convoy stopped, and everyone dismounted, clearing the flanks for possible ambushes. The combat engineers went out to investigate for bombs.

"I got fresh dirt, possible wires out the sides," he reported. He continued tracing the dirt trying to expose wires, walking a safe distance away from the suspected mine in the road culvert. "Absolutely! We got an IED."

Snap, snap, snap.

"Contact, north! Contact, north! Enemy shooters. Looking!" a voice yelled as dirt exploded around the Canadians from bullets skipping across the fields.

The foot soldiers dove to the ground and crawled into tactical observation positions on the backside of the grape mounds. The LAVs remained stopped and swung their 25mm main guns north to scan the enemy.

"Contact, FAMs on the backside of the wall, 200 meters, marked by my fire," 22 called over the radio.

Kawump, kawump, kawump.

The main gun exploded, ripping 25-millimeter rounds against the wall. The Canadian soldiers also fired, adding to the huge explosion of dust on the hard clay earth wall masking visibility of the enemy.

Slayer 14 was embedded with the company. He was the direct link to the fire control center at the TOC.

"14, send in the contact report to the TOC. See if we can get some support in here," the major hollered on the radio.

"Slayer TOC, this is 14. We gotta TIC in progress. Multiple FAMs north of our position. IEDs implanted. Request helicopter overwatch," he yelled over the radio.

"Roger, 14, stand by," TOC responded from KAF.

Reg Desert

"Shakedown 25, TIC in progress," the radio broke out. "Proceed 3 kilometers north of Madras, India 22A taking fire."

"Roger," I acknowledged then contacted India 22A. We were returning from escorting Blowtorch near Sperwan Ghar. He had returned to KAF solo. We were about to conduct some training in the Reg Desert.

"22A, go for Shakedown," I asked.

"Shakedown, this is two niner (29) . . . I am with 22A." The voice puffed as if out of breath. "I have dismounted my LAV and rejoining my foot patrol units on the grape rows at grid reference QQ44409052. Request overwatch. We are engaging enemy to the north with 25 millimeters and small arms, join from the south."

"Roger that, niner. I'll be in your location in two minutes," I answered.

I looked down to enter the coordinates then realized that I recognized the numbers. That's the Nakhoney region, again. I looked up toward Nakhoney. "I got it, guys. See the smoke and dust ahead? That's the 25 millimeter impacting something," I called.

The rest of the crew acknowledged. We closed rapidly as it was only a few minutes away.

"I can't see our friendly troops yet. Can anyone see 'em?" I frantically queried. I needed to be ready to shoot, and I had to make sure the infantry were not in my arcs of fire.

"Niner, it's Shakedown. I'm visual with your LAVs. Where are your dismounts?"

"East-west line 200 meters east of my LAVs." The voice was faint and still huffing. He was running and trying to yell over the radio simultaneously.

As we closed to 500 meters from the exploding dust, Snapshot called out.

"I got them, right ahead, prone position facing north on the grapes!"

"Visual." I saw the troops; my suppressive fire plan immediately formed in my head. There were bullet splashes landing all around them. On the west flank, the ground commander, Niner, was still running through the field almost like he was dancing in the bullet splashes around him, barely eluding them as the dust puffs followed him along the grape row.

"Fuck! He's under fire. Where are the bad guys?" I hollered.

"Niner, take me onto the target. I got a building, a wall, and multiple hit points in my field of view," I asked over the radio.

"We started taking hits from the wall. It's obscured in dust, 200 meters north," Niner reported. "The FAMs are between the wall and the building north somewhere!" he yelled.

"The wall was only a couple of hundred meters away; it was entirely engulfed in exploding dust from the LAVs firing 25millimeter cannon at or near it. The splashes of bullets were flying near our helicopters and on the ground near the troops. I realized that I was going to be exposed to enemy fire as turned along the forward line of troops.

"Right gunner, the wall marked by LAV fire, give me suppression on it! Possible enemy targets behind it," I ordered.

"Tally target," Snapshot called and released a five-second spread of bullets, joining the infantry's fire onto the wall. If anyone was behind it, the downward trajectory should suppress them.

"Check fire. I'm breaking left." The guns stopped.

Professor was directly behind me joining in the attack pattern. He was in the exact position I expected when I rolled out to reengage the enemy. I could cover his six o'clock as he broke contact.

"You visual with, Prof?" I called to the left gunner.

"Visual, Prof. Friendlies, tally target," Zorg hollered.

"Stand by," I called. The smoke was clearing near the wall. All the fire from the troops below was redirected 500 meters further north on the compound.

"The wall is clear from what I can see!" called Zorg. "No target behind it."

I relayed that information to Niner.

"Roger that, Shakedown. I need you to advance forward and see if you can pin down multiple shooters in the vicinity of those buildings marked by my LAV fire," Niner stated. I could hear and feel the concussion the of the 25-millimeter cannon firing 75 feet below me, the smell of cordite permeating the battlefield.

Thump, thump, thump.

"Roger," I responded. "Prof, let's set up a high orbit around those compounds and try to PID with the camera. The LAVs can still suppress if required."

I was concerned about the ricochet of the 25-millimeter cannon. Just the rebounding stray bullet had the potential to rip through the helicopter even with us at several thousand feet.

"Proceeding overhead. Can you check fire on the LAV?" I requested.

"Roger that," 22A acknowledged.

It was quiet. Both the enemy and the friendlies stopped firing. Niner's targets vanished; obviously they went into hiding. However, now without positive identification of the targets, we would not be able to fire.

We orbited the compounds for ten minutes looking for people and studying the POL. No one was around, and no shooters popped out. The infantry slowly advanced on the buildings, but the IED discoveries greatly slowed their advance.

"I got FAMs in black man jammies," called Zorg.

I looked down; two men walked out of the backside of the building and went in different directions from each other. I advised the panting ground commander.

"Roger that, Shakedown. We cannot engage now. No PID. We are advancing forward," the commander called.

"That's the guys, Cap. I know it," Zorg called.

"I know! But we lost PID. We don't know if they are shooters or farmers being coerced to walk out," I stated.

"This is fucked!" Zorg retorted. Everyone was frustrated. Our hands were tied, and it was obvious they were the shooters. However, there was always the slightest doubt preventing the engagement—the Taliban exploited that.

"Two more!" Irish called. He saw another set of men come out and also disperse slowly through the streets.

"Niner, this is Shakedown. Two more are dispersing. Total four men."

"Track them as long as possible and report," he requested.

Professor and I pulled high in the sky and observed with our MX-15 optics. We relayed the numerous locations to Slayer, hoping he had an available UAV that could continue tracking after we departed.

"There isn't another goddamned person in this entire village. It's usually busy. I know those are the guys. These ROE are fucked. When can we start returning fire?" Zorg was upset. He continued to vent as we monitored the Taliban slithering away.

"Shakedown, Slayer wants you. Another TIC in progress. Thanks for your support. Next time, guys! Niner out," the commander stated; his voice surrendered the pursuit but content none of his team was hit.

I switched radio frequencies and called Professor to change frequencies to prepare for the next TIC. I looked at the troops below. They were defiling into another IED search pattern as they advanced toward the enemy. It was apparent that the enemy intention was merely to taunt us through a minefield of IEDs. Now the task was to find and disarm the IEDs before they injured any locals. The battle was suspended, but the campaign of winning the hearts and minds through IED removal was resurrected—for the moment.

Chapter 31

Haji Sofi

"Hi, sir," I greeted Skipper as he arrived to the X-ray ramp TOC. Skipper was standing in the hall outside operations.

"Evening, Steve," he stated. "Come with me." He gestured me over into lit area outside the back door.

I sighed as he knew what was coming. Not too sure how Skipper was going to address this issue. I was getting charged for my day off.

"Let me show you something." He pulled out his Browning pistol and showed it to me. "Read the bottom," he stated.

I turned his pistol over and read the sticker label on the bottom.

"CO 408 SQN TF FREEDOM, SKIPPER, $100 REWARD IF FOUND."

"Does yours have this?" he asked.

I twisted my mouth and shook his head. "Nope."

"From what I've heard of the general's charge parades so far, you're probably looking at about $500 . . . Dumb ass." Skipper laughed. He had a knack of laughing off the events that were administratively required but saved his focus for things that were operationally serious. His laughter at my embarrassment was reassuring.

"A hundred-buck reward? It's a lot cheaper than $500 and no charge report! Now go inside. Carry on." He smiled.

"Yes, sir. Thanks, Skipper," I responded respectfully. "Wait just a second." I reached into my flight suit lower pocket and pulled out a piece of paper. "Can you sign this as having disciplined me?" I handed him my misdemeanor for walking in the dark without a light after the rocket attack.

He snatched it from my hand, swearing under his breath as he signed the document.

"Thanks again, boss. Appreciated." I laughed, showing him my zipper flashlight indicating it wouldn't happen again.

TOC

Northeast of Frontenac on the far side of the Dalah Dam and Arghandhab Lake was a small village called Haji Sofi. It was isolated from the other communities, making it an ideal secretive location for making homemade explosives or HME. HME was used in the IEDs that killed thousands of people every year throughout Afghanistan.

Task Force Freedom was tasked to escort an American Infantry unit, a small company of men with interpreters and ANA into the town. They would sweep through at first light and exploit any HME factories they found.

The mission was for Chinooks to insert the troops thirty minutes before first light. Shakedown's mission was to escort the Chinooks, mark the landing zone, and then stay on protective overwatch for the infantry during the sweep mission.

Professor and I had the escort, the insert, and the first watch for a few hours before being ripped out by Grumpy and Big C. We started our mission as a night observation section without the Chinooks. We proceeded to a position about 8 kilometers from Haji Sofi and scanned the area with the MX-15. We looked at the town for unusual heat signatures, POL, and then scanned the landing zone to ensure it was safe.

"Looks good, Prof. I don't see anything unusual. You?" I radioed.

"Nope, looks good. Shall we go meet the Chinooks at the rendezvous?" Professor asked.

"Roger that," I responded. Irish steered the aircraft high towards the middle of Arghandhab Lake. At Frontenac, with the MX-15, I could see the two Canadian Chinooks loading troops then lifting to meet us.

"Butch, I gotcha visual. Joining your six o'clock," I stated.

"Check that," Butch answered.

"Awe, damn it. I just lost a tube on my goggles," I cursed as my left eye NVG tube failed. "I'll try to fly off one."

"Shit, this is no good! I'm getting a splitting headache," I noted after a few minutes of trying to fly on one tube.

I tried to just use the one goggle and then go unaided (without goggles) and use the MX-15 in infrared for situational awareness, but the combination of one eye on a goggle and the other blacked out but focusing on the peripheral light of cockpit instruments was straining. "Irish, you'll have to fly all this for now." I tilted my goggles up to relieve the stress.

"Cap, you'll have to use mine," Zorg stated and came forward. "We only have thirty minutes until light. I'll be fine. But you need to see."

"Okay, if we get into a fight, I'll have to direct your PEC2 laser onto the target and call you to shoot," I stated and told the plan to Professor. Who responded back with a chuckle after he found out I had been flying for ten minutes with only one tube.

"Zorg, we'll switch after the insertion. Blowtorch is two minutes back. I'll suck it up until then," I briefed.

"Shakedown, this is Blowtorch, I gotta vehicle moving up this valley south of Haji Sofi. It's the middle of the night on a back road. Unusual," Butch called.

"Roger that. I'll GPS mark it. Thanks," I responded. I quickly swung the camera onto the vehicle. It was a motorcycle. It was stopping, and the rider was getting off. It was about 4,000 meters from the village but behind a large mountain range.

Professor orbited several kilometers away, and his laser marked the landing spot guiding the Chinooks. They landed a few hundred meters east of the town, and about eighty troops egressed from the rear and established their defensive perimeters immediately. Once the Chinooks departed. We immediately began radio check in.

"All units, this is 6 (the American major in command), check in," a serious voice sounded over the radio.

"1."

"2."

"3."

"4." Different patrols checked in sequentially.

"Roger that, and Shakedown, check in," he added at the end.

"Six, this is Shakedown, sixty minutes playtime, sixteen thousand rounds, seven six two tracer with two times MX-15 optics," I reported.

"Roger that, Shakedown. What do you see?" Six stated. He was focused and urgent.

"We have nothing. No hot spots. No POL. Your avenues to town look clear. Nothing unusual on each objective," I reported. The ground commander had passed us a map showing all the buildings. Each building had a reference code so it could be easily referred to if something unusual occurred. Each code was programmed in the MX-15, so I had to only push two buttons, and the camera would swing and lock onto the building.

"Roger out to you. All units. Move out!" he ordered.

I observed four individual streams of infantry filing into various access paths toward the village. They moved forward to the edge of town then paused, waiting for official sunrise before advancing into the town. They weren't breaking in, just knocking on doors (called a soft knock) and visiting locals. However, they wanted some element of surprise, or IED manufacturers would escape. The ANA and interpreters would assess the reactions of locals.

Additionally, an elder from Shawali Kot was to meet with Six about one hour after entering the town. However, he was nowhere in sight.

"I gotta squirter," I called, looking through my MX-15. "Six, I gotta guy who has left the town on the north side away from you. He is proceeding through the wadi and toward the lake."

"Roger, keep track and advise," Six responded.

"Here ya go, Cap. NVGs." Zorg came forward.

"Thanks, Zorg." I removed my pair and installed the working pair. "Oh, that feels much better, almost instant relief on my brain."

"The sun should be up in about ten minutes anyway," Zorg responded.

As the clock ticked past official first light, the radio broke alive with orders. "Move in!" Six commanded. From the air, all eighty troops advanced into the town slowly and started sweeping the streets and focused on suspected HME factories and compounds. It wasn't long before the first contact was reported.

"Six, this is 2. IED," the radio sounded.

"Roger that. Engineers go help 'em out."

Over the next twenty minutes, numerous other IEDs were found in positions to protect certain homes. Then they found a small factory.

"Six Alpha, you go take control of that factory. I will be at town center waiting for our guest," the major told his second in charge.

"Shakedown, you still tracking that squirter?"

"Roger that," I answered.

"I am expecting the mayor of Shawali Kot to be here any minute. He is to cross the river 6 kilometers northeast. Can you go investigate?" he asked.

Professor already had those coordinates in his MX and scanned the area from his current location. "No vehicles sighted," Professor informed.

"I know y'all got optics, but can you go and phis-i-cal-ly look," Six stated in frustration. He seemed anxious.

He had several IEDs already, a squirter and a late VIP who was important for the entire mission. Being a local elder, the people would respect him as opposed to the major, an American Infidel.

Professor and I flew over to the area. The sun was above the mountain and started lighting up the valley. There were no vehicles at the coordinates. However, about 10 kilometers in a different direction was snake of dust rising through the desert aiming toward Haji Sofi. We flew over to investigate.

"Six, no cars at the RV point. However, I got a convoy of nice vehicles coming directly toward you from the Kot," I informed.

"Roger that. Check my squirter," Six advised directly. This became our job for the morning; he kept us moving all over the place attaining information. Meanwhile, his temper was rising and more threats kept surfacing making his posture more at risk. Yet, our team could do little to find anything concrete to support him with anything other than our standby status and overwatch.

"Six, this is 2. No one owns this IED factory. They are claiming it is an abandoned house."

"Bullshit! Wrong answer!" Six responded in his perturbed Southern accent. "Keep questioning them," the radio ordered.

"Six, this is Shakedown. I have the squirter. He's walking toward the lake still. Not making much progress, but he's about 2,000 meters west," I informed. "Looks like he is just trying to avoid the show."

"Roger that. Thank you," stated Six more cordially.

We continued surveillance of critical compounds while tracking the squirter. He had difficulty walking through a wadi and rough terrain. The closest roadway was about 8 kilometers north. And the lake head from the Dalah Dam blocked him from going west. He was obviously suspect and either avoiding the Americans or trying to draw them in.

The ground commander continued his search. "2, this is 6. Ask them who that squirter is."

"All call signs, this is Sapper (counter-IED). Gonna blow the IEDs in one minute. Shakedown, back off 1,000 meters. All call signs acknowledge," the engineer broke over the radio to advise everyone that there would be a few explosions as they detonated the HME they had been securing. Each sub-unit responded in turn.

"Cool, we finally get a fireworks show!" I called over the radio then led Professor away from the explosion.

"All call signs, detonating in five, four, three, two, one," Sapper called.

A few seconds later, a few small puffs went off in town. It was an obvious explosion but nothing dramatic.

"What the hell was that?" called Zorg sarcastically. "We make a bigger poof than that when we land!"

"That was sure a lot of foreplay for a little bang!" Professor announced on the private radio frequency. The crew laughed.

"Six, I have I-comm chatter coming in. Ready to copy?" a new voice announced. It was the intelligence operator working with the ANA terp listening to cell phone communications for anything pertinent.

"Go for Six."

"I-comm chatter reads, 'they are coming along the wadi now and into the compounds.' I-comm out."

"6, this is 2," the platoon leader interjected. "They say that the man does not own the house. He is a duck hunter."

There was a pause, and the radio voice exploded in anger.

"All stations and call sign 2. Bullshit! It's not duck season. It's not fuckin' ducks they are hunting. It's us they are huntin'—stay focused. We are being watched. Most likely from the hills. It's the only place to make those observations from. We've discovered a factory and numerous IEDs. Watch yourselves. Shakedown I want eyes on those hills to the south. Anyone moving? I want info now! Out!" Six ordered.

"Roger that," I stated. He was sounding spooked. Shit was happening at the ground level that we were not privy to.

"Prof, he's getting stressed. Let's split up, and I'll take the base up to 700 feet. You take the ridgelines. Let's stay on the north face and sweep 5 kilometers either side. I'll start on the west end."

"Roger that," Professor responded as our two choppers proceeded west and tight against hills. I flew close to the mountains looking at caves, paths and behind rocks for possible hiding spots. Professor followed but about a thousand feet higher along the ridges. We scoured the ridge and hills for movement. The radio sounded with continual frustrated chatter between the infantry units below.

"Contact," Zorg called. "One o'clock, 1,500 meters. Halfway up I can see several men in jammies—white."

I looked over and noticed the speck of white appear around a ridge. Irish steered that direction as I passed the info to Professor.

"I got the ball on them," Professor announced. "Three shepherds and some goats just sitting there; they are around the corner but looking toward Haji Sofi."

"Keep observing. See if they appear to be communicating," I stated and passed the info to Six.

"Roger that, Shakedown. Sweep closer to the village, and I just got report the mayor should be here momentarily. His convoy is coming from the north now. Go identify."

"Check that," I responded.

"Let's poke closer to town and go find that motorbike again. If we can track a trail from the motorbike to the ridge, we may find someone," I stated to Professor.

"I-comm chatter update, 'They are coming from the river toward you,'" reported the intelligence operator over the radio.

The ground commander had gathered some information and realized that his troops coming up from searching the wadi could only be seen from within the town or the ridgeline directly south of the town.

"Shakedowns, the dicker has to be in town or immediately south on that ridge," Six reported. "It's the only place he could make those observations from. Not the goat herders."

"Roger that, Six. We are going over the ridge toward the motorcycle we spotted earlier, and it was being driven during your insert. It's in that observation line. We'll follow any paths from there toward the town from the bike," I called in my plan.

"Roger that, Shakedown. That has to be our dicker's bike…or the duck hunter's."

We crossed the ridge and located the motorcycle using the GPS fix on the MX-15.

"There it is," called Snapshot. "Come right," he directed.

"Got it," called Irish. "I'll set up a left orbit and find a path."

"Thanks." I focused the camera on the bike, recorded it, and then scanned along some trails to the ridge using thermal scan in the dirt. The sun had already masked the thermal contrast so footsteps wouldn't show up.

"Can't see steps, so I'm just scanning the ridge for possible observation spots," I informed. Irish adjusted the flight profile, making it easier for me to scan.

"Prof, go trail loose. I'm climbing back up to scan the ridge," I announced.

"Roger that. I still have nothing," Professor announced.

As we crossed the ridge, Zorg spoke. "I got two caves to the left. They look deep enough to hide in."

"Roger. Irish?" I stated, implying to set him up for further scanning, which they did.

"Prof, I've marked a couple of caves, but I can't see any movement. Let's go look for the convoy and scan back to here from a distance. Maybe the dicker will stick his head out when we move away." I stated.

"Check that."

We proceeded north; I reported the information to Six. He was still elevated. Understandably. He had probably been in Afghanistan for a year, most likely coming straight from Iraq and was getting a little exhausted from being blown up all the time. In his view, there was no "winning hearts and minds"—it was all survival.

"The convoy is at the river now. There are six men crossing the river. And if that is the mayor, he'll be pissed off because he just fell down and is now swimming," Professor reported. Laughing.

"Look at that. They are all on the bank now trying to dignify themselves. Oh, this isn't going to be pretty," I answered back.

"Six, this is Shakedown. Your VIP party is at the bottom of the wadi, 600 meters east walking up. They crossed the river at the wrong sport, fell in up to their necks; they're soaked," I radioed.

"Son of a bitch. Call sign Three. You're closest. Pulleese go escort our dignitary," Six stated emphatically.

Moments later, the two parties met, exchanged pleasantries, and immediately continued to the commander who was in the village center. They all met, and within a minute, the radio broke out.

"All parties, the mayor wants all men rounded up and brought to the center for a shura," Six radioed.

I observed the troops with ANA poking into each compound in what apparently was the announcement of the mayor of Shawali Kot wanting the meeting. Men began to meander out to the center of the village, and a circle formed.

The mayor was in the middle of the circle with the commander. He was addressing all the men in the village. Then he went and started talking directly with them. He went from man to man, apparently discussing the situation with the mayor.

"What the fuck, look at that!" I called to my crew in disbelief. "Is the mayor beating that man?"

"Just a few slaps it would appear, sir!" Zorg stated flatly moving forward to watch the TV monitor. "Far from a full beating," he snickered.

"Prof, you seein' that?" I radioed.

"Oh ya! I'm zoomed in," Professor responded to watching it on camera. I knew that the gunners in his aircraft would both be forward in the cabin laughing over the reality TV show. "This is awesome. Just need some beer and popcorn," he added jocularly.

"Six, this is Shakedown. Send a sitrep," I asked, wanting to know what's going on.

He responded quite calmly. "Apparently the mayor is upset to find out about the dicker in the hills, the lying, the IEDs, and the HME and doesn't believe the locals. He's an amazing actor. Stand by. He's approaching."

I watched the apparent elder approach the commander in the middle. They talked and pointed toward the hills, where the caves and motorcycle were, as the radio broke out.

"Shakedown, five-liner," Six sated.

Five-liner! I was perplexed. Where was the buildup to a fire order? I was about to be given fire orders and didn't have a clue what the target would be. The caves? The apparent duck hunter? What had the mayor, the major, and the terp figured out?

"Go for Shakedown," I replied.

"Shakedown, this is Six, cleared to engage and destroy the motorcycle approximately 4,000 meters south of this location," he ordered.

Before I could respond, Professor announced, "I'm in!"

I pondered for a moment. Was this legal? Was this a viable target? It's no threat—or is it? What's the worst that could happen? I recalled seeing a similar motorcycle for sale on the boardwalk—$80. Okay, if wrong, it would cost me $80 to replace it. For $80, it would be fun.

"Six, this is Shakedown. Check, we are clear to destroy the motorcycle. Back in five minutes with a BDA (battle damage assessment)," I responded.

Irish turned toward the ridge, and our two choppers climbed over.

"Prof, let's do a few passes to ensure no Bedouins are around and then get it on film. One burst for each gunner. Just to make sure that is!" I gave the plan sarcastically.

"Roger that. We're in position," Professor answered.

After a scan and the fire orders were given, the initial shots were from both left gunners; the fuel tank was ignited and exploded. An orange fireball burst in the valley followed by black smoke as tires caught fire. We reversed course for a second pass. As we approached and prior to firing, a second small explosion occurred, more like a puff kicking dust and white smoke into the air. The gunners joined in with further Dillon fire.

"Awesome! Did you see the secondary explosion?" Snapshot called.

"Ya," Irish called.

Zorg was forward. "I think it had HME in the side bag that was ignited. Report it to Six. They'll check it out later."

We returned and then reported the destroyed vehicle to Six. We reported the secondary explosion too. Six was elated. He could see the smoke rising from behind the ridge.

"You guys have fun?" he asked.

"Absolutely," I called.

"We're starting to get somewhere down here. Thanks, guys," he responded.

He sounded a little more cordial. It wasn't the first time I had heard emotion from the troops below; it wouldn't be the last. I don't think most people will ever understand the stress that an infantry soldier endures everyday. They say its hours and days of boredom followed by moments of extreme intensity, then repeat. Shit can go sideways in a matter of seconds, you must trust your fire-team partner and keep them alive. It's the only job they have: they accept the adversity, train intensely, refine their skills so to keep their partner alive—the toughest job on the planet, in my opinion. And it isn't for those faint of heart, without humor nor without compassion. There is a lesson in that.

"Shakedown 25, this is 30 Flight, you ready to RIP out?" I heard Grumpy check in to relieve us.

"Hey, Grumpy. Glad to hear you." I brought Grumpy up to date with everything that had happened and then passed him over to the Six in a formal tactical introduction.

"Steve, this is Grumpy. We have a convoy of vehicles a few clicks north across the wadi. Are those in need of eradicating as well, since that seems to be the theme?" he asked sarcastically. He knew those were the mayor's vehicles; and I knew the mood of Six. Any suggestion that those were targets would probably leave his diplomatic efforts in turmoil.

"Ahhh, roger that. With the mood the client is in, you probably shouldn't go there," I advised. He concurred. We proceeded to KAF.

Chapter 32

June 21: Lest We Forget

It was fighting season. The mood had switched over the past several months. The opium from the poppy resin had been harvested and sold for the heroin revenue used to finance the Taliban army. Farmers that had no peacetime intention traded their shovels for RPGs and AK-47s. The war was on. The Canadian Task Force commander visited all the fighting units including the First Aviation Battalion, Task Force Freedom to brief the changes in ROE (rules of engagement).

"Ladies and gentlemen, we have suffered through three seasons of counterinsurgency operations, COIN. We have made great strides in gaining the trust of the villagers where we patrol. We have given some stability. Yet the insurgency continues and the Taliban are standing to fight instead of hide. What this mean to you"—he paused, looking at all the aviators, especially the section leads with weapons release authority—"have a wider approved scope to determine enemy behavior thus allowing you to shoot. You know your enemy and you know their games. They can't hide in plain daylight behind that shovel anymore; the criteria now allow you to take them out."

He took another moment to ensure the seriousness of these words was being absorbed. "You now have authority to use lethal force to pursuit a known Taliban regardless of whether or not he holds a weapon, but be careful and continue to be professional. When in doubt, don't pull that trigger, but I reiterate, it is fighting season—we are at war." He stared at everyone. There was silence. There would be discussion. We would sit over coffee and review all the encounters we have had to date and rerun to different outcomes in our minds. It changed the game.

Over Kandahar City

"Blowtorch 60, this is Slayer. I got a TIC in progress in Nakhoney. I need your Shakedowns. Can you release them?" Slayer called to Butch.

It was a routine escort mission, and the three helicopters were just crossing the high ridgeline south of Kandahar en route to Wilson, a one-hour round trip, very safe.

"Stand by, Slayer," Butch responded then continued on a different frequency to Scrappy in operations.

"Scrappy, I'm good to go if you approve," Butch stated.

"Roger that. Steve and Prof, go to India 22 and help out. Butch, be careful!" Scrappy ordered. Something was different in the tone of his voice. I knew he watched the text TV and had a different insight into activities; I could sense it.

"Steve, switch to Slayer. Go get 'em!" Butch radioed, knowing us Griffon pilots preferred to get down and dirty as opposed to flying his wing.

"Fuckin' A. Butch is awesome," Zorg yelled as the two helicopters veered to the left toward Nakhoney. It was less than five minutes flight. I could see the village outline from the top of the ridge.

"Slayer, go for Shakedown 25," I eagerly radioed.

"TIC in progress. IED ROZ. One KIA. Contact India 22 to coordinate," Slayer stated calmly.

"Did he say KIA?" Snapshot asked.

"Yup. Wait." My heart jumped up in my throat and shivers went through my spine. I needed more info.

"India 22, this is Shakedown checking in," I asked.

"Shakedown, I need some surveillance and overwatch on my patrol. They are 1,000 meters south of Madras. IED attack has killed one of my men, and they are under small arms fire from the west." The commander was emotionless.

The Royal Canadian Regiment had just taken over from the Princess Patricias. They had assumed control of the area that would be one of the deadliest areas in Afghanistan over the summer season.

"India 22, this is Shakedown, roger. Four minutes to go," I responded.

Professor dropped into my trail and ready to immediately adopt a fighting attack pattern. He knew I would go immediately into the fight.

As soon as I could see the friendlies, I didn't hesitate to get rounds down range. An attack brief might get done, but if not, Professor knew what to do—no hesitation.

"Visual troops, 1,000 meters, one o'clock, Cap," Snapshot yelled.

"Got 'em, thanks. We'll fly north-south patterns over them. Watch left and right, but shots are coming from the right, over to the west," I cautioned.

Zorg stood up and looked through the front window to orient himself.

"I'm visual too, Cap," he called, saving me having to reorient the left gunner. Everyone was ready to fight.

"Prof, we'll do a figure eight over the troops. All effects if required are anticipated west. Watch for shooters," I radioed.

"Check that."

"India 22, send an update," I asked the ground commander.

"Shots southwest. No PID at this time. Find me some PID!" The ground commander was direct.

As we approached the area, the reports continued of shots being fired at us. We scoured the southwest looking for any movement, gun smoke, and flashes but saw nothing. The Taliban were good at concealing themselves.

"I'm pushing further west a few hundred meters, Prof. Go higher and overwatch. See if we can flush him out."

"Roger that, Steve," Professor responded. His aircraft pooped up higher, and I veered to the west, flying the guns.

We flew fast and jinked the aircraft but not so abruptly that my gunners didn't have full arcs to lock onto a target. Professor had a more vertical view overhead at several hundred feet. If any of the aircraft were engaged, one would break away drawing fire, but the other Griffon would counterattack. The aircraft breaking away would immediately rejoin to double the fire intensity.

"Shakedowns, you must be right over him. Shots have stopped. Keep overwatch in that area," India 22 commanded.

I expected shots to riddle holes in my helicopter. I tucked my shoulder into the armored seat as my head popped out, scouring for a target—anything. But the shooter hid. He was dug into a hole under a grape mound, and there would be no way to find him. They would just lie down and stay there for hours. They had IEDs around them for protection and dickers far away to keep them informed. Since they were in dugouts under the dirt of the grape rows, IR cameras wouldn't find them.

"Shakedown, how much playtime?" India 22 asked. He had to formulate a plan.

"Forty-five minutes," I answered.

"Roger, I need to evacuate my casualty. Can you pick him up? Where can you land?" he asked.

"Stand by." It was hot. I didn't know if I had the power to get out. I was greatly limited. I called Scrappy and explained.

"Ops, can you get a Chinook here to extract?" I stated.

Scrappy was following on the command net and already trying to coordinate the Chinook lift. There were no Chinooks available, and even if they could get one, it was too large a target for the middle of an insecure area. If they could get them to Madras, over a thousand meters away, it may be workable.

"I'm working on it with Task Force Kandahar HQ. Stand by," Scrappy stated. He was coming up with solutions despite the high risk and limited helicopter resources for the Task Force commander.

He responded within a minute. "Negative, Steve. You guys extract. Find a spot, maybe Three Hills. Is that secure enough? Can you do it?" Scrappy asked.

"Roger, we'll do it," I answered.

"India 22, can you guys get to Three Hills? We'll extract there," I asked.

"Give us about fifteen minutes," he responded. They had a 400-meter walk to carry their fallen. He had to reorganize the troops in order to carry him out while also defending against further attack.

Three Hills was a raised platform and very dusty. We would be pedestalled once landed, easy to shoot. The troops had to cordon off the area, find arcs of fire to protect everyone, and secure the LZ. Additionally, Professor would provide overhead cover.

"They're moving!" Zorg called quietly.

I watched the entire patrol start northbound slowly through the heat and dust. Several men picked up their fallen comrade and carried him and his gear.

We continued patrolling the area, placing an armed defensive barrier between the suspected area and the infantry procession, ready to respond. No shots were fired. Absolutely no normal pattern of life in the surrounding communities. Everyone knew it was a fighting day and stayed off the streets. The shooters and dickers stayed concealed.

The cockpit was quiet. Six brother soldiers were carrying the deceased. Flanks covered by the others, switching as they became exhausted. I was humbled, angry, and vigilant.

The blast was from a wall IED, about shoulder height. It was powerful enough to destroy a car. He didn't suffer. He didn't know what happened. But his comrades did. They had watched.

"They almost have it secure, Prof. I'll go in from the east and egress toward the FOB in the north. I need some pressure on the wadi west and southwest. I'll be wide open," I explained my concern.

"You got 'er," Professor answered.

"Shakedown, area secure. Come on in," India 22 called.

"Roger that. Inbound"

"Irish, I have control." I steered the Griffon low level and flared quickly at the end to make my exposure time less. There would be another massive dust ball, but it would help mask us.

"Dust ball forming and by the cabin, 5 feet above," Snapshot called.

I had a specific spot and allowed the aircraft to settle onto it, losing all visual references in the last foot of descent. We felt the aircraft lurch to a halt in the moondust.

"25 is down," I called to Professor, so he knew I was okay.

"Zorg, step out and help them. They're on the left," I stated.

"Already out, Cap." Zorg coughed.

I looked over my left shoulder and saw Zorg approaching the men through the dust, revealing his regimental patch. It seemed to be sign that he was a brother, not a stranger, and that their fallen would be escorted with dignity under his watch. He grabbed one end of the body bag and lifted it onto the floor of the griffon.

Snapshot had moved across and pulled the soldier through, placing a seatbelt from a floor ring over his body to secure him. The casualty's impromptu pall bearers reached out to our passenger. I couldn't see what they did—a pat of compassion? Blessing? I don't know. It was surreal. Their heads were low, faces flaccid with exhaustion, tears, fear, horror stained with dust and sunburn—stoic.

Another soldier, a senior warrant officer, grabbed them and with some hand gestures reminded them it was time to get into a defensive position. The war was still on; they were more vulnerable with a helicopter in their position. Shots were expected.

He then looked at me and spun his hand in the air signaling for me to get out—now!

"Let's go, guys," I called. "Cabin area."

"Right gun ready, left gun ready," Snapshot and Zorg called.

"Lifting, with a right turn out." I started to pull in collective, creating another explosion of dust as I inched across the ground, falling over the edge of Three Hills toward the wadi. The aircraft shuddered at maximum weight to gain flying speed.

We burst through the dust bubble and skimmed across the trees toward Steel Door, a few hundred meters west of FOB Madras. On my right, the few soldiers at the FOB stood quickly to attention, saluted, risking their lives for that moment to pay respects, then dropped back behind their berm.

"Prof, you have the lead and the radios," I sighed somberly.

"Roger that," he responded.

It was the quietest flight I had at war. We flew high to avoid enemy fire. We weren't hunting anymore today. I heard Professor's voice now and again on the radio, breaking the sound of wind and engines. It was peaceful for the moment, flying toward the east morning sun. Ironically, it was a beautiful sky but such an ugly, deadly earth.

"KAF tower, this Shakedown 25 Flight," Professor's voice broke the meditative silence.

"25 Flight, this is KAF tower. Altimeter two-nine-eight-six. FARP or X-ray, sir?" Tower called.

"Shakedown 25 is now Angel 25 Flight. Request direct Role 3 hospital," Professor answered; his voice was humble.

Tower's voice changed. "Angel 25, you are cleared south ramp arrival direct Role 3," he continued. "Paciderm 11, please orbit and come in behind Angel 25. Gunsmoke 26, hold present position for Angel 25. Longknife 11, please orbit north. Come in number 3 behind Angel 25." KAF tower kept clearing the way.

My heart throbbed. Everyone was quiet and humbled. The event tears a person in half. It is such a massive honor to carry your brother out of the field of battle. But he's dead. Why should I feel honor when his family is going to feel nothing but pain and suffering? A mother's worst fear. A spouse's heart shattered. A child's dream turn to nightmare of confusion.

The other aircraft circled for the two minutes it would take to allow our unencumbered approach, showing respect for the fallen Sergeant McNeil, ending his first trip toward the highway of heroes.

I'll never forget you. You are of the people I have never met but feel such loss for. Each Remembrance Day, I think of you.

Chapter 33

June 26: Lest We Forget

The last week of June and the first couple of weeks in July were life-changing events. I had seen death, misery, and suffering. It never ended—the same fighting and explosions everyday: death, innocent WACs as human shields, maimed children—young girls at schools being killed—tribal society with archaic methods of punishment. That was from an overhead exposure. I couldn't even imagine what a foot soldier had to deal with every day.

Nakhoney

Professor and I were tasked with overwatch in the Nakhoney area (again). We were patrolling South Nakhoney when the radio broke out.

"Shakedown 25, this is Slayer. TIC in progress. Can you respond?"

"Go for Shakedown," I confirmed.

"TIC in progress, multiple IED strikes, 3,000 meters southeast of Bazar-e Panjwaii. Contact 21 to coordinate," he stated.

As I started to plot the grid, the numbers made me realize they were very close. I directed Irish to steer around Mount Salavat and looked toward Bazar-e Panjwaii. The thick black smoke was seen rising above the valley floor from 8 kilometers away.

"Irish." I looked at my copilot and pointed toward the smoke. He immediately steered toward it.

"Slayer, contact smoke, switching frequencies," I answered.

"Oh, that's not good," Snapshot called.

"Oh no, no, no," Zorg added. We all felt it. Something was wrong, gone bad.

"India 21, this is Shakedown checking in," I called. The radio was frantic.

"21A, start moving east toward that village. Somebody fuckin' knows something!" a voice yelled.

"21B, get the casualties stabilized. Dustoff inbound. Cordon and secure an LZ now."

"21C, 21C? 21C? Report." The radio was silent. It would never respond again; destroyed.

"Fuck! 21D. Set up a block and observation west. Now!" he continued yelling commands.

"Shakedown, I got two times LAVs burning, multiple IED strikes. No shooters. I am securing the immediate area with a section. Another section is advancing on the village to the east. I have possible dickers there." His voice was getting emotional. He was stressed. "I want you looking for any dickers in the west. There is a suspect in the north-south wadi about 1,000 meters over. Find me something!"

"Shakedown 25, roger out," I answered. He was irate. Professor flew in behind me and started using the MX to scan from trail position. We listened to the commander—distraught. Payback was in his voice.

We joined in a high overwatch to observe the POL. It was the middle of a large open desert, a construction project that had been going on for months, building a paved road north to south to join Road Lake Effect to Road Hyena. It had just been cratered with a massive explosion. Two LAVs were destroyed. No Afghan people were visible, except for in the compounds of which the closest was a thousand meters away, perfect dicker distance.

"Is everyone okay? Is everyone okay?" Zorg's voice had a genuine concern; the objective warrior's voice was fading. His frail humanity was screaming to come out—it alerted me.

"I don't know the situation yet, but the commander sounded pretty distraught," I answered. "We are looking for insurgents, dickers. Just keep your eyes out."

The radio kept blasting out orders. "21 Alpha, this is 21. Get into that village right fuckin' now and start hard-knocking! Someone fuckin' knows something!" he blurted over the radio. He wanted doors busted down. It was the only obvious place from which a dicker could attack.

"21 Alpha—roger out," his subordinate acknowledged. A few moments later, a group of about eight dismounted Canadians and some ANA soldiers started jogging toward the village on foot.

"Shakedown, I need overwatch until the Dustoff (medevac) gets here. I have multiple wounded and some KIA." His voice was pitched with those last words. Dustoff wouldn't land unless the area was secure, and they had armed overwatch—that was us.

"Roger that," I answered. "Moving to the village to the east."

We orbited and started observing the compounds where 21A was advancing. There were a few people watching from the walls—kids. They seemed more curious than dickers. The infantry would have to visit door-to-door and investigate.

"Our troops are approaching. All we can do is watch for dickers and squirters. Maybe someone will try to escape," I announced.

"Did they get out, Cap? Did they get out?" Zorg repeated.

"Zorg, the blast was massive! Face it. Some didn't get out! The blast killed them before the fire!" Snapshot tried to comfort him. The flames and smoke rose ferociously from the two LAVs on the road, alongside a crater. There were Canadian troops scurrying around the burning LAVs. They were applying first aid to casualties preparing them for helicopter evacuation. Some were lying, a few sitting. The commander kept vying for results.

"Ya, the shock knock 'em out. That's what happened," Zorg told himself out loud.

"Watch your flanks, buddy. Is it clear left?" I asked, hoping to refocus him.

"Ya, it's clear left," he said stoically. "Clear left," he repeated monotonously.

The LAVs continued to burn. There was no way to extinguish the massive flames. The black smoke marked the IED blast and could be seen a dozen kilometers away.

"There's your answer, Zorg. The company commander said there are KIAs. I don't know anything else," I stated bluntly. Irish looked at me.

"I don't think that's what he means," Irish stated.

"I don't know, Zorg." I raised my voice. I couldn't do anything. I felt helpless. More death. No enemy contact. Another hit-and-run. This time it was big. Zorg just wanted to know if they got out of the LAVs. That bothered me too, and I did not want to talk about it. I had to stay focused.

"Shakedown, this is Dustoff. I'm one minute back from the east. Is the LZ secure?" the incoming Blackhawk helicopter requested.

"Roger, there's a marker on the east side of the burning LAVs. Friendlies patrolling the village to the east 1,000 meters, and no FAMs spotted. Quiet POL," I reported.

"Roger that!" Dustoff responded.

The large helicopter wasted no time and flared off its speed, plunking itself on the LZ marked by the infantry soldiers below. It was on the ground no more than a minute before lifting off again, climbing toward KAF to Role 3.

"Shakedown, this is 21. Do you have anything to report?"

"Negative, a few kids looking over the wall of the village. West is clear, no squirters," I answered.

"Roger. Slayer is sending Longknife 12 inbound to replace you. You are cleared off task for refuel. Thanks. 21 out." He sounded resigned.

I thought there would be more than one Blackhawk load of casualties to come out from two LAVs.

"Isn't Dustoff coming back? Have all the casualties been evacuated?" I asked.

There was a long pause followed by a forced flat voice. "Not everyone could be extracted. That's all I can evacuate for now," the major stated flatly.

"Oh no, oh no, oh no!" Zorg called out.

"It's all right, buddy. They died instantly!" Snapshot tried to comfort him with logic.

I nodded to Irish to take the section home. It was another quiet trip to KAF. Irish and I focused on discussing the patrol that was searching for dickers, trying to steer away from discussing the LAVs.

We landed and shut down. Zorg never called clear left as he usually does.

I stepped out of the helicopter. Zorg was usually bounding to meet me, sometimes helping with my armor and door; he wasn't there. I removed my helmet, slid the armor back, put on my sunglasses, and then walked a few steps back to see why Zorg hadn't been clearing his Dillon gun. Zorg was still on the gun. Frozen. Helmet and facemask still donned.

"Zorg, you okay? Look at me!" I panicked.

The Dillon was still armed and ready. I sat down slowly beside Zorg and put my hand on his shoulder. With my other hand, I lifted the firing blade, disabling the weapon and ripped the belt of bullets from the feed. I pulled the trigger and cycled the remaining bullets through without firing them to clear the weapon.

I saw Hawk walking toward the gun pit and, with panic in my voice, yelled, "Hawk, Hawk, help me!"

Hawk jogged over. I removed Zorg's facemask and helmet. His face was stunned, eyes glared over. He wouldn't blink. He was in shock.

Hawk immediately knew something wasn't right. Our eyes locked; I nodded my head toward Zorg.

"Hey, bud. What's the matter?" Hawk said as he took over. "Let's walk it off."

"Thanks, Hawk." Zorg looked at him and answered with his eyes glazed. "Will there be a ramp ceremony for that girl that got stoned?"

"Probably, buddy," Hawk answered. That girl was stoned six month ago. Zorg had been to several ramp ceremonies since we were here. And now he would be going to several more—all within several days of each other.

"We lost a few more good soldiers today, Hawk. I don't know who. We just spent an hour watching LAVs burn," I filled him in.

Hawk's eyes swelled up. His neck straightened as he gathered strength. He took a deep breath and walked away with Zorg. "Can you get the padre, sir?"

"Yeah, I'm on it." Professor and the other crew came over enquiring. "What's going on with Zorg?"

I looked at Hawk and then at Professor. Hawk had one of Zorg's arms over his shoulders, helping him walk. I could see the padre jogging over at the other end of X-ray ramp. I looked at Professor and stated, "We lost more than just the LAV soldiers today. Zorg's done."

Note:

"This book is fiction based on true events. This chapter is to emphasize that it was a horrible, soul-breaking day. I'll remember it forever."

"Medics join the military to help people and often work under the symbol of the cross. They are respected to treat friend, foe, and innocent victims without prejudice. Medic Master Corporal Kristal Giesebrecht and Medic Corporal Andrew Miller, lest we forget."

Chapter 34

Trapped: Answer to Chapter 2: Summer in Salavat

Salavat Patrol 22A

"Sergeant! Where are those dickers?" yelled the platoon commander.

"Shakedowns are still tracking them. Two in the grape hut over there." He pointed to the clay building about 300 meters west. He was on the radio talking to the helicopters. The valley filled with the noise of the engines from the two Griffons flying above. One was low apparently darting at a potential dicker, the other high doing circular orbits, tracking the situation.

"When is the goddamned counter IED team getting here?" The platoon commander was frustrated.

"They are on the way, but it's slow going. IEDs everywhere today."

"Keep the guys clear of the ones pinning us." The commander pointed to the known IEDs in the immediate area. Everywhere they tried to move, another ambush was waiting. And a dicker was watching them, ready to detonate the explosion when they got close enough.

"Captain, are those Griffons going to shoot?" a journalist asked. He was embedded with them and observing the situation. His head was down, covered. Sweat and dust from a recent explosion formed mud streams on his brow. He made notes in a pad trying to focus on his job while fully aware of the corpse of an ANA soldier lying beside him a few meters away, victim of the IED.

"Nope," the sergeant answered. "Every time choppers get here, the Taliban stop shooting, hide their weapons, pick up shovels, and walk away without ever getting shot at—they'll buzz around for an hour, but nothing will happen. At least we'll get these IEDs neutralized without getting shot at."

The platoon commanded was on the radio. He lifted his chin away from the microphone and yelled, "Heads down. Shakedown's rolling in hot!" Everyone did the opposite—stood up.

"*BBBBBRRRRAAAAAPPPPP.*

A deep throaty sound echoed through the valley of two Dillon guns opening up on the grape hut where the dickers were hiding. Explosions of dust rose up from the grape hut and then raced down the road, apparently chasing a target behind a wall from the platoon's view.

Freedom Operations

"Shakedown 25 is going hot!" Scrappy stated in surprise, reading from the text screen. "Get Butch."

Butch and Scrappy, as well as the other operations staff, listened to the situation develop. Scrappy had updated them all from the beginning:

"Butch, twenty-five minutes ago, an IED killed an ANA soldier on patrol with 22 in the Salavat area. The troops have been pinned down and were waiting for a counter-IED team from Masum Ghar to defuse the bombs. The team is slow as they are also running into IEDs en route." He paused, pointing the map from Masum Ghar to the area of the explosion. "25 and 26 are on overwatch. They isolated two dickers and are engaging."

"Who's the team?" Butch asked.

"Steve and Skipper has Professor's crew," Scrappy answered.

"Better tell Professor to get in here too. He'll wanna know what's going on with his crew," Butch suggested.

Scrappy nodded over to the Radop to silently delegate the task.

Professor came in. "So what's up?"

"Steve and Prof engaging in Salavat," Scrappy stated.

"That's my crew! I'm missing out," Professor stated. "Are they okay?"

"Yes, Steve just gave fire orders. 29 agreed," Scrappy added. It fell quiet; they were watching the text lines on the battle board fill and waiting for the subsequent radio report from our team. They listened to the radio chat between Skipper and myself.

"Squirters east!" Skipper yelled over the radio.

"Roger—tally, dropping to your six o'clock and firing!" I answered.

All the 408 Squadron Ops staff looked at each other, hoping to hear only positive reports. There were always risks of small arms or RPG attacks toward the helicopters.

Salavat

One of the Taliban had run toward a road wall to take cover. The gunner from Skipper's Griffon, Ricky, led a dust trail of bullets up which exploded around the man who had dove to go under a wall where an apparent escape hole was built. He disappeared in the dust as he rolled through the hole.

The other man looked over his shoulder and watched his colleague dive to apparent safety. He ran toward a compound 100 meters south. Skipper was at the wrong arc to engage the target, so my crew did.

"Gunny, fire before he gets to the compound!" I ordered and pulled the aircraft higher to ensure a straight down shot. "Fire!"

The ground erupted in dust behind the man and then engulfed him. Gunny stopped firing. The man kept running. "Did you get him? He's still moving!" I observed. "Oh, I got him, sir," Gunny stated stoically and observed. The gun didn't fire anymore.

The man started to slow. He jogged. He walked. He stood still and then walked a bit further. He moved toward a stream about 40 meters up the road and went out of my view under the branches of a large tree. I thought Gunny missed. I thought the Taliban soldier was going to "pretend to be a farmer" as he went under the tree. I felt frustrated after all this—IED pinned troops and a dead ANA soldier. And he was going to get away. Gunny knew different.

As I flew through half the circle, I saw a man, but his clothes were solid orange.

"Fuck! I lost PID. Where's the man in the white jammies?" I stated.

"Skipper, I've lost PID. My guy with the white shirt is gone. Maybe he escaped into the compound. I only have contact on a FAM with an orange shirt," I radioed excitedly to Skip.

There was a pause.

A calm, informative reply came back from Skipper. "That's your dicker. He's bleeding out."

I calmed. Everything made sense as I sank in my seat. "Gunny, check fire. The guy is no longer a threat," I stated softly. I had to continue with the procedure of battle. "Roger that, 26. Check fire."

"Roger" was the answer.

"Freedom Ops, this is 25, contact. Battle damage assessment. Two times FAMS engaged. One times FAM killed, one times FAM unknown. He escaped under a wall near north side of grape hut. We are continuing to monitor POL for India 22 and doing BDA (battle damage assessment)," I reported to operations. Operations had been listening all along, but this formalized the sequence of events. I then repeated the information for India 22 trapped below in the unexploded IEDs.

"26, I'm going in with MX low to verify BDA. Give me overwatch," I told Skipper.

I maneuvered the aircraft around, observing Skip who climbed above. He was watching for any other insurgents who would possibly take advantage of my slow-moving helicopter. I came into a high hover taxi while Irish put the MX-15 camera onto the man, now hunched over in a wadi near the compound. A strap of a weapon, AK-47, showed under his wet garments. However, he was still.

I noticed the water. It was green upstream and then changed color; it was red—all red. Downstream, the entire wadi for the next ten meters had been saturated with the blood of another victim of this war. He was dead.

"Okay, let's go. He's done," I stated and then flew off. "Skipper, I have a confirmed KIA in the wadi," I stated over the radio.

"Roger that. Close to bingo fuel, five minutes remaining for playtime," Skipper answered.

"Same. I'll check out with 29," I answered.

"29, one FAM at grid QQ41649008 in the wadi. Killed in action. The second dicker took rounds but is in the grape field at QQ41599020 coming toward you. We are bingo fuel. Need to return to base KAF," I reported.

We flew near the troops who were still on the rooftops being cautious of the IEDs still around them. India 22 had just lost one colleague to the Taliban. No remorse, only cheers directed toward our mission. They were all on the roofs jumping and holding their rifles high. It was relief to them. The pressure of being ambushed was relieved . . . for now anyway. The journalist wrote notes.

We landed at X-ray ramp. There was excitement but also emotional exhaustion. As I went to put my gear away at the sea cans, Big C was sitting there in the shade cleaning his gear. He had just completed another mission himself, a veteran of many tours overseas. I noticed his smile, and despite his happy demeanor, I empathized with the downward bend.

Chapter 35

Join the Army

More Done by 7:00 a.m. Than Most Get Done All Day

"Hey, Prof, you ready to go?" I asked, entering the operations center.

"Yes, sirree," he responded, spitting into his cup. His brow raised in concern.

"We just have an escort into Salavat today. It should be a quickie; and then some overwatch for 2 Company," I stated monotonously. I was thinking about Zorg.

"Ya, what's the matter?" He asked, he saw a look in my face. "Ah, yes, Zorg. No, he isn't doing too well. He's tired. He's going home. Gunny will be working with you," Professor sympathized.

I contemplated for a moment. I knew he was exhausted. Emotionally. Mentally. He saw more in his infantry days before he even got here. Now add all these experiences. Gunny was a great gunner, one of the best. But I still felt a bit of loss as Zorg departed.

"Ya, figured so. I'll go see him later before he gets on the plane." I inhaled, nodded, and mentally moved forward.

"We better get ready. Scrappy is waiting to brief us." Professor nudged me out of my contemplation.

Bazar-e Panjwaii

Lieutenant Davis had been leading a platoon near the village of Bazar-e Panjwaii since 3:00 a.m., a standard patrol. They departed from Masum Ghar and patrolled around the village investigating possible IED factories near the southern edge of town. Basically, another ordinary mission on an ordinary day in late July.

It was a low dust morning with bright blue skies and a beautiful brown-orange horizon from the sun rising intensely in the East—as always. By 6:00 a.m., the temperature was passing 30 degrees, the troops soaked in sweat from two hours of patrolling.

India 21 was Davis' call sign. He was in charge and tasked to patrol the compounds along the heavily treed wadi to the southern edge of the village.

"Joey, work along the wall westbound," Lieutenant Davis yelled to Sgt. Joey Foster. He pointed his hand in the direction to lead the troops.

"2, this is 21," he reported to his headquarters over the radio. "We're proceeding down Charlie-Charlie-One to search the next sector."

"21, this is 2. Roger that," the voice on the radio from Masum Ghar acknowledged tracking Davis's patrol.

They proceeded through an unoccupied compound, which led them to a wall paralleling the wadi. The wall was 4 feet high along a rooftop. It allowed them to look down into a thick-wooded wadi from a height of about 4 meters. The wadi was only 10 meters away, paralleling them on the south flank.

"Sarge, watch that green zone," the LT cautioned as he paused at the opening from the compound to the wall. He looked at each soldier passing through to check on them and give additional instruction if he needed to.

"Watch your spacing and watch that wadi," he advised to the troops, stepping by. He was concerned, but it was normal. They were used to the anxiety.

Tim was a young private. Young—yes, but he was a four-month veteran of these foot patrols and was a good soldier but exhausted, as usual. He was behind Sarge who was the leading along the wall. It was quieter than normal. Usually, birds were making noise along the wadi this time of day. But it was quiet.

He looked down watching his boots make little explosions of dust. He could hear his heart beating with each step. He was exhausted and thus became mesmerized on his boots; each explosion of dust was making little clouds. He remembered how new his boots looked when he first arrived in Afghanistan; now they would never pass inspection. He chuckled at his faultless noncompliance.

"Hey, Sarge. I got dust on my boots!"

Sarge shook his head, took a puff on his smoke, and exhaled with a half grin, "Smart ass."

Crack! A piercing sound rang in Tim's ears as pieces of rock blasted hard against his face. He regained attention, realizing the wall beside his head was exploding from bullets and spraying clay fragments into his face. Small craters appeared to be forming in front of his eyes, throwing chips against his ballistic goggles. The sound clarified and loudened. *Snap, snap, snap!* He could hear the bullets whipping by his head.

He felt his right arm being pinched as his body fell heavy to the ground. It was Sarge pulling him down behind the wall.

"Contact left, contact left!" a voice yelled from behind him, snapping him out of his daze.

He looked up to where his head had just been. It was exploding as bullets hit the wall. The gravel continued to snap off his goggles, and dirt filled his mouth.

"Returning fire!" the light machine gunner yelled from 30 feet behind him. *Ptump, ptump, ptump!* The sound of short bursts blasted into the wadi.

"20 meters in front of Timmy! Man in black pajamas! Fire," Davis yelled out the contact information for his troops. They tried engaging, but the Taliban target was concealed in the protective cover. He could escape from the patrol's view and pop up, returning fire at will.

"Fuck! Where'd he go?" Sarge yelled as Tim popped back up into action. "Suppressing!" *Bang, bang, bang.* His C7 rifle ripped out twenty rounds to the movement in the wadi in front.

"I dunno—I'm looking," Tim replied. He was angry now. "That fucker tried to shoot my head off!" He realized now that he was reoriented.

Ptump, ptump, ptump! The gunner continued to suppress the area where he last saw the Taliban fighter.

Snap, snap, snap! Shots were returned from the trees.

"Take cover! Where is that fucker?" yelled Davis. "Just keep your head down—start rotating observation. Johnny, call it in!" he ordered to the FAC patrolling with him.

"2, this is 21. Contact, wait out . . ."

Reg Desert

My crew departed KAF en route to escort a civilian resupply helicopter to Salavat. Because of all the recent enemy activity, Salavat was assessed as a red FOB, as were most in Nakhoney and the lower Panjwaii District. This required all unarmed civilian helicopters to have armed escort for landing. Otherwise, it was to be a mellow trip for the final few days in theater before I went home.

Most of our thoughts were directed toward decompressing in Dubai—vacations and cold beer—not on the Taliban. So to meet a civilian chopper for a simple escort would be a nice way to begin transitioning off the tour. Professor and I planned to meet them at 7:00 a.m.

"Right-left gunners, cleared to test fire," I stated to the gunners, allowing them to conduct a routine weapons check. It was six thirty.

BBBBRRRRAAP.

"Left gun ready, Cap," Gunny stated.

Burp! I didn't like that sound. I looked over my shoulder to Snapshot.

"Right gun, jam!" Snapshot reported.

"Git 'er fixed. We got a few minutes before we have to be in location," I stated.

We had to meet the helicopter at 7:00 a.m.—sharp. The civilian chopper did not have secure communication, only a standard air traffic control radio that the Taliban could monitor. They would make one call just before diving out of the sky from 10,000 feet once Shakedown had secured the area.

"No prob, Cap. It's a bad one. Gotta pull the blade apart and rebuild. Give me a minute," Snapshot informed that his jam was more than a quick fix.

"Shakedown 25 Flight, this is Slayer TOC. TIC in progress," the radio interrupted. Slayer's tone immediately transformed the mood of our crew. The team was used to this and more than ready. It was fighting season.

"Go for Shakedown," I responded.

"Shakedown 25, India 21 near Bazar-e Panjwaii under attack from small arms fire. Can you respond?"

"Roger that." I pointed with my hand in the direction to fly for Irish. I got a thumbs-up in return as I continued on the radio.

"Shakedown 25, contact India 21 on frequency 42.25."

"Romeo Tango for Shakedown. We'll be there in about ten minutes. Switching frequency," I acknowledged.

"Snapshot, how's that fuckin' gun?" I yelled, concerned he wouldn't have it ready in time for the fight.

"I got it together. Can I test fire?"

"Roger."

Burp! I was twisted around to watch. I got frustrated. Snapshot didn't hesitate for a second, immediately going into technician mode putting his engineer skills to work.

"Don't stop. It'll be ready!" Snapshot yelled bluntly, frustrated as his gun failed a second time.

I looked forward and plotted the grid information into the GPS and programmed the MX-15 moving map display. It looked to be in a compound from the map overlay information I had.

"Okay, guys, the grid is just on the southern edge of the Bazar-e Panjwaii town about a two clicks east of Masum Ghar," I stated over the intercom then paused and looked to the area to find it. I pointed my fingers. "Along the south side of Bazar, running east-west is a wadi," I continued to orient my crew. We were looking for the Canadian patrol. "Going out on the radio."

"India 21, go for Shakedown 25," I initiated.

"Shakedown 25, this is India 21. We are a patrol of twenty-five dismounts on the southeast side of Panjwaii on the edge of town near the wadi. We are currently fixed along a wall at grid QQ34599175."

"Wait out!" I answered.

I plugged the detailed information into my computer and set the navigation system for Irish.

"They're on the needle," I stated to Irish, indicating the GPS instruments showed the bearing and distance to the friendly forces. Irish could arrange his flight profile by the electric information as well as looking out to the area.

I responded. "Roger. Contact your location, not visual with you yet," I advised the troops on the ground.

"India 21, roger. Call when you are visual with me," the infantry voice informed.

I was about 3 kilometres back from the area. I didn't want to delay. Immediate suppression would be required.

"21, can you put smoke on the target?" I asked, hoping to get all the crew looking exactly where the target was.

The Patrol

"What's going on, Johnny?" Davis yelled over to his FAC.

"Shakedown is inbound and wants us to smoke the target."

"It's 20 fuckin' meters away! My smoke launcher will overshoot, and I can't get a smoke can through the tree canopy." He paused for a second. "Shit! Those fuckin' chopper guys can never make things easy."

"I got this L-T," Johnny stated.

"Shakedown, it's Johnny here. How copy?"

"21? Johnny sniper?" my voice responded. "Whatcha doin' down there?"

"Out for a walk with da b'yz Shakedown. I know your voice. I gotta situation here. We need it tight. I know you can do it. Who's the shooters?" Johnny asked.

"Snapshot, Gunny and Hawk's in 2."

"Alright, we're putting smoke out but it won't be close enough. Follow my talk-on from the smoke," Johnny stated.

"Roger that. Lookin' for smoke," I answered.

"Tim, smoke the fuckin' target with the 203 (grenade launcher), ASAP," he ordered.

"Oooookkkayyy, Johnny." Tim's sarcasm responded. They both knew it would overshoot. Tim loaded the canister, aimed, and shot. *Thoof!* The round penetrated right through the trees and continued across the wadi and into an open field and began spewing out red smoke.

"Contact red smoke!" Shakedown's voice could be heard over the radio.

"Shakedown. Reference red smoke?" Johnny asked.

"Contact red smoke," my voice answered.

"From red smoke, move toward me by 80 meters," he directed. There was a pause on the radio.

My hesitant voice came over the radio. "Okay, 21, Johnny, I am visual with you now, and 80 meters back from the smoke is a tree line in the wadi directly beside you! Confirm the target is in the trees about 10 meters from you?"

"Roger that. A-firmative! The tree line beside me is your target. Cleared to suppress. All effects south of me," he answered.

"Jesus Christ, guys, keep your fuckin' heads down. We are inbound hot," my excited voice responded.

Johnny looked at the L-T and Sarge and held his thumb up as he ducked down.

In the Helicopter

"The target is right beside them in that wadi. Be careful Gunny," I yelled at the crew.

"Prof, did you copy all?" I asked my wingman. "Roger that— it's fucking close," he responded, cursing for the first time I could remember in theater.

"There's the target area, boys. Inbound hot," I stated over the intercom. "Figure-eight pattern right turn execute. Left gunner, you're first, turning inbound—hot," I immediately repeated the command over the radio, so Professor knew the plan. Irish immediately banked the Griffon and rolled out directly toward the enemy directly over the friendly troops about 50 feet above them.

"Visual friendlies, tally target," Gunny stated.

"Once over the troops, cleared to fire," I ordered and then switched onto the radio.

"Two One, inbound hot." It would be raining fifty rounds per second momentarily.

"*BRAAAAAAAAAAP!*

Gunny walked about four hundred rounds of ammo through the trees, almost shooting straight down, sweeping back and forth using the Dillon like a broom to clean up the Taliban filth that hid below.

"Out of arcs, checking fire," he called, stopping the gun.

I watched the tracers of Professor's aircraft start firing as we banked hard right to reattack.

"You got the Griffon and the friendlies?" I asked Snapshot.

"Roger. Tally target, Haycee!" Snapshot lined up his onto the target. He pulled the trigger.

Brrraaapp! Burp! About twenty-five rounds burst out, and it jammed. "Fuck! Jam!"

"Right gun jam," I yelled over the radio. The enemy soldier would have ample time to target the Griffon and return fire once they realized I was incapable of shooting.

Professor's Helicopter

"Lead has a jam. Hawk, do you have the target?" Professor yelled to his gunner, realizing my ship was vulnerable.

"Visual friendlies, tally target," excitedly announced Hawk.

"Fire," Professor ordered.

The Dillon burst alive, saturating the tree line with hundreds of rounds. Hawk carefully guided the stream of bullets into the wadi. He could see dust and slivers of wood exploding.

The helicopter veered left, flying directly over the Royal Canadian Regiment patrol below. A soldier, Tim, was watching until it started raining hot shell casings off his helmet. He ducked and covered his bare neck to prevent them from falling down his back. The tree line exploded, and instead of dust from the wall bouncing off his face, slivers from the tree line were exploding over the troops.

"Check fire!" Professor yelled as he veered away. I had reversed my turn and was joining the re-attack.

"Gunny, your target when Professor clears," I stated.

As Professor's helicopter passed just to the left of Gunny's gun sites, he pulled the trigger. He carefully swept the tree line, diligent of the friendly forces. On this pass, he emptied almost one thousand rounds and accurately suppressed the area. The sound of the Dillon could only be broken by a voice screaming on the radio.

"Check fire! Check fire!" The rain of bullets, nearly two thousand five hundred rounds in a few seconds, was very close to the infantry below. The patrol didn't expect the volume of fire and were growing nervous from the bombardment of bullets, dirt, and wood chips.

"Check fire! Check fire! Shakedown . . . He's not shooting anymore," the radio yelled.

I was concerned. "Is everyone okay?"

"Roger that. I don't have contact anymore. We'll attempt BDA (battle damage assessment) but expect IED, so it may be awhile," Johnny answered, indicating he would look for a dead body.

"26, you copy? Check fire," I asked Professor if he acknowledged.

"Roger that—check fire."

Patrol

Sarge looked around at all his patrol mates. He wiped the sawdust off his glasses and called out, "Everyone okay? That was bloody well danger-close suppression, I'd say! Shit!" They chuckled with excitement.

He nodded his head as he heard the sequence of "rogers" coming in from his troops. "That Taliban guy is either deep in a hidey hole, long gone, or Swiss cheese!" he exclaimed as he called out to his patrol leaders to conduct a battle damage assessment. He picked up the radio and called to the Griffons.

"Shakedown, it's two-one. We're doing a BDA. Can you stay on overwatch and advise?"

"Roger that!" I responded.

In the Air

"Go trail high. We're gonna scout the wadi and area for any damage," I stated my plan to Professor.

"Roger." Professor zoomed up high to about 700 feet and circled, covering my scouting mission.

I saw a man in black about 300 meters west along a bridge crossing the wadi. He slowly moved out of the wadi and chatted with another person who came out of a compound. They observed our helicopter as we observed them.

"You guys think that's him?" I asked as Irish as he circled the man.

"Yup, maybe, but what do we do? He's moving slow. Think we tagged him?" I asked.

"I dunno," Snapshot answered. "But he's not a valid target anymore."

"I know. Let's monitor," I noted.

"India 21, 300 meters west. Now on the north side of the wadi is a FAM black pajamas, moving very slow, possibly damaged. I suspect that's your guy. No PID. We're monitoring," I reported.

"Roger, contact on that individual. We got it from here," the LT answered.

"Shakedown two - five, this is Freedom Ops, send Sitrep!" Scrappy's voice protruded over the radio.

"Ops, Shakedown Two five flight had contact with one times FAM in support of India Two-one at 0653 hours. Two thousand five hundred rounds, seven-six-two expended. Continuing to monitor. Currently lost PID and no BDA available," I reported.

"Roger, we got the Russians waiting to descend into Salavat. Are you able to get over there now?" Scrappy asked.

"Roger, on our way," I stated. I advised Professor and the LT that we had another task and departed. Professor had called up the Mi-17 Russian aircraft and told them to stand by for two minutes.

We went in low and aggressive to Salavat and set up and search pattern. We looked for any suspicious activity and ensured the pattern of life was normal before allowing the big Mi-17 to descend. I think with the Dillons echoing across the valley not ten minutes earlier, the POL would be quiet. Not a person considered threatening was out. No dickers. We cleared the Russian Mi-17 helicopter into land. Two minutes later, the large white beast lifted out of the massive dust cloud and lumbered back into the sky.

"I guess that's it, boys," I stated over the radio. "It's 7:08 a.m. Let's go get breakfast before the North DFAC closes."

"Roger that," a sigh replied over the intercom. Everyone needed a break. It was a busy forty-five minutes.

The eight of us met on the ramp together to chat before we walked over to the DFAC for breakfast.

"Fuck, you shoulda seen the troops below when I opened up," cheered Gunny. "One hand over the neck, duckin' low, and the other hand pointing toward the threat. Got some thumbs-up too! Fuckin' A!"

"I'm sorry, man!" Snapshot stated.

"Shit happens. Snapshot, you taking Veronica to the shack to get 'er fixed?" He was already in the process of dismantling his gun.

"Yup, on my way." He was disappointed that he tried but couldn't get her working properly. Gunny followed him. "I'll help ya, Master Corporal," he called.

"That's why we work in twos—mutual support," Professor closed.

"Well done, guys. Mission successful. Let's go fill in the engagement paperwork and grab some breakfast before it closes. I'll be a few minutes with Scrappy, so I'll see you all at the DFAC," I stated.

"Guys, remember that our replacements from 430 Squadron start arriving today for training. Share some stories, motivate them, or scare the fuckers!" I laughed, remembering my introduction from Chipper almost a year earlier.

Professor and I walked into the operations center. The cool blast of air-conditioned air soothed us as we sauntered through the door in our sweat-soaked flight suits. Our faces were red from months of Afghanistan sun and jawlines more chiseled, showing 20 pounds of lost weight from sweat and stress. Our faces were stoic from months and from many events like today.

A routine engagement in the midst of an airborne escort mission was the pinnacle standard for checking an aviator's ability during training in Canada. But here, it was a normal daily routine.

Roto 10, Task Force Faucon (Falcon), was now in the briefing theater across from operations. I could hear Skipper welcoming his replacement aircrew through the open door. As they walked by, I acknowledged the colonel.

"Morning, sir!" I stated as I walked by, turning into operations across the hall.

"Steve, good shoot again today," Skipper called out. "Let's wrap up at 1300 hours after lunch—lethal force debrief. Get your team together and advise Scrappy." His tone suggested this was routine—almost was.

I paused and looked into the room of pale, white faces with the occasional nervous grin of recognition. Anxious large eyes gazed upon Skipper and me. I paused and smiled back as I saw myself there through Chipper's eyes a year earlier. Someone had returned from Roto 7.

"Hey, Tourn-a-key!" a vaguely familiar face stated. "I told you dat you no have dem on very long," he added. It was a Devil's Infidel returning.

I smiled at him and nodded and then reached to touch above my knees where the bands would have been. I reflected and answered, "Welcome to fighting season, guys. I'm so glad you're here, so I kin go howme now." I looked at him mimicking a French accent to remind him of this situation a year earlier, and continued to the CO. "Roger, sir. See you at one o'clock."

I continued into operations where Scrappy greeted me as he usually did after a heightened mission. "C'mon, let's go!" Scrappy interrupted my thoughts. I followed him outside. The smell of the porta-potties nearby began to fill the air as they brewed in the sun.

"Everyone okay in Panjwaii?" I asked of India 21.

Scrappy smiled and nodded. "Yup, they're fine. Now, one last time." And he pointed to the pull-up bar.

Chapter 36

Decompression—Recompression

I waded through the warm waters of the pool in the Arab Emirates. It was 44 degrees, yet the water was refreshing. The Arabian Sea was a bright blue background over the horizon behind a swim-up bar and grill.

Behind me was a burnt mountain range along the orange desert on the east coast of the Arabian Peninsula. A short string of resorts established along the beaches, allowed Western activities (booze, bikinis, and dancing) without the repercussions of Islamic Law. Ahead of me at the in-pool bar was the jocular sound of the first group of Canadians shipped out of KAF.

"Hey, Cap, whatcha drinkin'?" Ricky hollered.

"Definitely something," I answered. I hadn't thought about it. But I knew it would relax my mind for the first time in a year. "Diet Pepsi," I stated. "And Jack—"

"Bartender, may I have a double jack and Diet Pepsi for my friend here please?" Ricky quickly deflected the statement into a beverage request.

"So what is the mission count?" Hollywood swam up and switched the conversation to data for his journal.

"One hundred ten mission days outside the wire, not including test flights. Five hundred forty flight hours," I proudly reported.

"One hundred eight, five hundred sixty—almost the same," he responded. "I guess we pretty much all got the same, except I also got shot down and blown up. Awesome!" He clenched his fist, pumping his elbow by his side, proudly trumping my stats.

Irish swam up and leaned back with his elbows on the side of the pool bar, "This is surreal."

"Ya, it is kinda weird being here, pampering ourselves. Yesterday we were dodging bullets – literally!" I replied, looking at him. We had difficulties merging as a crew initially in the year. We were cut of different cloth, but he was a good man. I was hard on him all the time.

"I'm sorry I was such a hard ass," I said.

"Ya, you were a bit of an asshole at times," he answered back. I glared back at him but couldn't help to laugh. He was right. I smiled. "Whether you believe it or, I do get it." He added taking a sip from his mini- umbrella, covered drink. I smirked at his umbrella. He caught my expression, "That's what I'm talkin' about," he smiled holding his glass up to cheers against my JD. I smiled.

"It was good to work with you. It took awhile to sort our shit out... but it was good," I nudged his shoulder.

"Will you two kiss and make up, let's drink." Snapshot interjected.

"And will you be our wedding photographer?" I responded as I put my arm over Irish to make him uncomfortable.

"Irish retreated, "Screw off you two!" Then splashed us both initiating some returns from Snapshot and Ricky.

"Whoa whoa, enough," I yielded to defend my JD and Pepsi from the pool water explosions. The boisterous play slowed as we regained composure. Snapshot was gathering his thoughts.

I looked at him knowing he was recollecting. "We have come a long way. Can you believe that two years ago we were learning gunnery for the first time, and planning training camps in Suffield and Arizona?"

"Ya, and a few days ago we were spraying tree-lines to suppress enemy shooters and pulling dead Canadians out of the battlefield," he recollected. "How do we go back to normal?"

"Ya, what the fuck is normal?" Hollywood added taking a sip of his drink. He turned to the bar with his back towards us in contemplation.

Snapshot had that same look on his face that I had seen months earlier. I remember the first time he was trying to sort it all out; when he froze at the TOC realizing a sniper did kill a FAM he spotted.

"You alright?" I asked smiling.

"Ya, just reflecting on a lot of stuff. I had a great tour; it was an awesome experience. I wouldn't trade it for the world," he paused. All the jocularity had departed as he took a deep breath, "And I get to go back to my family." He said slowly, nodding his head in a sort of unworthy shame. "After I spotted my first enemy dicker -- and called it, soon after the target died." He looked at my eyes. "How many enemies did we spot? Challenge? Engage? How many?" He took a drink to calm his realization. "Dozens? Hundreds? And how many did they kill? How does this ever stop?" he continued.

"I dunno…It's okay man.," it's all I could think to say as I rest my hand on his shoulder to comfort him.

He looked back intently through my soul. "That's the problem. That's what they are gonna say. It's okay. It's okay. But not everyone gets to go back to their families; and for what? Cause it's never gonna stop."

Gunny patted him on the shoulder and bowed his head, then humbly swam away. Hollywood was nodding his head while listening at the bar, he pulled his shades over his eyes, hiding his soul. Irish walked to the beach. I hopped up on the underwater barstool beside Ricky and Hollywood; I sipped my drink. I thought about his words. I just watched the pool, and drank. 'It's okay.' I pondered. Death.

After an hour or so, other Canadians all gathered around sharing stories of the past year. Drinks were going down quickly with a little food that the bar offered as a neutralizer of the liquor. It was the first time we had been given an opportunity to relax in, well, over a year— more like a year and a half including the training. It was all over. We had seen and done a lot. Many things we wish we hadn't seen, but it was part of the job. We were trying to accept that.

But that was why we were here. Decompression. The time at the resort was called decompression training. Mostly everyone wanted to just go home. But the military would not allow that. We were expected to pamper ourselves and receive numerous psychological lectures regarding what we could expect to experience postwar. We were briefed on symptoms to be aware of as well as resources that were available through the padres, social workers, and medical professionals in Canada. There were also crisis hotlines available. But first, the authorities knew we needed a few days to get some information and get a grip. So the war was beginning to wind down.

The next morning, I woke up around ten o'clock. My head was thick with an alcohol induced skull cramp, and it took a moment to get oriented. There was no laundry line hanging above my head. I was not in KAF. Ah yes, Dubai. I sauntered to the lobby where I knew espresso and croissants could be found. I sat down, slowly sipping my caffeine, and read a newspaper.

"Morning, boss!" It was Gunny.

"Morning. Join me?"

"I'd love to." He sat down. We focused on avoiding our heavier discussions of the evening and chatted about the later frivolous portions of the evening. We bantered lightly about the activities we were going to do today. Ricky briskly walked over with a serious look on his face.

"I just talked to our liaison officer. A Blowtorch has been shot down. They don't know about casualties yet," he whispered seriously.

"Son of a bitch," I whispered. I got up and left the table. I went directly to my room and connected to the Wi-Fi. I e-mailed Skipper. He was still in KAF. He would be discreet, but he would also let me know so I could pass it on.

"Steve, lost a Chinook to an RPG near Bazaar-e Panjwaii. Everyone okay. Safely back in KAF."

I finally exhaled after what seemed to be two hours of holding it in. I went outside to the pool where others were obviously talking. I shared the news. It spread quickly. There was relief; but as expected, lots of speculation.

"I'm going to the bar to start over. Last night didn't count!" one of the gunners stated as he started wading through the water toward the swim-up lounge.

I went to my room. I isolated myself the second night. There was too much spinning in my head. I ordered room service and e-mailed friends and family at home. I switched my focus. I occasionally looked out my balcony window to see many Canadians getting spooled up for another night of fun. Some waved at me to invite me down. I waved it off. I needed my own time tonight.

I lay in my bed and stared at the ceiling. I thought about Snapshot, Irish, Zorg, and Gunny. Almost a year in theater, I reviewed almost everything in my head—death, pain, suffering. For what? I was a bit angry at God. I know in the Book of Genesis it says that God gave mankind free will. I didn't know whether to be thankful or angry at him for that. I fell asleep.

Chapter 37

I Think I'm Home

The entire trip home from Kandahar, including Dubai, was surreal. During a forty-eight-hour period from KAF to Dubai, we had experienced a rocket attack and a ground attack on base by a small section of Taliban. That occurred while waiting at the TLS (terminal called Taliban Last Stand) to depart on the C-17.

Apparently, a brave young Canadian soldier was driving an infantry LAV out of a wash bay. He saw the ground attack starting and radioed in the invasion to HQ. Command asked if he was loaded, to which he responded yes.

The ground attack was quickly suppressed as 25-millmeter cannon fire from the LAV turned the Taliban attackers into a cloud of pink mist. We heard the gunfire at the TLS while waiting to depart—to us it seemed routine but delayed departure for a few hours.

Four days later, after Dubai, I woke in a blur, in the very civilized town of Lahr, Germany. I jogged through a manicured forest and stopped to have coffee and pastry at a local restaurant before embarking on another aircraft to Scotland. I remember how clean and civilized Germany was. It made me despise the Taliban even more. It made no sense at all that they would not want to cooperate and create a beautiful social and secure environment. Why poo-pond and dust when you can have of the smell newsprint, greenery and fresh baking?

After that, we leap-frogged from one hand-shaking ceremony to another so Canadian dignitaries could get their publicity with a bunch of leathery vets, who just wanted to go home: Trenton, Ontario, and Edmonton International Airport.

A half hour later, our detachment of about sixty personnel boarded a bus and had a police escort through Edmonton to the hangar in Namao, where our families were waiting at 12:30 a.m. This was the real reception—real families, real tears. I held my children and hugged my wife. I couldn't tell if it was real. I was finished. I survived. I went home.

A few days had passed, and I tried to function. I was a stick in the family spokes of progress. They were functioning without me.

Yesterday, the important decisions were about life and death—identifying Taliban, evacuating dead and wounded, watching patrols, and responding to lethal ambushes. Now the important decisions of home life were to ensure the garbage was out and the kids weren't late for school. Ironically, equally important, one was for the prevention of death, the latter for the sustainment of orderly life.

I was elated to be home yet stoic. The neighborhood welcomed me. Yellow ribbons were on the trees, and they held a block party in my honor. I just wanted to confess my sins and talk about battle, but no one would understand. Some just did not want to hear. I was happy yet far from relaxed.

A week later, I was going through paperwork that I left prior to deploying—notes for my spouse about accounts, mailing addresses, and insurance forms for medical claims that required my signature. And then I came across an envelope. "The envelope." My death letters. I froze.

Prior to deployment when training in the United States, Skipper looked at all of us anxious aircrew and gave us the lecture.

He said, "Guys, you have to write your letters. You have to accept your death, your impermanence. This can help you release your fear so you can focus on your mission. Your mission is to make sure you live and that your crew lives to return to their families. But your crew is your family now, and their lives are your mission. Write your letters."

I took the envelope and walked into the backyard to be alone. I sat down in a chair by the fire pit, lit a small fire, and opened the letter.

To my children:

When I was young I had a big fight with my brothers. I told them that I hated them. My mother pulled me aside and sternly scolded me. I'll never forget the look in her eyes when she told me that I was never ever allowed to hate anyone. Never hate.

I always remembered that. If I do not come back from Afghanistan alive, remember to love and only love. The reason I am in that part of the world is because some people have learned to base their lives on the promotion of fear and hatred.

You have the blessing of not having to live this way. I am overseas to fight against this, just as your forefathers fought against this in their time. We have a life and a culture that is blessed to be free and secure. It isn't perfect, but it's good. You are good—great. I volunteered to protect this way of life so that you can be free to live in love, free of fear.

I have had a great life. I am happy. Even now I am happy. I am even happier to have had the blessing to love you. Do not be sad. Do not hate my enemies. There is a difference between stopping them and hating them. I don't, so you shouldn't. Please don't waste the freedom and security we have. And honor me by honoring the words of my mother.

Dad

I wiped the tears from my eyes, sobbed quietly, and leaned forward. I held the note over the fire pit and lit one end of the paper with a match. I watched it burn.

Several gentle hands came and rested on my shoulder. I turned, and all my children were there looking. They didn't say anything, just saw me crying. They embraced me. I looked over their shoulders to see my wife's tearful empathy. She smiled. I was finally home.

"I spent a year in Afghanistan yesterday."

The end.

"I hate war as only a soldier who has lived it can, only as one who has seen its brutality, its futility, its stupidity."

—Dwight D. Eisenhower

I recall flying the Commander of the Canadian Army, from Wainwright to Edmonton around 2008/09 prior to deploying. I am paraphrasing the conversation but to summarize it, he stated as he critiqued the thin metal Bell 412 helicopter. "I am really glad you guys are in supporting our troops, we need you there. Despite that, I'm in an armoured APC travelling around that battlefield and still feel vulnerable. But you guys, flying around in this thin skin piece of tin, I think you're all a little nuts. Regardless, we are really glad you there; you make us feel much safer when you are overhead." He made me feel appreciated and proud that day.

In conclusion, Canada, America, Allies, Team Shakedown—it was an honor to serve you, and I would do it again . . . with a little push.

Glossary

ANA
Afghan National Army. The soldiers that NATO is training to eventually take control of their nation.

AO
Area of Operations. A term describing a geographical space where a nation or combat group focused their work.

ASE
Aircraft Survivability Equipment. The electronic warfare stuff on the helicopter, basically flare, rocket, and missile detectors. Three second warning to live or die.

BDA
Battle Damage Assessment. A report given following a battle to give operations information.

BUB (Battle Update Brief)
A formal brief of the situation in an area of activity. Refers to friendly, enemy, air force, and indirect fire activity in the immediate area. An Infantry BUB may also include his/her plan and how we (helicopters) will fit into it.

CALL SIGN
The name someone is called over the radio.

CHINOOK
A military CH-47 helicopter; can lift up to 20,000 pounds or forty-two troops.

CO
Commanding Officer. The lead pilot in the squadron.

COMPOUND
Home of local Afghanistan people. They resembled compounds as they were walled of hardened mud around a yard with small living quarters inside. The walls could often be unto 3 meters high. Often large numbers of compounds joined together with access to each other, creating villages or even cities.

CONTACT
This word is spoken when you see something but not designating it as friendly or enemy, i.e., "Contact house" means I see the house.

DFAC
Dining Facility. There were four main DFACs on base that the Canadians ate at.

DICKERS
Enemy person reporting on friendly activity for malicious intent. The enemy uses "dickers" to observe where friendlies are located and subsequently signal triggermen to detonate IEDs or commence attack.

EC DAY
Equipment Care Day. Every fourteen days. A day of minimal tasking giving the troops a chance to have a slower pace, a barbecue, and a breath.

EOIR
Electro-optic Infrared Sensor. Usually refers to an electric eye ball for long-range scanning. Infrared capable—it sees heat imagery in the dark—and targeting for some aircraft. Capable EOIR platforms are the Kiowas, Apache, UAV, and yours truly, Griffon with the MX-15.

FAC
Forward Air Controller (or JTAC)
A specialist embedded into a forward area with direct communication with artillery and fast-air helicopters. A FAC is beside the ground commander and ready to call in whatever the ground commander needs for air or indirect fire on an objective.

FAM
Fighting Aged Male

GOLF
Radio talk indicating an artillery unit (guns).

GPS
Global Position System. Navigation system.

GRAPE HUT
A huge mud structure often three stories tall. They were often half to one meter thick in places and hard like concrete. The Taliban used them as bunkers to hide and fight from.

GRID REFERENCE
An alphanumeric sequence of numbers that identified an exact location on the ground.

GRIFFON
A military Bell 412 helicopter. Lift up to 3,000 pounds, mostly ammo. In Afghanistan, two to four passengers maximum, seasonally dependent.

IED
Improvised Explosive Device. Used HME (homemade explosive). Primary weapon of terror for Taliban and insurgents.

INDIA
Radio talk indicating an infantry unit.

INT
Slang for intelligence. This could refer to the product or the person giving the int.

JTAC
See FAC.

KAF
Kandahar Air Field

LT
Lieutenant. A rank or position. Soldiers in a unit may refer to their platoon commander as LT or captain rather than sir or name.

MOAC
Mother of All Coffees: Green Beans special, 28 ounces. Coffee with four shots of espresso.

MX-15
A Westcam product that greatly enhances visual surveillance in the helicopter. Military and police units use them globally.

OPS
Slang for operations. A place where all activity was coordinated.

PID
Positive Identification. A term used to track and maintain a target. PID *must* be established and maintained prior to engaging with lethal force.

POL
Pattern of Life. A report about what kind of civilian activity is occurring, normal or abnormal, hiding out in the open.

PREDATOR/PRED
An American UAV.

RADOP

Radio Operator. Also keeps information and war log in the ops center and makes coffee. Does everything—gets food, cleans, sets up camp. Courier. Unsung heroes when they are good.

RAMP CEREMONY

A formal memorial service to honor the life of the fallen as he/she boards the aircraft to go back to Canada. Usually, thousands attend of all nations as a voluntary gesture of honor and respect. During my tour, the ramp officials often kept people out because more people showed up than ramp space was available.

RIP

Replace in Position. Often helicopters flew into the battle to replace another team that was out of fuel.

ROMEO TANGO/ROGER THAT/I UNDERSTAND

I understand.

ROZ IS HOT

Restricted Operating Zone. It is of defined dimensions where only those persons authorized to enter may do so.

RFL (Restricted Fire Line)

This is a line on a map in which a person cannot shoot across or move in some cases.

SAFIRE

Small Arms Fire, like AK-47s or C7s. Usually refers to anything under a .50-caliber.

SAMEO

Squadron aircraft maintenance officer. Lead maintenance authority at the squadron.

SHAMUS
Call sign for American Kiowa teams. Kiowa OH58D models with forward-firing .50-caliber and 2.75-inch rockets. Also had electro-optic eyeball on top for long range targeting and surveillance. Aka: Top Hat

SNAFU
Expression: Situation Normal (but) All Fucked Up.

SNAKE EATER
Slang for Special Forces soldiers.

TANGO
Radio talk indicating a tank unit

TERP
Interpreter, usually of Pashtun tongue that could listen on radio and tell the Canadians what the Taliban were saying.

TIC
Troops in Contact. Means they are usually exchanging bullets with the enemy.

TLS
Taliban Last Stand. The airport terminal where everyone gets off the aircraft on arrival and departure to theater. The TLS is where the final American/Taliban fight was in the early 2000s before KAF was taken over.

UAV
Unmanned Aerial Vehicle. Canada used UAVs for observation and intelligence gathering. American UAVs also maintained a strike capability.

WACS
Women and Children. A definite no-shoot criteria. Often called to let other shooters know there was potential to harm women or children.

WADI
Name for a river or creek.

WAIT OUT
Radio word to say, "I'm not answering yet," "I need to get more information first," or "I am busy."

X-CHECK
Execution checklist. This is a piece of paper listing all the activities to execute at specific times. It's to coordinate complicated missions with many players.

Printed in Great Britain
by Amazon

10460642R00207